BATTLETECH

THE CORPS

BATTLECORPS ANTHOLOGY, VOLUME 1

EDITED BY LOREN L. COLEMAN

BATTLETECH: THE CORPS
Edited by Loren L. Coleman
Cover art by Florian Mellies
Interior art by Alan Blackwell, Eldon Cowgur, Dale Eadeh, Aaron Harris, Harri Kallio, Chris Lewis, Duane Loose, Brad McDevitt, Ben Myers, Matt Plog, Klaus Scherwinski, Anthony Scroggins, Franz Vohwinkel
Cover design by David Kerber

Printed in USA.

Published by Catalyst Game Labs,
an imprint of InMediaRes Productions, LLC
5003 Main St. #110 • Tacoma, Washington 98407

CONTENTS

(CONTINUED)

FOREWORD

LOREN L. COLEMAN

"The two most powerful warriors are patience and time."

—LEO NIKOLAEVICH TOLSTOI

Forgive me. I can't help quoting from dead Russians these days.

Occupational hazard.

Before you begin to think that writing (or editing) somehow requires a degree in foreign literature, I should try to explain.

You see, the anthology you hold in your hands right now is just the latest link in a long chain of events that stretches back over four years. Longer, really, if you start at the point where my writing career and the *BattleTech* fictional universe collided. Not quite the Big Bang, but at least a medium-sized one.

We met. We fell in love. We enjoyed a lot of fights together.

Well, wars, actually. Planets were invaded. Military forces hammered at each other. Empires rose and fell. It was a lot like high school dating.

At that time (four years ago) I was presiding over what felt like the end days of *BattleTech* fiction. FASA Corporation had closed its doors, and my final hurrah was to wrap up twenty-plus years of fiction novels with a final trilogy. The year was 3067 (by the *BattleTech* timeline). I barely managed to bring to a close the Steiner-Davion civil war, tying up as many loose ends as possible. I typed *"THE END"* and sent off the file.

But we weren't finished.

The creative people in charge of *BattleTech*—and I was privileged enough to be considered one of them—had set up so much more. There was the Word of Blake Jihad about to kick off, which would have included nuclear holocaust, ravaged star systems, assassinations, and the dissolution of the Free Worlds League, just to name a few highlights.

Happy times.

Alas, it seemed not to be. WizKids had already put into place their time jump to the Dark Ages era. The publisher (Roc Books) voiced no interest in continuing a "Classic" line. Everyone seemed content to burn out the Civil War, and let wounded princes lie.

It was frustrating, and I complained (albeit softly) to those who would (and were forced to) listen. There just didn't seem to be an answer. So I let it rest. Though I did keep thinking about it, certain that there had to be something more. I stewed. I planned. I waited.

Patience.

And time.

Because then something strange happened on the way back from New Avalon. I came up with an idea. *The* idea, as it turned out. And, with some friends, I started up a small internet venture known as BattleCorps.com.

BattleCorps.com became the home for the "Classic" fiction universe. A way to get out those final (important!) stories, and to keep playing in the world where I had spent a great part of my career. It took over a year to fully launch the site, going live in the fall of the year 2003 (by the real world timeline).

Those first months were full of battles won and lost. Fortunately, I did find other writers who were just as devoted to the new campaign.

Our early stories roamed the entire timeline, the breadth of the Inner Sphere, and even managed a quick detour to the Clan Homeworlds. We explored the boundaries of loyalty *and* treachery. Of personal honor and cowardice. Of military

A RACE TO THE END

LOREN L. COLEMAN

GAN SINGH
CHAOS MARCH
12 OCTOBER 3057

It might be the last DropShip on Gan Singh.

Their final chance.

Wrenching at the controls of her *JagerMech*, Leftenant Kelly Van Lou struggled forward against the tangled jungle that covered most of the continent of Pandora. Shrill alarms wailed in her ears. Broken fronds streaked her ferroglass shield with green smears as sporadic laser fire burned through the leafy canopy around her.

Ruby-bright energy splashed armor from her BattleMech's shoulders, its arms, its chest.

She tasted the warm, dank air, poorly filtered by her cockpit's life support system.

Missiles corkscrewed in from her right, slamming into a palisade of majestic cypresses and thick-boled banyans strung with creeping vines. A few warheads dropped low against her legs, shredding the angular guards that protected her knee joints and lower actuators.

Her stride hitched, stumbled, and then caught up as she shouldered her way into a marshy glade. Planting her spade-shaped feet into the loamy, black soil, Kelly checked her HUD and found Hauptmann Roland Mills—her company excellence and political subterfuge. Enlisting soldiers, civilians, politicians, pirates.

Warriors, all.

These are the stories you will read in this anthology.

A collection from our starting months. Beginning with a handful of abandoned warriors, embroiled in the desperation that surrounded the forming Chaos March. Ending with a new, never-before-published story in the ongoing tale of one of the Inner Sphere's most beloved characters, Aleksandr Kerensky.

The warrior who taught me to love (and quote) dead Russians.

Like I said. An occupational hazard. And as such, let me leave you with one final thought:

Upon the brink of the wild stream
He stood, and dreamt a mighty dream...

—ALEKSANDR SERGEYEVICH PUSHKIN

commander in the Third Donegal Guards, and her friend—still limping along a half-klick behind. Well out of danger. Tightening up on her triggers, she snapped up both long-barreled arms and went looking for trouble.

Long licks of bright yellow flame flashed out of her *Jag*'s autocannon as she spent hundreds of rounds into the greenery, implementing her own plan of deforestation. Twenty-mills riding over powerful, ultra-class Nova fifties, the hot metal chewed through thick vines, splintered tree branches into kindling, and rained pieces of shredded fronds over the ground. The powerful, cutting streams walked destructive lines in a narrow arc, reaching out, searching for either of the two 'Mechs in between her and the DropShip.

She found the missile-casting *Dervish* when a leafy screen of branches exploded under her devastating assault. Autocannon slugs hammered against its chest, as if drawn by the gauntlet and sword set over a Davion sunburst. The insignia was one Kelly knew well—had called an ally only a few days before, but none of that mattered now. In scant seconds, the proud crest of the FedCom Corps had been chiseled away to a battered ghost of its former glory.

Too late to stop.

The *Dervish*'s chest caved inward over the fusion reactor. Golden fire blossomed inside the mangled cavity. It spread quickly. The 'Mech's head split open as the warrior ejected, rocketing up and away from the dying machine.

It was the last thing Kelly saw before the fusion-bright flare consumed the BattleMech. The force of the explosion blasted apart trees and scorched a great deal of underbrush to instant cinders. It rocked her *JagerMech* back on its heels as the ground trembled violently.

"Kelly!" Roland's voice crackled to life over her comms system. "Flash and smoke near your position. Can you see it?"

"Not anymore," she said, voice-activated mic picking up her reply.

Spots swam before her eyes, and she blinked away the aftereffects of the glare. A few curly strands of her platinum-blond hair tickled along the side of her face. No reaching them through the heavy neurohelmet she wore, but a practiced

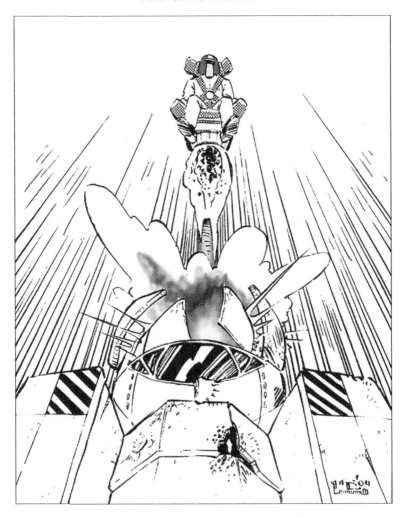

head shake matted them against the sheen of sweat on her forehead.

Whatever had been sniping at her with lasers had taken off. The *Dervish* was also gone except for pieces and parts scattered around a smoking crater. A leg, severed mid-femur, leaned up against a bamboo thicket. There was a titanium strut impaled through a nearby banyan. A few determined licks of flame crawled along the scorched trunks of some ironwood, but she doubted it would go much farther. The jungle was far too wet from the recent days of rain.

Kelly throttled forward, cautiously. Suddenly, new warnings screamed for attention as a rust-painted *Vindicator* shoved its way through the bamboo, stepping out into the hole in the jungle cleared by the explosion. She brought up her autocannon, but the wailing cut off as the other 'Mech dropped its targeting lock and paused, ready but waiting. Orange-and-black tiger striping covered half the BattleMech's chest, like a pelt draped over one shoulder, but it had no insignia she could see.

Kelly paused, fingers caressing her triggers. The *Vindicator* took advantage of her hesitation and dove back into the jungle thicket. Northeast. Toward the DropShip.

The last one.

Roland had given her a moment to collect herself. "One of ours, or one of theirs?"

"Ran across one of both," she said. Then sighed. "It was a Guardian," she admitted, swallowing against a sour taste. "First FedCom."

"Damn it, K." He didn't sound mad at her, but at the Fates in general. They had tried so hard not to engage the Guardians. "Well, that tears it."

It's Roland's one fault, Kelly thought. Holding onto an idea of "us" versus "them," or Federated Commonwealth versus the Marik-Liao alliance. That might have been true six months ago, or even six weeks, when the alliance offensive was chewing through the Sarna March. But Katrina-*verdammt*-Steiner tanked that idea when she called home all Lyran commands and the local defensive network fell completely apart. So bad, in fact, that a few stragglers got left behind in the confusion, including the Seventh Company of the Third Donegal Guards.

Roland's company had been deployed to Gan Singh, to try and coordinate with the First FedCom RCT. Only the Guardians were already gone. All they found were a few forgotten warriors—cast-offs or AWOL, didn't matter—butting heads with local militia-turned-mercenary.

The Donegal Guards company either missed the recall order, or it had never been sent once General Hammerskjold decided to cut his losses and return to Lyran space.

Kelly could only wish him a prime location in the deepest circle of hell.

A new silhouette flashed across her tactical screen as Roland limped his *Penetrator* up from behind. It looked quite a mess, with its right leg fused into an awkward steel crutch and several lengths of mossy vines draped over its ruined arms.

"What are we waiting for?" he asked. "Let's go, K."

She very nearly smiled at his forced *esprit de corps*. But six dead friends and four MIA in the last five days was enough to sour anyone's mood. From city to spaceport to remote landing zone, Seventh Company had tried to make rendezvous with any number of outbound DropShips. Always too late. Always forced back by Capellan or mercenary outfits with greater firepower or a larger expense account.

But not this time, she promised herself. *Please.*

Throttling forward into an easy walk, she took the lead against his best speed of thirty kilometers per hour. They struck along the trail blazed by the fleeing *Vindicator* and crossed their fingers.

For the next ten minutes, their luck held. No weapons sniped at them from the dense jungle. Roland pushed his *Penetrator* up toward forty kph as the trail made for easier travel. Kelly began to hope.

"Think we can afford passage?" she asked. Neither of them speculated the DropShip captain might call allegiance to any one faction of Gan Singh's three-sided battle. These days it seemed "every man for himself" was a predictable situation.

"We can barter against any ransom paid by the Third Donegal. We can deal away what's left of the *Penetrator.*"

He'd never once threatened to put a debt against her *JagerMech.* The *Penetrator* was a newer and much more valuable machine, but hers had been in the Van Lou family for three generations. Leased into Lyran service, but still hers. Roland would rather give up a piece of Lyran state property, and suffer the reprisals, than divorce her from a piece of family heritage.

It was the kind of thing he did without thinking, and for that, if nothing else, Kelly would stick by her hauptmann's side, no matter what.

That's what kept her anchored at his side when the sky fell in on them a moment later.

There was very little warning. A glimpse of smoke through the tree canopy from one of the Pandora jungle's many logging slash burns. A tremble in the ground that might have been artillery fire, might have been the first powerful flare of a DropShip's fusion drives lighting off. A screen of ironwood bounced back their active sensors until the last moment. Then they pushed through, and into the chaos of battle.

The DropShip was there all right, ninety meters high, its drive flare washing its underside in white-hot fire. It squatted on the blackened fields of a deforested plateau. *Seeker*-class, and painted a familiar blue-gray. Kelly Van Lou needed only the briefest glance to recognize the shamrock crest of the Donegal Guards, and the scales of justice that were the personal insignia of Third regiment.

A good thing, because a brief glance was all she got before a crossfire of lasers and autocannon converged on her location. The lasers scorched the soil at her feet while hard-hitting slugs beat a damaging tattoo across her *Jag*'s lower waist. The fire had come from two machines painted the blue and gold of Federated Commonwealth RCTs. A Behemoth assault tank and an *Enforcer*.

Their second salvoes went after a *Panther* painted dark, cerulean blue. Nothing she recognized. Another mercenary, or a wayward Capellan perhaps.

All told, there seemed to be about a dozen 'Mechs and half that number in vehicles jousting over the black-scorched ground. The DropShip laid out suppression fire from its upper weapons bays. PPCs stabbed down at the non-allied BattleMechs. They left the FedCom warriors alone. Wave after wave of long range missiles pounded machines into scrap and battered the ground into ruin. More than a few, Kelly felt certain, would spread Thunder munitions out into an ad hoc minefield.

Kelly stepped in front of Roland's *Penetrator*, protecting it while holding her fire. FedCom RCT forces had the advantage on the field. And so long as a mercenary did not target her, she would not target them. Dialing over to the protected frequencies of the Third Donegal, she waited to see what sense her captain could make of the situation, listening in as he identified himself.

"Captain Mills?" The reply washed out in static as the lightning blasts of several PPCs ionized the local atmosphere, one from a nearby *Caesar*. It made communications difficult. "We...no Mills listed...deployed to Gan Singh."

Deployed or not, Roland's name should be on the Guards TO&E. And Kelly recognized the voice, even through the communications haze. "Jollena?" First mate Jollena Marksower, from the *Lamprey*. "Jolly, it's K. Kelly! And Roland. You have two tired Guardsmen here looking for evac."

Only one of the *Lamprey*'s ramps was still down. Secondary bay. Big enough to hold a couple of BattleMechs, if they could get them aboard.

"K?" There was a pause. The nearby *Caesar* turned its weapons toward the Guardsmen, and Kelly drilled out return fire with her autocannon as a way to shove it back. "Kelly Van Lou, what in the Archon's name are you doing out here?"

"Taking a sightseeing tour! What the hell does it look like?" Kelly had heard the shock in the veteran spacer's voice. How badly had wires been crossed if their own DropShip crew did not know what forces were on planet? And where was the captain? "We need a safe route to board, and good covering fire."

The same *Vindicator* from earlier dodged out of a tight situation and ran back toward Kelly's position. It hesitated as she drew her crosshairs over it, lighting it up, then deliberately turned its back on her to challenge a pursuing *Jenner*. Over an open channel, an accented voice let them know "If you want a piece of the DropShip, form up southwest and get ready to cover our drive."

"We're getting more than a piece of it," Roland said coldly. "Stay out of our way, and we may find room for you."

It wasn't exactly their call to make, of course, but Kelly approved. A tentative agreement was better than nothing. The DropShip crew had already made some kind of pact with the FedCom, after all.

"Suit yourself, then." It sounded more like a threat than an allowance.

Then again, a hot battlefield was not the best place to make new friends.

"K," Jollena finally returned, "pull up northwest and come straight in at the ramp. We're out of here in five, so move it now."

"Straight at the ramp?" she double-checked.

"Move it!"

The *Caesar* and a blue-and-gold painted *Rommel* also shifted in that direction, but not so close to prevent the Guardsmen from moving. Roland led. Kelly stalked at his side, uneasy.

"It would be a lot easier if you brokered a truce between the FedComs and the mercs," she said over an unsecured channel. She warned off a too-close *Panther* with a quick stream of light autocannon fire digging in at its feet. "Make a second trip. Offer to send back a larger DropShip."

"Not happening, Kelly. *Way* too much bad blood now."

Kelly nodded. "Captain feel the same way?" she asked.

"Just get up here," Jollena ordered. "We'll deal with the mercs next."

It all hung on one word. *Next.* Not *later* or *eventually.* Also with the obvious cease-fire arranged between the *Lamprey* and the Guardians, and the way in which the mercs had tried to warn them. It all added up.

After a week of non-stop fighting and several days of only being able to trust the men and women at her side, Kelly's paranoia had grown acute. Sharp enough to recognize the trap being laid out for them as they moved into range of the DropShip's weapons.

The last DropShip on Gan Singh.

Every man for himself.

"Roland. Roland, fall back now!" The dry, metallic taste of fear crept into her mouth. Slamming her throttles against their reverse stops, she backpedaled the *JagerMech*.

Almost too late. The DropShip's weapons hammered down around their position as the *Caesar* and its support tank pushed forward. A pair of PPCs slashed at the legs of Kelly's

'Mech. Aligned crystal steel melted and splattered over the already-scorched earth of Gan Singh.

Missiles hammered around the *Penetrator*, but not so bad as the Thunder-deployed minefield would have been had they walked into the *Lamprey*'s waiting embrace.

"Kelly?" Roland staggered back, getting out from under the DropShip's weapons. "What?"

"Cast-offs. AWOL." No difference now. "They've quit the Donegal Guards, and they're not going to want us telling tales about them. Tree line, now!"

Her commanding officer was not one to bandy about with the order of rank when good advice was being given. Kelly let him slip behind her, and used her autocannon to push back at the charging *Caesar*, buying them seconds only.

With more BattleMechs sliding up in their direction, the two Guardsmen might have made a bad end of it if not for the mercenaries. The *Vindicator* and a *Blackjack* also painted with the Bengal pelt suddenly turned in their direction and sprinted inside the *Caesar*'s line of retreat. They savaged the Rommel, blasting one set of armored treads clean off and freezing the turret inside a ruined track. Then they turned up from the *Lamprey*, and came at the *Caesar* from behind while Kelly pushed forward to catch the RCT machine in a pincer.

The 70-ton machine held on for a few long heartbeats, then broke for the DropShip in a circuitous path that avoided the scattered Thunders and left the slower mercenaries behind. All of the RCT machines fell back, heading for the final ramp.

The scattered mercenaries, with two of their small number out of position now, let them go. Within moments, the DropShip had buttoned up and was blasting itself clear of Gan Singh.

Kelly Van Lou watched it rise into the air, soon losing itself behind a white tuft of clouds. Her breath came short and sharp, and had nothing to do with the hot, humid air in her cockpit. It had everything to do with the hollow pit deep in her gut. *If the Donegal Guards could turn on each other,* she wondered, *what's left for the now-estranged Lyran Alliance and Federated Commonwealth?*

As if in answer to her silent question, her communications board lit up on an unsecured channel. "We picked up some garbled transmissions." The accented voice from before. The *Vindicator*'s MechWarrior. With a moment to weigh it, he sounded Slavic. Maybe a native of Gan Singh. Maybe not.

"There may be a DropShip set down on the northern coast of Pandora. Near the city of Myros. The last DropShip on Gan Singh," he said tiredly as the remnant mercenaries gathered near their position.

Of course it was. That was the nature of battle and politics, after all. Always one more chance. If you were smart or lucky, or both at the same time. "Working together for this one might be in our common good," Kelly said, then waited for Roland to make the final call.

"It's a ten-hour push," he said slowly. "We can do it without sleep if you can."

"Sounds like a plan." The *Vindicator* turned away to the northwest, and struck out with a determined stride.

Roland switched over to a secure frequency. One reserved for Third Donegal Guards, Seventh Company. Maybe the last time they'd use it. "Did they just become one of ours?" he asked. "Or did we become one of theirs?"

"Right now," Kelley answered, "I think we all belong to Pandora. And Gan Singh." She pushed into an easy walk, keeping pace with the limping *Penetrator* as she switched back to a common frequency. "Maybe it's time to see what's left on this world," she said. "What we have to work with."

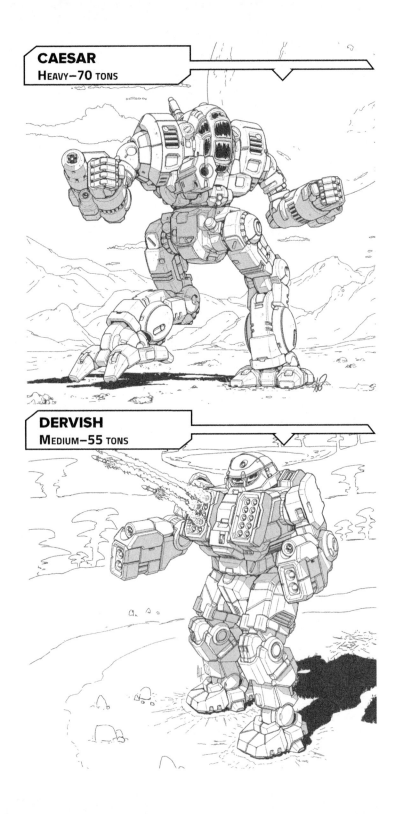

CAESAR
HEAVY—70 TONS

DERVISH
MEDIUM—55 TONS

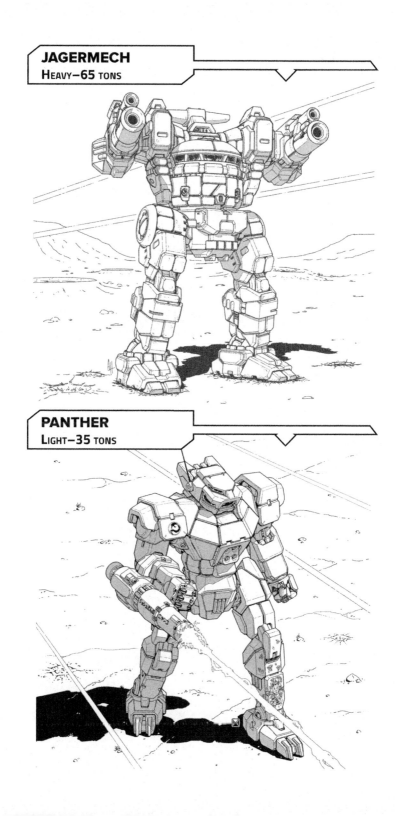

JAGERMECH
Heavy—65 tons

PANTHER
Light—35 tons

PENETRATOR
HEAVY—75 TONS

VINDICATOR
MEDIUM—45 TONS

DAMAGE CONTROL

ILSA J. BICK

**SCORPIUS PLANUS
THUBAN
BOLAN PROVINCE
LYRAN ALLIANCE
9 SEPTEMBER 3064**

There was a muffled roar as heavy cannon fire punched the sky, like the distant growl of thunder. An instant later, the floor of the medical Quonset twitched and jumped under her boots, and Dr. Elizabeth Trainer felt her heart slam into her throat. A steely talon of panic dug into her chest, and she clutched at the edges of the chair where she sat.

Relax. They're still more than twenty klicks away. She dragged in a deep, calming breath, and instantly regretted it. The Quonset's cooling units were going full blast, but the air was heavy with ash and the stench of rancid sweat, rotten eggs, and something sweet and burnt. It reminded her of pork roasted on a spit, drizzling juices into sputtering flames that licked along the meat.

But she knew the smell wasn't pork.

The front lines were to the east, on the black basalt expanse of the Scorpion Plains that spread around the base of Scorpius Mons, Thuban's highest volcano. The Plains—a vast, ruined landscape of lava hummocks—were riddled with steam plumes and sulfur vents. And that's where the soldiers and BattleMechs of the Twenty-third Arcturan Guard were fighting and dying in a battle against their brothers, the warriors of the Eleventh Arcturan Guard. It was a battle Trainer could smell and hear and feel but, mercifully, not see because she was so afraid that Jonathan might be there, in the thick of it.

Oh, God, please keep him safe...

A man's voice—tremulous and very frightened—cut into her thoughts. "I...I don't know what happened. It was as if I'd been airdropped into hell."

Trainer blinked back to attention. The MechWarrior was perched on the edge of a cot, his head bowed. His right knee jiggled up and down like a piston. Trainer sat on a chair she'd pulled around to the captain's cot. There were no offices in the Quonset, so a psychiatrist had to make do. Now, she crossed her right leg over her left, and clasped her hands over her knees.

"I know it's hard, Captain Stanton," she said, keeping her voice as calm as she could, even though she felt a slick of clammy perspiration along the back of her neck. "But you'll be better off if you talk about it. I know that talking makes it more real—"

"Christ, yes," said Stanton, jerking his head up in a sudden, spastic movement. His eyes locked onto hers. His eyes were very blue, like Jonathan's: the color of sky on a cloudless afternoon. But that's where the resemblance ended.

Stanton had been found, unresponsive and nearly catatonic, in the cockpit of his *Zeus*, a kilometer from their unit. Medications—not many, because she wanted him lucid—had relaxed him, and he was looking a little more...human. Not like the frightened animal they'd found. Still, there were purple smudges under his eyes that gave him a haunted, wild look. The med techs had stripped him out of his battle gear, and she saw that his camo t-shirt was sopping wet with sweat, the fabric clinging like a second skin to the muscles of his chest. A cigarette he'd lit but not smoked was tweezed between the first and second fingers of his right hand. White curls of smoke spiraled from the tip in sinuous ribbons.

Grimacing, Stanton screwed his eyes shut and slapped the palm of his left hand against his forehead. "It's like, they're pictures...they're here, in my head, right behind my eyes, and when I talk about it, I see it. I smell it, and I can't move, I can't..."

"Stanton." Trainer took her hand and gently pulled Stanton's arm away from his face. She could feel him shake. "Captain, open your eyes, and look at me." She waited until Stanton did and then she tightened her grip on his forearm. She had to appeal to honor and duty; she had to inject the sense of his importance into his psyche like a hallucinogenic drug. Manipulative? Of course, but this was civil war.

"Stop." She drilled him with a look. "Stop. This. Right now. You understand me? You pilot a goddamn *Zeus*. You're a *warrior*. Shakes or not, you've been trained to do a job, and, by God, you're going to do it. Because we need you, Captain. You can't afford the luxury of withdrawing from the fight."

"Luxury." Stanton's chin quivered, and she saw the shine of sudden tears in his eyes. "Don't you think I know that?" he said, and she heard his shame. Stanton looked away, then seemed to remember the cigarette in his hand. He sucked greedily; the tip glowed hot red and, in another moment, twin streamers of blue-gray smoke jetted from his nostrils.

"Look," said Stanton. He swung his head back, and she saw that while the tears were still there, he'd regained some of his self-control. *Good*, she thought. *Got him crying. Halfway there. Now, got to pace this just right.*

"I..." he said again, his voice clogged with emotion. "I don't expect you to understand. But these were...are my friends, and the simple fact is that we've never been trained for... for this."

"You're a soldier."

"Sure, but trained for a real war, not...this! I haven't been trained to fight, to...kill my friends, my...damn it," he said, and now a single tear crawled down his left cheek. Stanton's face was still grimy with black ash from the battlefield, and the tear left a solitary, white track. "That's our sister regiment, the Golden Lions, out there. Doctor, I trained with some of them. I know who they...what their *faces* look like inside those machines. Those are people in there."

Oh, my darling Jonathan, are you out there, are you safe? "We all know people, Captain," said Trainer, keeping her voice as steady as she could. *Focus, focus on the mission!* Her heart felt as if a fist had grabbed hold and squeezed. "We all have friends...and now it's hard, but they'll kill us if we don't kill them first. They're the enemy."

"But they're *not*," said Stanton. His lips were shivering so much that when he took another pull from his cigarette, the tip bobbed up and down. "They're still the same people. It's the damn politics that have changed, that's all. This isn't a war about principles; there's nothing just about it. It's simply killing."

"And that's why you froze?" Trainer asked, choosing another tack. They could discuss the illegitimacy of a civil war all day and, while she agreed, they'd get nowhere. "That's why you ran? That's why you left your infantrymen to fend for themselves?"

"I..." Stanton's mouth opened, but nothing more came out. After a few seconds, he scrubbed his lips with the flat of his left hand. He looked away, but not before she saw the emotions chase across his face: fear, shame. Despair. "I'm tired," he said, finally. "I want to be left alone for a little while. Please."

"You know I can't do that."

"Please." Stanton's expression was fierce, and she saw that his left hand was fisted, the skin over his knuckles white from tension. "Just for a little while." And then, in a low murmur: "You don't know what I've done."

"And what have you done, Stanton?" When he didn't respond, she touched his shoulder. He flinched. "What have you done?"

"No." He seemed to shrivel into himself. "No, I can't. Not... not now. I don't," he pressed his fists to his temples. "I don't want to *think!*"

"About what?"

"No, please, can't you leave me in peace? Please, just go away," Stanton whispered. His eyes snapped shut then bugged open, as if he couldn't stand what was in the darkness before his eyes. "*Please.*"

Trainer debated then pushed up from her chair. She felt as if she were very close to getting at the terrors bouncing around in Stanton's mind. But while she had to wiggle into his head and twist his thoughts to serve the mission, she couldn't afford to break him. "All right, Captain. But be very clear about this. My job is to get you back to duty, pronto. Yours is to fight. Everything else—love, friendship, compassion—is a secondary consideration. Hell, they're not even on the damn list."

They locked gazes for a few seconds. Then Stanton said, "I was wrong about one thing. You know what I said before? About it being like hell?"

He dropped his cigarette, then crushed the smoldering butt against the concrete floor with the heavy wedge of a MechWarrior boot. "It was worse."

"Your hell's inside you, Stanton, and you'll beat it," Trainer said, unsure if she believed this. "You're going to go out there and fight...and you're going to be fine."

As she turned to go, Stanton said, "I want to ask you a question."

She looked back. "Go ahead."

"How can you do this?"

"Do what?"

"This." Stanton looked around at the cots, the other soldiers. Men, women. "How can you stand to look me in the eye and assure me that all's right with the world when tomorrow I might destroy someone who was..." He broke off, sucked in a breath, then said, "When tomorrow I might be dying in a pool of my own blood...and all because of you."

For a moment, Trainer didn't know what to say. If she were truthful, she wondered this herself. She cleared her throat. "I'm just doing my job," she said. It was like a mantra that kept her sane. "Now...you get some rest. You'll be fine, Captain, you'll see."

Stanton stared at her for a long moment. "That's so easy for you to say."

She left the usual orders for Stanton with the nurses: clean clothes, a hot meal. A mild sedative and some rest. She debated about ordering a stronger medication, but decided against it. Better to let Stanton grapple with his demons with a clear head than with a mind fogged by drugs.

At the door, she stopped and glanced back down the long stretch of cots in the Quonset. *Only five days of fighting, and we're jam-packed and just getting worse.* The Quonset was ten meters wide by forty meters deep and filled with a double row of cots, one row to a side. The fresh arrivals, those medevaced from the front lines, lay on their cots, hands folded over their chests, and stared at nothing. There were empty beds, but that didn't mean she didn't have patients. Those soldiers who had been on-site for more than twelve hours were put to work: cooking, hauling supplies, cleaning. They were kept here for thirty-six hours, perhaps forty-eight. Then they were sent back to fight.

Damage control: If the term hadn't been so accurate, she would've laughed because it sounded like something one did to fix a machine. But it was accurate because the military was a machine, and they—her patients, the 'Mechs, her—were the cogs that made that machine go. Long ago, the armed forces on Terra had given what psychiatrists like her did the nickname "three-hots-and-a-cot." Someone had figured out that the best way to treat combat fatigue was not to medevac soldiers far from the front lines. Taking them away from the action was actually debilitating and reinforced their sense of failure. The best option was to treat them as close to their fellow soldiers as possible, to keep them involved in doing a soldier's work while driving home, over and over again, that they had a duty to the other men and women who were doing their jobs. Oh, yes, fear was fine. Fear was normal and, in fact, it was abnormal not to be frightened out of your wits in battle because a man or woman had a pretty good chance of dying.

So, she acknowledged her patients' fears; she empathized with the sudden, sometimes shocking revelation of their own mortality—that they might be dancing on the razor's edge between life and death, a difference that could be erased in the blink of an eye. She helped them through all these things—with kind words or harshness when she had to, with rest, clean clothes, a hot meal. And then, she sent a soldier back out to fight, and maybe die.

She despised what she'd become. The perversity of what she did. Every minute of it.

Trainer pushed out of the Quonset and into a blistering hot late afternoon at the lip of the Scorpion Plains. There was that constant pulsing roar of autocannons, and the vibrations from the battle were so much stronger outside that she felt them shiver up her boots and into her calves and thighs. The med unit was close enough for her to see the tiny hump of the mountain rising to the east. As she scanned the misty summit, she caught glimpses of the insect-like figures of BattleMechs boiling over the black rock, like ants dislodged from a hill.

She felt her blood chill in her veins. She hadn't been able to make out any 'Mechs on the summit yesterday, but their presence confirmed her worst fears. The Eleventh, led by Colonel Linda McDonald, was continuing its relentless advance. The Twenty-third was low on 'Mechs, and that was why even a single soldier like Stanton was so vitally important.

She turned her back on the volcano and stared out past the small village of Quonsets and tents to the middle distance. Not an inspiring sight: More lava flows, marked here and there by spiked stands of silver swords, the only plants that could survive on the lava field. The sun was very hot—it hadn't rained on the Scorpion Plains for almost a month—and her body responded to the sudden change in temperature by popping out little beads of sweat that trickled between her shoulders and wet the pits of her arms.

The stench of battle was so much stronger out here, she could taste it: ash and grit and something oily. She made a face, spat out a gob of gray-tinged saliva. She was tempted to go back into the Quonset, or maybe head over to her quarters and duck into someplace relatively cool. But she had a lot of work to do—the soldiers just kept coming—and then there was the medical unit's general briefing for later that evening. She really didn't have the luxury of time.

Luxury. That's what Stanton had said. What had made a battle-hardened man like Stanton crack? Trainer fished out a packet of cigarettes from her left breast pocket. She rarely smoked, thought it was a filthy habit. But smoking helped mask the taste of death in her mouth. She lit the cigarette, then smoked for a few moments, staring at and thinking of nothing, letting her mind drift the way the smoke billowed then dispersed on the wind. But then her restless thoughts settled on Jonathan.

Her vision suddenly blurred as the tears came. Stanton was the trigger, probably. They had the same eyes... Most days she was able to clamp down on anything to do with Jonathan, although the nights were hard. She sucked on her cigarette, savored the burn a moment, and then let the smoke go. Her left hand inched to her neck, and to a length of gold chain pooling in the hollow of her throat. She ran her fingers over the chain and felt how the gold was warm from her skin, then let her fingers trail over the pendant: a diamond in the shape of a single tear.

She remembered when he'd given her the necklace: five months ago in April, not long after the disastrous campaign at Tikonov, where Victor's forces were forced back into Lyran space. She remembered hearing the sizzle of rain against stone outside their window. A light breeze fluttered the curtains, and she smelled water and wet leaves. They made slow, lingering love, taking their time, delighting in the taste and feel of one another. The sheets felt cool, and in the dim light of a single candle, Jonathan's skin glowed a rich warm amber.

"I have something for you," he said and fastened the chain around her neck. The diamond caught the light, like a tiny comet. He touched the diamond with his finger then pressed his lips to the dome of her right breast, then her left, and then, last of all, her lips. "A diamond lasts forever, and so will my love for you," he murmured. "I want you to remember that, Liz, no matter what."

And she'd known at that moment what was going to happen. Still, she pulled him close. His skin was smooth from their lovemaking, and she inhaled musk and the faintest hint of sweat. They were silent for a few moments. Then she said, "You're going away, aren't you? You've decided to..." She couldn't say the word "defect," not just then, so she didn't.

He didn't answer at first, just traced the length of chain along her collarbone with a finger. Her eyes burning with unshed tears, she waited him out.

"Yes," he finally said. "I'm sorry. But after Tikonov, the way the war is going...Liz, I don't think Victor's right. I've given it a lot of thought and I'm not sure his claim is...authentic."

"And Katherine's is?" She wanted to be angry. She wanted to shout and tell him that he'd lost his mind. But she couldn't do any of those things.

He'd sighed, then rolled onto his back. "I don't know anything anymore. But I have to do what's right, what *feels* right. This...the Twenty-Third, fighting for Victor... Liz, I can't stomach it. I can't pretend loyalty to a cause I don't think is just."

She propped her head on her elbow so she could look into those intense blue eyes. "What about us, John? What am I supposed to do? Resign my commission? Report you?"

His eyes held hers. "You could. You know you could. I'll be a traitor."

"Terrific." She gave a bleak laugh. "They'll execute you and pin a medal on my chest. What kind of choice is that?"

"Then come with me," and then when she'd shaken her head, his hands gripped her biceps. "For God's sake, why stay? What's here for you?"

"My duty, John. My job. And I believe in Victor," she said. Her heart raced, but she kept her voice steady. "Besides, my oath is just as important as yours. You're not the only one with a conscience. I have to do what *I* think is right. Defection isn't, and there's no way you can make that choice right, not for me."

"And if the Eleventh and the Twenty-Third..." His voice was husky with emotion. "Liz, if it comes down to a fight, Lyran against Lyran, regiment against regiment...?"

"Then we do our jobs, John," she said. "We follow orders. We hope for the best."

"Oh, God," he said, pulling her down onto his chest. She nestled there, her ear pressed against his heart. She listened to its strong, steady beat and, for the moment, felt her fears recede. His hands stroked her long blonde hair, the back of her head. "It won't come to that. I promise."

"You can't know that," she said, and now her tears came. "It's not your promise to make, John."

"I know." He lifted her face and framed it with his hands. "But this is, Liz. This is my promise to you." And then he'd kissed her fiercely, hungrily, his need flowing into her.

They hadn't spoken again after that for the rest of the night—at least, not in words. She'd fallen asleep in the circle of his arms but the next morning, when she woke, he was gone.

Only five months ago. She closed her finger around the diamond pendant and pressed it to her lips. *Love is forever, my darling; the war isn't.* But there was no end in sight, and now she was on one side, and Jonathan was on the other. Her gaze swung back to the distant mons, the tiny 'Mechs. She saw a plume of smoke rise, and the wind reached her; there was a sound of thunder, and she smelled ozone, vented coolant, and the stink of sulfur.

I wish it would rain. I wish it would rain and wash away all the blood and the stench, and then the world would be clean, and we could start again, forget this horror.

But it didn't rain. She really didn't expect it to. Trainer finished her cigarette, then let it fall to the hard earth, and ground it to dust beneath her boot.

"I won't kid you," said the colonel, looking at the various command staff assembled around the table. He wasn't a tall man and his scalp was capped with a shock of white, unruly hair that always seemed like it needed a good brushing. His gray eyes sunk into his face from too many hours tending patients, and he looked as if he hadn't slept in a month. "The situation's bad. Command hasn't been able to slow McDonald's advance at all. There's a real, imminent danger of her people breaking through our front lines."

"Well, then we needed to start evacuating yesterday morning," said Dale Ramsey, who was seated next to Trainer. Ramsey was the unit's chief surgeon: a small, bantam-rooster of a man with a thatch of fiery red hair. "The OR's hopping. I can barely keep up, and my patients are packed tighter than sardines in post-op. If you're really serious about evacuation, then we need to start sending people out now."

The colonel sighed. "I wish it was that simple. The reality is Command won't spare us the transports because they're already in use." There was a general buzz of conversation around the table, and the colonel raised a hand. "Hold on, people. There's more. The scuttlebutt is that the retreat's already begun. Happened last night, under cover of darkness. A splinter of the Twenty-Third peeled off south, and they're about ten klicks away now and going fast. There's still a forward unit, a token force on the volcano spearheading the offensive against McDonald, but they're spread thin. And the bad news is we stay put, right smack dab in the middle."

"To fight another day?" asked Ramsey. His tone indicated just what he thought of that plan. "What, we're the bait? The sacrificial lambs?"

The colonel bobbed his head. "That's about the size of it. We run for it, and the Eleventh might suspect that we're not throwing all our man- and firepower at them here. Call it a diversionary last stand. We've got lots of wounded, plus anyone we can get well enough to send back to the forward line, so we can keep things looking pretty darned busy. By the time the Eleventh gets here and figures out that we're not actually shooting, Command's betting we'll have bought the splinter group time. So, in the end, Command will have conserved their healthiest soldiers and gotten them the hell out of here."

"While we do what?" asked Trainer.

"Our jobs," said the colonel. "No matter what, we've got to stay put. We've got patients to tend to who can't be moved. They need us."

"We need back-up," Ramsey said. "And some firepower would be nice. I don't much like the idea of defending my patients with a laser pistol, or serving as target practice for some *Banshee*. And what about that nice big *Zeus*? We've got all that power out there and no one here qualified to pilot it. Are you telling me Command's going to leave it behind?" When the colonel nodded, Ramsey blew out in exasperation. "Well, Christ Almighty, then how about sending a MechWarrior our way?"

"No can do. In a more normal war, where we had a bit more time, didn't have to cut and run, what with Command trying to cover Victor's tracks, maybe. Hell—" the colonel exhaled a laugh, "—can't believe I even said that. Whatever flavor war you call it, a soldier ends up just as dead. Anyway, I can't argue with you, Ramsey. 'Mechs are damn valuable, we all know that. But Command's pulling out so fast they can't even spare time to button their flies, much less hustle a pilot our way. And you, Ramsey, will defend your patients with your trusty laser pistol *only* if you are fired upon. No one engages *anyone* except in defense of a patient, got it?" The colonel gave each of the medical staff a hard stare. "I know this is a tough one to swallow, but you'll do your jobs, I know that. Now, everybody, go get some sleep. Dismissed," he said, and then added, "All except you, Major Trainer. The rest of you can go."

Ramsey shot her a look with raised eyebrows. Trainer responded with a slight hike of her shoulders. The colonel waited until the others had filed out, then closed the door to the command conference room.

"Sir?" she said, standing with her hands clasped behind her back. Not quite at attention, but not at ease either.

The colonel waved a hand. "Sit back down, Liz," he said, sliding into a chair himself. She did. He gave a slight groan. "God, I'm getting too old for this. Okay." He rubbed his face. "I'm going to give it to you straight. We're going to lose this in a big way. My own assessment. Command thinks they can salvage something? Christ, they're dreaming. This won't be the last stand, but it's probably the second-to-last."

She'd half expected this, but now that the words had been said—really out in the open—she felt her heart go numb and a feeling of something cold as glacial ice settle into the pit of her stomach. "If that's true, why are we staying? Why not say to hell with it and evacuate now?"

"Because we haven't gotten the go-ahead, for one, but that's not a real reason. Hell, I'd move us in a heartbeat if I could, but we don't have the people-movers, nothing that can really get us out of here, pronto, and I'm not leaving one of our patients behind."

"What about DropShips?"

"Already asked, already declined." He chafed his biceps with both hands. "I think the simple truth of the matter is that if these soldiers are too banged up to fight, then Command's going to call it a loss and keep on going."

"So we're written off? But what about our patients? They're not statistics. They're men and women!"

"They're casualties, Liz. We all are. It's damage control, pure and simple. You want to stop hemorrhaging, you got to control whatever's bleeding you dry. Well, we're bleeding out men and materiel on this offensive. Command's not going to pour more resources into this end of the Twenty-Third, that's all there is to it. They've calculated the odds and figured it's better to cut their losses."

"And leave us behind, with nowhere to go," said Trainer, bitterly.

"Like I said, chances are McDonald's forces are going to march in here and take us all prisoner. Good for our patients, bad for us, but at least we'll be alive. That's something." The colonel screwed up his features. "But there's one more thing, Liz. I need you to get *your* patients up and out."

"Out? You mean, as in back to the front lines? But you just said..."

"We need to maintain the illusion that we're making a fight of it. Pull out too many people, and McDonald will figure it out, and you can bet she'll come running. Never met the woman myself, but she's got a rep, and on the basis of what's flowing down that volcano, I believe what I hear." The colonel sighed, shook his head. "It's hell; I know, Liz. I don't like it, but I can't argue with it. Look, those boys and girls out there, *your* patients, they're Command's best shot."

"They're convenient cannon fodder, is what you mean," said Trainer. Her voice was saturated with disgust. "Colonel, you're ordering me to send those men and women off to die—*to prolong a battle we're going to lose eventually anyway.*"

The colonel ducked his head in agreement. "I wish I could say it was otherwise, Liz. But I need you to do this. Ramsey, his patients are too damn banged up to help Command any. But yours can. You just got to push them a little faster."

"How fast?"

"I want them out day after tomorrow."

"The eleventh." Trainer exhaled. "That's fast. Some of them only came in this afternoon."

"I know that. And there's one more thing. Stanton: It'd be real nice if you could get him up and moving back to the front line. Shame to see a 'Mech just sitting, and it's no use to us, anyway. Might just give McDonald's forces the wrong idea."

"You mean that we might put up a fight." Trainer gnawed on her lower lip, then shook her head. "The problem is I don't think he can. A lot of those kids, probably I can get them out. But something's really got Stanton by the throat."

"Something you can medicate?"

"It's not that type of sickness. Anyway, any medication that strong, and you can forget his being able to walk, much less pilot anything. Stanton's got a...soul sickness."

She was dismissed a short time after. It was a moonless night, and she almost didn't see Ramsey waiting for her outside. He peeled away from the side of the command Quonset.

"Well?"

Trainer jammed her hands in her camo trouser pockets and shivered. The desert cooled off at night. "It's bad."

"Hell. Got a smoke?"

"Sure," said Trainer, taking out her pack and tapping out a cigarette. There was a small metallic snick of a lighter, and then she saw Ramsey's face, a ruddy mask, as if a switch had been thrown by the tiny flame as he lit up. His face was lost in darkness again as he cut the lighter.

"That stuff'll kill you," she said, tucking her pack back into her breast pocket.

"Huh. Sound medical advice," Ramsey said around his cigarette. A puff of smoke shot out of the corner of his mouth. "That is, if our brothers and sisters of the Eleventh don't first." He inhaled, held it, then blew out. Trainer's nose tingled with the scent of burned tobacco. "What's the story?"

She told him. When she finished, Ramsey was silent, and in the darkness, she saw only the orange glow of his cigarette, and to the west, the sparkle of weapons' fire. She heard Ramsey drag in a breath, then say, "Things must be worse than bad."

"I'd say so." She turned back to Ramsey. "You going to fight?"

"You mean, defend my patients with my trusty pistol? I don't know. We pick up a weapon, then we're fair game."

"And if we don't, then we get to trust Lady Luck." Trainer sighed. "You think we're going to get out of this?"

"As in with our skins?" Ramsey flicked his cigarette into the darkness. The small orange dot arced like a tiny meteor and disappeared. He blew out a streamer of smoke. "I think the answer's pretty obvious, don't you?"

The next afternoon, dark clouds gathered on the horizon, beyond the mountain. Maybe some rain, finally.

She sat across from Stanton, who was huddled on his cot. The MechWarrior looked like crap. He was unshaven, and his steely-gray hair was mussed. The nurses said he'd been restless during the night and unable to settle down, even with a sedative. He'd been given a fresh change of uniform, but he hadn't washed, and his clothes smelled sour. His eyes were staring at some spot on the floor in front of her boots.

Sighing, she put her hands on her knees. "Captain, you can stay mum for as long as you like. But I can sit here, too, because that's my job. Now, that means if you won't talk to me, then you're giving me no choice." Empty threats, she knew. She had no intention of drugging him. What purpose would it serve? But she had to try.

"You have a choice," said Stanton suddenly. His gaze crawled up to her face. "You're just choosing one way over another."

Good, keep him talking. Better to fight than sit and stare. "Oh? Tell me my choices, Captain."

Stanton exhaled a laugh that was mainly air. His lips were cracked. "You could leave me alone. You could walk away. You don't want to know what's inside in my head, Doctor." His bloodshot eyes roved away a second, then returned. "You just don't."

"You don't know that. I'd like you to trust me."

"Why?"

"Because I can help."

"How?"

"Well, by talking, I think you'll feel better and—"

"Listen to yourself." Stanton's lips widened into a strange grin. "You're such a hypocrite. At least, I'm honest about my kind of killing. I get into my 'Mech. I blast someone to hell before he can blast me. But you." His gaze clicked down to her boots, then back to her face. "You call yourself a doctor, but you're just a killer. You pull the trigger every time you send one of us back to fight."

Trainer felt herself flush. "We're not talking about my job." She licked her lips. "We're talking about—"

"Killing," said Stanton. "We're talking about what you do. We're talking about what I've done."

Trainer keyed in on the words. "What you've done. You've said that before. You said that I didn't know what you'd done. What would happen if I did know, Captain?"

"I don't know." Stanton looked askance. Trainer saw the small muscles working along his jaw. "Maybe it's more that if I say it, out loud, it becomes real. Not that you can judge me any more than I hate myself."

Trainer sensed she was close to something. "Why? Why do you hate yourself, Captain? What have you done that's so terrible?"

For a moment, she didn't think he would answer. And then his face quivered, and broke apart, and he was crying from what she knew was an awful, limitless grief.

An overwhelming feeling of compassion for the man washed over her. Tears stung her eyes, and she blinked the tears back. "Captain," she said. She put her hand on his knee, just the slightest touch. "Captain, tell me."

"I..." Stanton said, his chest heaving, his voice hitching, "I...I killed...I killed the enemy."

"But, Captain, you—you were just doing your job."

"No," said Stanton, and the haunted look of loss and misery in his eyes would stay with her for the rest of her life. "No. Not when it's... your daughter."

No. She was prepared for anything, but not this. Brother against brother. Father against daughter. And Jonathan against... Horror left her numb and speechless, and she could only watch Stanton weep out his grief and loss. A little while later, she ordered sedation for Stanton, and then she left the Quonset. She couldn't bear anymore.

That evening, at dusk, she stared at the volcano. The flow of casualties had diminished—either because they were getting luckier, or there were no more soldiers to kill. The clouds were closer now, and there were lightening-like tracers of weapons fire all along the near slopes of the volcano, as if a swarm of fireflies had gotten loose.

McDonald was coming. And if Jonathan *was* with his regiment? Or if he lay dead on the battlefield? How would she know? She felt helpless and so small she wanted to curl up into a little ball and hide.

Stanton's *Zeus* stood a kilometer from the camp: a brooding, hulking, silent machine.

No casualties arrived the next morning. The bank of clouds Trainer had seen advancing the day before filled the sky, their underbellies heavy and gray.

By ten, McDonald's forces were spreading across the Plains like a wall of advancing water: two *Banshees*, a *Berserker*, and lastly, a *King Crab*. Foot soldiers and armored tanks milled around the legs of the 'Mechs.

The camp had a deserted feel to it. The patients they couldn't move were gathered into three Quonsets. Sidearms were distributed. Trainer put hers in a desk drawer. Ramsey strapped his holster around his waist. Trainer arched an eyebrow when she saw that. "I thought you didn't want to get shot at."

Ramsey shrugged. "Never hurts to be prepared."

They stood together, watching the machines and soldiers come. Trainer craned her neck. "I don't see any of our 'Mechs."

"That's because there are none left," said Ramsey. He turned aside and spat. "Hell." And then he shaded his eyes; it wasn't very bright out, but the gleam of the diffuse light of the morning off the advancing 'Mechs set up a white glare. "Oh, Jesus."

"What?" Trainer squinted. "What is it?"

Ramsey pointed. "Look."

Trainer's gaze followed in the direction he indicated, and then she gasped. "Oh, my God."

It was Stanton, sprinting for his 'Mech, too far away for anyone to stop him.

"Stanton!" Trainer screamed. *They'll think we're going to put up a fight!* "Stanton, stop! It's too late for that! Not now, *not now!*"

But either Stanton couldn't hear, or didn't care, because in a few moments, he disappeared into the bowels of his *Zeus*. Trainer waited in an agony of suspense through a minute, then two. There was a loud whirr, and then the *Zeus* quivered to life.

Horrified, Trainer watched the huge machine's cockpit pivot in a hot start protest of metal and gears. Its huge legs creaked, then pedaled in a backward walk. It lumbered around to face the oncoming army, its arms up and extended. There was a flash, and then Trainer was nearly blinded by a ruby-red blaze of laser fire from the *Zeus'* left torso.

The laser ripped across the right leg of the nearest *Banshee*. There was that peculiar shriek metal makes when it's being torn in two, and a smell of ozone in the air, and then the *Zeus* followed with another sizzle of laser fire that cut a swath across the *Banshee*'s chest. Caught off-guard, the *Banshee* teetered back and slouched right, its weight buckling its damaged right leg. But then there was a high hum, and Trainer watched as the *Berserker* put on speed and flew forward, its massive titanium hatchet upraised.

"Run!" Ramsey shouted.

Trainer felt as if she'd been jolted awake. She spun on her heel just as the *Berserker* reached the *Zeus*. A lance of laser fire from the *Zeus* went wide, and then the *Berserker*'s hatchet came smashing down, caving in the *Zeus*'s right shoulder with the first blow.

Suddenly, there were shouts; medical and support personnel went flying off in all directions; and the air was filled with laser and weapons fire from the advancing soldiers. Slugs whistled by her ears. *My God, McDonald thinks it's a trap, that we're trying to trick them!* Trainer's burning lungs pulled in air that was choked with smoke and the scent of burning flesh, and she sprinted for the far side of the camp, aiming for the relative safety of the medical Quonset.

She almost made it. Then, suddenly, she felt a blossom of pain bloom between her shoulders. Screaming, she staggered, and then another burst of weapons fire caught her in the back and chewed her flesh. The force of the blow spun her around. She crumpled to the ground, blood gushing from wounds that had pierced her back and exited through her chest. In a few seconds, the front of her uniform was soggy with bright red blood.

Jonathan... With the last of her strength, she turned her face to the sky. Her vision was constricting now, the world shrinking down to a narrow pinpoint. She felt unbearably cold, and then she began to shake as her blood pumped out onto the dry, black, thirsty earth. She couldn't move. Even blinking was an effort. Her mind felt sluggish, as if she were winding down like an old clock whose gears had simply worn out. In a few seconds, and probably less, she knew she would slip into a deep, long, dreamless sleep, and she wouldn't wake up.

The last thing she saw were the dark underbellies of the clouds, avatars of the approaching storm.

Colonel Linda McDonald's boots crunched over the ruins of the medical unit. She'd dismounted her *King Crab* as soon as she'd reached the medical complex. Anger boiled in her gut in counterpoint to the water bubbling in the steam vents beneath the black basalt plain. What a waste of lives! Even though she'd realized the *Zeus* had been the only bit of 'Mech weaponry, it had taken her too many precious moments to relay orders. By then, the damage had been done.

She'd already made a survey of the casualties on the volcano itself, lumbering over the hardened lava flows in her

King Crab. She'd picked her way over and around ruined bodies and machines on a battlefield, but that had been a real fight.

But not this. This was a massacre. McDonald's jaw firmed as her gaze swept over the debris and the broken, shattered corpses of patients and medical personnel flung into haphazard piles of bedding and bloodied bandages. Her people were already going through, recovering remains and zipping them away in black bags. There were some prisoners—patients, mainly, although she spotted one physician, male, red-haired, his uniform soaked with the blood of those he'd tried to save. But it looked to her as if the rest of the command personnel were dead; McDonald had already seen the body of the unit commander, a colonel she didn't know (a blessing), bundled away. Just beyond, and to the right, next to a smashed Quonset, was the body of another officer: a woman, her long blond hair dyed rust with blood. A physician, from the look of her uniform.

She directed her gaze toward the destroyed *Zeus. The maniac who started this mess.* The 'Mech lay on its side, the cockpit caved in and its belly ripped open by laser fire. God, if she'd only gotten control of the situation sooner, they might've been spared all this.

She heard the crunch of boots and turned to see one of her best pilots—the one who had piloted the *Berserker* that had destroyed the *Zeus.* "Peterson," she said. "You have a report?"

Holding his neurohelmet under his left arm, Peterson, a swarthy man with intense blue eyes and black curly hair, saluted with his right. "We've secured a perimeter, Colonel. I think it was just this one 'Mech. I'm sorry."

"Not your fault. You were fired on; you returned fire. How were we supposed to know?" And then, because she couldn't stand the taste of her own anger, she said, "God, what a waste! The Twenty-Third had to know that leaving their wounded..." She stopped when she saw that Peterson's gaze had flickered right, toward the ruined Quonset. "Captain?"

She watched Peterson take a single, unsteady step forward, then two, like a BattleMech with a faulty gyro; his neurohelmet dropped, unnoticed, to the shattered earth; and then he broke into a run.

"Captain?" she called again. "John?"

But Peterson didn't stop. He reached the body and stood there for a long moment, looking down at the woman. And then it was as if his strength gave way, because he swayed and tottered. His knees folded, and he sagged to the earth. He gathered the body of the woman into his arms, and then McDonald saw his shoulders begin to shiver.

She came up behind Peterson. "John," she said, and put her hand on his shoulder. She felt a long shudder ripple through his body, and even though she couldn't see his face, she knew he was weeping.

"Oh, Liz," she heard him say, his voice clogged with grief. "Oh, no..."

Understanding blazed through McDonald like a shaft of sun piercing thick clouds. *Dear God.* McDonald looked down at the woman in Peterson's arms. Her skin was white as marble, and her lips were parted slightly, as if she were about to speak. Her chest was shredded and so saturated with blood and gore that McDonald caught the odor of wet copper. Through the blood, she saw the sparkle of a diamond in the shape of a single tear.

Slowly, McDonald turned and walked away and gave Peterson the privacy of his grief.

Overhead, lightening flashed. There was a roll of thunder that echoed through the ruins and shook the ground. And then it began to rain.

BANSHEE
ASSAULT—95 TONS

BERSERKER
ASSAULT—100 TONS

KING CRAB
ASSAULT—**100** TONS

ZEUS
ASSAULT—**80** TONS

EIGHT NINE THREE

STEVEN MOHAN, JR.

GAINES
ALTAIS
LYRAN PROTECTORATE
5 JUNE 3039

Hikotoro Yamashita strolled toward the front gate of the Gaines Port Authority, nodding and smiling pleasantly at his death as if it were his oldest and dearest friend.

Right now his death was dressed up like a Lyran soldier, a twenty-year-old boy with hard eyes and a suspicious hand on the holstered needler at his hip. The soldier stepped out from a small guard shack. "You there, stop."

Yamashita obeyed, carefully lowering the burlap sack he carried to the ground. The bottles inside clinked together as the sack shifted. "*Ohayo gozaimasu.*"

The soldier's face twisted in confusion. "What?"

"*Sumimasen*—uh, excuse me, uh, Sergeant." Yamashita said, deliberately misstating the man's grade.

"It's corporal," the man snapped.

"Oh. I apology. I didn't—"

"Your name," the soldier said brusquely.

"Watanabe," said Yamashita cheerfully, handing the man his forged papers. "Kiichi Watanabe."

The soldier took a couple steps back before he glanced down at the papers. Smart.

Yamashita was careful not to glance at the gate as the soldier examined his papers. Instead he looked up at Big Smoker, the immense cinder cone that loomed over the horizon. A wisp of gray smoke curled away from the volcano's summit. Yamashita sensed the mountain's anger, smelled it in the sulfurous stink that soured the perfume of a late spring day, tasted it in the fine grit carried on the wind.

It was an evil portent.

Ukawa would've said this was a stupid stunt. But then Ukawa was dead, killed when a Lyran tank's PPC bolt blasted through the bulkhead of his APC, turning everyone inside into a fine red paste.

Most of Yamashita's comrades were dead. The rest were gone: the last DCMS unit on the planet had been evacuated the week before, leaving Altais to the Lyran Commonwealth. Yamashita was stranded on an enemy-held world. The smart thing would've been to go to ground.

Yamashita was never one for doing the smart thing.

He glanced at the corporal. The soldier was dressed in well-worn fatigues, the patch on his right shoulder marking him as a member of the Eighth Donegal Guard. Yamashita noted other things about that uniform: the astringent smell of Altaisian mud, a scorch mark on his left boot, a faded brick-colored stain over the right arm.

This guard was a combat soldier, one who'd survived this long by being careful and smart. He wasn't going to stop now just because his officers had stuck him in front of a gate.

This was going to be hard.

"Okay," said the soldier, handing the papers back, "what's your business here?"

"I'm here to see the Port Commissioner."

The soldier studied "Kiichi Watanabe" for a moment. Yamashita's hair was slicked back, and he wore a dark suit jacket with long sleeves, a garment obviously too hot for the day. "Watanabe" looked like a shady businessman.

Which was not so far from the truth, after all.

"Is he expecting you?" the soldier finally asked.

The question was a trap, an invitation to lie.

Yamashita played his only card. "No. But I guarantee he'll want to see me."

The soldier's eyes flickered to the sack resting on the ground. "What's in there?" He bent down.

"A gift for the Commissioner. Four bottles of New Ross Private Reserves, the finest wine on Altais."

"*Four* bottles?" asked the soldier, obviously noticing the fifth bottle in the sack.

"*Hai*, four." Yamashita smiled gently. "Each worth a couple hundred C-bills."

The soldier's gaze flickered back to the guard shack. Perhaps he wondered if there was enough to share with his comrade. The soldier pulled a bottle from the sack and held it up. Sunlight filtered through the ruby-colored wine. "I'll need to verify your identity."

"Of course," said Yamashita easily.

He'd make it through a fingerprint analysis or a retinal scan, but there were other checks, more basic checks, and if the soldier realized Yamashita was a soldier of the Draconis Combine, he would meet a sudden and violent end.

If he was lucky.

This thought didn't trouble Yamashita overmuch. He had learned to live with the reality of his death as one learns to live with the weather. Some days it rained and some days it did not, and since you could never tell beforehand which it would be, the wise man was always prepared for both.

Besides, there were secrets to be learned, if one had sharp eyes.

After patting down Yamashita, the soldier pulled an optical scanner from his belt. "Hold still." He brought the device up to Yamashita's left eye, pressed a button, and studied the readout. "Kiichi Watanabe," he said softly.

The soldier stared at him for a long moment with those hard eyes. Yamashita tensed, waiting for the order to strip to his waist or roll up his sleeves.

Instead, the soldier turned and bellowed, "Comstock!"

A Lyran PFC stepped out of the guard shack. "Aye, Bernie?"

"Take this gentleman—" He glanced at Yamashita. "—to the Commissioner's office. If he gives you any trouble..." The soldier didn't finish, instead flashing a tight little smile.

A cruel smile.

Neither Yamashita nor the PFC had to ask what that smile meant.

It was a long walk from the front gate to the Commissioner's office, and Yamashita spent every bit of it watching and listening.

A LoaderMech painted heavy-equipment yellow bent to pull shipping containers off a line of parked trucks, setting each of them down on the ferrocrete deck hard enough to produce a long, hollow *bong*. Longshoremen in hardhats scrambled to unload the containers while bored soldiers looked on.

Most of the containers were marked "*Willas*" or "*New Ross*," meaning they had come from one of the planet's spaceports.

But not all of them.

Yamashita watched the longshoreman unload a series of trucks marked with the seal of the Lyran Commonwealth.

Working quickly, longshoremen unbolted the shipping container from the first truck. An overhead crane riding on rails fifteen meters above the port's deck centered itself over the container. Riggers moved in and attached wire cables to the lift points. The crane hoisted away, lifting the container smoothly into the air. When it set the box down again, more workers pried it open.

Yamashita caught a glimpse of what was inside as he and the PFC walked by.

A rack of short-range missiles.

It was the same drill with the next three LC-marked boxes.

But not number five.

The fifth container was moved to a different spot altogether. As a special military shipment, it wouldn't pass through customs.

Yamashita would've bet quite a lot that container number five didn't hold short-range missiles.

The office was a long, narrow room with one wall fashioned entirely from ferroglass, so the Commissioner could look out over the port. Yamashita was careful to take a chair facing away from the window, even though he was itching to watch the port's activity.

Because he was itching to watch the port's activity.

The Port Commissioner, Colonel Rudolf Drescher, seated himself behind a mahogany monstrosity of a desk. The other officer in the room, *Hauptmann-Kommandant* Angus MacPhail, remained standing, his face carefully blank, his only concession to comfort the fact that he leaned stiffly against the wall.

"Well, Mr. Watanabe, you talked your way past our guards," said Drescher. "That's impressive enough. What do you want?"

Drescher was a big man, big and soft around the middle, 120 kilos of muscle running to fat, all of it stuffed into a dress uniform. His dark hair was regulation, but only just.

This was a man who enjoyed the finer things in life. And although he was a Lyran officer, he was not a member of the Donegal Guard. He was a logistics expert, brought in to manage the Altaisian ports.

Exactly the kind of man Yamashita had hoped for.

Yamashita shrugged. "What does any man want? The chance to do a little business."

MacPhail leaned forward. "And do ya expect us to believe ya have no loyalty to the Combine?"

Yamashita glanced at MacPhail.

Unlike Drescher, he was a lean whip of a man who wore fatigues without any adornment at all, not even a regimental patch. Except for the subdued insignia that indicated his rank, the *Kommandant* was a cipher. This was the kind of man who traded in secrets.

Exactly the kind of man Yamashita feared.

He met MacPhail's eyes. "I don't know what the war means to House Kurita or House Steiner, but to me all it means is a change in market conditions." He glanced back at Drescher. "One that brings opportunity."

Drescher and MacPhail exchanged a look that spoke volumes.

These two men didn't like each other.

"What did you have in mind?" Drescher asked softly.

"I can get things," said Yamashita.

"Aye," said MacPhail tightly. "Ore from the mining concerns. Equipment from the factories."

"No." Yamashita shook his head. "Nothing of military value. I'm talking about luxuries. Wine. Altaisian caviar. Spiced beef. Diamonds. Saltgrass."

Drescher leaned forward. "In exchange for..."

"Off-world luxuries. We sell them here for a healthy markup and split the profits. I pay you in Altaisian luxuries that you turn around and sell off-world for another big profit. You win twice."

Drescher sat back, his face suddenly blank. Yamashita could almost see the numbers percolating through the man's brain. "Most interesting," he said softly.

That was too much for MacPhail. "Gods, man," he snapped. "This is a Combine citizen—"

"A *former* Combine citizen," said Drescher. "Altais is now a protectorate of the Lyran Commonwealth."

"Just so," said Yamashita.

"Ya canna trust 'im. Give me a few hours with 'im, Colonel, and we'll see just exactly what he is."

Yamashita sat up a little straighter. If Drescher passed him into the Kommandant's custody he was done. MacPhail was not a man he could keep secrets from. Yamashita knew this at some deep level, but he would not allow himself to *really* know it, would not reveal himself through fear.

I am just a simple businessman, he thought. *One who cannot even tell the difference between a sergeant and a corporal. Crooked,* hai, *but in a way you can understand and exploit.*

"What's in the bag?" Drescher asked.

Yamashita reached down and pulled out a bottle of wine. "A gift." He handed it over to Drescher. "A token of good will."

The man studied the bottle with the gleam of avarice in his eyes. They had a deal. Yamashita could feel it.

"What happened to your finger?" MacPhail asked.

A shiver wriggled down Yamashita's spine.

"What, this?" he said as coolly as he could. He held up his left hand, revealing a pinky that had been severed at the first joint. "An accident. I used to work in a factory. It happens."

"Aye," said MacPhail coldly. "Especially on this world."

Drescher put the bottle of wine down and sat back in his chair, a new calculation plain on his face. "This is quite nice," he said, not even looking at the wine, "but if we are to do business, I require more."

Yamashita's stomach clenched. He knew exactly what the colonel was suggesting. He wanted a name.

If Yamashita didn't give him one, Drescher would turn him over to MacPhail to sweat one out of him. And if he did give him one, he was a spy and so, again, MacPhail.

Either way he was a dead man. All because MacPhail noticed his finger.

"I am not a spy," said Yamashita stiffly. "But I have done business on this world a long time. I know who the players are. Recently, some new names have surfaced, rather, ah, rapidly."

"Oh," said Drescher easily, "who in particular?"

"Sumiko Tawara," said Yamashita. "Junshi Nomo. Charles Hanson."

Tawara and Nomo were innocents. But not Hanson.

Hanson was a *tai-i* in the service of the House Kurita's feared Internal Security Force.

If the names were all valueless, Drescher would conclude Yamashita was an agent protecting his network. If the names were all ISF, Drescher would know Yamashita was an agent spooked into betraying his people. If there were a mix, Drescher *might* decide that "Watanabe" was just a businessman who'd noticed some things.

Drescher peered at Yamashita for a long moment and then he stood, leaned over the desk, and shook his hand. "Shall we drink to our deal?"

The wine was sweet and full-bodied, with a note of ripe raspberries and a rich, leathery bouquet. Drescher seemed to enjoy it very much. MacPhail didn't have any.

When Yamashita stepped out of the Commissioner's office, he knew he was lucky to be leaving with his life. This was going to be a dangerous business.

Absentmindedly, he pulled up his right sleeve to scratch an itch, revealing a dragon tattoo the color of sapphire coiled around his wrist.

After leaving the port, Yamashita caught a bus across town and transferred twice to lose any tail, stopped to eat at a Thai restaurant just to be sure, and then stopped at Body by M.

He slipped in the side door, strolling past a score of housewives in leotards doing aerobics to the driving beat of the latest jazzpop hit.

Yamashita hated to give Ikeda any credit, but using the health club as a front had been a stroke of genius. It was the last place anyone would suspect of housing an anti-Lyran cell.

The club was a brightly lit place full of potted ferns, the smell of sweat, and frumpy people chasing after beautiful bodies. The owner, Margit Devaux, was a real fitness expert who saw it as her mission in life to help people lose those few extra pounds.

It just happened she was also a patriot.

The club was so far beyond reproach that two members of the occupation government worked out here. Ikeda and his three lieutenants had memberships, too, and the thought of the occupiers working out next to ISF always made Yamashita smile.

He did *not* have a membership. There was no point. The elaborate tattoos covering his back, chest, and both arms would instantly mark him as *yakuza*. And from there it was a short leap to the conclusion that he'd served with the First Ghosts, the *yakuza* regiment that had been all but wiped out at Carlingford.

Yamashita slipped down a side hallway and tapped a six-digit access code into a keypad beside the door to the storage room. The door clicked open and he stepped inside, surprised to find himself alone with cases of power shakes and bottled water. Yamashita frowned.

Where was Ikeda?

Not one to waste an opportunity, he walked across the room and punched a second combination into another keypad, popping open Margit's wall safe. He reached beneath the pile of contracts and cash receipts until he found a slim blue folio.

He pulled it out and flipped it open.

The ISF had broken the encryption on the black box fax machines the Federated Commonwealth used for secure comms. The DCMS had been fortunate enough to capture one of the black boxes during the Fourth Succession War. The folio contained the latest intercepts. Yamashita pulled the first one out.

"You're not cleared for those," said a gruff voice.

Yamashita flinched. To rifle through ISF secrets was to invite death. Or worse. Still, he looked up and said, *"Kashira."*

Ikeda scowled as he closed the door behind him. "What?"

"'You're not cleared for those, *Kashira*,'" said Yamashita. "I am a Talon Sergeant of the Draconis Combine Military Service, and I will thank you to address me as such."

Ikeda grunted.

Yamashita would never get the respect he deserved from a man like *Tai-sa* Kazutoshi Ikeda, even though he and his brothers had paid for it with their blood. The colonel was an old-line conservative, unwilling to acknowledge the worth of a "gangster thug."

The irony was Ikeda tolerated Yamashita for the same reason he despised him: he was *yakuza*. Yamashita had been born on the street, and could get anything. Ikeda was happy to rely on Yamashita's skill, but he'd never show him any sign of respect.

It was an old issue for the *yakuza*, long regarded as the dregs of Combine society. The very name "*yakuza*" came from the Japanese words for the numbers eight, nine, and three, a losing hand in the traditional card game of *Oicho-Kabu*.

No one believed in the *yakuza*.

Except Theodore Kurita. The Combine's *Gunji-no-Kanrei* had given the *yakuza* the right to fight for their nation. And because of that, Yamashita would bear any burden, pay any price to justify the *Kanrei*'s faith.

"You're late," said Yamashita.

Ikeda stalked across the room and jerked the folio out of his hands. "Planning to sell these secrets to your friends?"

"I have no friends on Altais," Yamashita shot back, "only loyalties."

Ikeda shoved the folio back in the safe and slammed the door. He was a short fireplug of a man. His iron-gray hair was cut in a military crew cut, and he wore a stylish blue suit that fit him badly. He looked exactly like what he was: a military spook. It was a wonder the Lyrans hadn't picked him up already.

"I hear you were down at the port today," Ikeda said.

Yamashita nodded. "I saw some interesting things."

Ikeda inclined his head.

"The rumors about the JumpShip command circuits are true. I saw them unloading military equipment from containers marked with a Lyran seal. Probably rushed here to deal with the Second Ghosts before they evacuated."

"So?"

"*Jigoku*," Yamashita snapped. "We have to do something."

Ikeda shook his head. "The best we can do is gather information and feed it back to the DCMS."

"Listen, Altais is the deepest penetration of the Commonwealth Thrust. They're going to use this world as a jumping off point to attack Algedi and Rukbat, Alya and Shitara, maybe even Tsukude."

Ikeda's eyes narrowed. "How do you know that?"

"I can read a chart. The point is they're going to use this world, and we have to stop them."

"What you're talking about is suicide," said Ikeda indignantly. "That's why the world government surrendered. Why the Second Ghosts cut and ran. We don't have the forces to fight them on Altais."

There's always a way to resist, Yamashita thought, *if you're not too stupid to see it.*

"Did you see anything else?" Ikeda asked gruffly.

"They're smuggling."

Ikeda offered him a contemptuous smile. "A fact I'm sure you found most interesting."

Yamashita said nothing, but thought, *You bet I did.*

"I also heard you made a deal with Commissioner Drescher."

Yamashita snorted. "Well, you don't think I got in by politely asking for a tour, did you?"

Ikeda's jaw set. "Hanson was just arrested. That's why I'm late."

Yamashita blinked. "What?" The lie was so good he almost believed it himself.

Ikeda leaned in and jabbed a thick finger into Yamashita's chest. "If I find out you had anything to do with his arrest, I'll turn you in to the Lyrans myself."

And then he turned and stalked off before Yamashita could speak any of the false denials that came automatically to his lips.

Yamashita first noticed the tail when he was coming out of a meeting with an agent for an *agrat* farm, the taste of salty black eggs still heavy in his mouth. The *agrat* was a local pseudo-amphibian about the size of a monitor lizard, whose eggs were supposed to taste like sturgeon roe.

Yamashita didn't know if they really did or not—he'd never tasted real caviar—but the fact that some thought so made the contract he'd signed for 200 kilos of Altaisian caviar very valuable.

He was making a killing. Even considering Drescher's cut, he'd made more money in the last month than he'd ever made before.

So this was why people became collaborators.

Yamashita watched the tail out of the corner of his eye. A young man with short, blond hair who'd tried to dress like a local, but missed the mark.

One of MacPhail's.

Yamashita had taken a cab to the meeting, but he decided to walk a couple blocks and look for a likely place.

He ambled past an open-air fish market, where native blue snappers and six-legged crabs were laid out on beds of shaved ice. People crowded round the displays and called out their orders. Bills flashed back and forth.

Yamashita pushed his way through the crowd and glanced back. He'd lost the tail.

He sighed heavily.

Yamashita doubled back and pretended to examine something the fishmongers called "prawns" but looked more like roaches to him. After a few moments he saw a familiar blond head in the crowd.

He walked past the fish market, paused to window-shop in a little jewelry store, and then ducked down a side street that turned out to be a blind alley.

Perfect.

Yamashita glanced around like he was lost. His right hand drifted down to the small of his back, where he felt a little patch of slickness beneath his shirt.

How long was this going to take?

He heard a small sound behind him. He didn't turn. Instead he muttered, "I'm sure she said this was the place."

Something hard and heavy smashed against the side of his head and the world dimmed. Yamashita lurched to one side and fought to keep his feet.

He staggered around and threw a punch in a random direction, landing a glancing blow to his attacker's jaw.

It wasn't enough.

Another blow slammed down, the ground rushed up to meet him, and—

Yamashita had a nightmare about being beaten, blows raining down again and again until he curled up into a ball on the floor and just took them. Later he woke up and found out that it hadn't been a dream.

A tight pain in his chest told him they'd broken two, maybe three ribs. His mouth tasted like blood, and the blurry vision in his left eye hinted at a detached retina.

But the worst was his head. Whenever he moved, molten agony shot through his skull, incandescent white light filled his vision. Concussion.

Or worse.

He reached back to touch the small of his back and found they'd stripped off his shirt, no doubt looking for the tattoos they knew had to be there.

Hopefully they hadn't looked too closely.

He lay there for a long time, his body and face pressed against the cold concrete floor, eyes closed, waiting for what came next.

After a time a voice said, "It seems ya dinna lose your pinky in an accident after all."

"No," Yamashita croaked. He didn't open his eyes. Didn't look up to confirm that today his death had dressed up like Angus MacPhail. It was enough to hear his voice.

"You're *yakuza.*"

"*Hai,*" said Yamashita in a gravelly voice that hurt his throat.

"First Ghosts or Second?"

"First." Yamashita slowly opened his eyes and saw a blurry shape.

The shape nodded. "I especially liked the bit about the health club. Course it dinna do any good in the end, but no doubt yer a clever jake."

Yamashita said nothing.

"We've rounded up all yer friends. Rest assured, ya won't die alone, man."

"I can—"

"Can what? What do ya have to trade this time?"

"Sabotage," Yamashita whispered.

There was a long silence from the MacPhail-shape as he thought this through. "A nice try," he said finally. "But before we're done, you'll beg to tell us all about it. And even if ya dinna break, sabotage is something we can find ourselves. Have ya got anything else?"

Yamashita fell silent.

"That's what I thought. You'll never see the outside of this cell, Watanabe, or whatever your name is. I promise ya that."

"Drescher won't—"

MacPhail's harsh laughter cut him off. "Colonel Drescher is in no position to help ya now. Trust me." The blurry shape stood. "May as well rest. We'll talk more later."

A door clicked shut, and Yamashita drifted back into comforting oblivion.

For some amount of time Yamashita couldn't even guess at, the world turned off. And then someone bent over him, a dark shape blocking the bright glare of the naked bulb overhead.

Yamashita tasted something cool and clean. The man was trickling water into his mouth.

He grunted and rolled over onto his side.

"Oh, so you're awake," said a voice.

"Hungry," Yamashita croaked.

"Sure, I'll feed you. The Kommandant says you have to be strong enough to talk."

The guard turned to pick up a tray.

Yamashita reached down to the small of his back and felt the slickness there. He peeled back the two sheets of plastic, one from the other, careful only to touch the edge.

"Here we are," said the guard.

Yamashita's stomach growled at the thick smell of beef stew.

The man set the tray down.

Yamashita moved like lightning. He ripped the decal off, lunged forward, and slapped the plastic surface against the man's face.

The guard stumbled backward and fell. The decal was coated with a fast-acting neural agent; the guard never had a chance. He collapsed, overturning the tray, and spilling beef stew all over the cold, hard floor.

He lay there seizing violently for a moment, and then he was suddenly, terribly still.

Yamashita staggered to his feet and almost blacked out. He stood there for a few minutes, breathing hard, clawing his way back to reality.

Then he bent down and picked up the guard's M&G flechette pistol.

An exact replica of one of Yamashita's tattoos—an orange tiger—marked the dead man's cheek. It was masterful work. Even looking for it, Yamashita had a hard time seeing the nearly invisible plastic.

But he found it at last and peeled up the decal. Then he turned to go, leaving MacPhail with nothing but a dead guard and a mystery.

Two days after escaping from MacPhail's safe house, Yamashita recovered enough to drag himself up the five flights of stairs that led to the top of an abandoned factory a couple klicks from the Gaines port. He hobbled past long-silent air handlers and exhaust fans until he reached the building's edge.

Today, Big Smoker was silent and still. Yamashita hoped it was a good omen. Hoped all he'd paid had purchased the prize he sought.

He raised binoculars to his face and looked out over the port. He was too far away to see much detail, but what he could see brought a grim smile to his lips. The Lyrans had set up a vast field of shipping containers. Box after box lined the tarmac and they were opening every single last one of them.

Even better, they had crews inspecting military equipment. Heavy tanks, APC's, even BattleMechs were getting the once over.

No doubt looking for sabotage.

Yamashita could've laughed.

Until he heard the *click* of a round being chambered. He slowly lowered the binoculars and extended his hands so whoever was behind him could see them. Then he turned around.

This time his death was dressed up like *Tai-sa* Ikeda, pointing a weapon straight at his head.

So the old bastard had survived after all. Yamashita had to give the man points for that. "How'd you get out?"

"MacPhail suspected you all along. I read about it in the intercepts. I just had time to destroy them and get clear."

Yamashita puffed a mouthful of air out past his lips.

"They found the cell through you," said Ikeda. It wasn't a question.

Yamashita glanced at the gun in Ikeda's hand, then nodded. He didn't feel like begging for his life. He doubted it would do any good anyway.

"*Yakuza* scum," Ikeda whispered. "I *knew* you were no good."

Yamashita said nothing. What was there to say?

"I told you if you betrayed us, I'd give you to the Lyrans."

Yamashita shook his head. "If you have to kill me, then pull the trigger, but don't undo my work."

"Your work," Ikeda sneered.

"Some men think war is a matter of honor and valor. Men like you think it's the interplay of secrets. But what war is, the thing that's truly at its heart, is logistics."

"I know that," Ikeda snapped.

"No you don't. You just think you do."

Ikeda scowled.

"Have you ever moved a thousand keys of heroin? A shipment of bootleg trivids? A container full of mil-grade needlers?"

"Of course not," Ikeda snarled.

Yamashita raised his left hand with its severed pinky. "The *yakuza* take a finger to teach a lesson, so that it's never forgotten. Do you know what lesson I needed to learn, *Tai-sa* Ikeda?"

The colonel shook his head.

"I was late with a shipment." He paused and glanced at the port. "Logistics is life, *Tai-sa*. If you live on the street, you understand that more deeply than a man like you ever could."

Ikeda glanced at the port. "What did you do?"

"MacPhail suspected I was a plant from the beginning. I had to give them Hanson to let me in."

Yamashita saw Ikeda's face tighten, saw the gun shake in his hand.

"Drescher looked the other way because I made him a lot of money, but I knew MacPhail wouldn't let it go. I didn't want him to. For my plan to work, he had to catch me."

"And everyone else, too."

"*Hai*," said Yamashita with real regret. "I'm sorry about that."

"You betrayed us."

"Not betrayed. Sacrificed. Traded their lives for victory. What DCMS commander wouldn't do the same?"

Ikeda snorted. "Victory."

"I told MacPhail I had committed sabotage. He believed me because he found a real resistance cell. And for another reason. Because unarmed and badly beaten, I still found a way to escape. He had to believe I couldn't have done that without help."

Ikeda's eyes narrowed. "How *did* you do that?"

Yamashita remembered the mark of the tiger on the guard's cheek. "I used a weapon only a *yakuza* could use," he said softly.

"Or you're still working with the Lyrans, and all this is just an elaborate lie."

"Look out there, *Tai-sa*!" Yamashita shouted, stabbing his binoculars in the port's direction. "They are searching through every container, disassembling every weapon system, looking for sabotage that doesn't exist. It will take them at least a week to figure it out. I, working by myself, have halted the entire FedCom advance from this world for a week, and all it cost was the lives of five operatives."

"A *week*," said Ikeda dismissively.

Yamashita said nothing. *Yakuza* heard many things others did not hear, and he had heard a word, a secret word.

Orochi.

Yamashita did not know what it meant, and he did not want to know. All that mattered was the *Kanrei* had found a way to save the Combine, if only his soldiers could buy him the time to execute his plan. The week by itself might not be enough.

But it was a start.

"So you are a hero, then." Ikeda's voice shook with fury. "I should let you go. You should get a medal."

Yamashita met Ikeda's angry gaze. "Do whatever you must," he said calmly to his death. "I am *yakuza*, and it is my honor to serve the *Kanrei*."

Then he turned his face away and raised his eyes to the summit of the great volcano, waiting without fear for whatever would happen next.

ISOLATION'S WEIGHT

RANDALL N. BILLS

JACOB'S MOUNTAIN
TORTINIA
KIAMBA
BENJAMIN MILITARY DISTRICT
DRACONIS COMBINE
15 APRIL 3067

Lieutenant Cameron Baird watched as the odious-black smoke trail dissipated on the stiff mountain winds. Burning debris rained down across several kilometers. It looked as if the sky was bleeding.

"Can you believe that?" His comm system crackled to life as James broke the silence. "Wow. Too much."

Wow? Watching a Clan *Broadsword*-class DropShip falling through a cobalt sky had been sobering, true. Like a flaming thunderbolt tossed by Zeus's own hand. But Cameron read deeper. What the hell was a Ghost Bear force doing raiding Kiamba? What could be of interest to a lone DropShip on Jacob's Mountain? Surely they could care less about elements from MacLeod's Regiment of the Northwind Highlanders.

He shivered, though he knew the cockpit didn't hold a chill, and would soon be anything but cold. He hated it here. Hated the snow and the isolation from anything living beyond the small force around him. Hell, he would've preferred Hecate's

Swamp to this eternal cold. But not James. Wherever the action was.

Had Cameron ever been that young? That naïve? He hoped not.

"Yes, James. Wonderful." Did the boy hear the sarcasm? Probably not. The starch of his new cooling vest—handed to him, what, six months ago upon graduation from the NMA?— probably pushed up against his ears, making it hard for him to hear anything. Beyond his own voice, of course.

Cameron couldn't help but let a quirky smile spread his slim lips, a sparkle flashing in hazel eyes. He knew a certain lieutenant colonel who had shepherded a younger, stupider Cameron through *his* first year after the Academy. Who almost throttled him on at least ten different occasions. At least.

Cameron reached forward and toggled from the topographical map that displayed across the secondary screen, to radar, as the ghost of Geoff McFadden's words seemed to rise up like holography, temporarily blotting out the forward view screen and the snowy terrain beyond.

"When you're a leader, you lead and protect. One comes with the other. If you can't protect those under your command to the best of your ability, if you can't lead them to be leaders themselves—well, then you've got no business wearing The Bars."

Always the capitalizations in his voice.

Geoff's words seemed to echo in the confines of the cockpit. The man had been the father he never knew; regardless of the weight, Cameron tried to carry the responsibilities he now held with the same dedication and honor his mentor did. How could he do anything less?

The radar began sweeping, pinpointing Caden's lance, Geoff's Old Guard lance and the lance on loan from the Third Proserpina Hussars. Twelve 'Mechs—several green warriors. What would they find over the hill? He checked his secondary monitor and radar screen once more, which showed a pair of *Tatsu* aerospace fighters whipping away at well over Mach two, vanishing over the mountain.

"Thanks for the fire, Hussars. Kind of cold up here." Lieutenant-Colonel McFadden's voice broke over the comm.

Cameron smiled and checked the radar to see Geoff's lance the next ridge line over, but more importantly, several hundred meters closer to the crash sight. He shook his head, feeling the comforting weight of his neurohelmet. "Going to get yourself in trouble, boss," he said, but softly enough not to activate his own mic. With that flight actually attached to the Hussars' Third battalion, and O'Riley's touchiness over having to do combat exercises—regardless of how few were involved—with *mere* mercenaries in this northern, frozen wasteland, Cameron just knew ol' Harrison would make his voice known. Later, of course. Always later. And much worse than the original offense.

You'd think the Third Proserpina were a Sword of Light regiment for all their prickliness.

"No problem, Old Guard. Glad to bring a match to the barbecue. Just make sure what we tossed onto your grill is crispy black when you're done. *Hai*?" The unknown pilot's voice boomed laughter, lively and good-natured. Cameron felt shock. No way could he be part of the Hussars.

"Okay Highlanders," Geoff's strong voice began, "they've downed some bad guys. Time for us to put them away. Move forward at best speed and engage at will," with the unspoken line *before the Hussars lance has all the fun*. A series of affirmatives echoed across the comm.

Of course, Cameron would've loved to be taking command of this by himself, but with the Old Guard command lance on hand to help smooth the training issues between elements of MacLeod's Third Battalion and the Hussars' Third...well, he couldn't be happier to have the old man along for the ride.

Cameron reached over and pushed his own throttle forward a half, sending his *Wolverine* into a smart step forward—difficult through the deep snow. One of these days he really did mean to send a surprise gift to the quartermaster who'd managed to acquire several of the new WVR-8Ks from the DCMS. He'd been in it less than a year, but knew already he never wanted to pilot another machine. He could've probably gotten one of the Clan machines taken off Huntress due to his credentials at the Academy, but he felt confident nothing would've felt this good. This right.

"Okay, boys," he spoke up to his own lance, "you heard the boss. Bad guys over the ridge and we get to clean up the mess. Provided the fly boys left us any scraps."

Although he was serious, the responding laughter felt good. With the way the DropShip had come down, he wouldn't be surprised if they found nothing but a black smear against pristine white.

Ten minutes passed way too slowly. Manipulating pedals and joysticks to maneuver through the thick powder and heavy woods, he kept an eye on the radar, which showed almost a dozen green darts moving forward to the guesstimated position of the downed craft. With the high iron-content of the mountain, good readings of what they would face were simply not coming in. He knew the DropShip held a capacity to carry five Clan 'Mechs. But how many of them could possibly have survived?

The Old Guard made contact first; the heavy boom of autocannon fire echoed across jagged rocks and lonely copses of trees as McFadden drew first blood with his *Hatchetman*. Cameron's own lance simply couldn't move quickly enough, and McFadden wanted a taste of action before the Hussars. Typical.

"Okay boys. Let's show 'em youngbloods can keep up with geriatrics."

He stomped down on his pedals and vented plasma lifted his 55-ton machine into the air, sublimated snow blasting around him in a send-off halo. He landed smoothly and launched again, just about cresting the ridge where the battle unfolded. Then remembered only Karli's *Starslayer* mounted jump jets. Ben's *Hollander* and

James' *Wolfhound* didn't have the benefit, and he couldn't leave them over the ridge.

Had to lead. Had to protect.

"Come on boys. I know the Academy gives you better pilot training than that. Let's get a move on, eh?" He tried to infuse as much good-natured humor into his voice as he could, tried to hide his worry. Regardless of the strides to narrow the technology gap between the Clan and Inner Sphere, Clan 'Mechs still outclassed Inner Sphere pound for pound.

Geoff could pilot circles around almost anyone he knew, but depending on what lay over the ridge...Cameron's own lance could make all the difference.

Flashes of sapphire and ruby lit the sky over the ridge, along with the detonations of multiple heavy explosions. Cameron gripped joysticks in sweat slicked hands. Willed his lance to move faster.

"They've got some serious life left in them." Geoff's voice startled him with its immediate urgency. "If we don't take down that *Mad Cat*, and I mean now, we're going to be in a world of hurt. Lance, target the *Mad Cat*. I'll deal with the *Rifleman*." The comm descended into a low babble once more.

A *Mad Cat*! Damn. A *Rifleman*? His mind swirled. *What the hell?* Did he mean a Rifleman IIC*? Why would the Clans be fielding an Inner Sphere design?*

He had to wait. A single 'Mech might not make the difference, but a lance would. Beside, he couldn't leave them. Had to lead.

He stared at his radar, demanding it provide more information. Suddenly he realized at least one of the Hussars had been able to move around their own ridge onto the plateau and appeared to have engaged as well; the tag read *Tai-i* Matsu. His assault *BattleMaster* would lend considerable weight to their side.

His own lance finally pulled even. "Okay boys, over the ridge and give 'em everything you got," he said. Cameron prepared his weapons to follow his own advice and ignited plasma once more, sending his *Wolverine* up and over the ridge...to hell.

Spread out before him, a small, but terrifyingly urgent battle unfolded on the under-sized plateau. The downed DropShip still burned, sending up a huge bloom of smoke; a fallen *Thor* next to the massive rent in the *Broadsword*'s flank told him not all the 'Mechs had survived. Yet a thousand meters in front of him held a *Mad Cat* and *Rifleman*, with an *Arcas* off to the side, all weapons blazing and hammering the Highlander forces and the Proserpina *BattleMaster*.

He saw the Rasalhague logo inside a bear's head outline on the machine: First Rasalhague Bears. The *Rifleman* addition to a Clan force made sense now

As Cameron brought his own machine down to earth once more with a last gush of flame and stretch of myomer, he watched as fire lit underneath Geoff's *Hatchetman*. Time seemed to dial down until he could perceive individual autocannon shells and PPC beams hung suspended in mid-air.

The *Hatchetman* flew forward on a collision course with the *Rifleman*. The *Rifleman* pilot simply squared its feet, lined up both rotary autocannons and let loose a barrage that practically obscured its outline. Twin, horrific streams of vomiting death slashed into the *Hatchetman*, tearing away at armor like a bear savaging its meal, mortally wounding the metal giant.

"No!" Cameron managed to scream, as time swooped back to normal.

With an expertise few might have managed under such circumstances, Geoff kept the *Hatchetman* on course as limbs began to rip away under the murderous fire. Like a metal rockslide, the *Hatchetman* crunched into the *Rifleman* with a sound that could be heard even above the din of battle. Both toppled over in a mangled heap of metal.

Cameron would never be able to remember the next ten minutes. A haze—formed of tears and rage—seemed to blanket out his perception. One moment he watched his idol (his father) die, and the next he stood over a fallen Ghost Bear machine, firing endless kilojoules of energy into the blasted scraps—all that remained of the *Mad Cat*.

As silence descended, shame replaced his rage. Geoff would be rolling over in his metal grave at such a loss of control. *He* had done what needed to be done. Had led.

Had sacrificed himself to protect his command.

Though Cameron had tried initially to do the same, he too easily fell off. Too easily besmirched the bars (The Bars) he wore. Too easily forgot his heritage.

He blinked away the tears and the last shreds of his incapacitating haze. His command needed him. They needed to mop up and find out what might be here that would tempt the Bears; the rest of the raiding force to deal with elsewhere.

He swallowed several times. Tried to set aside his shame for another day and opened a general frequency comm.

Time to lead.

BATTLEMASTER
ASSAULT—85 TONS

HATCHETMAN
MEDIUM—45 TONS

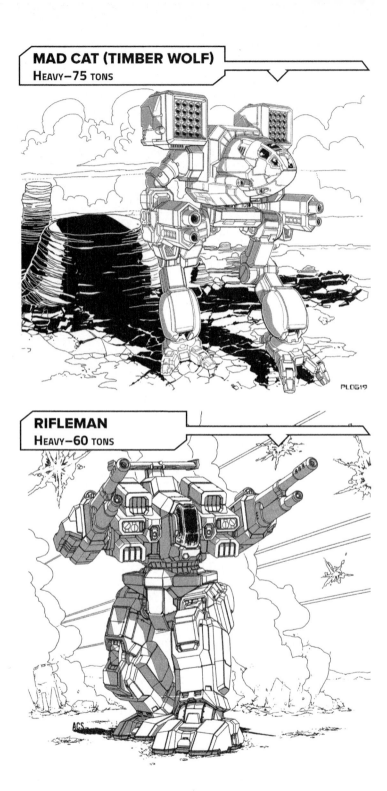

MAD CAT (TIMBER WOLF)
HEAVY—75 TONS

PLOG19

RIFLEMAN
HEAVY—60 TONS

ACS

WOLVERINE
Medium—55 tons

DESTINY'S CALL

LOREN L. COLEMAN

THARKAD UNIVERSITY
OLYMPIA
BREMEN
THARKAD
LYRAN COMMONWEALTH
2721

Alek heard Michael Steiner arguing with the nurse, swung his legs over the side of the cot and steadied himself against the nearby wall. The room tilted back and forth, sickeningly. He fought his rising gorge and held himself upright. He didn't want his friend to see him laid out like an invalid. Pity was one thing he had never seen in Michael's eyes, and never wanted to.

The university infirmary smelled of disinfectant and blood. The disinfectant was normal. The blood was his. Nurse Dragon had cleaned it up pretty well except for some dried stains on the front of his chambray button-up and the blood-clotted gauze packed inside each nostril. A wonder he could smell anything at all, really.

Footsteps in the outer hallway as they came toward the door of his room. Michael's pensive voice drifted in. "If he won't point a finger, there isn't much any of us can do."

"Scared?" the nurse asked.

A gentle laugh. "You don't know Alek. I wish we could scare him. Next time those boys might do permanent damage."

It was the work of a few seconds to pull back the white curtain that screened his cot from the rest of the room. Carefully he pushed up onto unsteady legs, drawing in a sharp breath as his bruised ribs protested. Rolling his right sleeve down over the bandage wrap, he fastened the button at his cuff. It took three tries. Alek brushed down some of his blond hair, covering the livid bruise swelling at his temple. There wasn't much he could do about his limp, or his face.

"So, what have we got in here?" Michael asked, stepping through the doorway. One hand smoothed his well-trimmed fringe of beard. A few gray hairs peeked through, but not many for a man of forty-five. Steiners aged well when they weren't sitting on the throne of the Lyran Commonwealth. With luck, Michael Steiner II would never bear that kind of weight. His older brother Jonathan was Archon, which allowed Michael to return to Tharkad University as a research assistant and, soon, the eccentric life of a celebrity professor.

An odd friend for twenty-year-old Alek to have made, but a friend nevertheless.

"Thank you for coming, Michael." Alek limped forward, trying to cover for his swollen right knee. "Let us get out of here, yes?"

"Hold it, *wunderkind.*"

Alek hated it when Michael called him kid. Their age difference rarely mattered—except when Michael wanted to make a point.

"I had to sign you out of here, since you won't take yourself to the hospital, and the university is worried about liability. Which means you go nowhere until I'm satisfied." He leaned forward, inspecting the younger man's face. "*Ja.* Those will darken up nicely, I expect."

Alek didn't care what his eyes looked like. He'd received blackened eyes before. Would do so again, most likely.

He looked past Michael at Nurse Dragon. Cynthia Durgen, the wonderful old battle-axe, had the same look of distaste she slapped on every time students carried him in from another hazing. Alek knew the look wasn't for him, but for the "don't ask" policy Tharkad University generally took toward such happenings. It didn't help that he pretended not to know who had come after him.

"Michael signed me out?" he asked, cutting to the bottom line. Lyrans understood bottom lines. She nodded reluctantly. "Then I'm leaving. Thank you for your attentions."

Michael fell into step with Alek as he limped down the hall and into a crisp Tharkad morning. Winter still had a stranglehold on late-arriving spring. The sky was a calm, anemic blue, but a rime of icy snow clung to the campus's park-like grounds. Alek stumbled as sunshine stabbed golden daggers behind his eyes. His temples throbbed.

"You look awful," Michael said, helping him down the non-skid steps. "Why do you let them do this to you?"

"'Not all of me is dust,'" Alek quoted. He shivered, missing the parka they had taken from him. "'Within my song, safe from the worm, my spirit will survive.'"

"Always back to Pushkin. Was he beat a lot as a young man too?"

Hero worship through masochism? Hardly. "That's not what this is about, Michael."

"I know what this is about," Michael said, stopping Alek with a hand on his arm. "You're young and brilliant, and they hate you for it." He let go of the younger man's arm. "They hate you, Alek. And they're spoiled mama's boys who think they can get away with anything. Or that Daddy will buy it off when they don't."

Staring out over the campus grounds, Alek refused to meet Michael's gaze. Other late arrivals slushed their way to class, hands thrust in pockets and breath frosting. One of them paused long enough to staple a plasticized handbill to a magnificent pine.

"Aren't they right?" he finally asked. "It's your world, Michael. I'm just a guest here."

Michael shook his head. "Well, some of our Lyran students have a strange way of showing their hospitality."

"They're Star League cadets. They belong to the entire Inner Sphere now." Which was as close as he would come to naming them. Alek figured Michael knew who they were, of course, but he wouldn't put his friend in the position of having that knowledge confirmed. His choice. His bruises.

"They're supposed to be professionals. You would be doing the Star League, and the Commonwealth, a great service by forcing them to deal with the consequences of their choices. 'Some sense of duty, something of a faith, some reverence to the laws ourselves have made.' Lord Tennyson speaks as true as any dead Russian poet."

Alek had classes this morning. He needed to get going. He drew upon Tolstoi. "'Everyone thinks of changing the world,'" He offered Michael a short wave as he headed off. "'No one thinks of changing himself.'"

"Are you sure you're okay?" Michael called after him.

Alek raised a victorious fist into the air without looking back.

But if he thought to escape on a position of strength, those desires went unanswered. Grabbing his 'corder and spare coat from the dorms and shuffling to class, his nausea increased. The final flight of stairs leading to the lecture hall swam before his eyes, and he nearly collapsed.

He felt bone-weary, but if he missed the entire Poli-Science lecture, they'd know they'd gotten to him. He hadn't stood up under two years of their "special attention" to lay down now, not with graduation so close. Elias Luvon and his friends would respect Alek's determination, someday. Maybe they would become better soldiers for it.

Elias was nearest the door when Alek slipped in at the back of the sloping hall, and his smirk faltered when he saw no hint of surrender in Alek's stoic gaze. Elias Luvon had strong, handsome features, and an over-inflated sense of his position at Tharkad University. He might very well be the Nagelring's top MechWarrior cadet this year, allowed to use Star League billets purchased at the university, but he barely held his own in academics. On merit alone he was likely failing Poli-Sci, but the class was considered a must for sons of noble families, and his father's latest endowment to the university guaranteed him a passing grade.

Alek moved by deliberately, barely avoiding the foot stuck out into his path. He rested against the side of a table two tiers down, vision narrowing into a long tunnel at the end of which he saw an open chair next to Gabriella Bailey. She was only two more tiers away, but it seemed awfully far.

"Hey. Alek." One of his classmates. Another senior. Brian? Alek rested against his table. Were they friends? "You okay?"

"Not all of me is dust," he said. Shaking his head clear, he shoved himself away and managed to descend the next two tier steps with great difficulty. He stood next to Gabriella's table, swaying, trying to blink his vision into focus. On the stage below, Professor Kleppinger droned on about the Davion succession problem being considered by First Lord Cameron. Would House Kurita be given claim to the Davion throne? No one knew.

But not all of Alek was dust. He knew that. Within his song, safe from...from the worm...

"Did you want to sit here?" Gabriella asked, motioning to the seat at her side. She glanced up at Alek and her eyes widened. They were hazel with green flecks, quite stunning— funny how he'd never noticed before. Brown hair, ironed straight. Voice like song.

"Within my song..." he whispered.

Gabriella looked worried. She started to get up, and that was the last Alek saw. He clenched his eyes shut as the room spun on its axis, and he clutched at one last coherent thought as if it were a lifeline.

"Michael...?" he whispered.

Then he collapsed into dust.

Three days in the hospital under observation, they ran a dozen "routine" tests on Alek, including a CAT scan and an advanced EEG. It also allowed time enough for two different doctors, Michael Steiner, and the Dean of Tharkad University to pay him a visit to let him know what was wrong with him.

"Subarachnoid hemorrhage," the doctor told him before being called out of the room.

Alek had resigned himself to looking it up when Michael showed to explain he had a cranial bleed putting pressure on his brain, but that he'd be fine. Later, Dean Caravel Albrecht nervously promised much the same thing, seemingly trying to convince himself as well. He'd also asked after who had done this to one of his students. Alek had shrugged.

"Does it matter?" He spooned up some crushed ice to wash the taste of medicine from his mouth.

"Of course," Dean Albrecht told him. "This is illegal."

"Only by a matter of degree," Alek said, still wielding his spoon. "If the law condemns and punishes only actions within certain definite and narrow limits, doesn't it justify, in a way, all similar actions that lie outside those limits?" Even paraphrased, the administrator of Tharkad University should recognize Tolstoi.

He didn't. "Commonwealth law would never condone such an attack."

"And a new medical library would never purchase a C- in Political-Science," Alek agreed with false *bonhomie*.

The Dean made his excuses and left not long after, no doubt wondering to whom Alek had been talking. Just as well he wasn't there when Michael came back, smuggling in a thick book of free verse and some spicy Skye-style pizza—although it did not require much smuggling. Who was going to refuse the Archon's brother?

"Not to worry, Pushkin," Michael told him. "They decided not to drill into your head. The bleed will reabsorb naturally, and you'll be out of here. That's all there is to it."

If that was all, then why run more tests? Psych profile. Reflex response. What more were they looking for?

He found out the next day, when Michael came back accompanied by a Star League colonel and First-Cadet Luvon. The colonel wore an olive drab dress uniform complete with Nagelring sash and a ceremonial sword. Elias Luvon wore cadet fatigues and a look of distaste. Alek's guard came up at once.

Michael introduced Colonel Baumgarten as part of the Eleventh Royal BattleMech Division, currently serving as commanding officer of the Star League's Nagelring Academy.

"You're in fine physical shape," Colonel Baumgarten said, glancing closely at a noteputer screen. The small device looked fragile in his large hands.

"That's reassuring," Alek said with a grim smile.

"It says here that you've had heart surgery. Fully recovered?"

He looked to Michael, but found no help. The pale scar across his chest might have alerted the doctors. More likely someone had dug into his records back on Terra. "When I was three," he finally admitted. "It took some time, I am told. I'm fine now."

"Good. Good. We have strict demands on potential cadets, after all. The Nagelring more so than many training academies. I have to say, your academic scores and Martial Aptitude Test results place you in high standing."

Which was when it dawned on Alek that Colonel Baumgarten—and Elias Luvon—were here to extend an offer into the prestigious Nagelring military academy.

Him! A Star League Defense Force military cadet?

"This is a joke, yes?"

Michael shook his head, but it was the colonel who answered. "No, son. No joke. When the local staff checked you over for cerebral damage following your fall, their examination recorded extremely well-developed motor-reflexes. They reported your results to us, as they are required to do, and we ordered additional tests while you've been laid up. Your nervous system is highly responsive. Perfect for a MechWarrior candidate."

MechWarrior! Alek sagged back in his bed. The offer rolled over him so hard it took a moment to realize that the Colonel had mentioned his "fall." The latest university euphemism for being soundly beaten, courtesy of Dean Albrecht, and maybe even another donation by Lord Luvon, Elias's father.

"No," Alek said sharply.

Elias was all smiles and bright eyes. The colonel might have been sucker-punched, a feeling Alek knew very well. "You...you don't want to think this through, son? We don't roll out the red carpet every day."

The last red carpet Alek had seen was the one he'd bled on. Now they wanted him to become one of them? "I understand the offer, Colonel Baumgarten. I have nothing but admiration for the Star League Defense Force as an entity." Elias glowered, no doubt feeling the verbal sting implied in Alek's careful compliment. "I do not believe I would make a good addition to the roll."

"According to our data, that wouldn't appear to be the case. It says here that your parents are both SLDF veterans. A trooper, your dad. Fine record. Your mother rose to sergeant major in military administration. I'd think they'd be honored to see their son follow in their footsteps."

"Ah, but Colonel," Alek's voice grew tight, "my parents would have accepted my original decision. I'm here to study history and poli-sci on a Star League scholarship, and glad for it. Education is also a weapon, sir. 'Its effects depend on who holds it in their hands, and at whom it is aimed.' Stalin."

Baumgarten reddened. "I'll have you know, 'that a sound military practice—'" he began before Michael leaped in to cut him off.

"Look, look, look, Colonel, you don't want to get into this. Once Alek pulls out dead Russians, you're fighting his battle." Even against a Star League officer, the Archon's brother could throw some weight. He steered the flustered man toward the door of Alek's room. "Let the boy think about it. He's had a hard week, after all—" his voice was lost outside in the passage.

The boy. Alek silently thanked Michael for the nice diminutive. He relaxed back into his thin hospital pillow for all of three seconds before realizing that Cadet Luvon hadn't followed the others out.

"Now you think you're too good for us?" Elias sneered.

Alek sat back up, reached for his glass of melting ice chips. He sloshed around the icy water. "I hope you aren't going to pretend you actually wanted me to accept," Alek said, then sipped around the spoon. "I'd be very disappointed."

"Why should I care what you think, *Terran*? Just because your "Royal" divisions think they run the Star League?"

The noble scion was picking a fight no matter what. Alek didn't need to provide more ammunition. "It's not what I want, all right, Elias? Let's leave it at that."

"You think we have nothing to offer a guy like you?"

Alek should have let it go. "Of course not." And, before he thought better of it, "After all, look what the military is making of you."

A pettiness buried deep within Alek took some pleasure at Elias Luvon's expression of outrage. He'd scored deeply with that remark, but it could hardly be called a fair fight. Elias studied to fight with weapons. Alek with words.

With exact military bearing, Elias toed himself about-face and stiff-marched from the room to catch up with his commanding officer. Michael passed him just outside the door. "Do I want to know what passed between you two while I escorted our good friend Colonel Baumgarten back to the waiting room?" he asked Alek as he entered the room.

"Just a difference of opinion." Michael winced, and Alek remembered describing his first set of bruises last year, shortly after his transfer, as a difference of opinion. "It's nothing."

"The last 'nothing' put you in the hospital," Michael reminded him.

"You think I didn't consider their offer."

Michael Steiner rubbed one hand along his beard, as if checking for exact edges. "I know you considered it, Alek. I'm just wondering if you gave them their fair due."

"If you can't beat them, join them?"

"Pushkin," Michael said, as if Alek had been quoting again. The two men grinned, and the somber mood evaporated. "Truly, Alek, there would be advantages, to the Star League as well as to you. Not the least of which is the more stringent rules inside a military organization that protect its own."

Everything you needed to know could, sooner or later, be found in Tolstoi. "'The two most powerful warriors are patience and time,' Michael." Alek rested back, exhaustion threatening to overwhelm him. "I already have them on my side."

But remembering Elias's expression, and the cadet's suddenly cold demeanor, Alek wondered if that was actually the case anymore.

Alek sat on the frozen ground, his winter gear safeguarding him from snowmelt, and leaned back against a massive cedar. A plasticized poster calling students to a pro-Skye rally protected his uncovered head from the tree's scaly bark. It was one of his favorite spots. Camped on the university commons right out in front of the main administration building, few bothered him here. Right now that was what he needed.

His breath frosted in front of his face, and he blew out a long, misty cloud of exasperation. Tension knotted behind his shoulders. His left ear still burned from being slammed hard with a lacrosse stick and his knuckles bled where he'd skinned them against the door on his way out of the dorms.

Served him right for letting the torments get to him.

He expected the hostile behavior from Elias Luvon and his cadet cronies, but what shocked Alek was how fast other students joined in after learning that he'd turned down a post at the Nagelring.

"Too good for a non-Terran academy," Elias spun it.

Patently absurd. Alek attended a non-Terran university after all. But still the feet thrust into his way and snowballs with rocks in them increased. Students took to kicking his dorm room door as they passed, making it hard to study for the preliminary exams being given this week. It finally drove him outside, hauling along his notes and data wafers, to relax for a few hours.

With his 'corder tucked safely away inside his carry-all pack, Alek untangled the wires and stuck plugs into each ear. Musical strains filled his head with deep viola and soft, whimsical flute, then the melodies faded into the background and Professor Kleppinger's monotone filtered in to explain the latest political fallout on Terra. A compilation of his own design: the soothing melodies helped him focus, allowing him to replay his Political Science lectures over and over.

This month's political dialog centered around two JumpShips which had been interdicted and destroyed by the Terran Hegemony's new Space Defense System. A problem with their IFF codes, by all reports. This was Alek's third time listening to the recording, but he couldn't help the way his heart pounded at the news. His parents had been outbound from Terra around the same dates, planning an early visit to Tharkad. The SDS wasn't supposed to challenge outgoing vessels, but the new technology was obviously unreliable.

Several of the House Lords were already positioning themselves politically following the disaster. Liao and Davion complained—loudly—that the defense system was unsafe, and that its early deployment violated common sense as well as long-standing restrictions. Takiro Kurita took a longer view, and simply wanted to know when the technology would be shared with militaries of the Great Houses. All three were stirring a strong public outcry.

"Of course," Kleppinger droned on, "it is unlikely that even such a tragedy as this will do more than spur local debate inside the separate Houses. Such is the absolute power enjoyed by First Lord Cameron."

"No power is absolute," Alek whispered to himself, closing his eyes. "Only corruption."

Though paraphrasing the nineteenth-century Lord Acton, he decided it was original enough to lead a paper on the subject and began to order his thoughts into a rough mental outline. Michael would give him a spot of grief over the non-Russian source, but the simple truth followed that Alek also studied in English, *en Français*, and was quickly learning *Deutsch*.

The musical composition had run into its third variation, and Alek into his second page of mental notes. He couldn't say how he detected the presence: A shadow against the back of his eyelids or a heavy footfall crunching down through the icy snow crust. All he could say for certain was that he suddenly knew that someone stood over him, and he startled to full alertness.

Gabriella Bailey stood there in parka, draped pants, and snow boots. Her hazel eyes reflected back a measure of uncertainty. "I didn't mean to scare you."

Kleppinger warned the class against accepting the media's analysis. Alek straightened up into a better posture, finger-combed blond hair back from his forehead. "No," he said. "I mean, it's okay."

Nodding, Gabriella sank down into the snow next to him, resting on her knees and the toes of her boots, settling back onto her calves. She wore her hair down around her ears today, and neoleather gloves protected her hands. "Quite the spot you've picked out. Needed a break from studying?"

"What makes you think I'm not studying?"

She grinned. "You had a relaxed smile on your face. I don't know anyone who smiles like that when plugged into a lecture. Not even you, Alek."

It was the most she'd ever said to him in one sitting. Alek certainly did not want to argue with her. But... "Here," he offered, pulling out his right ear plug. He passed it over, stretching the wire out of his pack. "Take a listen."

More for the sake of politeness than any real desire it seemed, Gabriella cupped the plug to her ear. Her eyes widened into doe-like pools. "Kepplinger...and Wolfgang?"

"Ulysses Rozz. Twenty-sixth century composer. He based his work off Mozart, yes. I mixed this myself."

She laughed, handed him back the plug. "That is so wrong."

Alek shrugged, pulled out his left ear plug with great care and a sharp intake of breath, and tucked both into the pack. "I can listen to it dozens of times, though. It makes it easier to...what?"

She cocked her head to one side, looking at him. "Your ear."

"My...? Oh. Yeah. Is it purpling up yet?" She nodded, glanced around uneasily. He tried to keep his tone easy, though the memory of the lacrosse stick lashing out at him in the corridor, driving him into the wall, was kind of hard to make light of. "It's not so bad."

Gabriella mimicked his lighthearted approach. "Don't you ever win a fight, Alek?"

"No one wins a fight."

"Is that another of your dead Russians?" Even she knew of his penchant for quotations, though Alek would have bet she hardly knew anything about him.

"A live one. Me."

That brought the smile back to her face. "You're very... complicated. For being such a straightforward person, I mean."

He shrugged. "Blame my father," he said, and she glanced askance at him. "I was very young, and...not always in good health. He would take me to the museums in Moscow. Russia had a very—" he reached for the right word, "—fractious history. There were purges. Massive oppression. And there were rebellions. But the strongest traits came from when the people endured. Seven hundred years later, you can still see it. *That* is a heritage."

Gabriella nodded. "He sounds like a man who would be interesting to meet."

"He will be here," Alek said. "He—and my mother—are traveling to Tharkad. They will vacation on some nearby worlds, and then return in time for my graduation. Perhaps you will meet him then."

"Perhaps I will."

Neither of them seemed to know what to say after that. The silence stretched between them, and then snapped like cold taffy. "Well," Gabriella said, "I just wanted to say that I'm glad you're all right. After your collapse in class last week."

Rising to her feet in graceful motion, she brushed away snow caked on the knees of her pants. Almost as an afterthought, she asked, "Are you going to the spring reception?"

A university tradition, hosting the Nagelring cadets in a large ballroom event. Archon Steiner would make an appearance. It was the largest social event of every year. "I don't know." Dark thoughts flitted through Alek's mind, knowing that Elias Luvon and his friends would be there in force. "You?"

"I was thinking about it."

Alek blinked his surprise. "You mean no one has asked you yet?"

She laughed. "Well, of course he asked. But I said... it doesn't matter what I said. I simply thought..." Gabriella laughed again, more quietly, at herself. "Oh, hell. Alek, I was hoping you'd like to go. Together. With me."

A flush crawled over the back of his scalp, and Alek climbed up to his feet. He didn't notice how his left ear burned anymore. He worried more about his dry mouth and a suddenly thick tongue. "I would—very much—like to escort you to the reception," he said formally.

"That won't create too much trouble for you?" she asked.

"No. Why should it?"

"Never mind." She shook her head—but her hazel eyes, they still worried. "I forget you're not part of the gossip underground. It should be fine." She shrugged. "So, it's a date. I'll leave you to your studies, and we'll talk later."

Alek might have left it at that. His brain was already working the problem, after all. He could have checked it out quietly. But the thought was only half-formed when he caught Gabriella turning away to leave, and he blurted out the question: "Who else asked you?" But he knew, he already knew.

Gabriella flashed a glance at the ground. "Elias Luvon."

And then she shrugged it off, leaving him standing in the snow beneath the tall evergreen, reminding himself over and over again the value of enduring.

Michael Steiner was far less sanguine, especially after hearing about it through staff gossip and not from Alek directly. The summons came as an invite to join Michael for lunch—not an order, but with Alek it carried the same weight.

He did not have so many friends on Tharkad that he could afford to casually refuse them.

So he sat on a stool in Michael's research library, feet tucked back, watching his friend pace the narrow aisle running between bookshelves and workstation. A forgotten manual lay open on Michael's glass-topped desk, its pages weighed down by a unique assortment of data crystals developed by the university in cooperation with a Lyran Commonwealth corporation—going to replace disk wafers across the entire Inner Sphere, Michael claimed. The crystals were lined up on both pages by color and, presumably, content.

All forgotten now, as the Archon's brother speared Alek with an unblinking stare.

"Do you like drinking your food through a straw?" he asked, a flush showing through his meticulous beard.

Alek rubbed at his jaw, massaging the dark yellow bruise he'd picked up this morning. He had seen the cyclist coming, but not the elbow. "I was careless."

"*Ja.* I would say you were." Michael plucked at his starched cuffs, tugging them out of his suit jacket sleeves. "Careless even to talk with Gabriella Bailey."

"I don't think this is so bad."

"Worse, Alek. Elias Luvon asked her to the reception, and she spurned him. If you think this will sit well with any Nagelring cadet once Luvon is through, you are sadly mistaken. For a history and PoliSci student, you can be remarkably short-sighted. Have you ever noticed that?"

"'How is it that little children are so intelligent and men so stupid?'" Alek asked back. He looked at the studying professor, grinned. "'It must be education that does it.'"

Michael froze, his face tightening down until his gray eyes disappeared behind narrow slits. Then he could not contain it anymore. A smile split through his beard, and a tight chuckle rolled out into a real laugh. "English lords, and now French authors. Alek, you will mar your reputation if you keep this up."

"Do not worry. I'm not finished with dead Russians."

Stepping over to him, Michael placed a hand on Alek's shoulder. "Just see that you do not become one yourself. All right?" Alek nodded, and Michael took that as a guarantee. "So, your parents make planetfall yet?"

He smiled. "Tomorrow. And I have three more prelims to get through before they arrive." Alek checked his watch. "Including the third part of Kleppinger's four-day miniseries. I should go."

"It's forty minutes until Gerald starts his...ah. All right. *Liebeskrank, ja?* You hope to find an empty seat next to your date for the reception." He exhaled a short, sharp sigh. "Very well. Go on with you. Just remember to duck now and then, and if Gabriella is wearing anything nice today, don't forget to say something about her shoes."

"Her shoes?"

With a shove, Michael propelled him from the stool and toward the door. "I'm beginning to side with Colonel Baumgarten. Maybe we are teaching you the wrong things. Or at least, not enough of the right things."

Alek shuffled toward the door, grabbing up his carry-all pack from a small end table. "There's nothing for me to learn from Baumgarten."

"If you really believe that, then you are most certainly right. 'A closed mind never errs, nor learns.' Tracial Steiner."

"Family's not fair," Alek called back, then pushed out into the corridor. He let Michael have that one. The prerogative of being part of a ruling House, you did get to win once in a while.

And the truth was always hard to refute.

The thought hung at the back of Alek's mind for his brisk walk over to the social sciences wing, haunting him, dredging up the ghosts of Colonel Baumgarten's offer and his father's commentaries, which had been delivered while the two of them explored Terra's violent past at museums and battlefield memorials. Was he being close-minded with regard to

Baumgarten's offer? Perhaps. But then he had never been one to put muscle (or metal) over mind.

Those most capable of wielding power were those least likely to desire it. To Alek, this was a self-evident truth. An article of faith. And faith was the force by which people lived.

At the same time, also according to Tolstoi, the sole meaning of life was to serve humanity. Did that mean Alek had to serve it in the most self-sacrificing method available? Or simply that he should always hold in mind his debt to the greater good? He sighed. The mills of philosophy could grind exceedingly fine.

"But safe from the worm, my spirit will survive."

At least through Kepplinger's Political Science class. Or so Alek thought at the time.

The lecture hall was only half-full, with most early arrivals doing some last-minute cramming from books, noteputers, or 'corders. The room smelled of flavored coffees, mulled cider, and nervous sweat. Styluses danced over paper, over screens, as timelines and tables were practiced again and again and again. This kind of frantic energy would not be seen again until final exams, though prelims were no easy slouch, as here students set a baseline for their finals grade. One could not improve better than a full letter grade over prelims, and the weighted average made it hard—but not impossible—to fail if one pulled an average grade now.

Gabriella Bailey already had a seat halfway up the stair-step risers, right on the aisle as she normally preferred. Elias Luvon sat next to her, straddling the chair backward with large hands gripping the backrest posts as if they were control yokes. Elias wore full dress uniform for today's occasion, including gloves and saber. A bit prissy, but he wasn't the only cadet who thought a strong show of military devotion might win points from an instructor. Gabriella saw Alek's approach and nodded to Elias, who stepped back up from the chair without so much as looking around. Alek stepped to one side, giving Elias room to pass.

Elias stopped in the aisle next to him, smiled when he saw the bruise darkening Alek's jaw. "I'd wish you luck, but you won't have any problems with a Commonwealth-level exam, will you?" Elias asked the question loudly, sharing it with the rest of the class.

His jaw ached for the first time since leaving Michael's office. "Commonwealth or Star League, I'd expect to have no trouble taking an exam for which I studied."

"Right. Studying. I forgot, thinking is beyond us dumb grunts, right?"

"I never said that." Alek saw several faces turn their way. Some curious. Some hostile. All right. A debate he could handle. "I appreciate your sacrifices, made for State and for Star League. Why do you feel my choices lessen yours?"

"Nothing you say or do lessens our honor!" Elias dropped one hand to the hilt of his saber, as if he might draw it to avenge his honor. Alek's carry-all was heavy on his shoulder. If he swung it hard enough... "The Inner Sphere does not revolve around Terra, you know." He stormed off, stomping up the risers to his usual seat near the top of the hall.

All a pose, Alek realized, *never a threat.* And Elias had got in the last word. He dropped heavily into the seat next to Gabriella. "I never said that," he complained softly.

"Why do you continue to fight with him?" Gabriella asked, never taking her eyes off the amber screen of her noteputer.

"It's a dialogue. Maybe someday he will actually hear it."

"I'm not so certain. But while you're waiting, you can quiz me." She shoved over her noteputer. "Political ramifications of the Periphery Unilateral Freedoms Act, as jointly proposed by the Capellan Confederation and Free Worlds League."

Which ate up the rest of their free time before Kleppinger closed the hall doors as his assistants paced the two main aisles handing out SAT-panels. The large green-screen display would be their only interface with the professor's testing program. Answers were shot by wireless into the mainframe, to be analyzed and graded later. Alek tore through page after page of questions, providing dates and names and, when called for, a political analysis of the situation.

So engrossed in the process was he, that at the first ringing tones he slapped his stylus down on the table thinking time was up. Then he realized it couldn't be. He was only half-done with the test.

Another series of tinny rings. Like a pager. A kind of warning tone. Alek looked at Gabriella who stared back at him. Students at nearby tables were also staring in his direction.

"What is this interruption?" Kleppinger shuffled up from the stage, his droning monotone actually holding a touch of irritation. He smoothed back a thinning spray of white hair. "Alek. Turn off your wireless. No pagers, no comms. You know the rules."

"Professor. I don't have a wireless."

Three electronic bleats argued, and Kleppinger frowned. "I'd like to think I hear the truth ringing in your words, Alek, but I doubt that very much. Stand up from your chair, please."

The professor checked Alek's seat, bending down on one knee. Another betraying chirrup. Kleppinger glanced beneath the table, reached under and pulled a slender noteputer free of its magnetic clamp.

Alek's stomach hardened into a fist of cold lead when he recognized the small device. His. The low-power light flashed in time with the next ringing alarm.

"I see," Kleppinger nodded. His pate flushed a dangerous scarlet beneath his thinning hair. "Can you explain this?"

Alek opened his mouth, but nothing came out. He had no breath to form the words.

"No matter. Let us save it for Dean Albrecht, shall we?" He caught Alek's slender arm in a grip that was strong for an aging academic, turned him away from the table and marched him up the risers.

Elias Luvon glowered from his seat near the door. "Studying, huh?" His voice was a little too loud. A little too pleased. "'Bout time someone found you out."

Alek had never felt an urge to physically hurt another person until now. His hands clenched into fists so tight his nails dug painfully into the soft bed of flesh in each palm. He considered launching himself across the table at Elias, sure that righteousness would prevail over academy training.

Before he could decide, Professor Kleppinger was dragging him toward the door, through it.

The elder man paused on the threshold. "The rest of you still have fifty minutes. SAT-panels will be collected on the hour by my assistants." Then he stepped into the corridor and gestured. "After you," he said coldly.

The door to the lecture hall closed with a heavy weight while Alek was only a few meters away.

The sound of finality.

Six hours into his academic review, Alek knew what a firing squad victim felt like.

The room Dean Albrecht chose was spartan and cold, painted an olive drab that someone, at some time, thought was a good idea. It smelled of floor wax and aftershave. Tharkad's pale sun shone through the room's single window, high on the left-hand wall so that no one could look out. Dust motes chased each other in the butterish sunbeams slanting across the floor.

Alek stood at the front of the room, behind a small metal podium on which rested a sweating pitcher of water and a single glass. His hands smoothed the edges along either side. He faced the seated board, which was now down to Dean Albrecht and Professor Kleppinger. Michael Steiner sat in as Alek's advocate, keeping the long process civil. Keeping his own counsel, Michael had also brought in Colonel Baumgarten, who sat in stoic silence through the entire ordeal, his falcon-sharp gaze pinning Alek to the wall, missing nothing.

Behind the board, his parents sat in straight-backed chairs, having delayed their travels to support Alek through his review. Dad rarely blinked, his blue eyes fastened steadfastly on his son, offering silent encouragement. Mom spent more time studying the academic board, seemingly amused by the entire process. Neither showed any doubt as to the outcome, and Alek was grateful for the strength of their belief.

"Another question," Kleppinger said, resting forward on his elbows. He looked down at Alek, a true accomplishment when seated. "Unless you need a moment to collect yourself."

"I'm ready if you are," Alek said. Kleppinger frowned.

Other instructors had arrived, asked their questions, and left satisfied. Kleppinger seemed to take this entire review personally. Alek remembered the professor's surprise—and suspicion—when told that his student would be let back into class pending a full academic review. It hadn't taken Kleppinger long to discover that Michael Steiner had gone to bat for Alek, vouchsafing his character and demanding the board prove Alek's need to cheat.

"The boy's own noteputer clipped under the table isn't enough?" Michael had later told Alek of Kleppinger's outrage. "His own fingerprints on it, and no one else's, I'm told."

Convenient that three of Alek's most serious on-campus enemies had worn gloves that day as part of their dress uniforms. He never once pointed a finger in their direction, though the broken lock discovered at his dorm room had argued part of his case for him.

"Is this question going to require another thirty-minute answer?" Michael asked, glancing at the slender watch on his wrist. "We do have a Spring Reception to ready ourselves for tonight."

Kleppinger drew himself up haughtily. "Perhaps we should be more interested in the ethical fiber of our student body than a social event."

"Quite right, quite right." Michael nodded. "I'm sure the Archon will excuse our tardiness." Michael did not go on at any length to remind the board members of his relation to the Archon. He didn't have to. Dean Albrecht took a long look at his watch as well, a gesture certainly not missed by Kleppinger.

"Very well," the Poli-Sci instructor conceded. "I'll keep this one short." He spread his hands over the table they all sat behind. "In the briefest answer possible, Alek, give me the founding political cause behind the last four decades of challenges from *ronin* Kurita samurai against Star League base champions."

Identifying the political foundations for current troubles was never an easy task, and would open a debate more often than ever reaching a consensus. Alek, however, was not one to shirk a challenge. "The Reunification War," he said at once. Then was quiet. He sipped his water. Waited.

"I'll ask you to elaborate *somewhat*," Kleppinger said finally with great distaste.

Alek set the glass back on the podium. "When Michael Cameron assumed the First Lordship in 2649, one of his first challenges came from Tadeo Amaris and the Rim Worlds Republic. Amaris had begun expanding his armies at an alarming rate. This prompted First Lord Michael into signing, among other laws, Council Edict 2650, dictating the acceptable size of any non-Star League military force. House Kurita's necessary downsizing of their army led to the *ronin*, or "masterless warriors" as they are called. Out of spite, under orders, or as a salve to their family honor, these *ronin* have been challenging Star League champions since 2681."

"And this relates to The Reunification War of the twenty-sixth century how?" Dean Albrecht asked.

Alek sipped again from his water glass. "The specter of another Reunification War no doubt loomed over First Lord Michael's decision to enact such military restriction in the first place."

"You propose to know the mind of the First Lord?" Kleppinger waved a hand, dismissing such a claim. "Your psychological skills aside, this would still seem a tenuous tie between events."

"'The processes of cause and effect among political circumstance are often legion, and nebulous, until viewed from a historian's perspective.'"

The professor scoffed. "Who said that?"

"Weldon Kleppinger, doctorate thesis, 2706."

Michael Steiner laughed, and Colonel Baumgarten dipped his head in a silent salute. Alek smiled. The academic gauntlet had been thrown down.

"And yet," Kleppinger rebounded on the attack, "you assert contemporary rationale for the *ronin's* activities. Spite. Honor."

"And being under orders," Alek reminded him, picking up his water glass. "But I never stated that these were contemporary issues. Even orders—if there were, passed through back channels—must have an historical context. These are the children and grandchildren of those who served under Leonard Kurita, who brought the Draconis Combine to the brink of war against the Star League in 2605."

"Leonard's Folly." Kleppinger nodded. "He died of a 'mysterious illness,' though it seems likely his replacement was engineered by...?"

"Siriwan McAllister-Kurita, after the *seppuku* of Leonard's sister—"

"Elaine Kurita," Kleppinger interrupted. Now the professor seemed to have something to prove. "She committed ritual suicide in shame for her brother's actions. But Leonard was too far unbalanced by alcohol and drug dependence to care, and his paranoia following—"

"Following an incident that took place in the High Council, where Leonard attempted to assault the First Lord with a thrown bottle and instead struck a guard, who fired out of reflex, wounding the Coordinator." Alek replaced his glass on the podium with a tired hand. "So we might as well say the *ronin* challenges were all for the sake of a wayward bottle."

"And that guard's name was... was..." Kleppinger trailed off helplessly, unable to say. Alek saw in his eyes, though, that he knew. Knew, and wanted to deny it.

Levering himself out of his chair with hands splayed on the table's top, Dean Albrecht rose. "I think we are at an end here, and this whole unfortunate misunderstanding can be chalked up to campus hijinks. Wouldn't you agree, Weldon?" Kleppinger nodded dumbly. "Alek, please accept the university's apology. Your scholarship stands, and your record will not reflect this incident."

He shrugged. The bitter taste at the back of his throat had little to do with victory, and everything to do with the crestfallen expression on Kleppinger's face. Maybe it had been necessary to push back so hard, but Alek had taken some measure of joy in it as well, and that seemed—now—inappropriate. "And my prelims? I never did finish them."

Kleppinger shook himself back to some semblance of decorum. He rose slowly. "Full marks," he promised. He seemed a bit taken aback when Michael Steiner offered his hand and a sincere thanks on Alek's behalf, but drew some extra strength from that, and left the room with salvaged dignity.

His parents came forward, offering handshakes and warm hugs, while Dean Albrecht passed a few comments with Michael and Colonel Baumgarten. "Did just fine," his father said. "What you had to do. Don't worry about the rest."

But Alek always worried about the rest. His parents knew that.

"You proved yourself a credit to the university," his mother reminded him. "That is what matters."

"Indeed." Colonel Baumgarten joined them. "A true credit." He introduced himself to Alek's parents. "I wish I could claim so much on behalf of the Star League Defense Force, but Alek is steadfast in pursuit of academia. He'd make a fine officer."

His father swelled with pride. "Told him much the same," he said, putting a large hand on Alek's shoulder. More than thirty years out of service, he still wore the same infantryman's flattop, and had a stiff military bearing. "Mother and I, both. But Alek, he is his own man. And has Tronchina's stubbornness," he quipped, glancing at Alek's mother.

His parents shared a laugh over that, and Colonel Baumgarten joined in politely. Finally, his mother made excuses for her and her husband both. "We should get ready. Dean Albrecht extended an invitation to attend tonight's reception as chaperones, so we shall. If you do not mind, Alek."

"Not at all," Alek said. He gave both parents another strong hug and watched them go. "I should be off to get dressed as well." But he held back just a moment, sensing a question in the Star League officer.

"You took Professor Kleppinger apart fairly quickly at the end," Baumgarten said. "I saw his shoulders fall, and knew he was finished. It made me wonder."

"What's that?" Alek asked.

"What the guard's name was who shot Leonard Kurita."

Alek paused near the door. Dean Albrecht waited off to one side to say goodbye to the colonel. He saw no reason to drag out another history lesson just now.

"Her name was Tanya," he said, then slipped out the door. The colonel could look up her last name himself. And he would, Alek knew.

He would.

For the most part, Alek had gotten used to the stares and whispers, the fingers pointed his direction as he passed tight knots of students in the halls or on campus grounds. He cataloged them in the back of his mind, parsing out those he felt might be a real threat from the students who simply enjoyed the petty torments of social segregation, and those who just didn't care enough to go out of their way. It was, he'd discovered over time, a kind of status in and of itself. To whom was he important enough to be worth disliking.

Walking into the university's Spring Reception with Gabriella Bailey on his arm earned him an entirely new level of attention.

A symphony breathed light melodies over the entire ballroom. Couples waltzed across a polished floor. Drifting slowly about the hall, roaming in between the refreshment tables and the receiving line already forming in anticipation of the Archon's arrival, students and soldiers formed larger islands of conversation.

Alek had early hopes of slipping into obscurity among the crowds, but those dreams were quickly dashed. They were a match meant to attract notice, it seemed; silent, thoughtful Alek escorting the stunning debutante. Gabriella's gown did not run toward any of the usual shades of blue, a color heavily associated with House Steiner and the Lyran Commonwealth. She had chosen a full-length emerald green with a slightly metallic sheen. A slit up the side flashed jewel-studded shoes and shapely calf. The back of the gown was strapless, entirely open down to the small of her back. Steering her toward the dance floor Alek's hand slipped across that expanse of bare skin. It left him feeling warm inside his suit of basic black.

Gabriella laughed at his blush, but not in an unpleasant way.

"Nothing like being the center of attention," she whispered halfway through a waltz, finally noticing the stares which followed them.

"It's your gown," he said. Though both of them knew it for a lie. Alek's past week, and his success at today's review board, was the hot topic of conversation in many circles.

"No." Gabriella took her hand from his shoulder for a moment, tucked a strand of hair behind one ear. "It's your dancing." Alek wasn't so certain she was talking about his waltz.

They finished their dance and one more, and then moved toward a refreshment table where crystal cups rested in a snowdrift of ice shavings. Alek found two non-alcoholic sparkling ciders. They traded stares with several other attendees over the rims of their glasses.

Women seemed to appraise them as a couple, reserving their approval or catty glances for them both, equally. Many of the young men looked in his direction with obvious envy, or elbowed a buddy and whispered an aside that caused jealous laughter. A few glowered darkly at the match. Most of these wore Star League cadet uniforms, complete with the Nagelring's blue sash tied around their waists with ends hanging down over their left leg as was allowed by tradition. Hands rested aggressively on saber hilts, and a cautioning flush warmed the nape of Alek's neck.

"You make it look so easy," Gabriella said, sipping at her drink. "I count a dozen pair of eyes boring into your skull, none of them exactly wishing you well, and you still look relaxed."

"You would like me to beat on my chest and make loud growling noises, yes?" The question made her laugh. It made a nearby Nagelring cadet frown, and Alek lowered his voice. "I can't help what they think."

"But doesn't it wear on you?"

Alek sipped the fruity beverage, let it play over his tongue and whisper down his throat. He smiled, almost sadly. "'Not all of me is dust,'" he quoted. "'Within my song, safe from the worm, my spirit will survive.'"

"I remember you saying that. Before. Or part of it, anyway." She set her empty glass on the tray of a passing server. "You draw a great deal of strength from the words of others. How do you do that?"

"I believe." Alek shrugged. "Because 'the writer is the engineer of the human soul,' I can decide how to influence the person I *wish* to become."

Gabriella's eyes softened, sparkled. Her lips parted in a light smile, showing a hint of white teeth. She leaned forward ever so slightly, then caught herself. "Take a walk with me?" she asked, nodding toward one end of the ballroom. Large doors opened through a glass wall onto a formal courtyard, and the university's gardens beyond.

He swallowed hard. "Of course."

Hand on arm they strolled along the tables, running into Michael Steiner and Alek's mother returning from the dance floor. It was Michael's first chance to speak with Alek since ducking out after the review. He buttonholed Alek while Tronchina exchanged pleasantries with Gabriella.

"Excellent work today, Alek. Old Weldon looked as if he'd swallowed a bug."

Uncomfortable, Alek shifted his weight from one foot to the other. His father turned up and lead his mother away toward the refreshment tables. Gabriella looked over and smiled a promise to him, then withdrew to leave him a moment with Michael.

"I really should thank you again," Alek said, "for sticking by me, pushing through the academic board review." He saw a shadow flit over Michael's usually amiable face. "What?"

"Well, I didn't push for that. My family connections notwithstanding, as a faculty member I'm responsible to support Dean Albrecht's decision. It was Colonel Baumgarten who actually swung some weight behind a board review, and got you the second chance."

Baumgarten? "Why did he..."

"Mostly because of your parents, and the fact that you are here on a Star League scholarship." He smiled. "The military looks after its own, Alek. Even when they don't necessarily want to be claimed."

And, Alek realized, Michael had realized well ahead of time that it might take Baumgarten to bring about a review, which answered Alek's question as to why his friend had brought in the colonel.

Alek wrestled with propriety and pride. It wasn't much of a contest. "Thanks, Michael. I owe you."

"*Ja*, you do, *wunderkind*." He tipped a wink at Alek. "You can repay me by suffering through the formalities and allowing me to introduce you to my brother at some point."

"Give me a moment to find my parents," Alek offered. "I'm sure they would consider it a great honor to—"

"At some point," Michael said again, interrupting. He placed hands on Alek's shoulders. "Never keep a lady waiting. Especially one in need of rescuing." He turned Alek to one side, pointing out Gabriella and Elias Luvon near the edge of the dance floor.

"Right," Alek agreed, trading clasps with Michael.

Elias had proffered an arm to Gabriella, holding it out for an awkward moment. She looked at him coolly. Alek walked up in time to hear him ask—not for the first time, likely—for a dance. "Alek can spare you for another two minutes, certainly."

"Not by choice, Elias." He slipped up to Gabriella's side, and her hands encircled his upper arm. It felt as if low voltage electrical currents played out of her fingertips, teasing and trembling his skin even through his jacket sleeve.

"You can't be gracious about this?" Elias glanced to one side, and Alek followed his gaze. Some of Elias's cadet cronies watched the exchange from the dance floor, already partnered up and waiting for their friend. "Just to show there are no hard feelings?"

Which was almost humorous, considering who offered the olive branch. Alek still harbored a coal of resentment for Elias's latest tactic, attacking him through his academic standing, but he banked it, smothering the angry burn in layers of calm reasoning. "You know what? There aren't any hard feelings. Whatever your problems have been with me, they're your problems. Not mine."

Elias had obviously thought he heard capitulation in Alek's words, and began to offer his arm again. But Alek shifted Gabriella back, putting himself slightly in front of her. "But those problems have nothing to do with Gabriella, either. And since I have never shown you hard feelings, I see no reason to demonstrate a lack of them now." He nodded deeply. "Good eve, Elias."

Escorting Gabriella away, he felt her reassuring squeeze on his arm. "Thank you," she whispered after a long moment.

"My pleasure."

And it had been. Where Alek had felt worse for Professor Kleppinger's discomfort earlier this day, he could only believe that Elias Luvon had earned whatever loss of face this evening had brought him. A strong man—a future leader of men— would learn from such an experience. Alek hoped Elias had such character in him.

Perhaps he should have known better and stayed more on his guard. But passing through the glass wall and onto the courtyard with Gabriella on his arm, it felt as if the day's entire troubles simply drained away. The crisp evening air stole their breath and gave it back frosted. Tharkad's legendary aurora borealis shimmered and wafted through the dark skies like a heavenly tide washing over a beach of black sand and brilliant diamonds. Couples stood transfixed by the stellar theater. Others strolled the brushed flagstone, and lost themselves among a spectacular collection of ice sculptures or headed out toward the university's winter gardens.

Alek and Gabriella took a slow turn around the yard, enjoying the frozen tableaus. They passed by a pair of ballroom dancers; the man wearing a frosted uniform and saber, bowing low to his lady in a formal gown and a necklace of faceted diamonds. They walked among crystalline swans and a forest of ice-captured pines. Deer stood proudly on glacier cliffs, their delicate antlers glittering like starlight.

Gabriella wore Alek's suit jacket over her shoulders for what thin warmth it offered against the night's chill. As the couple drifted further away from the lights and sounds of the reception, they also drifted closer together. Passing through a small alpine village, each building carved at one-fourth scale, Alek's arm stole around Gabriella and pulled her close.

They found themselves on a small patio, overlooking a short flight of steps leading down into the gardens. Alek wasn't sure what made him stop there. A hesitation in

Gabriella's step? A squeeze of her hand on his arm? Whatever the reason, he paused and she swung around to face him. Her eyes were wide and frightened, and also warm and inviting.

"Gabriella, I—" She hushed him with a finger held up to his lips.

What had he been about to say? An apology? Her slow smile echoed his thoughts. Neither one was sure. Neither one was willing to back away. She stepped into him, chin tilting up, and Alek caught her hands in his, holding them at their waist.

Then a new pair of hands gripped him on the shoulders, yanked him back.

"Now they are your problems," Elias Luvon whispered in his ear. And the cadet chopped Alek hard on the back of his neck, sending him to the ground with a violent shove.

His neck on fire with pain, Alek stumbled forward, heading for a tumble down the short flight of snow-swept stairs. Behind him, Gabriella called out a short, sharp, "Alek!"

Elias Luvon laughed.

Dragging his right foot Alek pitched himself to one side. He lost one of his dress shoes, but managed to catch the stone obelisk that began the courtyard wall at the top of the steps. One edge sliced skin off his right temple, scraped down the side of his face with a dry, sandpaper rasp, and chipped against his collarbone. Alek exhaled sharply.

Rough hands grabbed at him again, a pair to each arm, and yanked him away from the obelisk. Two cadets, among Elias's best friends and the ones who had been waiting on the ballroom floor as Elias asked Gabriella for a dance. They hauled him around to face Elias. A fourth cadet held Gabriella from behind, one hand clasped around either arm. Alek recognized him as well, from earlier at the refreshment table.

Gabriella's soft brown eyes were wide, and her arms puckered into gooseflesh from the evening cold. She had lost Alek's coat, which lay at her feet in a dark rumple. A lock of hair had pulled loose from her coif and lay down across her face. "Alek?"

He'd be all right. Probably. He felt the soft trickle of blood oozing down his face, dripping from his jaw. Bright red teardrops splashed down the right breast of his tux shirt, spreading into a stain.

"You're done, Alek." Elias's eyes were dark, and cold as any of the ice sculptures Alek and Gabriella had looked upon. "You couldn't even be a gracious winner this evening. Well, we're all tired of your Terran-elitist attitude. Your lack of respect."

"I can't understand it either." Alek shrugged one shoulder up to his jaw to blot the blood from it. "I mean, given my warm reception and—"

Elias skipped forward, saber jangling at his side as he brought a knee up to plant squarely into Alek's midsection. Breath rushed out in a violent exhale, and Alek sagged toward the ground. Only strong hands kept him off his knees, holding him above the frozen courtyard. A second blow was not as well-aimed, and Alek felt a rib snap with a bright thunderbolt of pain. He gasped for air, barely able to breathe.

"Hobnobbing with the Archon's brother." Elias paced back to his original spot. "Insulting the Nagelring. Insulting the Commonwealth." His list of Alek's wrongs, real or imagined, had obviously condemned Alek already in his eyes. "Thinking you were even worth her time," he said, staring at Gabriella.

"Worth my time?" Gabriella's tears were angry, not frightened. She struggled in the grip of Elias's crony. The dark-haired cadet glanced about warily, but held her fast. "I'd take Alek over some puffed-shirt 'Mech-head any day of the week, Elias Luvon."

Glancing back over his shoulder, Elias nodded sharply to the two holding Alek. One of them put a foot out in front of Alek, who struggled to regain his feet, and they both gave him a brutal shove. Alek sprawled forward over the courtyard flagstone, barely catching himself, grinding frozen gravel and ice into his hands. His left side spasmed as ends of his broken rib grated together.

"But he's so *clumsy*," Elias whined in mock incredulity. To his friends, he said, "Help him up."

They did so, one with a knee into his kidney and the other wrenching an arm behind his back until his shoulder screamed.

Alek grunted, refusing to shout in pain. Through clenched teeth he managed, "Can't imagine...what's come over me." *Faith is the force by which we live,* Alek reminded himself. And not all of him was dust.

"If he's so clumsy," Gabriella tossed back, all but shouting, "so undesirable, why did your commander offer him a position in the Nagelring?"

He felt a slight hesitation in the loose grips of Elias's friends. The cadet holding onto Gabriella also looked taken aback, doubt clouding his green, malachite eyes.

Alek gasped for more breath. The cold air burned harshly against his raw throat. "Didn't mention that to your friends, eh?" he wheezed.

Elias spun on him. "Shut up."

"No snappy comeback?" Alek stood under his own strength. His right foot burned with cold as the ice underfoot melted and soaked into his sock, but he ignored the needle-stabbing sensation. Breathing shallow, trying not to aggravate his broken rib, he asked, "No grand debate?"

"I'm not interested in anything you have to say, Terran."

Alek nodded. "Well, after all, 'a closed mind never errs, nor learns,'" he quoted.

"Another one of your dead Russians?" Elias scoffed.

"Not this time," Alek said, thanking Michael silently for the words. "Tracial Steiner. One of yours."

With Gabriella's help, he had gotten through to one of them. The dark-haired cadet holding onto Gabriella let her go. "Come on, Elias," he said, glancing about nervously. "That's enough."

Elias speared the other cadet with a severe look. "I'll say when it's enough, Patrick." Then he slowly drew his saber, letting the sword rasp free of its hilt in one long pull. "I decide."

Gabriella drew in a sharp breath, fear finally showing in her eyes. The two cadets holding Alek let him go. They hadn't signed on for murder, apparently. But then, neither had Elias Luvon.

No one else saw it in Elias' eyes. The desperation. The fear. Alek knew Elias wasn't about to use the saber. He was abusive and insecure, but he had not lost control of his senses.

He was posturing, pure and simple. Elias Luvon had a need to be respected. To be in charge. Alek found that sad, and not a little pitiful.

He was also very tired of being Elias's plaything, used as a means to the cadet's end. Shrugging away from the two cadets standing right behind him, he limped up to Elias. "You aren't going to use that, Elias." His voice was steadfast and certain.

Elias had a dead look in his eyes. He had backed himself into a corner, and knew it. "You don't know what I'd do."

Alek nodded. "You're going to be a soldier, Elias. A MechWarrior. You won't risk that here and now just to save face. Not with witnesses," he nodded to Gabriella.

"Who'd believe her?" Elias smiled cruelly. "Distraught and angry, found by four Nagelring cadets with her dress 'slipping' off and a Terran pawing her. Maybe her 'no's' were real... maybe they weren't. How were we to know, Alek? How were we to know?"

He meant to do it. Nothing with the sword—Elias seemed to have all but forgotten that as he crafted his latest piece of scandal and slander—but he could recover some poise by thrashing Alek further through university gossip. The feet thrust into his way, the thrown books and rude shoulders on the stairwells, they would never cease. Any "accidents" that befell him would be seen as deserving, to be covered up right away before any hint of the scandal made it into official records. If it ruined Gabriella Bailey's reputation alongside his, that didn't seem to bother Elias at all.

But it bothered Alek. More than anything else.

Bruises faded over time. Bones mended. But to hurt an innocent person for no other reason than she liked Alek seemed unconscionable.

"No," he said, shaking his head.

"Oh, yeah." Elias flipped the end of his saber up, tapped Alek lightly on the shoulder with it as if knighting him. "And you know," he whispered, "the more adamantly she denies it, the more people will believe it has to be true."

"No!"

Alek flailed out with his left arm, knocking the saber away from his shoulder with such violence it turned Elias halfway around from him. No one, especially Elias, had expected mild-mannered Alek to strike back. Not ever. Alek could have taken that moment to escape, so clean was the surprise. Grab Gabriella and run. Back across the courtyard patio, anywhere where others saw them, and could bear witness.

Instead, Alek took a full step across the line he had toed for so many years. The line which had grown thicker, more severe, in the eighteen months spent on Tharkad.

He grabbed Elias Luvon, taking thick handfuls of fabric in each fist, and *heaved.*

Elias staggered toward the steps which led into the university's winter gardens. Alek stumbled, lost his footing. Pain lit his left side as his knees slammed against the cold patio flagstone.

Through tear-filled eyes, he watched as Elias wavered dangerously at the top edge, sword slashing the air in front of him, as if trying to fend off gravity's clutches.

Then Elias fell.

Alek's breathing stammered, dredging in painful breaths and then exhaling small clouds of frost. He sensed someone drop down beside him, adding what warmth she could with an arm around his shoulders.

"Oh, Alek." The words echoed in his mind, but Alek drew no support from them. They were lost among a sea of chaotic thoughts and one dark, visceral image.

That of Elias Luvon. Sprawled over the lower patio.

A broken piece of his saber impaled through the right side of his chest.

The apartment, taken by Alek's parents so that they could be on hand for the inquiry, smelled of coffee and his mother's homemade black bread. The radiator rattled in the mornings, and there was never enough hot water to satisfy anyone, but for now it was home.

It gave him a place to rest over the weekend, nursing his broken rib and a deeply-bruised kidney. Retreating into his books, he memorized three new poems by Pushkin and long passages by Dumas and Shakespeare as well. None of them could scrub the image from of his memory. No matter how hard he tried.

He limped from his room only twice that weekend. The second time he met Gabriella Bailey at the apartment's door. She had tracked him down via Michael Steiner, Alek's first visitor after the incident. Gabriella stood in the hall and bit on her lower lip, trying to decide what to say after declining an invitation into the apartment. "Are you all right?"

He nodded. "You?" A shrug. "Gabriella. I never meant for—"

"I know." She cut him off with a quick shake of her head. Auburn hair whispered across her shoulders. The silence lengthened. She hugged herself around her middle. Awkward. Closed.

"Elias will be fine," she finally said.

Michael had already told him as much. Elias was in the critical care facility of the local hospital, in stable condition after the staff took care of some internal bleeding and re-inflated his right lung. He'd be there for several days, under observation. He wouldn't be coming back for classes.

Gabriella had heard the same thing. "Looks like you won."

It didn't feel that way to Alek. "No. I lost."

She looked down at the carpeted hall. "I can't get the picture out of my head. Everything changed so quickly." She looked up, her soft doe eyes full of uncertainty. "I wanted it to be different."

"Circumstance and accident often conspire against what we want."

She forced the ghost of a smile. "Who said that?"

"Me." Alek didn't smile. He had nearly killed Elias Luvon. Accident or no, it weighed heavily. "Gabriella. I—"

"Alek, I just wanted to see you. Tell you I wish it were different. Everything had been going so well. I want...wanted... but now..."

"I know," he offered, feeling very tired. "Me too."

"Thank you." She stepped into him, arms still between them as she leaned in close. Her breath was warm and sweet, and her eyes sad as she brushed dry lips over Alek's cheek.

It was his first kiss from Gabriella Bailey.

To say good-bye.

Alek spent most of his days in a virtual bubble of isolation. Mostly of his own doing. The Nagelring cadets pretended he did not exist, except for one who made a point of staking out the PoliSci hall and offering a formal apology first to Gabriella, and then Alek. Other students also forwarded tentative apologies for their previous hassling, or else wanted to hear more details about the night of the Formal, and thought Alek would be into the gossip. He ignored both equally.

Lunches were still taken with Michael Steiner, and it was through Michael that Alek forwarded his request for a meeting with Colonel Baumgarten. Michael had the impeccable manners not to say a thing at the time, though he invited himself along the following evening, showing up at the apartment with the colonel and a bottle of good Lyran wine as a gift to Alek's parents.

His mother played hostess, seating everyone in the small living room, passing out warm bread slathered with honey and pouring the wine. Alek's father stood behind his son's chair, hands on the backrest, encouraging but silent, as Alek first asked after Elias Luvon.

"Recovering," Baumgarten said. The officer still looked more like an accountant than a warrior, and ran through the report as if he were checking off a list. "Good prognosis for a full recovery. Very quiet about what happened that night. Refusing to meet with any other students or cadets. And expelled from the Nagelring."

"Expelled?" Alek blinked twice. After all the cover-ups and dismissed investigations, he had not expected that. Had not even wished for it, in fact.

Baumgarten leaned forward. "We put a great deal of stock in personal conduct at the Nagelring, Alek. Accidents and a few minor transgressions we might overlook. But a pattern of abuse?" He shook his head. "I would hope you thought better of us than that."

Alek took a small bite of the heavy bread, letting the honey sit on his tongue a moment before swallowing. "I think very highly of the Nagelring *and* the Star League Defense Force, Colonel. But who...?" He glanced at Michael Steiner.

Michael smiled serenely, very much at peace with himself. "Not a word from me, Alek, until Colonel Baumgarten asked directly. He already knew at that point. Apparently one of the cadets present that night came clean."

The dark haired one who had held Gabriella back. The one who had formally apologized to both of them.

He asked, and Baumgarten nodded. "Patrick Ward. *Ja*. On his testimony, the Cadet Honor Board also expelled the other two, who attempted to bluff their way out of trouble. Patrick is on probation." He set aside his untouched wine. "But you really didn't ask me here to go over Nagelring protocols, did you?"

"In a way, sir. Yes." Alek stood, glanced at his mother and father, who both smiled thin encouragement. They excused themselves from the room, leaving him alone with the two men. "I wish to formally apply to the Nagelring, per your earlier invitation."

Baumgarten did not appear surprised. "Lord Steiner suggested you might ask after that," he admitted. "I have to say, I thought it unlikely. I thought you did your fighting with words? 'Education is a weapon.' Isn't that what you said?"

That and more. Alek winced. "There is only a small difference between believing that, Colonel, and living by it. That difference nearly cost someone his life. When it truly mattered, I failed."

Michael shook his head. "You defended yourself, Alek. Don't beat yourself up over that."

"If I'm going to defend myself physically at all, I should learn how." That was the realization Alek had come to during his self-enforced isolation; that he had been fighting back against Elias Luvon for months without knowing it. Every verbal jab. His entire self-righteous attitude toward confrontation. And then, in a moment of frustration and anger, he had lashed out unconditionally. No thought or decision to it.

And that frightened Alek more than anything else.

Not all of him was dust, but he was not necessarily safe from the worm.

He tried to explain that to Colonel Baumgarten, who at least nodded as if he understood. "Still, you should think this over. Take some time, Alek."

"I hurt Elias Luvon without taking time to think. Colonel, I've made my decision. If the Nagelring will still have me."

Baumgarten stood, paced a tight box around the room while wrestling with the proposal. He came to a stop opposite Alek. "Technically, I cannot refuse you," he admitted. Though he certainly looked as if he wanted to. "I looked up her name."

"Who?" Alek asked, but he knew.

"The guard. Tanya. The one who wounded Leonard Kurita."

He sighed. "Yes. I thought you might. And I obviously know the story, Colonel. Kurita pulled a dagger from his robes and stabbed her to death before fleeing. Her family was later awarded the title Defender of the First Lord, and the right to attend any academy or university."

Baumgarten spread his hands. "You see my dilemma."

"Colonel. If you tell me here, in private, that I am not welcome at the Nagelring nor would I be of use to the Star League, I will accept that. I will not pursue it, even though it is important to me."

"Why, Alek?" The colonel pressed forward, eyes intent. "Why is it so important that you do this? As a politician or historian, you could effect such greater change."

Michael laughed softly. "Ah, Colonel. 'Everyone thinks of changing the world...'" he began.

And if Michael Steiner could learn Tolstoi, perhaps this effort by Alek wasn't so futile after all. "'No one thinks of changing himself,'" he finished the quote.

Baumgarten nodded slowly, digesting the words and never once breaking eye contact with Alek. He reached for the noteputer clipped to his belt, powered it up and pulled up a file. He showed it to Alek. The amber words glowed on the dark screen.

A formal contract, enlisting Alek into the Star League Defense Force, pursuant to his completion of training at the Nagelring military academy. It was all prepared, along with his identification number and full legal name, waiting for his thumbprint to seal the agreement.

Alek reached out and thumbed the pad, letting the small device take a full scan and DNA sample, turning it into an unforgeable verigraph document.

Alek watched as Baumgarten confirmed it with his print, and Michael witnessed with his. As simple as that. He had not expected fanfare or ceremony. There wasn't any. Just the mantle of the huge commitment he had just made settling over his shoulders with great significance.

"Not all of me is dust," Alek whispered, bearing up beneath the weight.

Colonel Baumgarten was the first to offer his hand. "Welcome to the Nagelring," he said, "Aleksandr Kerensky."

POISON

JASON M. HARDY

TUKWILA
TIKONOV
CAPELLAN MARCH
FEDERATED SUNS
21 FEBRUARY 3065

Seventy-five tons of metal should not be able to hide so easily.

Lukas looked through the shattered window onto the pockmarked street below, first north, then south. Nothing. He took a deep breath, but his pulse kept racing. Grit and oil coated his throat.

A moment earlier, a 'Mech—a *Rakshasa*, judging by the square missile launchers on each shoulder—had torn into the intersection just north of him, lasers firing. It had stopped, swiveled its torso, and scattered laser shots across the street, sending Lukas diving for shelter. A few blasts tore into the walls of the building serving as his bunker, but most flew past, leaving only yellow afterburn patterns in Lukas' eyes.

By the time Lukas realized he was still alive and returned to the window, the 'Mech was gone. He hadn't heard it move. 'Mechs could do many things, but sneaking quietly through city streets was not one of them. Yet this one was gone.

Of course it had moved on, he told himself. It didn't care about him. They weren't after him. They didn't know who he was.

He brushed plaster and glass dust from his pants, streaking the fabric with sweat. He shakily rose to his feet and poked his head through the ruined window. There was nothing—no 'Mechs, no infantry, nothing—on the streets below. At least, nothing he could see through the smoke and darkness.

Since no one was trying to kill him that second, Lukas took a moment to create his eighth survival plan of the day. The goals of his earliest plans had been lofty and, as it turned out, impossible. If they had worked, he'd be on a DropShip now, looking for a more peaceful place to stay until calm returned to Tikonov. Getting the rest he deserved.

But transport off the planet for a civilian was next to impossible while the battle raged. Transport for a civilian with forged papers (even high-class forgeries) was even more difficult.

He would not be leaving anytime soon.

Trapped on the surface, his goals shifted to trying to stay alive for a week, then to surviving the rest of the day. Now all he wanted was live another hour.

A cluster of missiles whined overhead, close enough to make Lukas flinch. He dropped to the floor again as they smashed into the roof of a building a block away. For the thousandth time that day, the streets of Tukwila shook.

Also for the thousandth time that day, Lukas Azhenov cursed military leaders and their pretended ethics. Put them in a quiet, locked room and they would drone on and on about the duties of a warrior and the Ares Conventions and keeping civilians out of warfare and other tripe, but as soon as they see an opportunity to gain an advantage on their enemy, all their talk flies away. Any civilians standing in the way of a strategically important goal had better get out of the way or get swept aside with the rest of the rubble.

Lukas always appreciated the honesty and directness of his kind of people when compared to the hypocritical nobility of generals and politicians. The underworld code was simple: anyone is fair game. Lukas, and people like him, did what needed doing, no matter whom was involved. Civilians, soldiers, or anyone else were all the same—if they were obstacles, they needed to be removed. One way or another. No nonsense about outside conditions or treaties or duty dictating what you can do or who you can kill. Anyone may become a target. That's the deal going in, clear and transparent, unlike the games and deceptions practiced by politicians.

Another cluster of missiles exploded, farther away than the first. The tremor that followed was barely enough to wobble Lukas' knees. Whatever was firing those missiles was not targeting him or anything nearby. It was time to move.

He stood and leaped toward the staircase he'd ascended five minutes ago, when he had first seen the *Rakshasa*. Entering the building had been a gamble—if the *Rakshasa* had spotted him, a few blasts at the already shaky structure would have taken it down on top of Lukas. He wished he could tell himself he had taken a calculated risk, but he hadn't. He had panicked.

He'd gotten lucky, though, and the *Rakshasa* had moved on, either because it didn't know where Lukas was, or it didn't care.

On the first floor, he stepped over collapsed steel beams, shattered desks, and large chunks of plaster—but no bodies. Most of the civilians had received word of the incoming troops before they arrived and were safely away. The military didn't seem too concerned about the few people left behind who never got the message.

Lukas knew he was partially to blame—the money he took with him from Luthien had allowed him to be indolent and less than watchful while on Tikonov—but he preferred blaming the generals and warriors who were busy reducing Tukwila to rubble.

At the exterior door, he poked his head out and scanned the street in both directions.

To the south, he caught a flutter of movement, ground troops crossing an intersection. They might have been as close as a quarter mile, but dust, smoke, and darkness obscured them. Lukas could barely make out their forms, so he knew he would be just as difficult to see.

He walked out of the door slowly, staying near any walls that still stood. His breathing was rapid, his ears heard only rushing blood. He ducked instinctively as a red laser flashed high overhead, but it was nowhere near him.

No other weapons fired. No one noticed him walking.

At the next intersection he turned west, away from battle, away from the Prince's Men. He couldn't risk running into their ground troops. If they knew who he was—they probably didn't, but if they did—Davion's troops would shoot Lukas on sight. If he was lucky.

After two blocks, he turned south again, walking slowly, swiveling to look north, then south, then north again so quickly that he started to feel dizzy. He slowed even more.

Patience, he told himself, *patience,* even though his heart and mind and muscles were straining to run until he collapsed.

He covered a mile in twenty minutes. Acrid smoke stung tears out of his eyes, washing clear trails through the grime on his face. He blinked, then rubbed his eyes, trying to get them clear.

When he opened them, it stood in front of him. He knew this humanoid shape well—a *Wyvern,* smaller than a *Rakshasa,* but, like any 'Mech, plenty big enough to take care of a single unarmored human. Smoke curved around its torso as it trotted through the streets, heading, like all of Davion's army, east.

Lukas jumped backward, his back flattening against a cool metal wall. He let the haze settle around him.

The *Wyvern* kept moving, a single beam of light from its head pointing forward, sweeping back and forth, illuminating the smoke and little else. The beam stayed ten meters above ground level, and Lukas exhaled a sigh. The *Wyvern* was looking for something taller than a single human. It was not looking for him.

The impact of the metal feet shook the road as the 'Mech drew near Lukas' position, then moved past. He watched the armored shins walk by, and the *Wyvern* didn't slow, didn't even look down. Then it was gone.

Lukas re-emerged from the shadows and continued south, still glancing over his shoulder every other step. But the explosions seemed to be getting farther and farther away, the battle moving east with the Prince's Men.

His pace slowed as adrenaline drained away. This wasn't the first time in his life he'd been on the run. He vowed it would not be the last.

Running from the military, he reflected as he tripped over a damaged piece of street that jutted upward, *is quite different from evading the usual team of assassins, vigilantes, bounty hunters, or mobsters.* Small groups could be tenacious, but much easier to evade than an entire army.

Maybe he should have stayed on Luthien, taken his chances with any agents the Combine sent against him. For all he knew, they never would have connected him to the assassination, and he could have retired with the money from the sale. There were plenty of places to hide on Luthien.

But then he remembered Celia, eight years ago. All she had done was sold a few secrets, troop movements, to Sandoval in the Draconis March. She'd barely made enough to pay for a few weeks of vacation. Minor league stuff, really.

But she'd disappeared. For months after she vanished, small pieces of her kept showing up across Luthien.

To the Combine, no treachery was minor.

If they had done that to a low-level spy like Celia, what would they do to him? They probably didn't have proof—Lukas himself couldn't be completely certain he'd even done it. But he trusted his gut, and it told him that he had played a part in one of the greatest crimes ever committed against the Draconis Combine. If some Combine agent had the same feeling, proof or no proof, they'd come after him.

He'd felt the heat approaching, received word through backdoor channels that investigations were growing more active, so he left Luthien, fleeing the Draconis Combine. He'd gone to the home he'd run away from decades earlier, only to have the Steiner-Davion civil war find him there. Now he was in the sights of Victor Davion's men, the only people who might want him dead more than House Kurita. If they knew.

There had to be somewhere he could go, a safe haven, a place to hide, anything to get away from the armies rushing toward him.

A rush of air followed by a series of clatters, like stones skipping across ferrocrete, made him jerk his head right. Where there had been nothing, half a dozen infantry troops, two clad in battle armor, walked down the street as fumes rose from their recently extinguished jump jets. A streetlight, its pole bent but its bulb still functioning, bounced light off their scratched armor.

They were a block and a half away, and Lukas' lower half was still enshrouded in smoke. They probably didn't see him. He squinted, trying to make out their markings. Narrow blue, wide white. Lyran.

But were they rebels or loyalists? In a civil war, even the generals had trouble keeping track of which regiments were on whose side. For a civilian, it was impossible. He wished he knew; if the troopers were loyalists, maybe he could go to them for protection. Let them know who he was, who he had killed, and he'd be fine. He'd just have to portray what he'd done as an act of war, the kind of thing they did every day. He wasn't a criminal, he was a hero. They'd understand.

He shook his head. They wouldn't. People like him were never heroes. If discovered and caught, they wound up in deep, dark holes. They were the dirty secrets of the universe, and most people wanted them to stay hidden.

Best to assume they'd be hostile. Staying near the ruined buildings on the south side of the street, picking his way through the rubble, Lukas moved east, away from the infantry.

They didn't follow. The troopers stood in the street, not in any sort of formation, talking with each other. A full day under fire is enough to scatter any platoon, and these soldiers were probably disoriented, confused, and weary. All that worked to Lukas' advantage.

He picked his way a block and a half ahead before the troopers moved. One of them issued an order. Lukas was too far away to hear what he said, but the commanding tone was unmistakable, and they quickly fell in behind him, walking ahead, drawing closer to Lukas.

He cursed. Normally he'd have no difficulty finding shelter in this city. He'd only been back for a year, but he had dozens of places to hide. The few good contacts he'd made in that time, though, were now either dead or fled and his safe havens buried under rubble. The rebels sweeping through Tukwila had destroyed the webs he'd woven—another reason not to feel bad for what he had done to their cause on Luthien.

The infantry was rapidly drawing close, their speed leaving him few options. He didn't want to be seen, certainly didn't want to be questioned by troopers. He had to stay ahead of them. He picked up his pace, made it to the end of the block, and turned south.

That was a mistake. After only half a block, Lukas saw a looming silhouette, well over ten meters tall—a *Zeus*—walk into the street about half a kilometer away. It turned and headed north, toward him, scanning the ground with a searchlight. Looking for infantry.

He turned, but only briefly. The infantry had arrived behind him, walking right toward the lumbering, heavy-shouldered 'Mech. Panic spiked through Lukas' head.

Insanity. Six troops didn't stand a chance against a 'Mech, especially one this size. The infantry should have turned back as soon as they saw it, unless the stress of battle had made them suicidal. But the troopers and the *Zeus* closed on each other, with Lukas squeezed between.

He didn't understand the troopers' decision to walk forward until he reached the next cross street and saw a smaller 'Mech to the west, crouched in the shadows of one of Tukwila's taller buildings. It was completely still, weapons poised and ready, aimed at the intersection where Lukas stood. He had seen this model before, with its bulbous legs and round shoulder turrets, but its name escaped his mind.

The *Zeus* was being lured forward so the other 'Mech could pounce. The trap was going to be sprung in the intersection where Lukas stood.

He had only one way to go—east, toward the front lines. Toward the explosions, the mortar whistles, and the screams. He'd endured that for ten hours today. He couldn't, wouldn't be able to endure any more.

The first shots fired by the infantry told him he didn't have a choice. Their SRMs worked as intended, doing no serious damage but angering the *Zeus*. It stomped forward.

Lukas ran.

He'd made it only a block before the intersection behind him exploded. A roar nearly shattered his eardrums and the ground heaved beneath his feet. He flew five meters, then rolled sideways across the ferrocrete. His legs and arms never stopped moving, and soon he was up again, running. Someone was dead in the intersection behind him, he was sure. But it wasn't him.

He was only conscious of smoke swirling around him, of his feet pounding the battered street. He thought of nothing but motion.

Two blocks later, his luck almost ran out. He heard the crackle of gunfire just as he entered another intersection— *look both ways before crossing,* some detached part of his brain told him—and he jumped backward and rolled behind the corner, out of harm's way. He didn't notice the crease of blood across the back of his left hand until he wiped sweat from his brow.

He looked curiously at the wound for a moment. He'd never been shot. Been a shooter, but never been shot. It stung.

He shook his attention back to the present, poking his head around the corner. It was bad. Infantry to the north. A 'Mech to the east, another south. And the survivors of the skirmish to the west would undoubtedly be closing in soon.

On top of that, he had no shelter. The buildings that used to stand on this block were no use. No doorways remained clear, no roofs were intact. The crumbling interior might kill him faster than the warring armies.

He felt his right hand fluttering. He looked at it, tried to will it to be still, but it kept twitching. He grabbed it with his left, held it tight, but it still twitched.

The temptation that had nagged at him since the rumors of Davion's flight from Tukwila rose again. All he needed to do was find some loyalists. If they knew who he was, if he could tell them the role he played in getting Davion to abandon his troops, he'd be a hero. It was just an act of war, he'd tell them. They'd listen. They'd understand what he'd done for them. The need for his secret contacts, for hiding places, for skulking through ruins, would disappear. Maybe, just maybe, they'd get him to a military DropShip. Get him off planet. Get him the rest he deserved. Hope, which had been pronounced dead as recently as half an hour ago, stirred lightly in his chest.

Of course, he hadn't really acted as a patriot, and he'd not given a thought to the Archon-Princess—or anyone else—when he'd made the sale that eventually drove him off Luthien. But no one needed to know that. He really didn't care about either side in this war, or how it ended, as long as it ended with him alive. Right now, his sympathies lay with the loyalists only because of his actions taken more than a year ago.

Someone had given Lukas a tremendous sum of money to buy two doses of fulmitoxin. The tremendous price had aroused his curiosity, but he had been in business long enough to not ask questions.

It was only much later, when the news broke, that he understood why so much money had been paid, and why he had been forced to flee Luthien soon after the sale

Seven months after he sold the fulmitoxin to a grubby courier whose headless body was discovered a week after the transaction, Omi Kurita was dead. Poisoned by fulmitoxin, reliable sources told him.

Lukas was willing to bet his life it was his carefully crafted poison in her blood. He had not been present to deliver the blow, but that distinction mattered little. He had made the fatal poison. He had, in essence, murdered Omi Kurita.

He pressed himself deep into a pile of rubble for shelter as lasers flashed overhead. Autocannon fire immediately followed, a few rounds smashing into the wall above Lukas. A large piece of stone fell, shattering on the pavement and sending shards into Lukas' exposed skin. Nearly a dozen pinheads of blood sprang up on his face.

That was enough. This was insanity. This was not what he deserved. He was as heroic as any man in this field—he'd taken out a bigger target than anyone, because his actions had taken Davion off the field. He needed to find someone. He'd make them understand. He'd make them remove him from the hell of battle. They'd have to. He was a hero. An unconventional one, maybe—he knew that people like him usually were rewarded with torture and death, not protection and acclaim. But this was different. It would have to be. He had helped this army, crushing the opposition's morale. They'd have to recognize what he'd done. Have to. It was what he had earned, and it was the only way he might survive the day. He just needed to find someone to talk to.

The 'Mech towered above Lukas, as if pondering what Lukas had said. He'd somehow found an officer loyal to the Archon-Princess, screamed himself hoarse getting the MechWarrior to see him, to listen what he had to say. And he had. He had listened. Lukas spilled the whole story. Now he just had to wait for the order to come down, the order that would finally get him the rest he deserved.

Lukas waited. How complicated could this be? The order was simple: "Take this man to safety." Five simple words, and Lukas would escape.

The 'Mech turned, pointed itself north, and walked away without so much as a gesture to Lukas. He watched in disbelief.

There had to be a mistake. He was a *hero*.

Gauss rounds sped overhead, flying into buildings with punishing blows. Smaller rounds flew lower to the ground, surrounding Lukas like a swarm of bees. And the 'Mech walked farther away.

Anger and fear rose together in Lukas' chest. How dare this pilot simply ignore someone of his stature? Who was he to leave him behind?

Lukas ran after him, a two-meter human futilely chasing a fighting machine five times his height.

After a half-kilometer of Lukas somehow avoiding the bullets and flying shrapnel, the 'Mech stopped. It stopped. The pilot must have heard.

Lukas shouted gratitude with his ruined voice, waving at the 'Mech as it twisted its torso. Salvation.

The side of the 'Mech exploded. Metal and white heat collapsed on Lukas.

He was on the ground. He couldn't feel his legs. The 'Mech he had pursued lay on its side, motionless, fifteen meters away. Another 'Mech —a *Wyvern*, maybe the same *Wyvern* Lukas had seen earlier—walked toward the metal corpse.

Lukas tried to scramble to his feet, but they didn't respond. All he could do was creep backward, pushing himself with his arms. The rebel *Wyvern* drew closer.

He had one last desperate idea. He still had something, something the rebels wanted. Information. They needed to know what he knew, he needed to tell them, that was worth keeping him alive, wasn't it? They'd listen. They'd want him alive. He could tell Davion's men whom he sold the poison to. They could use that to track the assassin. That would be enough. They would save him. He was worth more alive than dead. They may kill him eventually for what he'd done. But not today.

He raised one arm, propping his torso up with the other.

"Wait!" he screamed, but his voice was buried by the noise of battle. "*Wait!*" he screamed again. The *Wyvern* continued forward.

"I can help you!" Lukas screamed. "I can tell you things! Things you need to know!" The pace of the *Wyvern* remained steady.

Lukas was right in its path. The pilot probably couldn't see him, probably didn't care about anything lying on the ground. Lukas only had seconds.

"You don't know who I am!" he screamed. "*You don't know who I am!*"

The 'Mech, uncaring, lowered its foot.

RAKSHASA
Heavy—75 tons

WYVERN
Medium—45 tons

THE IMMORTAL WARRIOR AT THE BATTLE OF VORHAVEN

KEVIN KILLIANY

VORHAVEN
KATHIL
CAPELLAN MARCH
FEDERATED COMMONWEALTH
2 NOVEMBER 3062

The three MechWarriors ran ahead of her, their silver neurohelmets flashing in the sunlight. They were fast, but she was determined.

They would not escape the Immortal Warrior.

The three tried to trick her with a dodge toward the woods on the right, then dashed left. In an instant they'd disappeared behind a sharp corner of the cliff-sided mountain. Clutching her weapon tightly, she slowed and flared wide around the turn, giving herself room in case they doubled back and tried to dash past her in the opposite direction.

She needn't have bothered. The three had used her caution to gain distance and were now well ahead of her. She felt her feet thudding against the grassy soil as she churned her legs to maximum speed, closing the gap.

Suddenly the three MechWarriors stopped, facing the cliff-sided mountain. She saw them pull to attention and salute something up on the cliff. She didn't know why her targets had forgotten the Immortal Warrior was closing on them, and she didn't pause to see what they were looking at. They were in her sights and they were doomed.

Shrieking her best Immortal Warrior yell, she was upon them. She made a clean hit before they could respond. But, whirling and twisting, the MechWarriors danced away from her, laughing as they ran.

"I got you, Billy!" she screamed. "You're it!"

"Missed me, missed me!" Billy called back, not even slowing as he dodged around a knot of adults. The other two MechWarriors were already halfway to the food tent, the open vests of their Halloween costumes flapping about their arms.

"How goes the battle, Jessie?"

Jessie turned to face the mountain, and saw Grandpa on the porch.

"Billy cheated," she announced.

"I agree," Grandpa nodded judiciously. "You tagged him fair and square."

There didn't seem to be much to say to that. Billy and the cousins were now too far gone for her to ever catch them. Besides, her new uncle was on the porch with Grandpa.

Uncle David wasn't really a new uncle, of course; she'd seen pictures of him all her life. But he was a MechWarrior—a real one—and he'd been away since before she was born. She'd never really met him before the Halloween party two nights ago, and this was the first chance she'd had to look at him closely.

He looked like Grandpa, she decided, only a little shorter and his hair was not grey. She wasn't sure, but she bet he didn't have a brown circle with no hair on top of his head either.

"You going to eat that cinnamon roll," Uncle David asked, "Or just run around with it?"

Jessie looked down at the roll, which a moment before had been a weapon, though she'd never decided which one. It was smooshed slightly, the melted sugar frosting sticking to her fingers.

"Grandma made it," she answered.

"I was hoping she did," Uncle David smiled. She liked his smile. "I was also hoping you'd want to give it to me."

Jessie considered for a moment.

"I already had two," she announced. "And Grandma's got more."

"I'll bet she does."

Making her decision, Jessie climbed onto the porch and surrendered the roll to Uncle David. His hands were not as big as Grandpa's.

"Thank you, Immortal Warrior," he intoned seriously.

She giggled as she scurried into the house, propelled by a friendly swat on the bottom.

Billy was hiding from her again.

Jessie circled through Grandpa and Grandma's house, keeping an eye out for signs of her brother. She avoided the rooms at the end of the west wing. Aunt Grace and the twins had taken those over. They'd moved in nearly a month ago, right after the Halloween party where she'd met her new uncle, because Aunt Grace had said, "things were getting bad in the city."

She didn't mind the twins so much; they were too quiet to be very interesting anyway. But Aunt Grace was always cross, and saying how serious the situation was, and worrying about Uncle David. Even her mother had stopped trying to cheer her up.

She set thoughts of her aunt aside and focused on finding Billy.

He wasn't in the fruit cellar and he wasn't in the pantry. He wasn't under the library table and he wasn't in the little attic room with his comic vidbooks. She knew he knew better than to go into the guest bedrooms or the formal living room.

He must be hiding outside.

Jessie stood by the dining room window, considering. Outside, the sun was shining in a clear blue sky. No sign of the summer storms that sometimes blew down whole forests. It was a perfect day for being outside instead of in.

Her brother was a year and a half older than her, but he always hid in the same places. If Billy was hiding outside, he was either under the side porch, in the feed barn or up in the big lonely oak. That last was a favorite of his, because he could climb the rope holding the tire swing and she could not.

"Hey," her big sister Cassie called from the family room, "the video just went out!"

Jessie ignored her. Cassie watched too much video; all she ever wanted to do was watch kissy stories, anyway.

She looked toward the oak. Sure enough, the empty tire was swinging without a breeze. Billy was up the tree.

And a giant metal man walked over the hill.

Jessie blinked.

"BattleMechs!" yelled Aunt Grace from somewhere upstairs. "Not the Militia!"

Throughout the house, Jessie heard the grown-ups shouting.

"We're surrounded!"

"Where are the children?"

"Everybody, get to the cars!"

"No!" Grandpa's voice cut across the others. "They'll cut us down if we try to escape. Get into the storm shelter!"

"The children! Find the children!"

Whirling from the window, Jessie dodged around Cassie and ran up the stairs as fast as she could. She heard Aunt Grace call her name, but she didn't break stride.

Once in her room, it took her only a moment to find what she needed and less than that to pull on her bandana and loop an ammo belt across one shoulder. One minute after the metal giant came over the hill, the Immortal Warrior dashed from the kitchen door.

She could hear her mother's voice through the open windows of the house behind her, calling. She ran harder. No time to turn back now, there was a mission to accomplish.

The giant metal man, the BattleMech, was standing next to the big oak. It did not move. It just stood, watching the house while two other BattleMechs—one that looked just like it and another that looked different—fired their lasers again and again at Grandpa's crops. The AgroMechs and tractors were all smoking masses of twisted metal dotted about the burning fields.

The BattleMech had to see her, but she hoped the Immortal Warrior's armor would frighten it as she ran across the open ground. It did not fire. Or step on her when she ran in front of its toes. Her heart was pounding as she reached the base of the tree.

Looking up through the branches, she tried to find her brother. She knew Billy was up there, but she couldn't see him.

"Billy?" she called, straining to catch sight of him. "Billy!"

After a moment, her brother's head appeared over the edge of the broad branch the tire swing was tied to. His eyes were red and puffy, and he looked like he had been crying.

"What are you doing here?" he asked.

"I'm here to rescue you," she answered.

"Jessie, get out of here," he said. "This isn't pretend."

Jessie glanced over at the BattleMech, though from under the canopy of the ironwood all she could see was its lower legs. It was so big, and the house so far away. For a moment she couldn't breathe, it took a shuddering gasp to pull air into her lungs. She felt her eyes sting as tears threatened.

Jessie shook herself. The Immortal Warrior would not be afraid.

She looked back up at her brother, still watching her from the branch above.

"Get down here right this second, soldier," Jessie ordered in her best Immortal Warrior voice. "We've got a mission to complete."

"You're crazy, Jessie," Billy said. "Get out of here."

"Not without you."

Billy pulled his head back out of sight and for a moment Jessie thought she was going to have to yell at him again. Then his leg appeared over the side, swinging back and forth until his foot snagged the rope holding the tire swing.

In less than a minute he was standing beside her.

"That's a *Quickdraw*," he said, pointing to the BattleMech near them. "It's fast. There's another and a *Lynx* over there. That's three. Number four's got to be somewhere."

Jessie was uninterested in what the BattleMechs were called or where they were. The Immortal Warrior was on a rescue mission, focused only on the objective.

"We've got to get back to the storm cellar," she said.

"We can't," Billy said. "They'll see us."

"They saw me come out here," Jessie said, proud her voice stayed steady. She settled her Immortal Warrior helmet more firmly on her head and started toward the house.

"Wait."

Billy caught up with her and took her hand. Above them, the *Quickdraw* stood immobile, but they both felt it had eyes watching their every move.

"Don't run," Billy said. "Maybe they won't..."

At that moment the fourth BattleMech stalked around the corner of the farm house. Lower and wider than the *Quickdraw*, it looked to Jessie like a giant crab or bird. It swung toward them, fire flickering around little black tubes on its chest.

"Run!" Billy yelled as the ground between them and the 'Mech began to churn with machine-gun fire.

Jessie spread her arms wide, shielding her big brother with her Immortal Warrior armor, and ran for the house. She shrieked her battle cry at the top of her lungs as flying clods of dirt spattered against her chest and helmet.

Ahead, the cellar door by the kitchen stairs flew open. Grandpa was there, running towards them as pieces of the ground seemed to jump and shatter. She could see her mother behind him, calling something she couldn't hear. The world was full of a sound like thunder and gravel and the house seemed so far away.

Suddenly she was scooped from the ground, one of Grandpa's strong arms around her waist. She caught a glimpse of Billy, tucked under his other arm as he ran back toward the house. They were almost safe, but not yet. Something screamed through the air over their heads. A wave of hot air, like Grandma opening her oven, only hotter and meaner, swept over them.

Jessie kept her arms spread wide, protecting Billy and Grandpa as best she could.

Grandpa swung her up and around. The world seemed to tilt crazily and she saw a corner of the house and roof fly to pieces. Then her mother grabbed her, pulling her down into the cellar, hustling her toward the shelter. Behind her she heard Grandpa slamming the outer door and her brother's voice.

"I was trapped in the tree," he said. "There was a *Quickdraw* right next to me. Jessie came and got me."

Above them there was a great cracking and splintering. Jessie heard windows breaking and dishes crashing to the floor. The kitchen was going to be a mess.

Mother, holding one arm, half carried her and half shoved her down the shelter stairs. Billy came stumbling close behind, almost falling on the steep wooden steps.

"Everyone here?" Grandpa asked.

All around Jessie her cousins and aunts said "yes."

The room was big, but everybody was crowded close to the stairs, helping her and her mother and Billy get safely inside. Some held flashlights so they could see.

Grandpa slammed the thick metal door, throwing the lock and turning the wheel that slid bolts into the walls on either side.

Above them, against the door and ceiling, there was a bumping and thumping, like something big was stomping its feet. *That big crab-bird,* Jessie bet.

"So," said Grandpa, looking down at her.

Jessie looked up at him, looking like a giant in the dim light, and pulled herself to attention.

"Mission accomplished, sir," she reported.

LYNX
MEDIUM—55 TONS

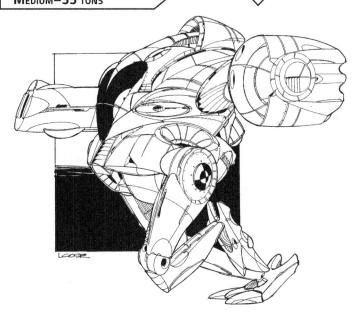

QUICKDRAW
HEAVY—60 TONS

GHOST OF CHRISTMAS PRESENT

MICHAEL A. STACKPOLE

FORD
BOLAN PROVINCE
LYRAN COMMONWEALTH
25 DECEMBER 3027

"T'was the day of Christmas,
   And all through the sector,
   Not a BattleMech was stirring,
   Not even a tractor."

Cadet Nelson Geist shook his head. "God almighty, Nelson, you're a horrible poet."

He dutifully tried to keep his mind on patrolling, but on Christmas Day that was almost impossible. The Techs had put a tinsel garland around the inside of the windscreen on his *Phoenix Hawk* and had hung red and green balls from instrument panel latches. Had they had the time, he was pretty sure the 'Mech would have gone out painted red with white trim and a big white beard, but it didn't because the Techs wanted to be home with their own families. They had, however, managed to make a huge bow out of red plastic and plant it on the 'Mech's head, which made the machine look a bit festive.

The decorations did make him feel good. As he was going to be entering his final year at the Nagelring—the Lyran Commonwealth's premiere military academy—he had been assigned to winter semester training with Gregg's Long Striders. The Striders had progressed nicely since the 3025 assessment that had listed them as a green unit. When the Fourteenth Lyran Guards were temporarily assigned to Gienah after the 3027 Galahad exercises, Ford became the Striders' domain.

He'd arrived barely a month before Christmas, and found the unit cordial, but very wary. As a young unit, they were sensitive about having some academy-rat show up and try to tell them how to do things. Nelson knew that wasn't his job, nor was it something he desired to do. He was there to learn, and did his best to earn the other warriors' respect.

He figured out almost immediately that an easy way to do that would be to volunteer for the Yule patrol. The day was normally split up into three-hour watches, with one BattleMech being assigned to a different sector. Nelson signed himself up for two patrols back to back and even ended up accepting another. Since his family was hundreds of light years away on Kooken's Pleasure Pit, he had no one to celebrate with anyway, so taking duty was easy for him.

More important to him, though, was the chance it gave him to log some serious hours in a *Phoenix Hawk*. From the time he was a young boy, he had found the very name of that 'Mech magical. He had read countless stories of battles in which the humanoid BattleMechs had performed heroically. The large laser held in the right hand provided long-range firepower, while the medium lasers mounted in each arm were good closer in. The *Phoenix Hawk* had twin 12.5mm machine guns in each arm for keeping infantry and light vehicles suppressed.

The main thing that had intrigued Nelson about the *Phoenix Hawk* was its jump jets, which allowed the machine to make crucial tactical advances and retreats during battles. If not for those jets, Davion *Phoenix Hawk*s would have fallen to Liao *Crusader*s at Lee II, and the Liao invasion would never have been turned back.

Nelson marched his *Phoenix Hawk* on through Alpha sector. The weather had turned cold and a light dusting of snow covered the whole area. "Christmas card weather," he had remarked to Leutnant Lukens when Lukens checked him out on the *Phoenix Hawk*. "When you're at home in front of the fireplace, I'll be out here enjoying the view."

Lukens had not offered to change places with him, which didn't surprise Nelson at all. Even though the *Phoenix Hawk* had been in Lukens' family for two generations—his grandfather had taken it as a prize in the battle for Loric in 2971—Lukens preferred to spend the time at home with his bride of three months. Having seen the Leutnant's wife, Nelson couldn't fault the man's choice of holiday diversion.

Nelson focused again on the viewscreen and saw nothing across the long, snow-choked meadow. He had been told that there was really nothing for him to worry about while on patrol. If House Marik was going to mount an assault, they would spend four days coming in from the jump point around the sun, so there would be ample warning about the invasion.

"Of course, he could face Anti-Nick and the Elves from Hell," Bronson, his Tech, had chided Lukens. "He'd love to find Cadet Geist here in your *Phoenix Hawk* and all alone."

Tom Lukens shook his head. "Not likely."

Nelson raised an eyebrow. "Anti-Nick?"

Bronson smiled. "Yeah, there's a group of bandits who have, from time to time, gone raiding on Christmas. Response time is low, lots of loot can be had. They're two *Locust*s and a *Jenner* centered up around a *BattleMaster*. A-Nick is the *BattleMaster*'s pilot. He speaks in rhyming couplets—a real nutcase. They've mostly raided far to the south, but..."

Lukens waved Bronson's concern away. "Some folks think they'll head north because the Fourteenth Lyran Guards are gone *and* the bank over in Harrison became a Commonwealth depository. They'd be nuts to try anything around the base here."

Nelson smiled. "I'll keep my eyes peeled. If I see them, I'll send out an alarm."

"Good, we'll all be ready to respond. If you see them, stay away from Anti-Nick and just track them. Good intel is better than a dead 'Mech." Lukens gave Nelson a friendly shot in the arm. "Especially when that 'Mech is *my* 'Mech."

"Message received and understood, sir."

Nelson glanced at the heat monitor. It was still down in the cool range, which he expected given the cold outside. He knew that in combat the jump jets, weapons, and maneuvering would cause heat to build up quickly. The targeting computer would begin to go. It would also cut his speed and, if it was high enough, could cook off machine gun ammo and even shut down his whole 'Mech.

"Shut down Lt. Lukens' BattleMech, you mean," he mumbled. He keyed the radio in his heavy neurohelmet. "Blitzen here. Sector Alpha is clear."

"North Pole to Blitzen, roger. Having fun out there, Cadet Geist?"

Nelson recognized the voice on the radio. "Bronson, you lose at poker with the CommTechs again? Must have been a hell of a hand to bet the third watch on Christmas on it."

"My full boat sank. Besides, gets me out of the house so my mother-in-law can't tell me I'm a layabout."

Nelson laughed. "So, was Santa good to you?"

"Not bad. I got a new set of actuator wrenches. If Santa gives you the 'Mech you were hoping for, I can fix it."

"No such luck, Bronson. Santa couldn't fit it on his sleigh."

"Next year, kid. You're a good pilot, they'll find you something when you leave the 'Ring."

"Thanks, Bronson. I hope you're right."

"I'm always right, Cadet. You should have let me fix you up with that old hangar door. You could just head up into the mountains and do some snowboarding on that 'Hawk."

"Too much eggnog isn't good for you, Bronson."

"Hey, there's enough snow out there for it."

"I'm sure the ski tourists will be happy. Me, I'm just working like you. Blitzen out."

Nelson cut the radio link and started down the length of the meadow. At its longest point it led into a hilly valley in the foothills of the Thunderbird Mountains. The valley sides became steep and a hundred meters up from the plain where he marched, dark pine forests grew thickly. Because the region on Kooken's Pleasure Pit where Nelson grew up was arid, he was not used to tall pines and tangled forest depths. They made him uneasy, and as the dying sun lengthened the shadows, he began to feel the hair on the back of his neck stand up.

C'mon, Nelson, it's a Christmas card. Be a good boy, check it out, and Santa will reward you. He smiled and shook his head. Unlike many other Cadets at the Nagelring, he had no family 'Mech waiting for him upon graduation. He'd get whatever the Lyran Commonwealth gave him, *if* they assigned him to a line unit. Guys with 'Mechs got those choice slots, whereas the *Dispossessed* or, like him, *unpossessed* warriors got to drive a desk until a machine opened up.

He took another long look at the valley. *It's still clear, Nelson. Nothing here to worry about.* He pushed his fears aside and headed into the valley. *You're in a 45-ton war machine. Nothing can bother you in this thing.*

Something moved ahead of him and stepped clear of the forest. *Nothing but a* bigger *BattleMech.* Nelson squinted out through the viewscreen. *That's a BattleMaster!*

Nelson keyed his radio to a short range, wide-beam broadcast. "Please identify yourself. You are on restricted territory."

"Ho ho ho, you'll die in the snow!"

Nelson tapped the side of his neurohelmet. "This is not the time for games. Identify yourself." As he spoke, Nelson dropped his crosshairs on the humanoid 'Mech. *Range is long enough for the large laser to be my best bet.*

"Anti-Nick am I. Prepare to die."

Hmmm, I may be a bad *poet, but apparently I'm not the worst* poet around. Nelson hit the firing stud on the joystick in his right hand. The pistol-like large laser in the *Phoenix Hawk's* right hand ignited a ruby energy beam that lanced into the *BattleMaster's* chest. A half a ton of aligned crystal steel armor ran in steaming rivulets over the BattleMech's breast. It melted through the snow, raising vapor columns that twisted around the *BattleMaster.*

The *BattleMaster* fired back with the PPC mounted in its right arm. The firing coils glowed an unholy blue seconds before the particle beam shot out. It crackled through the cold air, and despite missing the *Phoenix Hawk,* its hellish heat warmed the 'Mech's cockpit. The azure beam exploded a leafless tree, scattering burning wooden fragments to oppose the dusk.

Move or die, Nelson, he might not miss the next time. He punched both feet down on the jump jet pedals and braced himself. Twin tongues of silver flame boosted the 'Mech into the air. Scanning his holographic display for a landing, he got a good look at the battlefield and his stomach began to fold in on itself. *This is not good at all.*

Down on the ground, the pair of *Locusts* that worked with Anti-Nick started running from cover in the woods to his right. Their bobbing gait, caused because of the birdlike configuration of their legs, made them look funny and almost toy-like from his height. *But they aren't toys.* The medium lasers they sported were deadly and they could hem him in and herd him toward their large companion, the way dogs coursed deer to hunters.

He came down as far from the enemy as he could get, which put him on the edge of the upslope woods on the left. "Blitzen here, I have Anti-Nick and his elves."

"Sure, kid. Funny."

"North Pole, I'm not kidding. Sector Alpha, T-bird foothills." Nelson saw his large laser come back into service. *If the* Locusts *are here, where in hell is that* Jenner?

Out front he saw his 'Mech's shadow start long, then grow short as the *Jenner* jetted up from within the forest. Without conscious thought—thanks to endless drills at the Nagelring—Nelson stepped the *Phoenix Hawk* backward. He painted the *Jenner* with his crosshairs and kept the cross tracking it as the flying 'Mech overshot its target.

No one jumps on my head! Nelson squinted, watching the range finder figures fall. *You're mine now.* Keeping the enemy impaled on his sights, he hit two triggers and a firing stud.

The large laser skewered the *Jenner* with a ruby spike. Armor shards exploded from the ungainly 'Mech's left side. The two medium lasers Nelson had also triggered jabbed their red beams through the gaping hole the larger laser had opened up. Smoke poured from the wound and a secondary explosion spat out chunks of the 'Mech's titanium steel skeleton.

The jump jet mounted on the 'Mech's left side flared and died. The other two jump jets sputtered on for a moment and then died as well, leaving the *Jenner* airborne and slowly rotating to the left. The *Jenner* continued spinning as it accelerated, then it slammed into the ground on its left shoulder. One leg telescoped into the torso, but the left one snapped forward and sheared clean off.

As the left leg bounced away from the wreckage, Nelson blinked and stared at it. *I got it! I got it!* Years of drilling might have given him the skills, but all the simulations in the world couldn't match actual combat. The dryness in his mouth, the twisting in his stomach, the desire to see someone emerge from the wrecked 'Mech—none of that came from war games.

It's not stories anymore, Nelson. This is real and real serious.

Swallowing hard, he keyed his radio. "Bronson, I got the *Jenner.*"

"Sure, kid."

A keening whine rattled through the speakers in Nelson's neurohelmet. "This is no game, my honor you defame. *Phoenix Hawk*, you are mine to kill, which I now vow to do, I will."

"Cadet, if this is your idea of a joke—"

"Anything but, Bronson. Get me some help, will you?" Nelson stilled the shivers running through him. "I don't like the odds here."

"They'll be worse if you get the Leutnant's 'Mech hammered." Tension flooded through Bronson's voice. "Putting out the call. ETA twenty minutes. Think you can last that long?"

Down below him, in the valley, the two *Locusts* moved off and headed in toward Harrison and the bank. While he took some heart in the idea that he would only have to face one BattleMech, the fact that it was a *BattleMaster* killed any hope. The *BattleMaster* outmassed him by forty tons, had three times as many medium lasers as he did *and* had short-range missiles in addition to its particle projector cannon. He didn't even want to think about the differences in armor between the two 'Mechs.

"Maybe I can, but I'm betting your new spanners will get a great workout fixing this 'Mech if I do." He took a deep breath, then nodded. "The *Locust*s are headed for the bank. Stop them, will you?"

"Screw the bank, kid, or do you still have your Christmas Club account there?"

"Something like that. Do it, Bronson."

"Roger that."

Nelson tried to figure out if he had any advantages as he started his *Phoenix Hawk* back into the woods. He knew the cover would help conceal him, making him harder to hit. The *BattleMaster*'s line of attack was uphill, which would also help. He had a sneaking suspicion, given their first exchange, that he was a better shot, but the *BattleMaster*'s array of weapons gave Nick more chances to get lucky.

He searched his mind for all the technical data he'd memorized, searching for anything that might help him. *The PPC has a minimum effective range. Maybe I can use that...* Nelson peered out through the picket-line of trees between him and the meadow. *If we go toe to toe, I'm done.*

The *BattleMaster*'s long confident strides through the meadow did nothing to set visions of sugar-plums dancing in Nelson's head. Snow shot up and out from in front of its massive feet, dusted the 'Mech and settled in clouds on the its backtrail. As nasty as he knew the machine to be, the light frosting of snow and the way it moved made it seem grand and almost benign. He couldn't help but admire the machine.

Then the *BattleMaster* made a sharp parade turn left and headed straight in at him.

"Spoiling for a fight, on what should be a silent night!" Nelson shuddered as he realized he was talking like his foe, then started tracking him with the crosshairs. "If you're going to give me the shots, I'm going to take them." At range, he triggered the large laser and prayed for a Christmas present.

The ruby beam nailed the center of the 'Mech's chest. Sheets of armor, half-fluid and glowing warmly, spun away into the dim twilight. Nelson looked in vain for the same sort of critical opening his large laser had made in the *Jenner*, but he saw none. *That thing's got a lot more armor for me to burn through!*

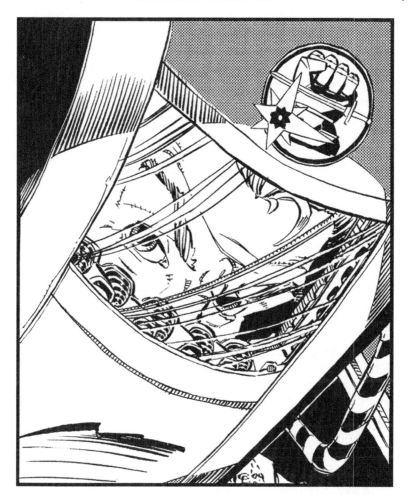

The *BattleMaster*'s PPC came up and swung in his direction. The azure fork of pseudo-lightning it spat out threaded
its way through the trees and savaged the *Phoenix Hawk*'s left
arm. Armor shards clattered off the cockpit canopy and rico-
cheted into the darkness. Nelson's damage monitor reported
the armor had been stripped clean off that limb. *One more shot
there and the whole arm is gone, along with a medium laser and
a machine gun. That would pretty much ruin my day.*

The *BattleMaster* charged forward, coming in at the
Phoenix Hawk at full speed. The 14-meter-tall war machine
battered trees aside, snapping trunks as if they were tinder.

Showers of snow poured down, reducing the *BattleMaster* to a grey shadow in a blizzard, but a shadow that always came closer, relentless and implacable.

It seemed for a moment to Nelson that Anti-Nick wanted to physically grapple with him and tear his 'Mech apart. Aside from the fact that Leutnant Lukens would have frowned on having his 'Mech broken that way, Nelson had no intention of letting that happen. In that sort of fight, his chances of survival would have been the same in or out of the 'Mech, so discretion definitely seemed the better part of valor.

He's a bad shot and... Nelson slowly grinned. *He's a worse tactician.*

As the assault 'Mech closed, Nelson stomped down on the jump jets. He launched his 'Mech skyward, but pulled his feet off the pedals almost instantly, abbreviating his flight. He grounded the *Phoenix Hawk* behind the *BattleMaster* and turned, giving him a clean shot at the *BattleMaster*'s pristine back armor. *I'll just die if I miss at this range.*

The large laser's beam slashed a huge gash in the *BattleMaster*'s rear armor, but failed to breach it. The twin medium lasers followed up on that damage, widening the gash and vaporizing armor. The reddish beams filled the center of the assault 'Mech with fire and Nelson saw internal structures melt in the backglow. He waited for secondary explosions or even a little shudder, showing he'd done serious damage, but got nothing.

The *BattleMaster* never even made an attempt at turning around to face him. The two rear-facing lasers oriented on the *Phoenix Hawk* and returned fire. One bubbled away armor on the *Phoenix Hawk*'s right thigh, reducing its protection by a third. The other beam drilled into the *Phoenix Hawk*'s left breast and carved a crescent scar into its armor.

Heat swirled up through the cockpit and sweat beaded on Nelson's exposed flesh. Between jumping and triggering three weapons, he'd pushed the heat up to sixty percent of maximum capacity. His crosshairs started tracking poorly, and he knew that his movement had been cut down. *If I don't get out of here, though, I'll have more problems than roasting to death.*

As the *BattleMaster* started to come around, Nelson hit the jump jets and launched himself skyward. Despite the added heat rushing up into his cockpit, he pushed the burn and sailed over the *BattleMaster*'s head and on into the woods. He cut the jets and braced himself for a rough landing.

He came down hard. Trees snapped in half and toppled over, but somehow he managed to keep the 'Mech upright. The snow that had laden the tree branches sheeted down over him, but he knew it would give him no cover. The heat did begin to head back down into green ranges, which meant he had his mobility back. *And I'm going to have to use that as best I can.*

The whole situation resolved itself very quickly and easily in his mind. He was playing for time. If his reinforcements intercepted the *Locusts*, Anti-Nick would break things off and retreat. Survival was the key, and the further along he could draw the *BattleMaster*, the greater the chances that the reinforcements would put an end to him once and for all.

There was no question in Nelson's mind that he was playing a very dangerous game. Reaching out with his left hand, he punched up a geographical survey map of the area on his auxiliary monitor and his sensors painted the oncoming *BattleMaster* onto it. Nelson kicked the *Phoenix Hawk* into motion, drawing his enemy away from Harrison and up into the mountains.

They entered into an absurd cat and mouse contest. Nelson risked the PPC by staying at longer ranges, but that kept him free of damage from the missiles and smaller weapons. His large laser did light up the woods, burning holes through the pine canopy. Rarely hit his foe, but often enough he lit a tree on fire. *If nothing else, it will be easy for them to find us.*

The *BattleMaster* kept coming and as the minutes piled one on another, Nelson began to believe he might actually survive. He tried to call out to Bronson, but the mountains broke up radio transmissions. This he really didn't mind because it also meant his foe couldn't inflict couplets on him. He had to wonder about his foe and his odd Christmas tradition of shooting and looting to celebrate the holiday. *It must make sense to him.*

Nelson realized he didn't want to know *how* it made sense.

He continued to duck and dodge and retreat halfway up into the mountains when he discovered he'd made a tactical error. His retreat had taken him into a narrow draw with sheer sides. While one jump could carry him to a plateau on the south side, another would not be enough to get him out. He was also certain the *BattleMaster*'s pilot wasn't going to let him jump behind him again for another shot at his back. By the time he discovered his mistake, he was too far in to get back out, and the *BattleMaster* appeared to seal the entrance and his fate.

"You can't run. You can't hide. Now this battle, we'll decide." The *BattleMaster* advanced slowly, coming straight up the middle of the draw. "Bad you're not. Take your best shot."

A million thoughts flashed through Nelson's mind. He could shoot, and might get lucky, but the odds were against it. Memories of exercises, of winter drills on Tharkad, of watching children play in snow and even the long treks he'd taken on skis across glaciers came to him. *If I had that hangar door, I might be able to snowboard right past that monster, just the way kids used to escape parents on holiday.*

Something sparked in the back of his mind, so he hit the jump jets and soared to the plateau. He landed and turned around, his 'Mech's left shoulder striking the rock wall behind him. Nelson looked down, and began to track his crosshair toward the *BattleMaster*, which had resumed its advance. *Clean shot. So tempting, but this isn't a day to give into temptation.*

"Nice escape try, but why? Even so high, you're just going to die."

Nelson shook his head. "Why the poetry? It's horrible."

Mock surprise ran through Nick's voice. "I thought it was festive. And it's not that bad."

"Yes, it is. Just like your aim."

"Let's hear you do better."

"Hear, no." Nelson shifted his aim point and raised the 'Mech's large laser. "See, you bet."

Nelson triggered the weapon and slashed the beam right to left, up through the darkness. Its verdant light illuminated the low grey clouds so heavily laden with snow. It pierced them and vanished, vaporized snowflakes drifting back up to condense again and fall.

"How cute, how quaint, a signal light. But there will be no help for you tonight." The *BattleMaster*'s PPC came up and the charging coils began to glow. "On that ledge, you have an edge, but one hit and it's a long fall."

"I may fall, but not tonight." Nelson brought the *Phoenix Hawk* down into a crouch and inched back, letting the ledge shield as much of him as possible. The *BattleMaster* stepped back, lengthening the range, but improving his angle. Nelson would survive Nick's poor marksmanship for one or two bursts, then Nick would get the idea of slashing away at the rock. Once that was undercut, Nelson and the *'Hawk* would come down in a 'Mech avalanche.

Fortunately, Nick never got the chance to figure out what he had to do to bring Nelson down. Even in his cockpit, with the wind howling and snow swirling, the low rumble came to Nelson. It grew, becoming equal parts tactile and auditory. It took a couple seconds more for Nick to get its full effect, sheltered as he was down in the draw.

And by the time he did, time had run out for him.

Having grown up in an arid region that never had much of a winter, Nelson Geist had had a lot of things to learn about winter and snow. Tharkad had plenty of both, and instructors at the Nagelring went to great pains to guarantee their cadets weren't going to fall prey to stupid things. He learned about frostbite and winter survival. He learned how to ski, both downhill and cross-country, and how to snowshoe. He even learned how to climb mountains in the winter and learned about the special dangers of generous snowfalls.

His large laser had cut through the clouds and burned into the mass of snow much higher up in the mountains. New snow over old created a fragile structure supporting a lot of weight. When the laser melted into that layer of old snow, the structure collapsed and with it came a lot of snow.

The avalanche picked up speed as it descended, sweeping rocks and trees along with it. The *BattleMaster* might well have been one of the largest land war machines ever created by the hand of man, but compared to the titanic forces of nature, it was something of a toy. Snow poured down into the draw in a frozen white flood. It slammed into the 'Mech's back, pitching it forward and face down. A rock the size of a small hovercar bounced up and off, then snow just buried Nick.

The snow kept coming, filling the draw. Nelson hit the jets as the snow lapped up at the ledge, but was able to land back down there easily. The snow came up to the *'Hawk*'s knees and was packed so solidly he had to kick his way clear to move forward. He sank down to mid-calf with each subsequent step, so he didn't venture very far.

He switched his scanners over to MagRes and got a clean picture of the *BattleMaster* laying face down, as if it were floating. *Floating at the bottom of a pool.* He dropped the crosshairs on the thing's head and keyed his radio.

"You're only going to be getting out of there with help. Surrender, and I burn you a tunnel to climb out. If you don't, I burn that tunnel through the cockpit. Answering me in rhyme is the same as not surrendering."

Nick's voice came back faint and weak. "If I surrender, you'll be taking my 'Mech away, won't you?"

"You've been raiding and ruining Christmases for years, and you want me to be sympathetic over your being *Dispossessed?*"

"That would be a no?"

"How right you are, yes sirree!" Nelson smiled. "Your 'Mech's gonna belong to me."

"My poetry wasn't that bad."

"Yes, it was." Nelson frowned. "You coming out, or do I radio the base and tell them to requisition a body-bag and a new *BattleMaster* cockpit?"

"Tell them to bring blankets. And brandy." Resignation flooded through Nick's voice. "I'm going to want a lot of brandy."

"You got it. You made the wise choice." Nelson fought and kept the laughter out of his voice. By the rules of combat, that *BattleMaster* would be his, which meant he'd get a good assignment in the LCAF. *With a 'Mech like that, anything is possible.*

"Oh, and Nick?"

"Yeah?"

"Merry Christmas."

BATTLEMASTER
Assault—85 tons

JENNER
Light—35 tons

LOCUST
LIGHT—20 TONS

PHOENIX HAWK
MEDIUM—45 TONS

ZEROING IN

A PREQUEL TO
THE LEGEND OF THE JADE PHOENIX

ROBERT THURSTON

When Joanna had been very young, her caretakers had worried about her sensitive side. While they believed a warrior-to-be should have an understanding of what it meant to be a human being, especially one fortunate enough to belong to the Jade Falcon Clan, they also felt that tender and compassionate emotions interfered with combat skills. Emotions were fine for those who washed out of training and entered a lesser caste, where some emotional engagement was extremely useful. The scientists, for instance, could not improve Clansmen without some insights into their nature. Artisans needed some feeling to create decorative objects. Technicians had to have a sense of the value of the BattleMech to suit the needs of the warrior, and thus had to understand the quirks as well as the traits of the warrior.

The reason Joanna could remember the issue of her sensitivity so well was that she did not have any of it left and could not recall what it had been like. She did not know how she had worked it out, or which life experiences had hardened her so, or who was the first to draw her monumental wrath, but now she liked to *think of herself as the nastiest warrior in the Jade Falcon Clan. And she was satisfied that many others thought of her that way, too...*

IRONHOLD
CLAN SPACE

What an exhaust fume of a place, Joanna thought as she entered her new quarters at the Ironhold training camp. A dark cloud seemed to hover in the ceiling shadows of the badly lit room of this bleak barracks. Spartan was all right for barracks, but this one outdid others in its sheer drabness.

Her cot, stripped down, with a bedroll at its foot, showed a definite sag in its middle, along with bent and nearly broken springs. The damn bed was ancient, the damn room with strips of wood curling off the walls and dirt streaks slashed across a bureau as old-looking as the bed, the damn dirty Jade Falcon flag hanging from an old rusty nail. How long had this portion of the facility gone unused? She would get her fledglings in here to work at once! Still, it was some welcome for her, the *stravag* Joanna who was feeling pretty *stravag* old herself as she dragged her *stravag* duffel bag through the room's *stravag* splintered door.

Old? How old? I have forgotten. I should be dead by now, felled in heroic combat. Or at least alive with a Bloodname. The Bloodname will come. It has to! She recalled when she had been young, twelve or thirteen (an eternity ago) when she had been a trainee herself—so eager, so determined, so certain. She had been the top trainee in her *sibko*, scoring high on every test, pummeling and flooring all the others in fights. In those days she had been cool, delivering blows with a smile, quite unlike the angry, sometimes furious warrior she was now.

Still, the two others in her *sibko* who had eventually won their Trials and become Mechwarriors along with Joanna had been less skillful than she, and yet they had advanced further. One had earned a Bloodname and the other would have but for her valiant defense of a mountain encampment, holding back enemy 'Mechs while the encampment behind her emptied of valuable scientists who had escaped in time, just before she had been blasted to smithereens by a lucky shot; even then she had gotten a line in the Falcon Remembrance.

I need my chance. But how, in a field of walking corpses like this Ironhold training camp, am I going to get it?

She took a few steps into the room. The floor creaked. Not just creaked, groaned.

Flipping open the bedroll, she flung its mattress onto the squeaking bedsprings and sat down. She tossed the duffel bag to the head of the bed, then put her own head into her hands.

She had never felt this empty before. Angry, yes, but not empty. It was as if she had been flung out of a waste chute and, instead of ending in the vacuum of space, had arrived here.

I should probably make the best of it. I should just buy into what Ter Roshak told me at his briefing. Talk about walking corpses. He is the prime example.

"Training *sibkos* may not be as exciting as staring down a 'Mech with only one PPC in operation," he had said as he rubbed his prosthetic hand with his good hand almost absentmindedly, "but you know what the manual says—it is just as important to the Clan as combat duty, *quiaff*? These kestrels are the future of the Clan. Few of them will succeed, not even enough to fill the vacancies available in Stars and elsewhere. But at least we know, if we do our job right, we will be sending out warriors so skilled they will keep the Jade Falcon tradition the best and fiercest of all the Clans."

He almost mumbled the speech. It was clearly one he gave to every new falconer, and some of it did not sound sincere, but maybe he had been right. Being a falconer was not the worst designation among Clan warriors, it just did not satisfy a real warrior, one who needed to slice a *Dire Wolf* in half with well-placed shots.

She sighed and began taking items out of her duffel bag. The few clothes—fatigues, field caps, old boots whose cracks were hidden by a thick coat of leather treatment—she carried to the bureau and deposited in drawers. Reaching into the duffel bag again, she felt her lock-box.

Stupid savashri. *No reason to lock up anything in this.* Carefully lifting the box out of the bag, she put it down on the bed and retrieved her keys from her jacket pocket. Maneuvering the key into the lock, she held it still for a moment, then—with a graceful wrist action—snapped the key to the right and the box sprung open with a *click* that sent some flakes of rust on the spring flying.

Inside were the few mementos she chose to carry from place to place. It was her ritual to examine them on the first day at each new assignment. The items would not have drawn much interest from a casual observer, most of whom might have classified these apparently unexceptional things as junk.

She reached into the box and ran her index finger through the stuff. A picture emerged and she picked it up. It was that old holographic picture of Lyonor. Joanna did not remember Lyonor looking so happy any other time, although she did have an unfortunate cheerful strain in her personality. Her small body was erect with characteristic pride, her crisp uniform was highlighted in a fiercely bright morning sun that, in the way she stood, cast her shadow in a long stretched silhouette behind her. Because of her thinness, the shadow's lines appeared to point at a distant high mountain. What in hell was the name of that mountain? For that matter, what was the name of that damn planet?

Walking with the picture to the dirty barracks window next to the cot, she looked out through its smudged panes at the training field beyond. In the distance, a falconer leaned toward a pair of trainees and was clearly barking at them, probably telling them what a bunch of inept *eyasses* they were. It was a pleasant sight, reminding her of the first and only time she and Lyonor had fought. It was not long before the taking of this picture on some other godforsaken planet.

THE PHOTO

Lyonor had lovely eyes. Everybody said so, even though it was unlike Jade Falcon warriors to make a compliment about any physical feature. Something about the eyes—their near-violet color, perhaps, or maybe the question that always seemed to be expressed in them—easily drew compliments from the toughest and meanest warriors. It had not escaped Joanna's attention that nobody ever said anything about her eyes.

Now Lyonor's lovely eyes were wide in fright. Joanna's outburst, over her drawing back from killing one of the freeborns that were part of the refresher exercise Jade Falcon warriors routinely went through, had unnerved Lyonor.

"Your autocannon was so close to his cockpit, almost touching it. You could have split that filthy freebirth apart and saved his 'Mech for later exercises. Instead, what do you do, *eyas*? You walk your *Summoner* back a step, slice off his 'Mech's legs and allow him to eject while you blasted his 'Mech into too many puzzle pieces to put back together. The *stravag* freebirth walks away and you get points off, and the unit loses the practice trial because of it, along with wasting a 'Mech. That was damn stupid, Lyonor. I was ready to pick you off myself."

Lyonor's dejection almost touched Joanna's sympathy. "I know," she said. "But I knew that freeborn. We drank together on another exercise just a week ago."

"I do not care if you took him into your arms and gave the wretched piece of trash the only good time of his life. I do not care if you admired his humor, or thought he was the most admirable example of a freeborn you have ever met, or he revealed himself to be to be a trueborn in disguise. You had to kill the *surat*. That is the point. You had to draw blood."

"Joanna, it was only an exercise, a—"

Joanna became enraged.

"*Only an exercise?* We learn by doing! And we acquire victories through skill. Or perhaps you do not think victories important? By the Founder, how do you expect to ever win a Bloodname with thinking like that?"

"I will win a Bloodname in my own time, Joanna. Or I will fail gloriously in the attempt. I do not have to breathe for it every minute of every day as you do. What is important—"

"Do not tell me what is important, *eyas*! I know what is important, *quiaff*? I tell you what is important. Got it?"

"*Neg*, I do not get it. I want a Bloodname, yes, but a Bloodname is an *honor,* not a battle medal. You do not just earn it for what you do, you earn it for what you *are.* You—"

"What? What kind of kestrel droppings is that? You're saying there is some sort of ethics in Bloodnaming? You're saying—"

Lyonor put her hands to her ears. "Please do not throw contractions at me, Joanna. You know I cannot stand that."

"Yes? Well, maybe you're—you are cutting things too fine. If an occasional contraction makes you hold your ears, maybe you are not meant to be a Bloodnamed warrior."

"*Shut up, Joanna.* I will get my Bloodname. You can bet on it. And I will get it soon, not when I am as old as you and ready to pack it in."

Joanna hit her with a backhanded fist across her face. Blood began to flow from the slash she had created on Lyonor's cheek. The other woman reeled backward, then rushed at Joanna, screaming like a falcon descending on its prey.

Although Joanna was able to reduce the impact of Lyonor's charge by dodging sideways, Lyonor slammed into her shoulder and spun her around. She stumbled. As she fell, she cursed herself for what it looked like. She did not like being seen as clumsy, although she knew she sometimes was.

Bending down and placing her hand on the ground to steady herself, she regained her footing, did a purposeful spin, and came up with her head against Lyonor's chin. The blow was so hard it seemed to rattle the teeth inside Lyonor's head. Arms flailing, and growling with the characteristic rumbling explosion of the Jade Falcon attack cry, the two sprung at each other, each showing a readiness to kill in their eyes.

Their fight went on for a long while, and both combatants were bruised and bloody for some time afterward. When each could not lift her arms any longer and their legs were too unsteady, they still flung weak blows at each other. One thing could always be said about Lyonor: she could not be intimidated. She would fight to the last, and this time was no exception.

After they were no longer able to fight, there was no immediate reconciliation. Instead, they went back to attacking each other with words. The argument between the two of them went on for hours, and only total exhaustion ended it.

For the next few days, they stayed in the kind of pain inside that recognized that their relationship would never be quite the same again. Still, they remained close and performed their duties well and often in tandem. A scar from their fight remained as a faint line on Lyonor's cheek. Scars were good, badges of honor for a warrior.

Right before the photo had been taken, Joanna and Lyonor had been laughing hysterically, which might explain, in the photo, the joy in Lyonor's radiant eyes. The scar on her cheek was so fresh, it showed up darkly on Lyonor's fair skin.

Strange, Joanna thought, *I did laugh that day. How often do I ever laugh? I cannot remember what we were laughing about.*

Walking back to the cot, Joanna smoothed out the edges of the photo and put it back in the lock box, underneath some transfer documents. Running her hand through the box's objects, her finger fell on a comb. She maneuvered it out of the pile and stared at it.

Although Jade Falcons were not known for skills in crafts, this comb approached beauty more than most of their objects. Made of a shell Joanna had found on a beach on the world of Strana Mechty, it had already had a comb shape, with a scalloped top tapering down to a flat thin surface.

At first she had just pocketed it, then found it a few days later when the fatigues she wore that day had reached the slightly odorous, slightly stiff state brought around by too many days of wearing. In readying the garment for laundering, she had reached into her pocket and pulled out the shell, now covered in patches of clinging lint. She wiped the lint away and was again struck by the nearly symmetrical shape of the shell, not only in its shape, but in the way light, thin gray lines ran across its surface in a design that looked as if it had to be crafted by hand rather than the erosion of sea waves.

She transferred the shell to the pocket of her clean fatigues and, two days later, happened on a village where a labor casteman, actually a specialist in etching designs on Jade Falcon medals, agreed to make a comb out of it for her. She remembered the man—a squinty-eyed freeborn with the kind of rough skin common to such breeding—saying that a comb was a good idea to straighten out Joanna's long, unkempt hair. She pushed him against the wall of his spartan, single room house, telling him never to talk to her, just do the job.

When she returned the next day, the man did not speak but merely handed her the shell, crafted into a comb whose teeth imitated the symmetry of the piece's overall shape. For a reason Joanna chose not to ask about, he had neatly painted a diamond figure, as symmetrical as the rest of the shell, in the center of the upper portion of the comb. She paid for his work with work credit—eliciting a surprise she ignored, since a warrior simply commands and takes—without complimenting the man's impressive skills.

The next time she visited the town, she could not find his house and was told he had died.

Sitting on the cot, listening to the springs squeak beneath her as she shifted her body, she recalled another day, one soon after their brawl, when she and Lyonor had been linked by the comb.

THE COMB

Lyonor's arm was broken, in a fracture too delicate to be immediately fixed, so she wore it in a sling. When Joanna came upon her, she was running the fingers of her good hand through her dark hair.

Joanna noticed her hair, which in Lyonor's strange, un-Clanlike vanity was worn longer than most, had lost some of its shine in the days since she had injured her arm in a simple fall off a ladder in a storage depot while searching for a new edition of the Clan epic, *The Remembrance,* to replace the one she had worn out; even more ironic, considering most considered the use of an actual hardcopy Remembrance superfluous.

"What are you doing?" Joanna asked, standing behind Lyonor.

She jumped, startled. "Do you always have to sneak up on people?"

"On the battlefield I will announce my presence. You, *eyas*, I watch with a Falcon's stealth."

Lyonor scoffed. "On the battlefield you have no choice, you mean. How in the name of Kerensky can you sneak up on someone while in a 'Mech which can be seen from kilometers away?"

"It can be done. Fog, snow, blinding rain. A sandstorm, perhaps."

"Telemetry can still detect you."

"Do not split hairs. And, speaking of hair, let me ask again, what are you doing?"

Lyonor held up the comb, one of the small, fragile ones issued in the kit of all warriors. Nearly half of its teeth had broken off. One of the remaining teeth dangled, ready to fall. "You ever try to operate one of these when you only have one good arm?"

"I do not try to, as you say, *operate* one of those much at all."

"I can tell. But some of us believe in grooming even when it is not time for a ceremony or ritual."

Joanna, resisting the urge to touch her own hair, shrugged. "You want help? Operating, I mean."

"You sure you know how?" Lyonor asked, handing her the comb.

Joanna waved it away, saying, "Not that one. Got my own."

Lyonor's eyebrows raised, clearly surprised Joanna would even carry around a comb. Staring at it, she started to smile, then took a better look at the item. Light seemed to flash off it, even though the sky, filled with dark clouds, hid the sun. Impressed by the piece's symmetry and its diamond symbol decoration, Lyonor allowed herself to do something Jade Falcon warriors rarely did—express an aesthetic opinion.

"That is pretty," she said. She touched the diamond design with her thumb. "Pretty. And strong, too. Looks unbreakable."

Joanna held it up. "Yes, it probably is. Turn around."

Lyonor took up her position, her back straight, her head slightly down. With her good hand, she fluffed out her hair so it hung down over her shoulders. Joanna smoothed its surface with her hand, noting that Lyonor's hair, even in disarray, felt smoother than her own.

Choosing some strands, Joanna slowly ran the comb through Lyonor's hair, felt its strong, smooth teeth disentangle strands of hair easily. The firmness of grip the comb allowed and the unbreakable strength of its teeth made the process of combing effortless. Gathering bunches of Lyonor's hair, she began creating order out of the mess.

As she was smoothing out the last strands, she heard a loud guffaw behind her. Whirling around, she saw Garvy, one of the most disagreeable warriors in her Star. He liked to provoke all the other warriors, said he did it to make them better fighters. Joanna could not deny that Garvy was skillful in his 'Mech cockpit. With his long, thin neck and body, he looked more like a seabird than a warrior, but in spite of his slim frame he could attack another with a special viciousness. His hawk-like face was distorted into a gleeful sarcasm.

"Wipe that smirk off your face, Garvy," Joanna said. "What is rattling your gyro, anyway?"

"You two. Such a pretty picture."

Joanna stiffened. In warrior circles, words like "pretty, beautiful, lovely," as applied to warriors, were usually setups to a further insult that would start a fight. Garvy had a mean look on his face. He probably had been drinking fusionnaires somewhere, and she and Lyonor were the first potential victims he had found.

"So domestic, *quiaff?*"

Another fighting word. The last thing a true warrior was, was domestic. Warriors did not live in households, and words like family often made them sick to their stomachs.

"You know what the two of you look like? Like a pair of freebirth villagers during a— "

And, of all the words in a warrior's vocabulary, the word *freebirth* was the worst. It could be, and often had been, an invitation to a fight to the death.

Joanna started to lunge at Garvy, but the strong, sudden grip of Lyonor's good arm held her back. "He is mine," she whispered. She stood up and wrested the comb from Joanna's fingers.

Lyonor did not lunge, did not even look menacing as she strode casually toward Garvy. There was a hint of a smile on her face.

"Garvy," she said. "Although you look like a canister mistake, you are a Trueborn warrior, after all. I respect you for that, and so I will give you a chance to perform *surkai*."

Surkai was an ancient Clan ritual that gave warriors a chance to extricate themselves from words or actions that had been too rash, too impulsive. When a warrior acknowledged *surkai* and asked for the forgiveness allowed by the ritual, the rash acts would be forgiven without penalty, without recrimination. Meaningless fights were useless, and *surkai* was a Jade Falcon way to eliminate them.

"*Surkai!*" he grunted. "I would not waste *surkai* on a freebirth like you."

Lyonor nodded, turned as if to return to Joanna, then whirled around, holding the comb straight out in the hand of her good arm, and aimed it at Garvy's neck. Its teeth broke the skin and she pushed it in. Lyonor wrenched it out and blood spurted after it. Garvy's hands shot to his neck to stem the flow. It looked to Joanna as if he were strangling himself.

Lyonor wiped the comb on her sling and walked casually back to Joanna. "Guess we should get him some medical help," she said, then looking back: "Or not."

"How about it, Garvy?" Joanna yelled. "Want some help? Nod if your answer is *aff*."

Garvy just looked at them, his eyes bugged out, and clearly was steadfast in his resolve not to answer her. His eyes glazed over, and he staggered. For a moment the eyes became clear, and he did nod, vigorously, then they returned to the glazed state and he fell. He must have been unconscious, because his hand fell away from the wound and the blood began flowing freely.

Handing Joanna the comb, Lyonor quickly ripped a piece of cloth off her sling and went to Garvy's side, where she knelt down and pressed it to his wound.

Joanna, remembering Lyonor's useless compassion when she had refused to kill that freeborn, wanted to kick Lyonor away from Garvy's body. On the other hand, she admired the quick, brutal way she had wielded the comb. There was hope for her yet. She was certainly the best warrior Joanna had ever taken under wing. She might just win that Bloodname she claimed not to want as desperately as Joanna did.

"Think we should save this freebirth?" Lyonor asked.

"Well, he is a warrior, and he is fairly skilled, and we would just have to train a replacement..."

"That is it, then. I think I can manage with one arm. I will take his head; you take his feet. Just a minute first, help me to do a field compress."

"With one good arm? Let me do it."

"*I can do it.*" Lyonor's voice was low but menacing, then her tone softened. "I can do anything, you know that, *quiaff?*"

"*Aff.* I do know that."

It was a struggle, but the two of them did manage a tight field compress and got Garvy back to a medic, and he lived to continue his usually drunken unpleasantness.

Joanna smiled as her thumb ran along the edges of the comb's teeth. They were not as sharp as they had once been, as they must have been when Lyonor shoved them into Garvy's neck. She shut her eyes and saw Lyonor again for an instant, on her face that curious combination of confrontation and respect toward Joanna, as if she realized Joanna had made her into the fine warrior she was. One of the best.

Maybe I do have a talent for training, she thought. *Maybe I do belong at this* stravag *facility.*

She flipped the comb back into the lockbox and was about to close it when a rare flash of light through the dirty window made something briefly sparkle in the box.

Pushing other detritus aside, she saw the piece of armor that was her most distressing memento. It had fallen from Lyonor's *Summoner* on the day Joanna learned what hell truly meant.

THE ARMOR

Twelve hours out from Tokasha, preparing for battle with the Ghost Bears, most warriors would feel elation, the call to Trial surging in their blood. But Lyonor had still been in a miserable mood, so much so that the scar Joanna had given her was a darker line than usual. She had not been selected to participate in one of the Trials of Bloodright rituals back home, and was bitterly angry about it.

Joanna, too, had not been selected, but that had happened so often she'd just cursed and vowed to find a way to get the Bloodname at any cost. Twice now she had joined the melee that would produce the thirty-second contestant, and both times she had been defeated in the melee's late stages, in each instance through a dirty trick rather than a one-on-one confrontation between warriors. She knew there was something about her ferocity that put fear into others and made them resort to trickery rather than go against her. She could try the melee again, but not this time around, she told herself.

They were in a DropShip, on their way to challenge the Ghost Bears for the legacy of one of their warriors. It was apparently from a genetic line worth fighting for, although Joanna never took much interest in that sort of thing. A fight was a fight, and she was always up for it.

"Damn it, Joanna," Lyonor said. "I deserved the chance at a Bloodname. Look at what I have done. Who is going, do you know?"

Joanna hesitated, deliberately extending the silence. She had to admit that Lyonor had certainly changed in her attitude about getting a Bloodname. The indifference to Bloodnames she had once professed had vanished.

"Tell me, Joanna."

"Garvy, I think."

Lyonor's remarkable eyes seemed to have a fire blazing behind them. She was clearly ready to destroy anything she could reach. And she did reach. For Joanna. She pushed Joanna away, and Joanna began laughing uproariously.

The laughter sent the anger right out of Lyonor. It was more of a shock than that of Garvy's selection for the Bloodname ritual.

In between bursts of laughter, Joanna said, "I was—joking. Lyonor, it is a joke, *quiaff*? Garvy would not be selected. I have not heard who has, but it would never be Garvy. If that happened, I would simply challenge him to Trial. And he would lose."

Lyonor lunged at her, but this time Joanna's laughter drew a vaguely disreputable Lyonor smile.

And a half-day later, the Star was assembled to fight in a battle over the Ghost Bear warrior's genetic legacy.

Ensconced in the cockpit of her *Hellbringer,* going through her weapons checklist while the 'Mech's lasers and PPCs were powering up, and the telemetry whirled and flashed in its activation of the 'Mech, Joanna had a brief thought of how odd genetic legacy challenges were. Yes, it mattered that her Jade Falcon Clan challenge for the nearly sacred ideal of a legacy. Yes, a warrior would have to fight for a valuable warrior's legacy to the death. Yes, Joanna would never scale down her efforts under even the most doubtful conditions.

Still—part of her mind wondered if such a skirmish over a legacy really was a proper occupation for a warrior. Skirmishes were, in a way, just rituals to keep warriors in condition, hone their skills with an imagined goal. The true goals of a warrior were matters like defending a city or planet from attack, attacking another Clan with the purpose of destroying it, conquering new worlds. Many warriors, Joanna imagined, dreamed of all-out war. It was the forbidden fruit. And its taste would not come today.

This particular skirmish was being fought on a vast, hilly plain spotted with abandoned archaeological digs. Joanna knew nothing about these digs or, for that matter, anything about archaeology itself. She knew a lot of strange, unkempt tech-caste people dug into mounds looking for lost artifacts from before the Clans, from the time of the Star League in Exile. Very few significant discoveries had ever been made in this region of Clan Space, but that did not stop archaeologists from trying.

The Clan Ghost Bear leaders may have chosen this area because they believed Jade Falcon warriors would be less effective in such strange terrain. To Joanna, this was not smart strategy. It was just another trick, like those of her victorious opponents in her two melees. No matter how familiar they might be with this planet, where Ghost Bear maintained some storage depots, it was uncomfortable to have to take note of holes in the ground while mounting assault or defense strategy. Anything that distracted attention from the fight irritated Joanna, even though she had been trained in all possible terrains and practiced hundreds of tactical situations.

Well, at least her Trinary had been bid into the skirmish, and she was happy with that. As they touched controls, her fingers actually itched with the anticipation of the coming battle.

"You daydreaming, Joanna?" Lyonor asked over the comm.

"Why do you say that?"

"You are standing still. We have been waiting for your signal for—well, for longer than I would like. Why do not we start?"

"There have been no orders from the Star Colonel."

"When have you been one to stand on ceremony? Or signals? Or even obeying a mere colonel, *quiaff*?"

"*Aff.* We will move."

Soon, Joanna's Star was crossing the plain, up small hills, down larger ones, and skirting the archaeological digs, which were at least spread far apart. As the Star advanced, Joanna saw the Ghost Bear 'Mechs gradually appear in the distance. At first, the 'Mechs, strung out in an uneven line, looked like toys that slowly grew larger as they came closer. And they were so far away their advance seemed agonizingly slow. There were so many heavy 'Mechs in the line they were slowing down the faster ones.

Joanna wanted to spring her own 'Mech forward, run right into the center of the Ghost Bear string, wreak havoc on its orderly arrangement, then burst past them, turn, and attack others from behind. It would instigate a grand melee, a free-for-all, much like the one she was missing back on Ironhold. A doomed tactic, probably, but she was tempted, just this once.

Before she could think any more about the Bloodname, the Ghost Bears opened fire. Joanna and Lyonor, both of whom had bid for particular enemy 'Mechs during the prebattle Ghost Bear advance, responded first, sending a flurry of PPC blasts that sent armor flying from the enemy each had chosen.

Joanna sent her *Hellbringer* lunging forward, zeroing in on an enemy *Mad Dog*. Her cockpit shook as the *Mad Dog* landed a glancing autocannon shot across her shoulder. She regained control in a second and rocked the *Mad Dog* with a barrage from both PPCs. Something was disabled in the 'Mech. Both its arms dropped, apparently useless, though their futile jerking movements indicated its pilot was trying, probably desperately, to lift them. Joanna took advantage of the moment and downed the *Mad Dog* with a powerful barrage.

Nearby, she saw Lyonor having similar success against a *Warhawk*. Her short-range missile salvo had made a good hit, and the *Warhawk* was staggering, ready to go down, which occurred after Lyonor's well-placed PPC bursts in the *Warhawk*'s gyro area.

On her forward screen, as Joanna quickly traced the action of the battle, she saw the Jade Falcons were holding their own against the Ghost Bears. As far as she could tell, each side had about the same number of fallen or clearly disabled 'Mechs. No one for her to challenge.

Looking out the cockpit for a visual check, she found too much smoke and fire to the left of her *Hellbringer* to discern many details. To her right, where Lyonor was now stalking her next target, the view was clearer, and Joanna could see all the way to the edge of the plain, where a tall, leafy forest seemed to rise toward a sky that was darkening fast. A storm was coming.

She hated storms. In fact, she hated any weather condition that distorted the view of a battle. There had been many times when, caught in a sudden heavy downpour or a blizzard of swirling snow, she had raged as the enemy seemed to shapeshift, become larger or smaller, lose all defining outline, fade in and out of sight. Although it might be just a Clan legend, she had heard Ghost Bears were particularly dangerous in inclement conditions.

She spotted a *Stormcrow* trying to blindside Lyonor, heading toward her with its typical quickness. Lyonor was bearing her *Summoner* down on a *Mad Dog* that had already suffered considerable damage, but had managed to down its opponent. She destroyed the *Mad Dog*'s right arm pulse laser, which sputtered flame. Nevertheless, it still came toward the *Summoner* steadily, if a bit slowly. The slowness also seemed to suggest this particular Ghost Bear pilot was in trouble but, with characteristic Clan persistence, would rather die fighting than take a brief and safe retreat.

This Stormcrow*'s mine, then,* Joanna thought, and started racing her *Hellbringer* toward the ambushing 'Mech. She pushed the 'Mech as hard as she could, trying to get every ounce of energy out of it. Instead, the 'Mech slowed down and became difficult to handle. Something in one the *Hellbringer*'s leg actuators must have been hit or chosen this *stravag* time to malfunction. She felt like she was heading toward the *Stormcrow* at half-speed, as if plodding through a field of mud. Frantically working her controls, she tried to increase the speed, but the *Hellbringer* did not respond. Twisting in her seat, she tried to urge the 'Mech forward with her body. If anything, it seemed to slow down more.

Ahead, Lyonor was in more trouble than she realized. Joanna tried to raise her on the comm, but all signals were being jammed, and all she heard was noise. She shouted a warning to Lyonor, hoping maybe her abrasive voice would get through all the static.

Whether Lyonor heard or not, she suddenly shifted position and shot at the *Stormcrow*. The shot went wide, but it diverted the *Stormcrow* just enough. It raced past Lyonor's *Summoner*.

It had also accomplished its goal in tempting Lyonor—tricking her—into firing on two different targets! By the rituals of battle, she had agreed to a two-against-one battle!

If the Ghost Bears could play such games—the same tricks that had twice cost her a Bloodname!—Joanna felt no shame in unleashing her full fury against them. A grand melee. So be it. She worked furiously at her controls, trying to get more power and speed out of the *Hellbringer*. Ahead, the storm cloud seemed to be racing toward them with the speed of a *Stormcrow*.

Edging her *Hellbringer* toward the *Stormcrow*'s path, she watched it begin to turn back toward Lyonor's *Summoner*. Its medium lasers were already engaged, sending bolts toward the *Summoner*. They went astray, but Joanna knew once the *Stormcrow* got into close range, it could be deadly. The red bolts seemed brighter against the dark, oncoming storm. Joanna could see the lines of rain, the tempest was that close.

Lyonor's concentration seemed to be on the *Mad Dog*, which was now reeling, ready to fall. In her mind, Joanna urged the fall with the same intensity she urged her *Hellbringer* onward.

As it fell, the *Mad Dog*'s pilot managed a strong green burst from its large pulse laser. Hitting Lyonor's *Summoner*, it sent pieces of ferro-fibrous armor flying. The *Summoner* rocked slightly at the laser's impact, but maintained its position as the *Mad Dog* fell in front of it, its head just missing the *Summoner*'s feet.

Lyonor should be proud of this one, Joanna thought. *Her combat skill shows she should earn a Bloodname.*

But the *Stormcrow* still headed steadily toward the *Summoner*. And the storm reached the area, releasing a downpour whose impact felt just as powerful as a hit from a PPC. And her *Hellbringer* continued trudging along, going into the heavy wind. Now it was not too far away from the *Stormcrow.* And Joanna hoped the enemy had not detected her approach.

A flash of lightning illuminated the scene in eerie colors. To Joanna, it seemed like a chalk drawing done by a child. The shadows on the *Stormcrow* seemed sketched on, with no relation to any object throwing them. Further in the distance, Lyonor's 'Mech was more like a smudge against the landscape, its edges uneven, as if the child wielding the chalk had not stayed within the lines.

In a moment, all three 'Mechs were in close proximity to each other. Joanna could see the silhouette of Lyonor through her darkened cockpit shield.

Power suddenly surged back into the *Hellbringer,* and it lurched forward. Joanna thought she might lose control, but with deft movements she manipulated switches and levers to steady her 'Mech. She felt it gradually pick up speed, as if finally responding to her growled urgings.

The pilot of the *Stormcrow* clearly had the *Summoner* in his sights, and more red bolts hit their targets, further weakening the 'Mech's armor.

Joanna could see Lyonor silhouetted in her cockpit, she could visualize the determination on the other woman's face as she responded to the *Stormcrow*'s assault with her PPCs. Aiming at the 'Mech's legs, her shots caused heavy damage to the left one, sending the *Stormcrow* staggering. It slowed down and its feet hit the ground at odd angles, reminding Joanna of the limp of a staggering drunk.

The storm got worse. The wind whipped the rain around the trio of 'Mechs, making them sway almost as much as a well-placed laser burst might have done.

Now the *Hellbringer* was racing along as fast as it had formerly been slow. Joanna struggled with her controls again. Something in the *Hellbringer's* leg actuators needed adjustment. She vowed that, as soon as the battle was over, she would get her tech on it right away to restore the equilibrium.

Her *Hellbringer* was now closer to the *Stormcrow* than it was to the *Summoner.* She could ambush it and down it before the pilot knew what hit him. Taking aim with her right arm PPC, she trembled slightly with anticipation as she neared the point at which, as her judgment indicated, she could release a barrage that would surely prove fatal to the *Stormcrow*.

Just before she took the shot, she felt the left side of her *Hellbringer* suddenly dip and go sideways. It was a moment before she realized it was falling and her PPC attack, instead of targeting the center of the *Stormcrow*, merely added to the damage on the Ghost Bear 'Mech's leg.

What happened before and after she crashed, she only sorted out later, when she learned her *Hellbringer* had indeed stumbled, and where else? On one of those damned holes left behind by the archaeologists. It was a fairly shallow one the *Hellbringer's* left leg had plunged into. Someone told her the leg came down so hard on the bottom that it unearthed some strange metal artifacts, but Joanna saw the story was clearly legend and gave no credit to it.

The *Hellbringer* staggered in reaction to the stumble. Joanna nearly steadied it but, as she tried to lift the left leg out of the hole, it stumbled again, on the lip of the hole. Frantically working controls, she could not bring the *Hellbringer* under her control and realized that the 'Mech might go down: *savashri*! As she attempted to raise the *Hellbringer's* arm and target other areas of the *Stormcrow*, she refused to eject and vowed to stay with her 'Mech all the way to the ground.

This last stumble finally threw the leg's actuators completely offline, and an alarm in Joanna's control panel showed the leg malfunctioning, shutting down. A strong push forward with the 'Mech's other leg dragged the damaged leg along for a step, but the right leg began to slide sideways in the mass of mud caused by the storm.

The *Hellbringer* pitched forward, out of control. Joanna struggled to will the 'Mech upright, but the machine continued to collapse. Rocking the throttle full foward, she got another good push from the right leg, thrusting the 'Mech further ahead.

As she was told later, Joanna's barrage as her 'Mech fell, both her shots to the leg and those on the *Stormcrow* torso, set the Ghost Bear 'Mech up for Lyonor's final attack, which sent the *Stormcrow* reeling forward. It should have landed on top of the downed *Mad Dog* at the *Summoner's* feet, again reenacting the traditional heroic picture of one 'Mech defeating another.

But it did not work out that way.

The *Hellbringer*, in spite of its collapsing legs, had been advancing at a stunning speed, and now hurtled forward, even as it fell. One Jade Falcon pilot who observed it told Joanna her 'Mech seemed to turn into a missile as it shot forward, its arc propelling it ahead on its own flight—a flight that sent it crashing into the *Summoner.*

Lyonor should not have died. It was just two 'Mechs crashing into each other, something that happened often enough in BattleMech combat. It was just a desperate final burst from the *Stormcrow's* lasers that penetrated Lyonor's already damaged cockpit as the two 'Mechs fell. It was just a damned combination of chance events that had sent the red laser burst through Lyonor's chest and then, if she had any life left in her, crushed her as the pair of machines fell into a shattering and shattered pile.

Lyonor should not have died. It was not logical. Joanna's *Hellbringer* should not have stumbled. It should not have even touched the *Stormcrow.* The *Stormcrow* should just have fallen into the traditional warrior tableau of battle. The *Summoner,* by all the rules of chance, should not have been in the falling *Stormcrow*'s path.

But it happened. It all happened. And Lyonor would never fight for the Bloodname she craved.

Afterward, the storm over, Joanna oversaw Lyonor's body being extracted from her *Summoner.* She knew from the onset that Lyonor was dead. Her face was peaceful, as if satisfied she had died bravely. The scar on her cheek was so faint now, Joanna could barely discern it.

She watched the body being carried away. *My mistake,* she thought. *If I had been late to the fight, Lyonor would be alive.* Then she seemed to hear Lyonor's voice in her mind, saying, *"Not your mistake. We fight, we die. Is that not what is meant by the Way of the Clans?"*

Every muscle of Joanna's body ached from being bounced around her cockpit. Her head was on fire with shooting pains, but she did not want to rejoin her unit just yet.

Joanna stared at the remains of the *Summoner* and saw it was now scrap, parts of it only usable for other 'Mechs. She remembered the last sight she had of Lyonor's falling *Summoner* as her own 'Mech crashed into it. Pieces of the *Summoner*'s aligned crystal steel armor had fallen all around, as if part of the storm.

Next to the *Summoner* now, she noticed slivers and chunks of the armor strewn around the fallen 'Mech. Walking a few steps, she noticed a flash of light, a sparkle, coming from one of the armor pieces. The piece's radiance made no sense. There was scarcely any light in the dark sky to cause the flash.

She leaned down and picked up the armor fragment. It was still warm from the battle. There was nothing interesting in its shape or in the battle scars on its surface, but it was from

Lyonor's 'Mech, so she put it in her jacket pocket and trudged on through the mud.

Now, Joanna stared at the armor piece, and considered tossing it. There seemed no reason to keep it. She really did not want to remember Lyonor anymore, not now or in the future.

She held it up, as if measuring it for destruction. She held it for a long while, then shook her head, and placed it back in the lockbox. She flipped the cover down and shoved the lockbox under the cot. It clattered on the uneven floor.

She considered taking a nap, but knew she would not sleep.

Glancing around the decrepit room, her home for who knew how long, she pulled on her gloves, strode through the doorway and slammed the door shut behind her.

Outside, the air was fresh, and a strong breeze hit her. She felt it rustle her long, dark hair. Strands of hair brushed against her neck and sent a pleasant shudder through her.

In the distance, she saw what she had hoped for, a group of trainees to kick around. Breaking into a run, breathing in the welcome fresh air, closing her hands into fists, watching rays of light rising off her gloves' metal studs, she zeroed in on them.

HELLBRINGER (LOKI)
HEAVY—65 TONS

MAD DOG (VULTURE)
HEAVY—60 TONS

STORMCROW (RYOKEN)
MEDIUM—55 TONS

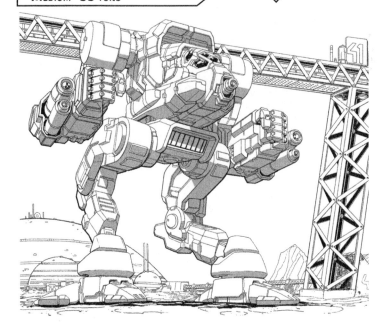

SUMMONER (THOR)
HEAVY—70 TONS

PLOG19

WARHAWK (MASAKARI)
ASSAULT—85 TONS

FOR WANT OF A NAIL

DAN C. DUVAL

RAMORA
OUTWORLDS ALLIANCE
10 MARCH 3067

Defoe eased the truck to a stop and set the brake. An early spring storm filled the sky with black clouds, and thunder rumbled back and forth between the hills and mountains surrounding the site.

The roadway ran straight up the side of the hill, from the Regimental Base at Danforth, and straight down the other, toward the next stop of his circuit. The Pegasus Scout Hover Tank was grounded into a cut made into the side of the hill, just below the crest where he had parked the truck.

He jumped down, walked to the back of the truck, and pulled his handcart from behind the cover shrouding the bed of the truck. He loaded the two big containers of spare components onto the cart and rolled it down the paved path to where the Pegasus sat.

The old scout tank had survived several battles, as evidenced by the streaks of rust that ran down from the weapon scorings on its armored side. Its engines had not been replaced at the last refit. To fund military expansion, President Avellar exported everything that would generate hard cash or needed goods, such as replacement engines. So the old hovertank had become a picket outpost, its engine compartment converted to hold tiny living quarters for its crew, and for the additional cabinets of electronics and optics that controlled the sensors scattered across the valley hilltops.

Active hovertanks smelled of lubricants, half-burned fuel, and the stale air from under the skirts; this unit smelled of grass, old earth, and maybe a malfunctioning sewage collection unit.

Defoe placed his access key on the pad next to the scout's hatch and typed in his clearance code. The hatch sank into the hull with a hiss and swung inward. He stepped through the opening and dragged his heavy cart into the darkness within.

As he turned, a voice said, "Jump, rook."

Defoe automatically caught the object tossed at him and it took him a moment to notice it was a grenade.

He flung it away and it rattled around on the floor of the scout's cabin, banging into one component cabinet after another.

Benny, the senior sergeant assigned this week, said, "Don't be such an ass, Hutchins."

"It was just a dummy. Not about to toss a live one to this rook. He might camp on it and try to hatch it." Neither of the two crewmen could be seen through the backs of their command chairs, but Defoe knew them both, had seen them every other day, every other week, for months now. Benny big, graying, and going to fat; Hutchins tiny, skinny, and seemingly putting more and more of his mass into the long, hooked nose that gave him a rat-face.

Nothing Defoe could do about it. It was bad enough that, despite the desire that sent him to enlist in the Alliance Borderers Regiment, he had ended up in the Third Battalion, the sole infantry unit in the armored regiment. Even worse, his performance in his early training had relegated him to support functions rather than the line units.

The first time he handled a live grenade, he had activated it and then fumbled the live round onto the ground. When the drill instructor shouted at him, he bent over, picked up the arming lever, and threw it over the safety wall.

If it had ended there, it might have been alright, but then Defoe had ducked, squatting right over the hissing, smoking grenade, and the DI practically had to throw him out of the way to flip the weapon over the wall before it detonated.

And the next time they gave him a grenade, he just froze.

The result was no Line, no armor, just spare parts and supply runs. Pure, boring, grunt work.

The cab of the scout consisted of the two command chairs forward, behind a wide belt of thick, armored ferroglass, both seats surrounded by consoles for movement, armament, and the many sensors. Immediately behind them, a small section of the decking had an engineering panel on one side and a fold-down jumpseat on the other, which the outer hatch swung into when it opened.

Aft of that, where Defoe stood, was the combination bunkroom-kitchen-commode-dining hall—this entire section would fit into his locker back at Danforth. Defoe had never liked this arrangement, where the commode acted as the base of the fold-down dining table. It would all be stripped out when—and if—the tank received a new engine sometime in the future.

The two operators spent a five-day tour in this box, never leaving it until relieved by the next crew.

Defoe flipped down the jumpseat and entered his clearance code on the engineering panel opposite. After the readouts lit up, he started a basic diagnostic of the sensor systems. One module lit up as requiring replacement and he powered down the sensor system, the consoles in the fore-cabin going blank.

Defoe confirmed the power-down on the engineering panel and popped open the indicated cabinet, revealing rows of components. He fingered the labels until he found the indicated component and pulled it from the slot. He tossed it on top of his cart and opened the front of the lower box, pulling a new unit from its slot. He placed it into the guides where the old component had been and jammed it tightly into the backplane. He swung the access panel back into place.

"Repowering the sensor system," he called, receiving not even a grunt. Hutchins appeared to be reading some sort of book on one of his consoles. The initialization diagnostic started automatically, just as it was supposed to, and Defoe stood up. "I'll go get your supply box while the diag is running."

He stood and tapped the hatch control and the hatch swung inward, Defoe stepping back to let it by.

He lifted his foot to step over the threshold when the consoles in front of the command chair lit up and klaxons blared in the confines of the tiny cabin.

Startled, the hatch swung shut for the emergency lockdown and bashed him full in the chest, flinging him back into the commode and on top of his handcart of spares.

Hutchins was shouting, "What the hell did you do, rook?" while Benny slapped at his consoles, shutting down alarms and starting the data dump to Regiment.

Benny smacked Hutchins with one hand, said, "Shut up." Then he shifted to the calm communication voice expected when talking to Regiment. "HQ, this is Burn 3. Showing ten, eleven, twelve targets—repeat, twelve targets—descending Placecard Six. Altitude scattered from 50K to 65K, hot descent. Data stream is active and remoted."

Hutchins turned in his seat. He waved a hand vaguely toward the aft end of the cabin and said, "Crawl into the bunk. Grab onto anything you can. If we get a near miss, everything will shake and rattle, and I don't want you landing on my head."

Defoe stumbled backward and almost fell over his cart. He stepped clumsily around it and fell onto the bunk, pulling his cart toward him and setting its feeble little wheel brake. Forward of him, he could see Benny and Hutchins pulling their chair straps tight, Benny maintaining a running commentary on the targets shown on the console displays.

The earth trembled underneath him and Defoe saw, through the ferroglass windows, the plasma plumes of descending 'Mechs, out in the distance, before the world in front of him exploded into light, heat, and screeching metal.

It seemed like a long time that he floated in the darkness, with no sound to disturb him, until a high-pitched keening started, far away, but still annoying. He let himself drift toward it, to see what it was but it was just more annoying there and he tried to drift away again, but the smell of smoke burned at him and the keening grew ever louder.

He opened his eyes on hell.

The ferroglass had disappeared entirely on Benny's side of the Pegasus, with chunks still hanging in the edges on Hutchins' side. The upper half of Benny's command chair was gone and blood pooled underneath it. A smaller pool collected beneath Hutchins. The keening was coming from there.

The forward view was empty of 'Mechs, and a fresh shower of rain obscured visibility into the valley. Still, Defoe could think of nothing but getting out. He didn't seem to hurt anywhere, so he pushed his legs over the handcart and almost dropped into the hole where the commode used to be, along with half of the communications panel in the floor.

He reached for the far side of the hole with his toe and then pushed himself upright, teetering for a moment astride the hole before he got his balance again. He slapped the hatch access pad. He heard the bolts release and saw the hatch start to swing inward, but it jammed, with just barely enough space to squeeze through.

He had put his shoulder into the crack when he heard Hutchins' keening turn into a howling speech-like sound, nothing a human being should be able to make.

"ROOK! You crap! You Clan-hump! You don't leave me here! You come get me! You shit, you come get me!"

Defoe froze. Hutchins. Hutchins was dead. The 'Mechs wouldn't ignore the Pegasus forever. In fact, the 'Mech that had blasted the Pegasus might be out securing the factory at the far end of the valley, but it would be back to make sure of its first shot on the scout. If he didn't get himself out, they were both dead. He moved again, trying to push his chest through the tight opening.

The speakers in the small cabin crackled and a voice emerged from the background hum. *"Burn Three. Burn Three. This is Hammer One. We have lost data feed and require targeting information on landed bandits. Burn Three acknowledge."*

Still stuck in the hatch, Defoe panicked for a moment before remembering that when the scout took damage, the comm channels would switch onto the open speakers. The Pegasus could still receive from Regiment, but apparently no longer transmitted. He looked at the hole in the floor. Probably not a surprise. He started his wriggling again.

"Defoe, you bastard! You can't leave me here!"

He stopped again. He was almost out. He could feel it. Almost through the gap. But Hutchins apparently couldn't help himself.

Run, his mind told him. *Run*, his body told him. Hutchins was dead.

He was dead, too, if he didn't move.

And move now.

He moved.

He pulled back into the cabin and stepped gingerly around the partly open hatch. The hot, bitter fumes rising from the hole in the floor made him dizzy for a moment, but he held on and set his foot on the other side, pushing off on the door to get himself upright.

He wanted to avoid looking at the remains of Benny's command chair—and of Benny—but a sick, perverted urge overwhelmed him and he looked anyway. Just a set of legs, strings of clotted blood hanging over the edge of the chair seat, while the rest of the chair was simply gone, along with the upper half of Benny. Defoe felt his gorge rise, but swallowed it back down.

Hutchins was little better. Arm gone above the elbow, and Hutchins trying to hold the blood back with his sole remaining hand. His leg on Benny's side was covered in blood, apparently the recipient of spalling and fragments from the bolt that took Benny. Hutchins' face was pale and his eyes were rolled back in his head. He had stopped screaming, but still muttered, "You shit. You come get me."

No way. Hutchins could not move from that chair, and no way he could get through the narrow opening in the hatch. The urge to run started to rise in Defoe again.

Before he could turn, though, the rain let up enough to show a 'Mech not more than a few klicks down the valley, heading toward the Pegasus' position.

On the console in front of Hutchins, a blue icon started to flash, a tiny square about a quarter of the way down from the top of the screen. It crept slowly toward the spidery X in the middle of the display, which represented the Pegasus. Weirdly, the same image appeared on the console in front of what little remained of Benny. The 'Mech was coming.

A reticule appeared from the edges of the display and shrank until it just fitted around the tiny blue icon, which then turned red. A mechanical voice said over the cabin speakers, *"Target locked. Missile battery ready to fire."* One of the buttons on the arm of Hutchins' chair flashed rapidly white to red and back, then settled to a slow red flashing.

Defoe was not in the Line, but even he had had some rudimentary training on the weapons of the Borderers. Push the flashing red button, and the Pegasus' battery would launch one salvo of missiles at the marked target.

Training also told him the tiny missile battery on the Pegasus would not do much against a 'Mech. Not to mention the target was well outside the battery's range; the hit must have damaged the targeting system as well.

Over the speaker, a voice said, *"Burn Three. Burn Three. This is Hammer One. We have baskets to give away. Need targeting updates. Respond."*

Defoe reached toward the flashing button, but Hutchins' hand knocked his away. He looked down at the man's drawn face.

"Mission. Recon. Report. Target for air wing. Shoot and we might...kill one, more behind. Need to report. Then shoot."

Defoe slapped the back of Hutchins' command chair. "No way. The entire transmitter section is a hole. I can't fix it."

He looked back. The hole was big enough. The components were all gone, but he had a full set of spares in the hardcart, which was untouched. But the backplane—the communications bus was gone, a fragment of the transmit section there, though the receiving section was clearly intact.

From the speakers, the voice droned on. *"Burn Three. Hammer One. Report. Require targeting information."*

There was plenty of information, the various displays showing all of the hostile 'Mechs, most converging on the United Outworlds Corps fighter production plant, nine kilometers away. And one still trudging toward the Pegasus, locked in on the central display.

And no way to tell anyone.

That old poem ran through his head, *"For the want of a nail, the shoe was lost; for the want of the shoe, the horse was lost—"*

For the want of a place to plug in, the battle was lost.

Bus. Communications bus. Transmit and receive both use the same antenna, which is tied to the same bus. Don't need to receive. Need to send.

No one had ever told him this should work, but it should.

The remains of the panel could not be raised while the exit hatch was open, though, so he slapped at the access pad and nothing happened. He shoved on the heavy door and it barely budged. He pushed again, harder, until he thought his back would break, but the thing barely moved. Way too slow.

He flipped down the jumpseat and sat in it, wedging his back against the panels behind him and his feet on the hatch. And pushed.

It gave, slowly, until it stopped with a *click*, now jammed neither all the way closed nor all the way open. No way he would be able to get out that way.

He stood up and looked out over the command chairs. He could probably climb out through the hole in the ferroglass, but Hutchins would never make it. And that took him closer to the 'Mech still coming up the valley.

He yanked at the floor panel, which held for a moment and then sprang open, almost clobbering him. The six receive modules, lined up and unmarked. All he had to do, supposedly, was to pull them and replace them with the six transmit modules. And the system should automatically feed the data from the sensors out to Regiment.

Though there was no way to know, once he pulled the receive modules.

He pulled one module after another, tossing them behind him onto the tiny patch of floor that neither the command chairs nor his own feet occupied.

Now he could hear the roaring crunch of brush as the 'Mech crashed through them, the distant *crack* as a tree resisted for a moment before giving way to the metal beast.

Why doesn't it just fire?

He pulled the front panel of one of the boxes on his cart open. Wrong one. He fumbled with the catch on the other box and almost pulled it off its hinges once he got the latch to release. The six transmit modules were lined up, one next to the other. He pulled the first and guided it into the first complete slot.

The crashing in the trees got louder, and now Defoe thought he could feel the impact tremors as dozens of tons of metal stomped forward, step by step.

One module after another, he shoved them into place, until the telltales next to the handles were lit on all six.

According to the theory, the Pegasus was now sending its latest data to Regiment, forwarded then to the incoming fighters.

In theory.

In practice, though, that red light was still blinking. Defoe scrambled to his feet, the discarded modules tangling his ankles, and reached for the arm console of Hutchins' command chair.

The 'Mech seemed to fill the entire viewing opening. *Too close*, a panicked voice said in his head. *With half the ferroglass gone, the missile explosions will fill the cabin with blast.*

The right arm of the 'Mech started to rise, covers snapping off small missiles in a launching pod.

Praying the targeting system still worked, Defoe slapped the flashing red button. The world filled again with sound and light and violent vibrations and the taste of blood and darkness and quiet.

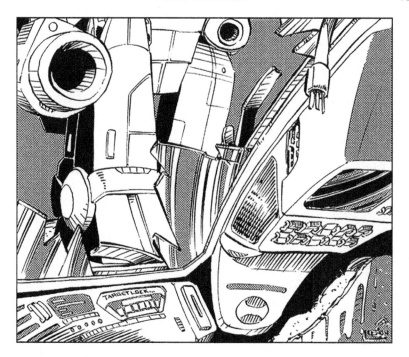

When Defoe awoke, he was in the hospital. The pale green walls and overly perfumed air (undercut with old decay and new antiseptic) were giveaways. Along with the bandaged arm hanging from a rack on his left side, its purple fingers sticking out of the end of the cast.

Defoe wiggled them, to make sure they were his. The fingers wiggled, and his arm suddenly felt like it was on fire. They seemed to be his.

A young man's face hovered over him for a few moments, then a cool hand stuck a thermometer patch on his cheek, and the face disappeared.

An eternity later, a different face appeared, the patch was peeled away, and another face replaced that one.

This last face hovered above a uniform tunic with colonel's tabs on its collar. Chairman Fitzroy Candly. Defoe had seen him once before, at a full muster of the Alliance Borderers. Colonel of the whole damn Regiment.

His voice was low and gravelly, as if he needed to choke down something in his throat. "You did well, Protector. We smashed them flat. The Third Air Wing took out the lot before they had a chance to damage the plant. We think it might have been a raid for engines. But, thanks to you, none of them got away, though we missed their DropShip.

"We couldn't find any markings on the scrap we recovered. Do you recall any markings on the one that hit you boys?"

Defoe made one attempt to shake his head and quickly gave that up as a bad idea. He tried to speak, to say "No," but he couldn't get out more than a croak. A very inarticulate croak. He'd barely seen the one that had seemed right on top of him. He sure as hell was not looking for markings.

The colonel flashed a very quick smile. "No matter. You will be debriefed when you are better able to talk. In the meantime, you rest. Get well, and we'll get you back in the Line."

Defoe tried to croak again. "Hutchins?" This sounded a little better than the last attempt. Still Candly only looked at him and Defoe tried to repeat himself. "Hutchins?"

The colonel grimaced and shook his head. "No. You were it. And you were pretty torn up yourself."

Defoe said. "I tried to run." When the colonel's face screwed up with confusion, he tried again, slower. "Run. Tried to."

The colonel leaned back and nodded. "You probably should have. I might have, in your place. When I was younger. But you didn't and we hurt these people badly. Twelve dead 'Mechs that we'll part out." He tapped Defoe's cast lightly. "Get well, soldier."

And his face disappeared.

Someone stuck a straw in his face and Defoe sucked feebly at it for a few seconds before giving it up. At the edge of exhaustion, he concentrated on breathing.

Had the colonel said, "back in the Line?" And "protector?"

Defoe felt an itch on the back of his left hand, the one hanging in the cast in front of him. The itch grew worse.

PEGASUS
HOVER–35 TONS

ART OF THE DEAL

LOREN L. COLEMAN

"Only after General Motors contacted Ceres Metals on [Vicore Industries'] behalf was the Capellan company willing to listen to Giovanni's proposal."

—Excerpted from Vicore Industries' "Phoenix Report"
1 August 3067

CERES METALS PLANETARY HEADQUARTERS
WARLOCK
CAPELLAN CONFEDERATION
7 APRIL 3065

Overseer pro-tem Nikolai Kwiatkowski shivered as he charged between buildings, slipping along the icy, unprotected walk. Frigid gusts whistled through frost-rimed metal framing the support structure meant for enclosing ferroglass, which was still waiting on delivery three years later. A strong blast of wind blew back his parka's fur-lined hood and ran cold hands down the back of his neck. Dry snow, as gritty as sand, stung his eyes.

Ducking forward, the large man weathered Warlock's arctic grip until he finally bulldozed into the rotunda door. The revolving entryway created a thermal lock for the proving grounds' Operations Center. Shrill alarms rang inside this building as well. Nikolai's thick glasses fogged over and he swiped at them with one hand. Ignoring the elevator, which only seemed to work on alternate weeks anyway, he took the stairs three at a time and arrived gasping for breath with his throat on fire at the second-floor observatory only two minutes after the first perimeter alarm had sounded.

"What in the Chancellor's great-and-worthy name is going on here?"

Not that anyone paid attention.

Sirens continued to blare in three discordant tones as technicians pulled out procedural manuals and argued over their instrumentation. One man switched his tracking station from direct feed video over to broadband satellite. His female counterpart switched it back. On their shared monitor, the image jumped from the blocky silhouette for a *Blackjack* OmniMech, rust-red and looking lost against drifted snowbanks and frosted conifers, to a tactical overview of the local taiga. A large, flashing red icon eclipsed one entire corner of the display. Then back to the *Blackjack*.

Hùn dàn niŭ-kòu tóu-bù! Bastard button heads! Nikolai reached over to the alarm panel and cleared the annoying sirens. Everyone stopped dead as if he had thrown the master disconnect breaker for their brains.

The overseer pro tem switched the nearby station back to satellite and pointed at the red icon. "What is that?" he asked through clenched teeth.

Jīng-lǐ Fen Xou, the operations manager, bowed perfunctorily. "DropShip," he said in his usual abrupt manner.

"One of ours?" Meaning one belonging to Ceres Metals or the planet's military garrison.

Xou shook his head. "Ours would not set off alarms."

They could, actually. The southern continent proving grounds were off limits on a live-fire day, such as this day with the BJ2-O undergoing its yearly retrials. But if the approaching vessel was a Capellan flight, it was not even trying to broadcast proper IFF clearances. With Warlock sitting so close to the Capellan-Federated Suns border, that likely meant a Davion DropShip.

Didn't the FedScum have their hands full enough with their civil war? They had to make Nikolai's life on this ball of ice more difficult?

Nikolai swallowed dryly. Help, he knew, was at least three hours away at the garrison post of Yumen. Where soldiers of the Confederation were treated to such luxuries as cafeterias, nightclubs, and the Canopian pleasure circus currently on-world. Ceres Metals' usual overseer, Nikolai's boss, was there as well. No doubt enjoying himself. Which meant responsibility for this breach would land squarely on Nikolai's shoulders.

"We have a visual," one of the techs called out.

Out of reflex, Nikolai looked out the large ferroglass window fronting the room. Snow flurries occasionally pelted the glass, driven horizontally by the sharp, arctic winds. Some of the larger flakes stuck, melting into long runnels that trickled toward the bottom edge. Visibility was intermittent, up to five hundred meters. Any DropShip visible by the naked eye would be landing right on top of them!

He moved to an auxiliary station, where the technician had selected penetrating radar. The computer painted an amber silhouette over the green-black scope.

Spheroid vessel. Military design.

Nikolai scrubbed his palms against the side of his trousers, drying away nervous sweat. Running the *Blackjack's* retrials by himself should have been another small stepping stone toward advancement. This was shaping into an administrator's nightmare.

Then the computer tagged the vessel as an *Intruder*—at 3000 metric tons, one of the smallest spheroid-class assault DropShips one could find.

"They assault Warlock with *that*?" he asked. A determined band of Capellan space-scouts could hold off any military force arriving in an *Intruder.* It could not even transport a single BattleMech.

Correction: it might hold *one* 'Mech if the cargo bay was refitted and you didn't load too much tonnage in the way of spare parts. Which was apparently the case, Nikolai saw, as a large shadow detached itself from the hovering DropShip and landed under its own jump jet power. The computer was having trouble placing it. Identification jumped back and forth between an old PXH *Phoenix Hawk* and one of the Confederation's newer 3L *Vindicators*.

"Where did that monster set down?" Nikolai asked sharply. "Is the DropShip landing anything more with it? Where is our garrison support?"

These people were not military-trained, and had not responded with good Capellan discipline to the emergency. But they knew how to get data when an oversight manager asked for it.

"Two hours for Yumen garrison," Fen Xou reported, answering Nikolai's last question first.

"DropShip is standing by. No other forces deployed," a technician at another workstation reported. "Enemy 'Mech is within two kilometers of our live fire range."

Within two kilometers of *Sao-wei* Cho Tah Men's *Blackjack*, then! "Have Cho move to intercept," he ordered. Perhaps all was not as dark as he'd feared.

"We are receiving a transmission from the *Intruder.*" A communications tech held up her hand for attention. "Vessel identifies itself as General Motors Flight One-one-three-eight-special. With...With the compliments of Governor Giovanni Estrella De la Sangre." She frowned. Then, "Message repeats."

General Motors? Nikolai sneered. Worse than the enemy, then. It was their competition.

"Whatever game this Estrella De la...whoever...is playing, I want that BattleMech destroyed."

The BJ2-O was on the grounds for its live fire retrial after all. And bringing the venerable *Blackjack* design back to the attention of the Confederation Armed Forces, with the military's recent infatuation with new technology, could not hurt the reputation of Ceres Metals.

Or his own reputation, for that matter. Nikolai suddenly envisioned this as his ticket off Warlock, the frostbitten *zhī-chuāng* of the St. Ives Commonality. Away from the snow and the icy winds and the long hours spent proving (or finding flaws in) someone else's designs. A post on beautiful, warm Capella would not be too much to expect. Even the world of St. Ives itself would be acceptable. With a nice promotion. Surely he could bargain that in as well.

Dreams which lasted until the *Blackjack* OmniMech finally made contact with the foreign machine.

"A *Phoenix Hawk*," *Sao-wei* Cho reported. "The computer cannot fix on the variant, but I recognize its profile. Something different... *Tā mā dè*! It has reach!"

Reach? Over the Omni? "What variant is Cho running?" Nikolai asked, moving to the corner of the room where technicians monitored tactical screens, tapping directly into the *Blackjack's* systems.

"Alternate configuration 'C', with double long-barreled autocannon."

A 3D, then? But only a single large laser? "Give me guncam feeds on monitors two and three."

New screens winked to life, showing fields of white interrupted by frosted conifers and tall, gangly winter hemlock. The image swung drunkenly as the *Blackjack* stalked forward, swinging its arms around to the right...in time to catch a blur of highly-polished metal erupting through a waist-deep snowbank.

A laser mounted on the back of the enemy 'Mech's right arm slashed angrily below the camera's eye. On the *Blackjack's* wire-frame schematic, the leg darkened by several shades of gray as armor puddled to the ground. The BattleMech retreated before Cho angled in with his autocannon.

"Freeze that image and clean it up," Nikolai ordered.

One of the techs did so. It was a *Phoenix Hawk*, all right. No mistaking the lines. But not a 3D; the armor looked reinforced, and more angular than the traditional design. Wide intake ports on the jump jets. Better weapons, obviously.

"Upgrades." He spat the word out with a bad taste. General Motors had been busy, it seemed. It would make the OmniMech's job harder, but would not make the difference.

Except *Sao-wei* Cho kept reporting a difficulty in acquiring solid target lock. "It keeps ghosting my sensors," he complained, suffering long-range strikes against his chest, his arms, and then a shoulder-to-shoulder slash that burned deep enough to melt through part of his engine shielding.

His return fire was sporadic, and mostly ineffectual. Flechette munitions sanded some armor from the *'Hawk's* left side, a bit more from each leg, but more often than not Cho ended up carving local conifers into kindling. Usually right behind where the *Phoenix Hawk* had been standing a moment before.

Nikolai stabbed angrily at the communications board, opening a direct channel to his test pilot. The officer was lower-grade, it was true, but his performance bordered on the embarrassing. "Quit sniping with that *hùn dàn* pilot and stand up to him!" It was rare for an administrator to intrude on any live-fire situation, but there was more riding on this than Cho's reputation alone. "Force him to stand and fight!"

It was a gamble, playing with a *'Hawk* that way. Fifty percent faster and sixty meters of greater reach with its jump jets, Nikolai risked letting the redesigned 'Mech slip behind Cho, where it could do a lot more damage.

Then again, as the Omni lost more armor from his left leg and lower waist, its rear-facing armor might just be stronger than whatever it had left up front.

The *Phoenix Hawk* let him come. It raced onto a dry expanse of hard-packed dirt and loose rock, swept clean of snow by the hard winds, and waited for the Capellan pilot. If Cho expected a great advantage in closing—or any advantage, for that matter—he did not see it. His autocannons continued to miss as often as not, while the *Phoenix Hawk* struck at him again and again. One ruby lance cut deep enough to silence one of Cho's autocannons, halving his effective weaponry.

The *'Hawk* had to be heating up by now, not that General Motors' MechWarrior ever let on as they continued to fire its large laser with regular accuracy.

It sparked a thought that worried at the back of Nikolai's mind. "Give me a thermal profile of that machine," he requested, feeling a dead weight settle deep into his gut.

"It will switch Cho over as well—" Xou started to explain, but the overseer pro-tem cut his manager off with a raised hand.

"Just do it!" he yelled as the *Blackjack* charged forward.

No, the *'Hawk* did not appear to be running hot. In fact, its entire heat-dissipation system appeared to be banked toward minimal output. It was a thermal image Nikolai recognized. So did the computer. Which was why it kept bouncing over to the *Vindicator* 3L variant.

Stealth armor!

"Cho! Cho! Break off from that '*Hawk*.'"

His order went out a few seconds too late. Medium lasers and machine guns tore at the *Blackjack* with savage strength. The ruby fury of its large laser slashed hip to shoulder, finishing off the OmniMech's armor.

Then another laser lance skewered the *Blackjack* just to the right of centerline. This time the enemy pilot found Cho's ammunition bin for the autocannon. Lacking cellular ammunition storage equipment, which could have channeled the destructive force out specially-prepared blast panels, the resulting fireball tore through the OmniMech's entire chest cavity. Golden fire erupted in a catastrophic failure of the fusion reactor system, and the guncam screens washed to static.

For a moment Nikolai thought he had lost his man as well as his machine.

Then the camera's eye switched to the safety network built into Cho's ejection seat. Nikolai watched the crash couch rocket up and away from the exploding 'Mech, leaving behind a mushrooming cloud which was all that was left of several million C-bills of Capellan state property.

Likely, all that was left of Nikolai's corporate career as well. He might be leaving Warlock, all right, but as something other than a civilian. Sending Cho in unprepared. Interfering with a live firefight. The Capellan state did not look kindly on failures of this magnitude. And the military would look for any reason not to blame their own man.

"Overseer," the communications technician said quietly, as if worried about disrupting the moment. She tapped the side of her headset. "We have a new transmission from the *Intruder*. They…They congratulate us on a well-coordinated exercise. And ask if we would like them to pick up our MechWarrior before he freezes to death."

Nikolai gripped the sides of the workstation as if his life depended on it, propping himself up, unsteady on his own legs. He had been staring at the death of his career. Now he

shook himself out of it, his corporate survival instincts kicking in and recognizing that—for whatever reason—a possible lifeline was being thrown to him.

By the enemy. The competition.

What was General Motors up to?

This was the most unlikely raid in the history of Warlock, if not the entire Confederation. Was there something larger in play here? He perked up. There just might be a chance to salvage something from the ruins.

"Yes," he said, slowly, thinking it out. "Tell them we are happy to have them return our test pilot. And if..." What was the name? "If Gioavanni Estrella De la Sangre has further need of Ceres Metals, then Overseer pro-tem Nikolai Kwiatkowski stands by to receive word."

"Governor De la Sangre's representatives are standing by at your convenience," the tech said after relaying the overseer's response. Putting one hand over her wire-mic, she looked askance in his direction. "Sir, what is this about?"

"I think," Nikolai said cautiously, "the most bizarre inter-corporate memo ever placed."

Which put Ceres Metals—and Nikolai—in one hell of a bargaining position. Warm offices on Capella might not be in the offing any longer, but neither, he hoped, was a cold cell on Sian.

He could get used to life on Warlock. *Either way,* he decided, *after this the job would be one hell of a lot more interesting.*

He just needed to keep his head above water, and one hand in the deal.

BLACKJACK
MEDIUM—50 TONS

PHOENIX HAWK
MEDIUM—45 TONS

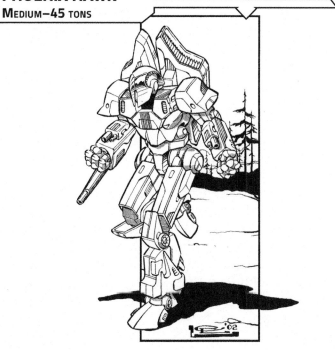

MCKENNA STATION

KEVIN KILLIANY

MCKENNA MARITIME ACADEMY
MCKENNA SHIPYARDS, KATHIL ORBIT
CAPELLAN MARCH
FEDERATED COMMONWEALTH
7 DECEMBER 3062

Armis Tolan hated planets.

Which surprised no one; dirtsiders expected asteroid miners to hate planets. What they never understood was why.

Most thought it was the openness, as though anyone pasted to the side of a rock could understand what open space was. Others thought it was being on the ground itself, but the novelty of walking on an unbonded particulate surface had paled halfway through his first visit to a planet at age five. It wasn't even the weight, though the monotonous drag distorting vectors at the bottom of a gravity well was annoying.

It was the atmosphere that scraped spacer nerves raw.

Even indoors, concealing the oppressively opaque sky, the air was wrong. Wild fluctuations in humidity, sometimes as much as two or three percent, shrilled failing life support to nerves reared in space, while airborne grit screamed overloaded filters. But worst by far were the uncontrolled breezes; each random breath had his every reflex leaping for a hull patch.

Armis could not understand why anyone would intentionally live on a planet.

Though he did concede some worlds were beautiful, if viewed from a sensible distance. Kathil, for example. At the moment it covered half his field of vision with bright golds and greens punctuated by brilliant white bands of suspended water vapor—clouds, he remembered. Nearly four thousand kilometers below him, it seemed close enough to touch.

Any other cadet would have taken a sled for the nine-hundred-meter trip from the loading gantry to the palette, but the Tolans had been asteroid miners for thirteen generations. Unless the task called for a vehicle, Armis simply free-jumped across distances that most people wouldn't chance without a shuttle.

Few miners left the asteroid fields to crew civilian DropShips or the JumpShips that plied interstellar space, binding the Sphere together. Fewer still went to Maritime Academies like McKenna, putting in the years to earn their Merchanter's papers—certification to tech the Kearny-Fuchida drives.

Most asteroid miners left their home systems because they wanted new and different lives. Others were like Armis—younger sons and daughters looking for a new system in which to establish their claims.

Every ship's captain knew the legends, that a miner was only passing through. But folklore also had it that miners were tireless workers and pragmatists who would spend decades finding just the right asteroid field, and give good value for their wages as they searched.

The legends, like all broad statements about a race or culture, were only true just often enough to keep them in circulation, which suited Armis just fine. Because of them miners were always welcome, and a miner with his K-F tech license from McKenna could pick his JumpShip.

Or he would have, before the situation became so complex. Now the merchant fleet, usually neutral in all conflicts, seemed polarized by the brewing political upheaval. Even among the Merchant Cadets, Armis found himself expected to declare for one side or the other—as though a

miner would care who the dirtsiders took orders from. He refused, of course. He'd even concealed his home system to prevent the others from assigning him an allegiance he didn't feel.

Swinging his arms with the unconscious calculation of a lifetime in space, he imparted spin. His view shifted from Kathil to the palette of machine parts he'd been assigned to secure. Today's exercise had the cadets rounding up cargo that had drifted free of the loading bays. Armis had never heard of such an event in real life, but perhaps DropShip cargo handlers were more lax than miners.

Content the palette was where it should be, he didn't counter his spin, letting inertia carry him in slow rotation. McKenna Station and the Shipyard were out of sight "beneath" his boots, of course, but he could see the flares of several worksleds nearby.

Most of the other cadets were working in teams—SOP on salvage/rescue. That no one wanted to team with Armis had not gone unnoticed. Admin had specifically ordered the team retrieving a nearby water cylinder to keep an eye on him.

These two, both planet-born, had taken a sled. Armis noticed that contrary to Academy regs, each wore mailed fists below their merchanters' patches. Lyrans. One was a sharp-faced woman whose name he'd forgotten, but the other was Brogden Baylor, the closest thing to a friend Armis had.

A giant of a man, over two meters, Brogden was from the Odessa system. Armis knew that system had been mined out for easily accessible metals generations ago. Just as his was, or would be within a few years. However, he'd heard several systems in the Timbuktu region were showing promise, yet were still wide open. If he wanted to get posted to a JumpShip headed that way, he might have to declare himself a Lyran at some point.

A ship burned a quick course correction about sixty clicks out. A *Mule*-class DropShip, from the size of the flare, not a troop ship.

Which was a strange thing for a merchant cadet to worry about.

Even at McKenna, where ship building tied it closely to the Federated Commonwealth, wars and the rumors of wars had seemed distant things. Stations, after all, were neutral territory. Particularly stations as vital to the entire Sphere as McKenna Shipyards.

That sense of isolation had been disturbed a week or so ago when Admiral Kerr, executive officer of the WarShip *Robert Davion*, had put off the ship's captain and over half the crew and taken the vessel out of dock. He'd blasted a DropShip that had challenged him to scrap and two other ships had pounded each other to ruin arguing over his right to take command.

Since then the ships around McKenna, both military and civilian, maintained an uneasy peace. Ostensibly they were all loyal to the Federated Commonwealth, but arguments and debates over who was the rightful ruler choked the comm channels.

Armis caught a glimpse of the WarShip on his next rotation. At this distance it was only a silver spark, of course, moving slowly up from the planet's south. Its transpolar orbit would fly by a few hundred clicks above their geosynchronous path, ten, maybe twelve, degrees behind the station.

In a position to keep an eye on things.

Some planet-born cadets insisted they couldn't tell a ship from the starfield beyond it, all the points of light looked the same to them. But none of them had any trouble spotting the eight-hundred-meter WarShip on its thrice daily rounds.

Realizing he needed a course correction of his own, Armis extended his arms again, moving them through less sudden arcs, and allowed the laws of motion to cancel his spin. Satisfied with his new orientation, he blipped his shoulder thrusters through a series of micro burns until he was targeted directly on the palette.

In his own suit he would have made the correction mid-spin, but the standard-issue cadet suit was not as responsive. Or as snug. At sixty-two kilos and one hundred seventy-three centimeters, Armis did not consider himself abnormally small, but whoever designed the cadet suits had apparently assumed no one under one ninety was interested in space service. Even with every strap cinched its tightest, he felt swathed in balloons.

Once he was posted to a JumpShip he'd have an issue suit, with much better tech than the Tolan family could ever afford, custom-fitted. Until then, he was resigned to looking like a child playing dress up.

Tucking his knees up, then bending at the waist—reflexively keeping net angular motions at zero—Armis oriented himself for landing. Essentially sitting with his legs extended toward the palette's upper anchor point.

The palette itself was a hexagonal box, four meters on a side and twenty meters long. This one, according to the manifest, was loaded with grain. Like most containers designed to be muscled in zero-G, it was covered with recessed tie points and hand-holds. This one also had a harpoon, a compressed air cannon that launched a two-hundred-meter adhesive tow line. A harpoon mounted on a palette made as much sense as a palette drifting free in the first place, but who was he to question the wisdom of the instructors?

Armis flexed his legs slightly at contact, absorbing some of his momentum even as he let the rest carry his upper body forward. Snapping his safety line to a recessed ring as his feet bounced clear, he let his forward motion carry him through a somersault. Stretching his arms akimbo, he brought his total rotation to zero just as his feet once again touched the massive ferrosteel frame. Only then did he engage his magnetic boots, letting the field anchor him firmly to the surface.

"Can't you ever do anything without showing off, Half Pint?" Demanded a voice over his suit speakers.

It was Brogden. Armis had looked up the term "half pint" the first time the huge Odessian had used it and discovered it meant 240 cubic centimeters of fluid. He had no idea what he had done to earn the nickname, but since Brogden evidently meant no harm by it, he'd accepted it in good spirits.

Turning, Armis found the water cylinder, actually an external tank for the station, a few hundred meters up orbit. Over fifty meters long and perhaps a dozen in diameter, it was bluntly rounded at one end and at the other sported a flared shroud that protected the valve mechanisms. Even with recycling and rationing, a lot of water was lost in a shipyard the size of McKenna.

At this distance, the other two cadets appeared perhaps a centimeter tall. The sled, tethered with enough space to give the station's grappling hooks room to reach the cylinder, was little more than a sliver of silver in Kathil's light.

"If you'd learn to think of yourself as several dynamic systems working together instead of a solid lump," Armis repeated for perhaps the hundredth time, "You'd waste a lot less energy."

"I like being a lump."

Armis shook his head, grinning despite himself. His reply was cut off by another cadet shouting over the all channel.

"They're shooting!"

"Where away?" asked Jenkins, who salted his speech with every colorful bit of navy jargon he'd learned from trivids. Common wisdom had it he'd need another decade's practice before he sounded authentic.

"Behind, down orbit!" the same excited voice answered. "The *Davion* just blasted something!"

Armis pivoted in place, wasting energy shoving against his magnetic boots. Just down orbit were two dissipating clouds of burning gas near a mote that could only be a DropShip. The ship was firing its lasers with apparently random fury. *Fighters*, he guessed, *too small to be seen at this range.*

A curse from Brogden and a flicker of light at the corner of his eye brought Armis' head around.

Against the blackness beyond the bulk of McKenna Shipyards, a brief spider thread of azure traced the space between two motes. A few degrees to the left another mote was bracketed by tiny flashes of orange.

"What was that?" Brogden asked on their workteam channel. Armis cut down the volume on the general frequency. It was a white noise of questions and exclamations anyway.

"An *Excalibur* hit another with lasers at eleven o'clock relative," he snapped, his words clipped with tension. "And an *Overlord* took missiles at ten."

"How can you tell who's who?" Brogden's partner demanded, her voice suspicious. "They all look alike."

"Standard orbital formation." Armis tried not to sound like he was pointing out the obvious. "The *Excalibur*s are in close orbit, the *Overlord*s farther out. Look at the relative velocities."

"Spacer voodoo," Brogden murmured darkly, aware Armis heard the aside as clearly as his partner. "Just take his word for it."

"Attention Merchant Cadets," Master Roberton's voice cut across the babble on the general channel. "All exercises are cancelled. Return immediately to station. Stand by for emergency rescue procedures."

They'd been expecting this, or something like it, since Admiral Kerr had commandeered the *Robert Davion*. But expecting it and having it actually happen were two very different things.

"McKenna Station, the Shipyards, and the Merchant Marine Academy are neutral," Master Roberton's voice was firm. "Remember that. When the time comes, we're going to help all who need it, regardless of their—"

An expanding ball of flaming gas threw an assembly gantry into sudden silhouette.

"They're shooting at us!" someone shouted over the chorus of curses.

They weren't, Armis realized. At least not directly. The flare was the *Mule* he'd seen earlier, mortally wounded and trying desperately to not collide with the shipyard. Spewing fire and atmosphere, the ungainly spheroid, a jagged rip laying its cargo bay open to space, twisted upward, trying to clear the construction frame.

It almost made it, would have made it if the hull had been intact. The ragged edge of the hull breach snagged the topmost gantry, ripping the hundred-meter structure from its moorings.

Armis was the first to realize where it was going.

"Brogden! Allison!" he yelled, remembering the woman's name at last. "Jump to your sled! Fast burn, eight o'clock relative!"

He saw the two cadets slap their belt packs, jettisoning their safety lines, and leap clear of the water tank. Their shoulder jets flared, seeming pitifully feeble before the ponderous approach of the gantry, but fast enough. One made the sled, dropping into the control harness, but the other arced suddenly to the left, swinging wildly away from the utility craft.

"Release your safety line!"

"It's got my leg," Brogden snapped. "Get out of here, Ali! Go, go, go!"

He bent, trying to reach the line fouled around his leg as Allison obediently gunned the sled. Scooting up and away, she headed down orbit, above the trajectory of the massive ferrosteel frame.

In deceptively slow motion, the gantry slammed into the water cylinder. The heavy metal frame bent, but only slightly, imparting nearly all of its kinetic energy. Brogden's safety line popped like a whip, jerking the cadet savagely.

The cylinder began to tumble down orbit.

Armis wasted a heartbeat determining it would pass about a hundred meters behind his palette before he could move. He swung the harpoon around and, calculating the vectors almost by instinct, fired the adhesive line across the cylinder's path.

Stooping quickly, he levered the quick-release catches anchoring the harpoon to the palette, letting his magnetic boots and back absorb the torque. Once it was free, he straddled the harpoon's support post, the square base behind his thighs.

Judging he still had about a dozen seconds, he let out the suit's leg cinches and triggered the patching foam. For once his size worked in his favor and the frothing sealant filled the space around his legs. His extra half dozen centimeters of padding gelled just as the harpoon line snapped taut.

Whiplash nearly separated his skull from his spine. He was sure that without the foam padding his legs would have broken.

Fighting the impulse to climb along the line hand over hand, he activated the harpoon's winch. Climbing would have been faster, but there was no point in arriving five minutes earlier if he was too exhausted to be any good once he got there.

"Brogden," he called over the team channel. "Brog, you still with us?"

"Huh?" Brogden's voice.

Ahead, Armis could see the cadet's suit still swinging at the end of its safety line. Neither cadet had enough mass to affect the water cylinder's course appreciably.

His comm unit flashed for attention. Academy administration on his individual channel. He chinned to the secure frequency.

"Merchant Cadet Tolan."

"Disengage, Tolan," came the order he'd expected, but not the Old Man. The Academy's Commandant never sounded that hard and clipped. "Let the rescue sleds do their job."

"Rescue sleds are out of position, sir," Armis replied. "Besides, it's too late."

Actually, it wasn't, yet; not for him. He had another twenty, maybe thirty seconds before his point of no return. But Brogden, tethered to the mass of the water tank, didn't have a choice.

"Cadet Tolan, this is McKenna Station Control." No wonder Armis hadn't recognized the voice. "You are ordered to sever that line. Disengage."

"No can do, sir." Armis was proud of his level tone. "I'm all he's got."

"Cadet—"

"Sir," Armis cut the officer off, "Impact was from up orbit. He's retrograde. I figure atmosphere in twenty minutes."

For a moment the frequency was silent. Did they really think he hadn't realized the water cylinder and Brogden had been knocked from orbit by the impact?

"We make it twenty-two minutes," the watch officer said at last. His voice was gentler. "What do you intend to do?"

"I'm giving that some thought, sir," Armis replied.

"Understood," Station Control said. "Let us know how we can assist."

"Aye, aye."

His point of no return, the last moment when he could leap free and not be pulled down into the atmosphere by the plunging cylinder, came and went unremarked. The winch still reeled in the line, its vibration an irritating itch through the suit and impromptu padding.

Armis was still twenty meters from the cylinder when Brogden came fully conscious. He announced the event with a string of curses directed at the fates, safety lines, his left leg, and space in general.

"Leg broken?" Armis asked when the other began to run out of steam.

"Yes, it's broken. Yes, I filled the leg with patch to immobilize it. Yes, I triggered the yellow pain injector, not the blue one, so I am still conscious and able to function and very aware I really want to take the blue pain shot, too," Brogden dispensed with the standard first aid checklist in an angry rush. "Where the hell is rescue?"

"I'm it," Armis answered.

Firing his jets, he abandoned the harpoon and leaped for the axis of the cylinder's tumble, the safest boarding point. Matching vectors was tricky; he was almost too late in swinging his legs up to absorb the impact. He hit with a jolt and nearly bounced free before his boot magnets engaged. Not trusting their power, he stooped quickly and clipped his own line to a safety ring.

Through his boots he felt the ring of the harpoon's impact. No doubt it was smashed, its casing no match for the massive cylinder.

He located Brogden's safety line almost instantly, which didn't surprise him. The fact that the other cadet was spiraling almost lazily behind the cylinder instead of swinging wildly through space had told him the safety line was anchored near the center of the spin.

Planting his feet widely to absorb torque, he began hauling the line in.

"What are you doing?" Brogden demanded through gritted teeth. "That's my damn leg you're jerking around."

"Simplifying the dynamics," Armis answered, grunting with effort. For a moment, he envied the planet-born their massive musculature.

At last he had the larger man in hand. Armis wasted no time in lacing the safety line through two pairs of rings, passing it across Brogden's body several times as he bound him securely to the cylinder.

"I'm getting tired of asking you what you're doing."

"Keeping you from bouncing around," Armis replied.

"I was fine," Brogden said. "Where the hell is rescue?"

"I'm it," Armis repeated.

Brogden digested that as Armis worked his way toward the valve assembly. From their perspective, Kathil rose at the blunt end of the cylinder and arced above their heads at dizzying speed before setting beneath the flared shroud of the outlet nozzles.

"We're falling," Brogden pronounced at last.

"Right."

The cylinder was tumbling fast enough that there was a faint sensation of "down" pressing him against the titanium steel as Armis reached the base of the shroud. That was nothing compared to the vertigo induced by the wildly streaking stars and blur of Kathil swinging past. He kept his eyes firmly fixed on the cylinder beneath his feet.

"You've got a plan." It wasn't a question.

"Going to use a simple reaction drive," Armis said, wishing he could wipe away the sweat seeping past his headband.

"Ah."

The shroud was meant to shield the nozzles and valves until final connection. It was designed to open out in sections, like the petals of a flower, as the nozzles and valves it protected slid into a gasketed port in the work station's hull. There was no way to either jettison the shroud or open it; he was going to have to climb inside to reach the water tank's controls. His job was made a little easier by the rings of handholds meant to facilitate muscling the massive cylinder through the last millimeters of connection.

Armis leaned forward, stretching himself along the grey metal, and gripped one of these tightly. "Unclip my safety line, will you?"

"You anchored?"

Safety protocols even now. Especially now.

"Yes."

"Line is free."

The electric motor at his waist retracted the line with maddening slowness as Armis counted his heartbeats. He figured he had six minutes in which to either succeed or fail. He knew the station gave him a bit more, but he trusted his instincts more than their calculations.

"How are you going to stop the tumble?" Brogden asked.

"Can't," Armis said simply. Catching the end of his safety line, he reached above his head, clipping it to the handhold.

"Loquacious," Brogden said. "Anyone ever tell you you're loquacious? You just talk too damn much."

Armis grinned. "Good to have you back in gear," he said. "You understand the plan?"

"You're going inside the nozzle shroud," Brogden answered. "You're going to manually vent water—we've got what, six thousand liters under pressure here? —and hope it's got enough thrust to push us back in orbit."

"We'd need three of these tanks to make orbit," Armis corrected. "I'm going for one bounce to buy us enough time for rescue to get here."

"One problem."

"One?"

"If the cylinder's tumbling and you're inside the shroud working the valves," Brogden said, "You won't know when we're pointed the right way. How will you know when to open and shut the valves?"

"That's why I brought you along," Armis explained. "Time our rotation. Shout 'open' and 'close' at the right times. Physics will do the rest."

"Wait, wait, wait," Brogden objected. "That's seat-of-the-pants astrogation. You're way better at that than I am. You sit out here and I'll work the valves."

"Even if both legs worked," Armis countered, "You wouldn't fit inside the shroud assembly."

He waited a moment, but Brogden had no answer for that.

Gripping the handhold tightly with both hands, Armis chinned his boot magnets off. The angular acceleration of tumbling cylinder immediately swung his body around. He barely suppressed a gasp of pain as his body snapped taut, his feet swinging against the wildly spinning sky.

"Hang in there, Half Pint," Brogden's voice was soft in his ear, as though the big man didn't want to startle him into losing his grip.

Armis grunted an acknowledgement.

One hand at a time, he reversed his grip on the handhold, twisting his body so he was facing the open maw of the shroud assembly. Pulling his knees toward his chest, he folded himself against the centrifugal force of the spin. It took far too long to get his feet inside the shroud, too long for them to kick against something metal and their magnets take hold.

For a moment Armis hung, his hands gripping the handhold outside the shroud, his boots anchored to some part of the plumbing mechanism within while angular acceleration tried to throw him into space, and caught his breath. Releasing one hand, he found purchase on the inner lip of the shroud assembly. There was a raised ring, part of the seal, a ledge about four centimeters wide he could push against.

Shifting his magnetic boots blindly from metal surface to metal surface, he pushed himself down until he could grip the end of the nozzle with one hand. Releasing the lip of the shroud, he began pulling himself further in.

Finally his back was against the cylinder itself, his legs astride the emerging pipes. The valve controls were almost directly in front of him, while the nozzles themselves were above—although it felt like below—his head.

Pulling a loop of slack in his safety line, still belayed to the handhold outside the shroud, he lashed himself firmly in place.

"In position," he reported.

"Great," Brogden's voice seemed faint. Armis hoped that was an effect of the shroud blocking transmission and not the man's succumbing to his injuries. "Open in nine."

"Ready."

There were four pipes and four valves, though Armis wasn't sure if that indicated four separate compartments inside the tank. He could reach three: one just to his left, the second directly in front of him, and a third a long stretch to his right. He knew the fourth was out of reach on the other side of the bundle of pipes.

Until he knew how long he had between vents...

"Now!" Brogden's shout interrupted his thoughts.

Armis grabbed the two valves closest to hand and yanked them open. Fortunately, they were simple open/close levers, not wheels, and full flow was immediate.

Now acceleration was added to the centrifugal force of the cylinder's tumble. Blood rushed to Armis' head as his suit creaked, straining against the lashings. A chill ache penetrated his suit and spread through his thighs as the decompressing water rushed through.

"Close! Close! Close!" Brogden's frantic shout came faintly. *Definitely the shroud muffling the signal,* thought Armis as he snapped the levers shut. The other cadet was clearly fully conscious.

Armis shifted his left hand from the first valve to the one directly in front of him and stretched his other to the valve at the far right. In case there were four compartments, he wanted to get the maximum thrust from each flow.

By the third revolution, Armis had the pattern. Every thirty-seven seconds he'd open the vents for six seconds.

The ventings—Armis thought of them as "burns"—seemed a little long to him, but he wasn't in a position to see what was happening. There was no choice but to trust Brogden.

After the fourth vent, Armis loosened the line holding him to the pipes. Keeping his grip through the fifth was difficult, pain shot through his lower back and already aching legs as the thrust tried to push him upward. The fact that he could hold on confirmed his suspicion that the force of the ventings had diminished.

As soon as the fifth vent ended, Armis scrambled awkwardly around the pipes in the confined space until the valve that had been out of reach was in front of him. The valve that had been to his left, the one he had only used once, was now under his right hand.

With no time to lash himself in, he jammed his right leg as far into a gap between the cylinder and the valve assembly as he could, twisting his foot sideways until it was wedged firmly. He hoped that would anchor him if he lost his grip.

He rejected triggering the painkiller against the inevitable broken leg. He needed to keep his mind clear.

"Now!"

Armis opened the valves. His grip slipped against the thrust, definitely much stronger than the last. He felt his right knee *pop* as it torqued violently. But his leg held, even as the wave of pain and nausea threatened to knock him out. He was still in position, still conscious, when Brogden shouted the order to close.

Cursing his earlier machismo, Armis quickly chinned the yellow injector. There was a sharp chill as the dispenser blasted microscopic crystals of medicine through the soft flesh over his jugular vein. A wave of giddiness passed through him as the powerful analgesic took effect.

As he lashed his good leg to a pipe stanchion, he realized the deadline had passed. They should have been burned to ash by now. Had they generated enough thrust to bounce off the atmosphere? Or had they only delayed the inevitable by a few moments?

Almost in answer to his question, the shroud behind him seemed to throb heat. *Intermittent friction,* he realized, *as the water cylinder tumbled through the outer fringes of the atmosphere.* When—if—they dug in a little deeper, the leisurely rotation would snap the other way with the force of an inertia ram. He'd be crushed to paste before he felt anything. Right now all he felt was heat, though there must be a lot of it if he could feel it through his back pack and shoulder jets.

His shoulder jets.

In a panic, he vented the jet pack's fuel reserves. There was no place for the mist of microscopic droplets to go inside the shroud, of course, but there was little danger of the loose liquid igniting. His suit would protect him against a burning cloud of unconfined fuel in any case. A fuel tank explosion would have cut him in half.

"Now!"

The icy cold of the venting water coursing between his legs contrasted sharply with the sweltering heat building up inside his suit. What was Brogden feeling, tied to the outside of the cylinder, unshielded by the shroud?

"Close!"

"You okay out there?" Armis tried to keep his tone light.

"A little lemon with a bit of butter," Brogden answered, his voice scratchy with static, "And I should be perfect. Somebody better flip me over before I burn on this side, though."

"Be sure to vent your fuel," Armis advised. "And fill as much of your suit as you can with patch to help insulate."

"Took the same safety classes you did, Half Pint," Brogden somehow managed a chuckle. "How's it look in there?"

"We're good," Armis assured him, as though he could see the gauges well above his head.

"Get ready," Brogden warned. "Now!"

Armis opened the valves, counting to seven before he shut them again. It was only after the rushing stopped that he realized Brogden had not given the close order.

"Brogden?" he asked. "You still with me?"

Static. Static and maybe a groan.

"Brogden!" Armis shouted, knowing his voice would be a scratchy whisper in the other's ear. If the other was in any condition to hear.

Armis hadn't been counting the seconds since the last burn ended. Without Brogden, he had no way of knowing when to open the valves again. He waited, straining to hear any sound from the other cadet.

Now? he wondered, trying to count back the seconds in his head. *Now?* His hand twitched on the valve control, but he fought the urge to throw them open. A vent at the wrong time could undo all work they'd done.

It had been too long. He knew it had been too long. He'd missed the moment to vent; he must have. He knew there was no way to way to see outside and trigger the valves at the same time, but he tried to think of one anyway.

Anything was better than sitting blindly in the dark waiting to die.

A cough on the radio, a gasp and then: "Now!"

Armis' hands already gripping the controls, twisted in a painful spasm, throwing the valves open.

"Close!" Brogden croaked.

"Good to have you back," Armis said.

"Yeah," Brogden answered tersely. "Hang on."

"What?"

"Hang—"

Armis was slammed back against the shroud, his ears ringing from the helmet's impact. Then he was slapped forward, his faceplate hitting the pipes so hard he forgot everything else in a frantic check for microfractures.

His radio light flashed for attention. One of the commercial frequencies, he realized.

"Brogden, I'm switching to channel L-four," he broadcast, and waited a moment for the other to answer. Silence.

With a sigh, he chinned the frequency selector. "Merchant Cadet Armis Tolan here," he reported crisply, or as crisply as he could.

"You the monkey on the valves?" asked an unfamiliar voice.

"Aye."

"Lay off. This is the *Castle Hayne*, we've got a grapple line on you."

Armis didn't recognize the name, but only a DropShip would have the mass to capture a tumbling water cylinder. Even one that was mostly empty.

"How's my partner?"

"We'll know in a minute."

There was another jerk; a second and perhaps a third grapple, Armis guessed. And faint clangs through the metal pipes; people landing on the cylinder?

There was a slight pause.

"His suit integrity's good, he's got pressure," said a voice. A female voice Armis thought he recognized. "His faceplate's fogging."

Armis nodded in the dark as he listened to them secure the injured cadet for transport to the DropShip. An inflated suit and evidence of breathing; anything beyond that was detail. Brogden was going to make it.

"Avast, Tolan!"

"Ahoy," Armis corrected Jenkins—for it could only be Jenkins—but not loudly enough for his mic to pick up.

"Stay clear of the shroud," Jenkins continued. "We're going to blow the bolts."

Not questioning how he was supposed to stay clear of the titanium steel plates which surrounded him, Armis hugged the pipes before him tightly.

"Clear!"

There was a pause, perhaps a dozen heartbeats, then the yellow flare of explosive bolts and the sky opened up around him. His vented fuel flashed, a pale blue nimbus that dissipated almost instantly. Then there was only space, *home*, black with cold and distant stars.

Twisting sideways, Armis tilted his head back, trying to see the DropShip that had rescued them. The *Castle Hayne* was the wounded *Mule* that had hit the gantry, which made sense now that he had time to think about it. It had been the only ship in position, already moving in their general direction. Of course it had scooped up the scattered cadets and come after the cylinder.

Suddenly the other cadets were around him. Alison caught his shoulders, bracing him, while Jenkins bent to work on his trapped and broken leg. He had never noticed the sword-and-sunburst patch on Jenkin's shoulder before. There were others, but he could not see their name patches nor their faces through the polarized ferroglass of their helmets.

Beyond them, the golden crescent of Kathil cut across the sky as the cylinder swung on its tether, blotting out the stars.

Armis pulled his mouth into a hard line.

He *never* wanted to be this near a planet again.

ECHOES IN THE VOID

RANDALL N. BILLS

**QUETZALCOATL SCOUT-CLASS JUMPSHIP VOIDJUMPER III
TRIANGULATION:
24.631 LY FROM MANOTICK
15.662 LY FROM GIBRALTAR
9.739 LY FROM SILVER
ABBEY DISTRICT, FREE WORLDS LEAGUE
6 JULY 3066**

"Just cannot be right. You go on an' check it again." The deceptively soft voice breathed across his neck, reeking of Tamarind dorith-jerky.

Colt wondered if Cap might be going senile. Serve him right; Colt couldn't stand the smell of the acerbic jerky, much less the way it made Cap sweat vile from every pore. (Colt never did figure out how the stuff could survive the air scrubbing so well.)

Then again, Colt just couldn't stand Cap, jerky or no.

He turned and did as ordered. After all, whether plying the waters of ancient Terra or the black voids of space, a ship captain was god incarnate. And on the *Voidjumper III*, that couldn't be more true.

No way would Colt Stevens be "accidentally" walkin' out an airlock!

He tapped on the pilot's console for almost five more minutes, the sounds echoing through the small confines of the JumpShip bridge. He turned to Cap, subservient look painted large.

"Captain, just not here," he said.

Could've been a funeral service for the sounds coming from the rest of the crew on the bridge. In his peripheral, he could see James and Teddy upside down above him in the microgravity, hunching until they practically kissed their monitors, while Jiptom and Santora, to his left and right, pretended as though they saw something more than endless blackness.

In the center of the bridge, Cap sat—a bloated spider jerking the strands of his web to keep his prey leery and scrambling for survival. The Lyran merchant fleet uniform he wore could've come out of the Second Succession War. The fabric was soiled, half-heartedly mended, and coming apart at the seams. His numerous jowls, filled with dirt, sweat, and who knew what else, were in sharp contrast to his almost boyish curly brown hair and pudgy hands—the right grasping a hunk of jerky like an oxygen mask during decompression. On top of it all, cunning eyes lurked, dark and beady, emotionless, dead.

Colt swallowed. Tried to imagine a cool breeze moving through the stale, regurgitated air of the star ship. "You been lied to."

Not a flicker on the Cap's face. Colt stiffened his resolve. This had to be it. The opportunity he'd been looking for. The Cap had screwed up too bad this time. Time to walk (no, roll!) the bastard out an airlock.

Colt licked his lips. He'd won a poker hand to get on this ship, and a silent tip to local authorities two years back had dumped the previous pilot into a rat's hole and him into this seat. One more bid...he could do this, right?

"Captain, there's no long-lost ship here."

"I tell ya, you had to see your face." Jiptom busted up laughing for what seemed like the tenth time.

Colt tried to ignore the moron, glanced at the controls of the long-range shuttle craft that entombed them. He trimmed the thrust and began another long-range scan of near space. The usual, comforting sight of myriad stars in the void, distant scintillating pinpricks awash in the blackness, did nothing for him now. He tried not to think about the absence of a burning ball of gas taking up a good portion of near space.

"Ya thought you gonna get hot n' heavy with an airlock. Right? I tell ya, I did. So did the rest." The guffaws filled the small cabin to bursting.

Glancing around at the cramped cockpit, feeling his flesh pushing against his bones, he couldn't stand it any longer. Colt flexed his ass and tried to push feeling back into flesh smashed into the tight-fitting shuttle cockpit for too many hours.

"I'll tell you, Jiptom! You keep flapping and you'll be the one shagging with the airlock...and you can bet *I'll* like the peepshow!"

The small, wiry man turned off his laughs and smiles like a c-bill run out on a trideo game. The too big eyes in the sallow face looked like a kicked puppy.

Damn, is he gonna cry?

"Look, Jiptom, sorry, man. You know how I get around Cap." He glanced down at the small device he clipped (hidden from Jiptom's view) to the under-edge of his pilot's seat. The warm green glow said no electronic listening devices were in play. Never could tell with Cap; he shivered at the idea he'd been sold a faulty device. 'Course, he'd have been cold and dead long before if that were true.

He glanced back to his left. Realized Pup-man would be under his command soon. *Have to keep the masses content, not just scared, Cap! Doesn't take much to content us. Couldn't even do that!*

"Jiptom. Okay, yeah. Thought Cap might be taking me for the long walk. Just uptight. You know I hate gravity."

The smile burst on his face like a zit; a relief, but not pretty. "No problem. I tell ya. No problem." He waved his hands almost frantically, and Colt could almost see his tongue wagging. Pup-man indeed.

"Hey, ya stood up to him. Told him what we all thought. I tell ya, ballsy. You know it straight. Take us to danger, no sweat, but make it pay off. We treasure hunters, right?" The mad laughter again. "Always gotta make a haul pay off. Or the cold-kiss for you. Yeah, ballssyy."

Colt rubbed his ear, slapped Jiptom on the shoulder companionably. The return smile and bobbing head looked more puppy-like than ever. A sickly itch crawled through his head at such subservience; tried to ignore what had just occurred on the bridge of the *Voidjumper* with Cap.

But never forget men like him were useful.

He glanced back at the console and tried to ignore his current situation. Closed his eyes momentarily. Tried to imagine the bulk of the *Voidjumper* around him, not this twenty-meter long delta-shaped craft of death; tried to feel the luscious lack of gravity, the floating sensation he'd signed on quick as you like with a passing JumpShip to always enjoy; to feel the climax of sex in zero-g (when Santora would give it up, bitch!): couldn't do it. Cap stuck him in this long-range shuttlecraft hunting down his nonexistent ship cause he'd spoken out. Never mind a half dozen other long-range craft from the *Voidjumper* were swimming the darkness, hunting for a hint of metal in the great void. He was a pilot, and Cap had to show him a lesson! Nothing he could do about it.

Yet.

The hours crawled by. Pup-man tried several times for conversation, but Colt didn't want it. Not only did he hate gravity, he had a case of claustrophobia. He knew grounders might laugh at him, considering he'd lived most of his life on a JumpShip. He didn't care. He knew the difference between a JumpShip and this pop-can, and right now he had one mother of a headache coming on like a Canopian whore looking to score.

"What's that?" Pup-man said.

"Uh?" He'd almost dozed, trying to escape hell.

"Something on the radar. I tell ya. Saw something." Dirty, almost scabrous fingers twitched above the radar screen. The slightest hitch showed for an instant, could've been a smudge on the screen.

Colt didn't think so. He leaned forward, stretched, craned his neck until it popped loudly, and concentrated. He finally patted the man on the shoulder again; adoration eyes. *Pup-man may be stupid, but he's got a good pair of eyes in that thick skull.*

Re-triangulating the scanners to focus on that particular quadrant, Colt's hands moved smoothly to the controls. Cutting off his main thrust, he used the latitude thrusters to nudge the tail end of the craft up off its current axis. He rotated almost ninety degrees horizontal and forty-five degrees perpendicular to the plane of current movement, overcompensating for the bleed off of inertia needed in their present direction. Grimacing, he fired a strong burst, pulling the craft out of its heading and shooting it in a round-house arc towards the new destination.

A small smile touched Colt's lips. He was still a damn fine pilot! Light-years better than Cap had ever been before he'd seized control of the *Voidjumper.*

'Course, Cap's information had been right—he gave that up grudgingly. Still didn't know if the money he paid for these coordinates would be worth it.

Another long hour passed; the blip grew larger. They pulled out past a quarter-million kilometers from the *Voidjumper.* Normally, such a distance from his womb would've spiked his headache, but the excitement grew. Not having the ship here would've been better. But having the ship here, and so far outside of detection range he actually might board it first and sack it before turning the info over to Cap? Yeah. Could work all by itself.

The hours passed, and the long-range shuttle closed to within a kilometer. The radar images simply hadn't made any sense, so they'd closed, decelerating across the torturous three hours, sore backs and sleeping muscles making nerves taunt and tempers fray.

Colt had been around the block once or twice, seen just about every type of JumpShip out there, even that funky *Hunter* they'd run into up Falcon way.

But this...

"Uh, that not right, Colt. I tell ya. What we looking at?" For some reason the man reeked of fear. Out of the corner of his eye, Colt could see the whites of Pup-man's eyes almost engulf his pupils.

The actinic glare of the forward bank of lights bathed a small portion of the...thing. He supposed it had to be a ship. But more like a mega-DropShip, or perhaps even a weird WarShip. His pulse quickened. A WarShip! What he couldn't do with...the idea died before fully forming. No weapon ports he could see. The armor configuration all wrong—too spindly.

No, whatever it was, it was no WarShip.

He massaged the controls and inched the shuttlecraft closer, turning it at an angle and slowly moving back along the ship.

The front of the vessel had the bulbous, cylindrical look common to most JumpShips, Though two large bay doors up front ruined a perfect fit, Colt still found it recognizable enough. The rest of the ship simply looked like nothing he'd ever seen. No long, smooth tapering lines. In place of what he expected to find, five mammoth cubes marched in a line, each slightly larger than the last; a massive cylinder ran from the front (what he assumed was the bridge), skewering the blocks, holding them in a straight line.

Colt punched in a quick code and the bank of lights swiveled slowly back and forth, revealing nothing but metal. No port holes, no bay doors, nothing. Even queerer, no docking collars. Just metal. He suddenly looked again, punched up the magnification.

Pitted. Cracked. Scoured. Almost crumbling away, as though ravaged by some horrible, metal-devouring virus.

"The metal..." he began. Stopped. Licked his lips with what felt like a scrub brush. Started again. "Jiptom, the metal."

The Pup-man looked at him, looked at the screen and back again.

He's got good eyes, but not much behind them. "Look at how pitted it is. How weathered."

Like a child, understanding slowly seeped in. Pup-man whistled. "Damn. I tell ya. Damn. That some old metal."

"Yeah. *Voidjumper*'s what? Three hundred years old?"

"I guess."

"Just about three hundred, Jiptom, and she looks like she just had a bottle smashed on her prow compared to this thing," he finished, pursing his lips in the direction of the ship.

As the light crept onto the final cube—Colt shook his head at the sheer size of the monster—some things immediately began to make more sense. His queasiness did a flip-flop as 'Mech-sized butterflies started dancing a jig.

"There's no jump sail array," Jiptom whispered in a hoarse voice.

Colt slowly swiveled his head towards Pup-man—perhaps not so dumb after all—swiveled back at what could not be.

The final cube was fully twice the size of the first, with three mammoth nozzles jutting out the end—interplanetary drives—something that only existed on a WarShip. Yet he'd bet his next haul's portion it wasn't.

Twin gaping wounds hove into view—told of death for this beast—mammoth holes that covered most of one section of the cube. His uneasiness expanded as it dawned on him the jagged sides peeled out, not in: internal explosion.

Course, all this he might swallow. After all, they were treasure hunters, pirates to some. He'd seen about everything you could lay your eyeballs on. But his JumpShip pilot mind couldn't tackle this one. Jiptom's words vibrated in his skull.

No jump sail array.

Not having a jump sail, he could buy that. The ship had been here a long time and if it sustained that jab in the can, the sail likely tore away. But not to have a jump sail array in the first place...

What the hell kind of JumpShip didn't have a jump sail?

He rubbed his temples as the headache continued its spike, eased back into his seat and tried to think. What were they looking at?

Did he still have his weapon to unseat Cap, or had this just grown beyond him?

If the shuttle created a sense of claustrophobia, the spacesuit defined the reality of it in hard edges; spikes that sank painfully into Colt's ability to concentrate. It didn't help matters in the slightest when the head-mounted lamps actually managed to make it *more* difficult to see anything. They'd both switched the lamps off for a moment, to see if that would help. The horror that engulfed them had them snapping their lamps back on before three terrible intakes of breath passed.

It started bad, and only got worse. Much worse.

"Man, Colt, we got to go back. I tell ya. Back. Got to go back." Even through the electronically reproduced sound, Pup-man's terror could be felt. If Colt ever had a nightmare as a boy about entering the belly of some unimaginably large beast, he lived it now. This second.

Damn Cap for making me do this. Making me have to overthrow him. Bastard.

"Pu—" he began, then cut himself off. "Jiptom, no sweat here, right?" he started again, rattled he'd almost let slip what he thought of the whiner. "You can make it happen. Bring it home. Think of the prize. Got to be something here to rock your world."

Jiptom's helmet stopped swiveling in fear and turned toward him. Nodded after a moment. "Okay. You bossman. The prize worth this danger?"

"'Course it is." *Damn well better be.*

After anchoring the ship to the outer bulkhead, the two of them had entered through the holes torn into the aft of the vessel, . EVAs usually didn't bother a shipper. However, when the stars looked like pinpricks in the blackness, and you realized how many light years away from a star and supposed safety you were...not many could survive that. Colt always laughed at such comments. After all, get a leak in your suit, lose your safety line or run out of fuel, and it didn't matter if you were hugging an atmosphere or plugging in the void, dead was dead.

This time around, however, for once, the pressure built, until he couldn't ignore it. Couldn't ignore this strange ship; couldn't ignore how far out of normal traffic lanes they were, with no safety net of a standard solar system; couldn't ignore trying to instigate a mutiny. Along with the claustrophobia, it almost made it more than he could bear.

Cap.

Only that word kept it all at bay. Allowed him to crawl over twisted, metal teeth and down into the beast's gullet. Course, having someone to browbeat helped.

Now, almost an hour later, after dropping some two dozen blinkers to light an escape route, the corridor simply seemed to go on forever. Three more hours, and they'd have to head back. No air.

They trudged on, time stuck between ticks, interminable. Finally, they came to a new hatch. New type, different metal. Colt could tell immediately a new section of the ship would begin here. The last block to the next? They already passed that point? He simply couldn't tell.

"We goin' in there, bossman?"

Colt could get used to that word. "Yup. Need to get to the front of the ship. Or captain's quarters. Something to tell us what the hell this ship is."

"Yeah. I tell ya, cap's quarter. Most ships have 'em in the same spot, right bossman."

"Except this isn't most ships." He didn't mean to bring back the unease they both felt.

"Let's do this," Colt barked. Grasping the wheel, he wedged his feet into the corner and threw his muscles into action. For several long seconds, nothing happened.

"Little help."

"Oh, course. Sorry man." Pup-man got on the other side, wedged his own feet and both poured it on.

Once again, nothing for several long seconds. Then, with a screech that brought to mind ghouls and banshees in forgotten graves, the wheel cut loose and slowly began to turn. Forcing it the entire distance, it finally un-dogged; another giant chore getting the hatch open as well.

Panting with the exertion, Colt stepped through and played his wrist-mounted lamp around. "What the—"

They stood on a catwalk—one of several dozen marching horizontally up the bulkhead—which ran around an immense chamber, might well fill this entire cube section. Though the high-powered light couldn't penetrate the dimness more than halfway, he could just make out the massive, cylindrical structure that pierced the center of the cube, passing into it and out of it; the Kearny-Fuchida drive?

Damn, damn big drive, though. What the hell? Has to be three times the diameter of the Voidjumper's.

Around the jump drive, a mammoth latticework rose, around which hundreds of colossal tank-type structures hung, like grapes on a vine. If they'd been on a catwalk above or below, there would've been no seeing the center, would've been blocked by the tanks which marched along the lattice work, all the way to the bulkheads, in every direction.

"I tell ya. That is one hell of a lot of fuel tanks. Why they need so much fuel?"

Colt jolted. Anger blossomed. How could he miss it? *'Course,* he consoled himself, *this room held a thousand times or more as much fuel as our own ship.* Had to be hydrogen fuel. For the destroyed reactors they'd seen in the engine cube?

An idea began to form.

Couldn't be. No way.

He turned to look at Pup-man. Slowly patted the man on his overly-padded shoulders. "Good call on the fuel. Didn't see it." Unlike Cap, he could admit a mistake when it didn't cost a thing, and further tied Pup-man to him. He smiled. Laughed out loud.

"Thanks bossman. Just called it like I saw it, I tell ya."

"Sure did. But I got a feeling coming on. Coming on strong. If this is what I think it might be, well, we just might make all the money in the world...by not touching a stinking thing."

"Uh?" Those confused puppy-eyes were back.

"I'll explain. Come on."

"I tell ya, bossman. Don't matter what this is. Cap ain't gonna let you leave it alone. He gonna sack it, no matter what."

"I got that covered. Money comes in all forms, Jiptom. And you don't always have to steal it to get it."

"I tell ya, bossman. Don't get it."

Colt wondered if the man might be a closet savant, or something. Showed brilliance now and then, but most of the time Pup-man seemed to run around with faulty sensors.

Standing outside the cap's quarters—stupid Pup-man couldn't bring himself to enter it—he smiled triumphantly. Held up the captain's log and tapped it, very carefully, against his gloved hand; never knew if it might just fall apart. And he needed it. Needed it to convince the rest of the crew.

The talisman to force ol' fat man out the airlock. And walk away rich as well.

"Think Jiptom. No jump-sail array. How can you be jumping without a sail?"

"I tell ya, ya can't."

"No?"

"No."

"What about charging with the reactor?"

Pup-man clumsily bumped his hand into his helmet, as though he'd tried to run his dirty hands back through greasy hair. "Well, sure, you can do that. But you run out of fuel awful fast if ya keep it going too long."

"Exactly. But the fuel. You saw it first."

"Fuel?"

"The fuel, Jiptom. A thousand times what our ship's got. Ten thousand. Wouldn't run out of fuel too quick, toting around that much."

In the strange lighting of his head-lamp, Colt saw the beginnings of understanding flicker on pup-man's face.

"Still, gotta have a jump sail," Jiptom insisted.

"Why?"

"Cause, a JumpShip has a jump sail. I tell ya. A JumpShip has a jump sail." He repeated, like a nursery rhyme.

"Only because it is the best way to do it, right?" Colt led him.

"Ya. Right."

"But what if the ship didn't have access to a jump sail?"

"Uh. Bossman, you confusin' me. What House or Clan don't have access to that when they build a ship like this? Big ship. Lots of tech here, though old-looking. Ship even gots itself a whole cube for people to live in." He looked up, happy-puppy eyes. "Remember the mummies. Want to take me one of those."

Sick bastard. "Jiptom, stop thinking about the mummies. I told you, leave it alone. Worth more if we don't touch it at all. I'm only taking the captain's log to convince the crew of what we got here." He may have come to trust Pup-man a little, but no way was he spilling about pushing Cap out the airlock.

A beeper went off; both men almost jumped into the air, only kept to the ground by their boots. Colt glanced at his wrist-comp. Couldn't believe so much time had slipped by.

"Gotta go, Jiptom. Oxygen burning away."

"Yea, thinking smelled too stale. I tell ya, too stale."

As they began the long trek back, Colt tried once more to make Jiptom understand what they'd found. Make him understand what it could do for them.

For him.

"WHAT!?"

Colt hated Cap, but he couldn't help be impressed with how much power the fat man could push into a single word. 'Course, he had a lot of mass to push with.

He'd had almost a full day to think about what he would do on the way back to the *Voidjumper*, including tearing out a portion of the console to erase their flight telemetry. And a good thing too, since Cap ordered him straight to the bridge. You could only delay something like that so long, but Colt felt he'd had enough time. Not all the crew knew, but enough. Key people. The smart ones. He'd laid the groundwork for months, cinching it with the log. Now it was time to simply face the Cap down. Move him down and out and dead.

"I said we're not going to touch the ship."

Cap didn't move a muscle, didn't say a word. But Colt suddenly felt as though the man grew several sizes larger. Something about the set of his face. Those dead eyes. For a moment, he almost wavered. Almost lost it.

Bossman.

The word echoed up. From Pup-man, of all people. Might as well have come from a dog...but the trust he'd earned. That was something. Meant something. For the long years Cap had ruled the *Voidjumper* with his fat, iron hands, not a soul on board trusted him. Yet in one outing, Colt had done more than Cap had managed in long years.

Colt smiled and this time, let it slide onto his face, a snake out of the grass, ready to strike.

The silence took on physicality, and seconds drifted into minutes. Something shifted in Cap's eyes. Colt couldn't tell, but something. For once, a crewman stood up to him. Fear only worked for so long, and Colt held the key. A dead ship, centuries old. And he wouldn't touch it. The smile grew into a grin, transformed his face.

For a first, Cap broke the silence. "You sure you be wanting to do this, pilot?"

Colt's smile turned predatory. *Never use my name, just like I never use yours? This crew'll damn sure know my name. Say it with respect!*

"You're through, Cap. Every dog has his day, and yours, fat man, is over."

A feeling he'd never experienced before surged. To face the man down, to unleash his pent-up anger and frustration. It felt better than any food, any experience, any sex he'd ever had. It tasted like...

Victory.

Quicker than he thought possible, Cap surged forward, his bulk actually undulating back in the micro-gravity as he tried to grab Colt. It almost ended right there. The crew might have believed him, but you had to face down your own trouble before they would step in. He didn't mind such an attitude. He'd had it himself, and still had it. Face the man down, but know the crew would back the move when needed.

Colt flexed his knees, pushed up hard. He came free of the deck and drew himself up into a cannonball as Cap practically flew through the space he previously occupied. His vile stench wafted after him. Did the man ever bathe? Ever!

Stretching out perpendicular to the approaching ceiling, he landed with hands stretched out behind him and legs bent back. Pushed off and shot toward the Cap's chair. Grabbed the edge as he neared. Expertly realigned himself and sank into its soft embrace. Santora couldn't match this feeling, this warmth, no matter how long she tried.

Cap hadn't fared so well. Fat and not nearly so agile, he'd tumbled into the jump computing console, his bulk almost enveloping the precious machine, before rebounding slowly. The man happened to snag the edge of the machine at the last second, bleeding off excess velocity, but he wasn't going anywhere.

Colt tapped the intercom. "Security, this is Colt, the captain. To the bridge at once." He made sure to keep the comm on.

The words were like climax. A quick tumble, and then the finale. At this point, watching the Cap take the long walk would be anticlimactic.

'Course, he couldn't help but rub it in. He had the right. Right? Colt used both hands to press himself into the seat, wiggled his back to readjust the dimples and folds to his own body, stretched like a cat settling in for the long haul.

"You see, fat man, you got to see other possibilities. Treasure hunting comes in many forms, and you don't always need to rape something to make money off it."

Those beady eyes stared back at him (they'd lost their power now!), but the man had enough guts to not say a thing. Not to babble. *He'd sent enough of us on the walk, he better not show any wobbling knees or red eyes now.*

Colt gave him a single nod for that—least he could do. Stretched his neck, continued.

"You see, we actually get to obey the law and make more money than we've taken in the last three years. See, what we got here is an archeological find. Yeah, say it with me, cause I'm sure you can't: archeological. That ship you heard rumors about. That ship no one seemed to be able to find? Well, it's not just an old JumpShip. It's ancient. One of the first. You probably never opened a damn history book, but I have. You see, according to the captain's log, that ship out there..." He paused for dramatic effect. "That ship is the *Liberator*, lost for almost a thousand years. Can't remember the date off the top of my head, but some time in the twenty-second century went missing. Twenty-second century!"

He looked around at the rest of the crew and saw some understanding. Many blank faces. Didn't matter. They'd all know soon enough. And he'd walk away with the ship, stronger loyalty from the crew than Cap could ever dream of, and the biggest haul they'd likely ever get.

He glanced back at the Cap, but couldn't tell whether he understood or not. Still that wall of flesh. No problem. He'd hammer it in.

"Fat man, we put that ship up to auction and every House in the Inner Sphere will be frothing at the mouth to buy it. Heck, even rich nobles and mega-biz will get in on the action." He barked a laugh. "Hey, might even get to meet ol' Rhonda Snord, 'cause you know how hot-to-trot the Irregulars are about shit like this. Hear she's hot too, even if she's over the hill." Several chuckles rumbled and he knew the job was done.

Just then, security moved onto the bridge. With a gesture he'd practiced in his dreams for too long, he waved toward the fat man. "Take him."

There were no brigs on this ship.

Before the man had even been taken off the bridge, Colt forgot him. Turned his attention to the task of organizing his crew. Got to maximize the information taken from the *Liberator* without bothering it; too much contact would drop the premium price.

For a moment, he cocked his head, as though listening for laughter in the void. A pirate actually doing legitimate work? Could those mummies have a clue what would become of them? Did they know after a thousand years since their death in the cold black, he'd make a pile of cash so rich bastards could snap holophotos of their sandpaper faces?

Colt shook his head and laughed at his own thoughts. Philosophy from him?

Why not? He was now the Cap, after all.

THE LONGEST ROAD

THE UNTOLD STORY OF
ARCHER CHRISTIFORI AND ARCHER'S AVENGERS

BLAINE LEE PARDOE

OVERLORD-CLASS DROPSHIP *COLONEL CROCKETT*
NEW AVALON
CRUCIS MARCH
FEDERATED SUNS
29 DECEMBER 3066

The *Crockett* quaked slightly as it punched through a pocket of clear air turbulence. For a moment, everyone's heart skipped a beat. If it wasn't turbulence, it could be an attack.

Captain Fuller, an old friend from years past, cast General Archer Christifori an unshaken nod. Archer remembered when Fuller used to react to every bump the ship took. That was before the war, before he became a seasoned veteran.

The heavy, almost sweaty air seemed to get more stagnant as everyone else wondered if they had been fired upon. Archer didn't worry. If Fuller wasn't worried, then he wasn't. This was not a normal landing. This was the big one, the big show, the one they'd all been waiting for. This was New Avalon. This was the end of a tyrant.

We aren't going to be shot down, not after all we've been through. God wouldn't let that happen. That's why we're here, now...for the end.

"We've got final clearance," came the voice of the comm officer.

"Penny for your thoughts?" Colonel Chaffee asked from his side. Archer turned to her quickly, absent-mindedly. He had forgotten she was there. He'd been so focused on their approach, he hadn't paid much attention to his surroundings. When he saw her face, he wanted to kick himself. Only an idiot would forget someone like her.

"Me?" he replied coyly. "Just about a hundred or so thoughts. How secure is the LZ? What about our decoy force on Graceland—how are they doing? What is the current status of operations on New Avalon? Are we too late? If so, is that bad? What if her side has the upper hand? How's that for starters?"

"I guess shouldn't be surprised that you had a few things on your mind," she said, smiling in rebuttal. "Par for the course."

He wanted to say more. A wave of emotion came over him, washed with memories of the last few years of his life. It had begun on Thorin. His sister Andrea had been killed by an operative of Katherine Steiner-Davion, who in turn pardoned the killer. The fighting on Thorin had been his entry into the Civil War on the side of Prince Victor. Thorin had been home. He had done his duty for the military in fighting the Clan invasion, and hoped to retire to the family business. He had become a businessman. The war had torn him away from all of that. Circumstances had forced him to take on the mantle of a warrior again.

There had been months of fighting on a half-dozen worlds in the Lyran Alliance. Hit-and-run strikes, constantly keeping the Lyrans off-balance and forcing them to send countless troops after him. Then he and his ragtag band, cobbled together from a dozen different units, had been sent to woo the services of Snord's Irregulars to Prince Victor's cause.

That had proven difficult. The elite mercenaries had nearly been wiped out in political maneuverings that had pitted Archer against them. It was pure luck he'd been able to sort through the mess and prevent their slaughter. Colonel Tasha

Snord now commanded the unit and kept them out of the civil war—a blow against Katherine's cause.

He'd hoped to be on New Avalon months earlier. But that was not to be. The Jade Falcons had slammed into the border with the Lyran Alliance. Archer had volunteered to go and try and rally support to stop them. He had forged an uneasy alliance with Adam Steiner, and caught the Falcons off guard by seizing the initiative and attacking their own occupation zone. A relative peace had come over the Lyran/Falcon border afterward.

It was a risky gamble that paid off. For Archer, it had been a gamble he had played with the blood of his men. His Avengers, "Archer's Avengers," had been decimated in the fighting. He hated that name, but didn't want to hit their morale by forcing them to rename the unit.

The last few years had taken their toll. He felt older than his years. Roles he never expected had been thrust upon him. There had been many times he was in over his head. Prince Victor seemed to have faith in him, when he didn't even have faith in himself. His troops had faith, too. In the end it was Katya's faith that mattered the most. It had helped him get this far. She had always been something more than just an officer. She was his confidant, his friend, the one person he fully trusted. He was counting on her faith in him to get him to the end.

Archer had thought about stopping, settling in on a world for a few months and rebuilding. Some of his officers had suggested it. But he couldn't. There was an appointment that had to be taken care of, a final mission. The death of his sister had compelled him into fighting in the war. Removing Katherine Steiner-Davion from power was the ultimate goal, and with the Prince driving to New Avalon, Archer knew where he needed to be—at his prince's side for the endgame.

Intelligence had said Katherine's agents were watching him, so slipping away was not easy. On Graceland, he'd used some of the local militia and some of the personnel to stay behind and create the ruse that the Avengers were still there. They paraded 'Mechs, stirred up dust, caroused in bars, and maintained the illusion of a presence.

In reality, the battered regiment that remained of his hodgepodge force had packed up and began the trek across the Inner Sphere. They rebuilt and recouped along the way. At two jump points, they met with friendly ships, picking up supplies and parts, and even a handful of troops for replacement. Snord's Irregulars had sent a ship to rendezvous with them at Northwind at the recharge point. Two of their MechWarriors had volunteered to come along, temporarily relieved of duty with the mercenaries. It was a gift from a dear friend, and he appreciated it. The sound of the troops cheering for their new comrades in arms brought a smile to his face. It seemed everyone that had a stake in the Civil War wanted to be there on New Avalon for the resolution.

Archer sighed and closed his eyes. So many dead. Katherine had an ocean of blood on her hands. The time had come to put an end to the war. She was a tyrant. For his sister, for his men and women, for everyone that that suffered under her rule, he was coming to New Avalon.

"I'm coming for you, Katherine. Going to make you pay," he muttered.

"What was that, sir?" Katya asked.

He opened his eyes. "Nothing, Katya. Just talking to myself, I guess."

"Right," she said slowly. "For what it's worth, Archer, I was thinking the same thing." She gave him a smile, warm, beyond friendly. For a moment, he allowed himself to think of her before the war, and even after it. Perhaps there was going to be some sort of life after all of this. Maybe, just maybe, she would be a part of that life.

"Sir," the comm officer called. "We are approaching the LZ. A private file has been transmitted for you. Orders, sir, and one more thing."

"What is it?"

"Sir, we just got these words: 'Welcome to the party, Avengers.'"

Archer smiled. Yes, indeed. But this was not a party, not a game. This was the last battle of the last war he would be called to fight in, or so he hoped.

"Signal back comm. Tell them we bring greetings from the Lyran Alliance, the Falcon Occupation Zone, and all points in between."

DARING FLOOD PLAINS
NEW AVALON
CRUCIS MARCH
FEDERATED SUNS
29 DECEMBER 3066

"Any word yet?" Victor Steiner-Davion asked as he raised his head from the holotable where he and the other officers surveyed the battle zone. Dust swept through the air as a *Cicada* kicked up a cloud of dirt, swirling through the interior of the HQ area.

"He's on his way," replied Kai Allard-Liao, walking over to the table. "He wanted to ensure his troops were billeted first." Kai smirked. They joked privately that Christifori cared more for his men than anything or anyone else. It was an admirable trait, but on more than one occasion he had kept Victor waiting.

Victor flashed a fast grin. He expected that from the general. "For that, I can wait."

Kai nodded and crossed his arms. "Have you given your idea any more thought?"

"You still worried?"

"You're asking quite a bit from him. After all he's done for us so far, you may be asking too much. The Civil War has cost him a great deal as well—his sister and all." There was a hint of hesitation in his voice, one the Prince did his best to ignore.

"I know, Kai." *I know all too well, this war has cost many of us our families.* "I know he wants in the middle of the big fight, but I need him to do this assignment. I know I'm asking him to go into harm's way one more time. But if he does it, he might just be able to help us bring this war to an end faster."

Another officer, his arm in a sling, stepped forward and snapped to attention. "Your Highness. Major General Archer

Christifori, sir," the leftenant said. Behind him, a man stepped forward and offered Victor a salute.

The man seemed older than the last time Victor had seen him two years ago. *The Jade Falcons will do that to you.* There was a little more white hair in his sideburns, and a wrinkle or two more. When they had last met, Archer had assumed command of Operation Audacity, a plan to blunt and drive back a Jade Falcon incursion into the Lyran Alliance. He had performed brilliantly, far better than Victor or his staff had anticipated. Christifori had punched into the Falcon occupation zone and forced them to pull back or risk losing their honor. More importantly, he had won over Victor's cousin Adam, denying Katherine vital political and military support.

As Victor looked at the faded jumpsuit the general wore, he could see the man was weary, almost sagging in his salute. His eyes were sunken, dark, with bags under them and crows-feet marking their ends. He had gotten a tan somewhere, one that was fading and making his face appear almost leathery.

"General," Victor said, planting a smile on his face, "I'm glad you're able to join us." He extended his hand and as Archer took it, Victor reinforced his shake with his other hand as well. "You look good for a man who's supposed to be on Graceland."

Archer allowed himself a brief smile. "I take it our little decoy still has your sister convinced?"

"Yes. Our own agents in MI5 say you are still back there, far from her prying eyes."

Archer looked around at the HQ area, then back to Victor. "I never thought I'd be back here again, on New Avalon."

That's right, he was in the Academy and NAIS. "I always knew we'd be here—again," Victor replied.

"Yes, sir. I'm sure you did." He glanced over his shoulder at a lance of 'Mechs in the distance. "I'll be damned. Is that our old unit?"

The Prince smiled proudly. "Tenth Lyran Guard. Fighting during the Clan invasion seems like a lifetime ago."

"Things were easier then," Christifori added. "With the Clans, you had defined enemies. Good versus evil; that's how it seemed anyway. You knew where you stood. Now with all of this—" He swept his arm out to where a salvage team was working to recover the remains of a destroyed Seventeenth Avalon Hussar's 'Mech. It had been a victim of the fighting the day before, and was now fair game for the technicians salvaging it for parts. The techs struggled with a stubbornly clinging strand of myomer that refused to let go of the actuator they were pulling out. "—you don't always know who the bad guys are."

Victor's voice changed tone. "I want to congratulate you personally on your operations against the Jade Falcons. You performed brilliantly."

Archer allowed himself a grin. "I appreciate the kind words, sir. But I assure you, I wasn't the driving force."

Victor nodded. "I know. If it's all the same, you still deserve the congratulations. Any man that can work side-by-side with the Wolf Clan, tangle with the Jade Falcons, and soothe the ego of Adam Steiner is a man who deserves congratulations."

Archer paused for a moment, drinking in the memories of the last campaign. "There was a price for that victory, Highness. We accomplished our mission, but the cost was steep."

"I haven't gone over your readiness reports," Victor replied. "What is your current status?"

"We started operations with three regiments, though realistically these were combined elements of militia, veterans, locals, a real cobbled together group. At this point, on paper, we're at regimental strength. That's on paper. Realistically, we've lost more personnel than equipment. The gear we do have is patchwork. I'm low on expendables and ammunition. If you want a realistic assessment, I would rate us at two reinforced battalions—tops." His voice was weary. His words seemed mixed with memories of the campaign, the fighting, the deaths and perhaps even worse.

Victor understood. He had seen war at its worst, and knew how commanders felt the pain of loss. It was something he had struggled with for a long time himself. First his father at the end of the Clan wars, a loss that seemed to hit him harder now that he was on New Avalon. The assassination of his mother, then Omi. Archer was older than he was, but was carrying the weight of the loss of his troops as if it was a physical burden.

"General, I need you to get what forces you can ready. We have ammunition, parts, and replacement MechWarriors. We need to get you up to strength."

Archer cocked his eyebrow as he looked at the shorter prince. "You're sending us into the fight so soon?"

"Not necessarily," Victor said. *Not the way you're hoping...*

"I'll need a little more than that, Highness," Archer replied. "Truth be told, my men are going to need more."

Victor understood. *That's what I like about him. He's a soldier's soldier.* "Archer, I want your men ready for a fight, but they aren't going in right away."

Archer crossed his arms and leaned back on his heels. "Details?"

Victor shifted his stance slightly. "General Christifori, since you joined my cause, it has been well-known that you've wanted my sister to come to justice."

"Her actions led to my sister's death." His voice seemed to ring with anger.

"I know." There was more Victor wanted to say. The list of his sister Katherine's crimes was long. The dead attributed to her arrogance was a list that cut a deep scar across the shattered remains of the Federated Commonwealth, now segregated into its original Lyran and Davion halves. "It is a fact that is also known to Katherine and her people. Our own propaganda department has made sure that your motivations are well known."

Archer said nothing. He was obviously taking in the information Victor was providing.

Victor continued, "We are going to covertly reconstitute your regiment, the First Thorin, the Avengers. Officially, we're going to disguise you as part of the Outland Legion, a ploy of hiding you right under my sister's nose. You will be seen meeting with a number of other regimental commanders, handing out orders, directing operations."

"Disinformation?"

Victor nodded. "My intention is to create the illusion that you are going to lead the final assault on Avalon Island and the palace. There are spies everywhere here. Your successes in the past, my known pretense for leveraging people such as yourself to render justice—it will all play well with her intelligence corps. MI5 is going to believe you will be leading the final push."

Archer uncrossed his arms and rested his hands on his hips. "Permission to speak freely, sir?"

His request caught Victor off guard. "Of course."

"Sire, I didn't come all this way just to sit on the sideline and be a diversion or some sort of intelligence ploy. I have buried my troops all over the Commonwealth and the Falcon Occupation Zone. I came to put an end to this." Christifori paused and let his words sink in. There was no venom in his voice, no demands. It was as if his emotions had been drained from him.

Victor understood. Like so many officers that had fought for him, they had lost a great deal—family, friends, livelihoods, all cast aside for him and his cause. Archer Christifori was not asking for anything more than what he had wanted from the very beginning of the conflict—justice.

"Archer," he said slowly. "You have my word. You'll be there at the end. There will be plenty of fighting for you and your troops. This isn't just a diversion; it's much more. You have my assurance that you'll be there when the curtain falls."

Archer sighed heavily. "Your word has always been enough for me. Very well then, Highness," he said saluting. "I'm at your disposal. Can you give me the details of what you have in mind?"

Victor saw a glint in his general's eyes, something of the determination that made Christifori so useful. "Archer, it would be my pleasure."

Archer's Avengers were deployed not far from their DropShips on a sandy plateau. Every time the wind swept their tents and 'Mechs, it kicked up tiny twisters of dust and dirt. The air was dry this season, and each breath made the fine dust stick to the roof of your mouth. The plant-life was sparse in this area of the flood plains, mostly scrub brush and saplings. It was not the paradise most people associated with New Avalon.

Archer walked to the campfire near the center of the camp and as he approached, he saw his officers rise to attention. He gave them a quick salute. Formality of this kind was not typical of his unit. *Must be the presence of so many regular army units...*

Colonel Katya Chaffee drank down her last gulp of coffee, shaking the last bit out of the cup at the fire, then walked over near him. He would have called it a saunter, but there was nothing exotic about it. Months of being in the field and aboard a DropShip had forced him to forget sometimes that Katya was a woman. The look in her eye was enough to remind him.

Maybe if this war is ever over...

"General," she said. "What's the word?"

He allowed himself a chuckle. "The word? The word is we are going to play a crucial and critical role in the eventual assault on Avalon Island."

"That explains the arrival of five trucks loaded with replacement parts," replied Captain John Kraff of the Muphrid Rangers. The Rangers had been the heart and soul of the Second Thorin Regiment...when that regiment had existed. The Jade Falcons had decimated its ranks. Now it was little more than a battalion of troops. "I don't think we've ever been this well outfitted."

"That doesn't bring back the dead," Katya added solemnly.

Archer had seen her gloom before. "Regardless," he said, "we have some major operations to plan. The role of the Avengers in securing a beachhead on Avalon Island is critical."

"We leading the way in sir?" asked Major Alice Gett.

"In a manner of speaking, yes. We will be landing six hours prior to the rest of the invasion force."

His officers glanced nervously at each other at that news. For a moment, there was no sound other than the noises of the troopers in the camp and the crackle of the flames as a log settled, sending sparks up into the darkness.

"Sir," Katya asked hesitantly. "Are you serious?"

"Yes, I am," he said solidly. "And if we do our jobs right, we can help bring this war to an end." Turning he scanned the eyes of his officers and made sure he had eye contact with each and every one of them. "We will have a secured briefing tomorrow to go over the operational plans. Get some sleep, and I will see all of you at 0830 hours."

Before they could rebut him, Archer pivoted and walked away.

They're good people. I need to ask them to take part in one more fight. That's all, just one more fight...

CAMP AVENGER
DARING FLOOR PLAINS
NEW AVALON
CRUCIS MARCH
FEDERATED SUNS
31 DECEMBER 3066

The dull, flat-green plexi-dome had guards posted all around it. A fine layer of dust covered it and was streaked where people had brushed up against the dome, taking the dust with them. As the ad hoc command center for Archer's Avengers, the roof of the small collapsible structure was covered with a prickled layer of antenna, stabbing skyward.

Inside, Archer stood at the holotable. Millennia before, a table covered with sand had served the same purpose—to allow a commander to model combat terrain for tactical planning purposes. The holotable was a familiar tool, but Archer found himself waxing nostalgic, wondering what it was like to use a good old-fashioned sand table.

While the hot sun beat down on the plains outside, the portable AC unit strained to keep the interior of the command center cool. His officers stood around the table, staring at the holographic image of the target—Avalon Island. Most had their arms crossed over their chests. They said nothing.

Despite orders, Captain Kraff had a cigar in his mouth, a thin wisp of smoke rising from it. It didn't reek like a cheap cigar, and Kraff was quick to point out to anyone that complained that he had stolen only the very best—the spoils of war.

There were a few guests in the room as well. They hadn't been introduced to the Avengers command yet. They stood out in that their olive drab jumpsuits, while worn, were not nearly as faded or patched as those worn by the Avengers. There were no signs of old patches pulled off as their affiliations and units had changed. Some of his people had handmade their lance or company patches and wore them proudly. The elbows of more than one Avenger uniform was threadbare.

Archer's people had been cobbled together from dozens of other units and retired veterans, all answering the call to support Prince Victor against his sister Katherine. While some had outdated uniforms, and a few still wore their spurs of the Federated Suns, all had one thing in common—a desire to see the war brought to an end, swiftly if at all possible. Archer was proud of the way they looked. It wasn't the uniforms that were important, but the men and women in them.

General Christifori leaned forward over the holotable, putting his palms on the edge of the three-dimensional map and leaning on his arms, over the terrain. He tipped his head back and let his gaze sweep the tight confines of the room. "First and foremost, let me say how proud I am of all of you. We've fought our way across the Inner Sphere to get here—at the right place, at the right time.

"The Avengers have been given a unique and special honor. We are going to lead the assault on Avalon Island. Our forces are to be the first ones ashore in the final assault against Katherine's forces." He didn't expect a cheer. These were seasoned military personnel. They had a pretty damn good idea of what they would be facing if they led the assault. He did hear a few mumbles.

"For intelligence purposes, we're officially being designed as reserve elements of the Outland Legion," he said, making eye contact with each of his officers. Reaching into his right flank pocket, he pulled out a wad of Outland Legion patches. "Sew these on, pass them out to the troops. Orders will go out to repaint our 'Mechs for the time being with Outland Legion colors."

"Sir?" Kraff said, taking up the patch as if it was manure in his fingertips. "Why all the cloak and dagger stuff? Outland Legion? That's crap in a can if I ever heard it. They're good and all, but we're the Avengers." His words were met with more than one nod of agreement.

Archer smiled. Pride in the unit was one of his cornerstones for holding his troopers together. "Just relax. It's temporary. When the time comes, we'll show Katherine our true colors. I can't speak for the rest of you, but I can't wait to get her panties in a bunch when she finds out we're here." As if to add emphasis, he winked at his officers who, in turn, took up the patches with a new sense of purpose and chuckled at his response.

"The shortest distance between Avalon Island and our current base of operations is Portsmouth. That is our target. We will hit the beach to the west of the harbor and city and drive inland, sweeping back into the city and catching it from the rear." As he spoke, Archer triggered the animation on the holotable showing where the landings would take place. A long, red arrow swept in behind the port city and punched into it from the rear flank.

"While we secure the port facilities, the Sherwood Foresters will punch in toward Reamuth and cripple the satellite relay station there. Katherine's intelligence people will expect this kind of surgical strike during the assault. The attack on that installation will have the net effect of creating a four- to five-hour disabling of Katherine's capabilities to get downloads from satellites while they reroute to secondary facilities." The image of Reamuth appeared, nearly five kilometers inland from Portsmouth. It was a short distance on the map, but the officers knew it was a long way to go. "For a while, they'll be blind."

"Sir," Major Gett of the Armored Company queried, "how long until the rest of the invasion force gets on shore with us? If we're the beachhead, I assume that they'll be right on our tails, ready to drive us back into the water."

Archer glanced at one of the visitors. "Major, this is a two-part operation. First part is us hitting and taking Portsmouth. Phase two is best left to our guest. It is my pleasure to introduce Kai Allard. Most of you are, I believe, familiar with his exploits on Solaris a while back."

General Christifori waved his hand to the officer, who gave him a slow nod/bow in response. The officers turned to the stranger that had been standing with them and gave him looks of acknowledgement and respect. Kai's reputation had easily preceded him.

"Thank you, General Christifori," Kai said, scanning the officers. "The Outland Legion never looked quite *this* good." The officers laughed at his words. "To answer your question, Major Gett, we will be following with the rest of the invasion force four hours after your initial landing."

"Four hours?" barked Captain Kraff. "Holy freaking crudstunk, might as well be four months. Those bloody damned troops Katherine has at her disposal are going to hit us with everything they have. Landing in Portsmouth will be like kicking a beehive. They'll come from everywhere to pummel us back into the sea. General, sir, you have gone out of your way in the past to piss her off. She's going to want your ass on her wall—sir."

Kai nodded. "True enough. In fact, we're counting on that."

"Sir?"

"This is a two-part operation, as General Christifori has pointed out. The first phase is the Avengers leading an assault force into Portsmouth and gaining the full attention of the defenders on Avalon Island. The second part is a deception campaign that started several weeks ago. The Avengers are not the main blow of the invasion, but a carefully crafted diversion. In the eyes of our enemy, you are the spearpoint. We're sending enough disinformation now to the other troops to convince them that no one other than General Christifori would be leading the initial landings."

"We're bait?" the usually reserved Thomas Sherwood asked, his eyes unblinking as he spoke.

Allard nodded. "In essence, yes."

"Crud," Kraff added. "I like the sound of 'diversion' a hell of a lot better than 'bait.'"

"Regardless," Archer cut in, knowing the commentary would go on for hours if he let it. "From what I've been told, an intelligence operation has been running to paint our force, specifically me, as the leader of the invasion. Most military people would assume the assault would come somewhere along the Portsmouth coastline. Katherine's defense is concentrating there. They'll be convinced I'm the key leader in the field. They will throw everything they have at us. They will attempt to shatter our beachhead.

"Don't kid yourselves, boys and girls; this is the reality of this mission. We are going to be the biggest damn target on Avalon Island. Katherine is going to come at us—at me—full force. She'll want my testicles on a platter. For four hours, we will draw their fire, suck them in, let them think we're a full-blown invasion. Then the *real* invasion force will hit the other side of Avalon Island."

Kai jumped in. "We know Katherine will respond to the real invasion, but it will buy us the time to establish the real beachhead and to set up the kind of defenses necessary for a campaign of this type."

Captain Kraff shifted his cigar to the other side of his mouth. "Don't get this wrong, sir, but what happens to us while you all pitch your tents and settle in?"

"You'll be extracted. DropShips and naval transports will come in, pull the Avengers out. Portsmouth would be nice to have, but is not necessary for the final operation. The beachhead on the other side of the island is what is critical."

Captain Joey Lynn Fraser of the White Tigers spoke up. "We're just one regiment. It won't take those people long to know how big we are. Once they figure out that it's just one regiment, they'll know it's a diversion, sir."

Kai held up a hand. "Under normal circumstances, you're right. However, we have a few little surprises. First, we have these MA generators. Magnetic Anomalies. They are small, but generate signals as if they are moving BattleMechs. The signals on long range sensors appear as several lances of 'Mechs of varying size. Properly placed and moved by infantry, they can confuse an enemy into detecting a significantly larger force."

Archer spoke up as well. "We are also going to have some comm units with us. They will generate simulated combat communication traffic. From the sound of it, combined with some of the jamming units we'll deploy, you'd swear you're facing five or six regiments worth of troops. On top of that, our positions will be urban in nature. Without a clear line of sight, it will be difficult for even an eyewitness to tell just how big the force is." He paused. Most of his officers nodded. Given the right circumstances, the plan had a good chance of working. Battle, however, often altered circumstances dramatically.

"How do we know that Katherine's people will take the bait?" Katya Chaffee asked. "I'm in intel and I have to tell you, it's a fickle business."

Kai offered her a thin smile. "I understand your concerns. We know they are monitoring all of our actions and key personnel. We are on New Avalon, after all. Your General Christifori will be meeting with a number of other regimental commanders and other leaders. News of this meeting here will reach them. We already have double agents that have reported they have noted that your units are undergoing a major refit right now. In fact, we're going to spread counterintelligence that states the General is definitely not leading the attack, knowing full well Katherine's people will suspect it is false.

"There's more. Katherine knows that for Prince Victor to claim a true victory, he must be true to this cause in the eyes of his people. General Christifori is the perfect tool for that. He is from the Lyran Alliance, making this less than an internal fight. He's been harmed by Katherine and has sought justice—and made it public. Our own public relations people have played him up. It's an easy story to buy, and one we will deny if asked—adding credibility to it."

"I guess," Chaffee added. "The only real question is, will it work?"

"It better," a new voice added from the doorway. Entering the inner tent dome was the short figure of Victor Steiner-Davion. The warm air seemed to jump five degrees at the sight of the Prince. Most of the officers had never seen him, or if they had, only from a distance. The abrupt Kraff slowly pulled the cigar from his mouth, the closest he got to a salute.

"I trust fully that the Avengers are up to the job we're giving them. I assume you all agree?"

There was a chorus of *"yes, sir's,"* barked in unison. Victor smiled, and warmly patted several of the officers on the shoulder as he strode to the holotable. "We are going to go out of our way to play up the minor role of the Avengers. But we've made sure the supplies and gear you've received are what we'd ship to a front-line assault unit. We know there are spies in our logistics chain. They'll get the word out to Katherine.

"As far as anyone outside of this room knows, this operation is not happening. You are to tell your personnel that your role in the invasion will be as a strategic reserve. Their spies will pick that up as well, and will assume that we are trying to deceive them."

Katya smiled. "Oldest trick in the book. Get someone to believe what you want by denying it."

"We're counting on it working," Victor added. "Even my visiting here today to speak with you is something likely to be observed and reported. Don't kid yourselves, there are enemies watching everything we do. We just have to turn that to our advantage. And trust me when I tell you there is more we are going to do to convince my sister that this is indeed the primary assault. By the time we are done, she will think of Portsmouth as the most important target on the island."

Archer smiled. *I'm counting on it, too. All of us are counting on this being successful. If it's not, we're dead.* "So there you have it—our role. You have the backing and support of everyone on the Prince's staff, and the Prince himself. Is there anyone here that believes we cannot pull this off? Anyone here that doesn't want to jerk Katherine's chain just one more time?"

"No. We're behind you, sir...Sire," Kraff added, giving the prince a glance. There were nods all around, confident nods. Even the usually reserved Katya seemed to grasp the eloquence of the plan.

"Excellent. Well then, it is New Years and we're on New Avalon. Next year, it and all of the Alliance and Suns will be free!"

There was a cheer around the holotable, one even Prince Victor joined.

Field Marshal Simon Gallagher was Champion for Katrina Steiner-Davion, Archon-Princess of the Federated Commonwealth. He wielded incredible power, but at the same time served at her whim, and there wasn't a moment they were together that she did not remind him of that.

Despite his loyalty, he knew that he was always one mistake away from termination. He had wanted many times to correct her use of her own title; the Federated Commonwealth was gone—a memory—but he said nothing. Best not to make waves. Men like Gallagher were not allowed to retire or walk away from their mistakes; they took them to their graves.

The conference room was dark, lights dimmed so that his holographic slide show in the center of the briefing table would show up better. It made reading Katrina's face difficult at best. It was just another ploy on her part to keep him off balance, this much he was sure of.

"What is Victor planning?" Katrina asked from her seat, elevated slightly higher than the others in the room. "And don't rattle off facts and figures, Simon, I want your assessment." There was a hint of bitterness in her voice.

"Highness," he said, clearing his throat, "we cannot ascertain for certain what your brother's plans are. But our experts in military analysis believe he will strike at the Portsmouth region, perhaps at the city itself."

"Why do you think that?" queried a smoother voice, that of Jackson Davion, the leader of Katrina's military forces.

"Distance and facilities-wise, it is the most logical location for establishment of a beachhead."

"And Victor will lead the assault," Katrina added.

"Not necessarily, Highness," Simon replied. He saw her eyebrow cock at his words. Yes, this was something she had not expected. "Remember my reports a few days ago about the Outland Legion being reinforced?"

She nodded curtly.

"Well, it appears your brother was attempting to mislead us. It was not the Outland Legion at all. Our agents have discovered that the unit there is Archer's Avengers—the First Thorin Regiment."

Katrina clenched her teeth and said nothing.

"More importantly, our recent intelligence operatives in Victor's camp indicate he has placed a high degree of emphasis on General Christifori and his Avengers." He tapped the remote control for the holographic display and the image of Archer Christifori appeared in the middle of the table, a giant floating holographic head.

"Christifori?" Katrina asked, half-spitting his name. "Him again? You'd think Victor would be tired of sharing the spotlight with this man. Isn't it enough that he lured that traitorous cousin of mine into keeping his units out of the fighting?" The reference to Adam Steiner's ordering a portion of the Alliance to stand down from the civil war was not lost on the small gathering. Katrina's ranting about the incident was legendary in the palace corridors. "You told me he was on Graceland."

"As we thought he was. It was a ploy, as is Victor's failed attempt to hide him right in front of us as part of the Outland Legion. Once again we have penetrated his veil."

"Hopefully not too late," she added.

"Indeed, Highness," Simon replied. "We are wise to not underestimate him. He was responsible for luring Snord's Irregulars from their contract with the Alliance. He has been a thorn in our side for some time. *And* he has been meeting three times a day with Prince Victor and his staff. These may be indications that he is the leader of the first wave of troops. What few assets we have in place show him to be conferring on strategic issues—things we'd expect to see from an invasion leader. We're confident Victor will be with the landing forces, but our intel points to Christifori leading the assault."

"Why him?" Jackson Davion asked.

"He has a grudge against the Archon-Princess," Simon said carefully, knowing he was on thin ice. "He claims she is responsible for the death of his sister."

"I'd never even heard of him until the last two years, let alone his tramp sister. What he thinks means nothing to me. He is simply a tool, a pawn in Victor's hands. What would I care about someone like him, a junior officer at best?" Her voice rang with contempt as she waved aside the allegation.

"I understand, Highness," Gallagher replied. "Nevertheless, the accusations have been made, and I'm afraid they have played well with the media. Adding to this, one of our operatives has learned that the holotable in his command tent has been used recently to go over terrain in and around Portsmouth. This only adds fuel to our belief that it is the target area."

"A ruse, perhaps?" Jackson added. "Victor has proven himself a formidable military leader. He could be fooling us, fooling your people, Simon." Unlike Katrina, there was no venom in his tone.

"I can't rule that out," he replied. "But you asked me my thoughts, and I have provided them as best I can. Our experts believe General Christifori will lead the assault in the Portsmith area. Victor will use him as a tool to show that this is a war, in his eyes, for justice. He's become quite media savvy, and will play that against us to take the hearts and minds of the citizens here on Avalon Island."

Katrina rose from her seat and all eyes fixed on her in the dimly lit room. She stared at the holographic image in front of her. As she rose and closed with the image, Simon could see the anger in her face.

"Very well, Simon. Portsmouth is the assumed target. We shall send additional troops there—not many, but enough. If you're right, they'll buy us time. If you're wrong, I want to be prepared for defense elsewhere. For your sake, however, I would not be wrong...

"And as for this General Christifori," she said waving her hand at the hologram. "I want him dead. When his broken body is shown on the newscasts, it will shatter the morale of Victor and his people. Let him see what happens to those icons that are held against me.

"In fact, Jackson," she said as she turned to her general, "I want you to assemble a team to do just that. When they come ashore, kill this Christifori...no matter what the cost."

UNION-CLASS DROPSHIP *LITTLE SORRELL*
OVER PORTSMOUTH
AVALON ISLAND
NEW AVALON
CRUCIS MARCH
FEDERATED SUNS
24 MARCH 3067

As the *Little Sorrell* swung wide of the landing zone, Archer double-checked the tension on the five-point security strap of his cockpit. His BattleMech, a *Penetrator*, had been rebuilt so many times he often wondered just how many of its components were original. *Do I really want to know?* It didn't matter, really. It didn't matter that it was built by the lowest bidder, either. What did matter was that he was armed with replacement Clan weaponry, captured in a previous lifetime when he had been in the Revenants, serving with the Prince.

His urban paint scheme of grays and blacks had been covered with the temporary insignia of the Outland Legion, but he'd had it replaced with his own regiment's markings again. If they fought, it was going to be under their own names. There was a comfort in fighting under his own colors. It was like being in a familiar chair.

Back then, he had been a young, wide-eyed officer, hell-bent for leather. He had fought the Clans, won, and then retired. War was gone for him. Then the loss of his sister. Her killer, pardoned by Katherine Steiner-Davion, had murdered his only remaining family member, and then the Archon-Princess had paroled the man who had committed the crime. Since then, all he had lived for was wrapped up in the events that were to follow this day.

The downfall of Katherine Steiner-Davion.

"Katya," he said on the command channel. "I show us closing in on the LZ. Are you set and clear?"

In their efforts to confuse the enemy even more, Katya Chaffee had drawn a critical role. She was not a MechWarrior by trade, but would be piloting a 'Mech today. It was a big one, hopefully safe for her.

"Roger that, General," she came back in the speakers in his neurohelmet. "I'm showing us on drop-standby. I've got this beast ready for action. I sure hope you picked the right person for this."

Archer allowed himself a chuckle. "It's got to be safer than piloting a command vehicle out there."

"You'd think," she replied.

NewArcher suddenly heard a metallic grinding, and saw the drop door in front of his *Penetrator* open up. Dirt and dust were kicking up. He could make out the cliff-tops where the landing zone was located. In the distance was the outlined shapes of Portsmouth City about a kilometer away.

Warning lights came on in his cockpit. Yellow—prep for debarkation. He switched to the channel for the rest of the command company. "Avengers, stand by for deployment."

The light turned green. The safety harnesses on his *Penetrator* released, and he tapped the foot-pedals. The gyro feedback was stable as he leaned forward slightly. They were in the right place, that was for sure.

"All right, Avengers, standard deployment, just like we practiced. Recon lance deploy to the north, command to follow."

He stepped out onto the ramp, and in three steps was on Avalon Island. Almost immediately he heard the familiar *ping* and *thump* of small arms fire slapping his BattleMech's torso. Pivoting at the waist, Archer saw the source, a small building near the LZ. Infantry, huddled inside, were firing at him despite the odds.

Waste of perfectly good infantry. He brought his pulse lasers online and using his joystick, swept the targeted reticle onto the small building. Archer didn't wait for a weapons lock. Hitting his secondary target trigger, he unleashed a burst of crimson energy bolts into the building. The small stone and brick structure seemed to pop. Smoke and steam rose from the debris. It didn't stand a chance, nor had the men hiding in there.

"Sitrep," he queried on the command channel.

"Sir, we've secured all five LZs," Katya answered. "We are showing indications of substantially more troops present than anticipated. Saber Beach LZ reports two companies of troops, 'Mechs, and armor attempted to swarm their LZ upon landing. Similar reports coming in from the White Tigers at Halo LZ."

"Sounds like someone knew we were coming," he replied, moving his *Penetrator* out. The *Little Sorrell*'s turrets were firing at some targets off in the distance, too far for him to make out even with the visual enhancements of his T&T system. Whatever it was, it was firing back at the DropShip, no minor accomplishment. *Maybe our little bluff worked after all.*

He switched to the broad command channel and set his comm unit to scramble. "Specter One to Avengers," he snapped as he angled further away from the DropShip. "Move out to your assigned targets. Be warned, we are getting signs of reinforced troops in the area."

He then sent an encoded message back to the command post near Portland for Prince Victor and his people.

"Red Rover, Red Rover."

Jackson Davion stared at the reports scrolling by on his screen. The map of the area showed the landing zones. Five, possibly six. Multiple reports of deploying 'Mechs. Despite moving in the reserve 4th Avalon Militia, a unit mostly made up of reservists and veterans, it was clear something was going on in Portland, and they were facing the invasion of Avalon Island.

Possibly...

Behind him, arms crossed defiantly, Katrina Steiner-Davion stood brooding. "So, Jackson, is this it, or is it some sort of ruse of Victor's?"

Jackson didn't look at her; he kept his eyes focused on the reports. "Someone is hitting Portsmouth, exactly as Simon had predicted. It seems to be multiple regiments, but right now there is a lot of confusion. We've tossed in the 4th

Avalon Militia, which is wreaking some havoc on whoever is landing there, but we can't be sure if this is a diversion or the real McCoy."

"Well, troops are deploying. Isn't that enough?" Her tone was demanding, it was always demanding.

Jackson didn't waver. "If it's a diversion, Highness, it could have us shifting troops that we need elsewhere."

"You're my Marshal of the Armies. What do you recommend?"

"Patience," Jackson replied. "Until we are sure."

The Militia *Gallowglas* swept behind the water reservoir tank just as it fired its ER PPC. Archer winced as the bolt of blue energy stabbed at his *Penetrator.* The shot went a little wide of his right leg, but an arc from the blast of manmade charged particle burst seared the paint on his knee joint. A small residual arc of blue electrical charge danced up the thigh of his 'Mech. *Too damn close.*

Archer swept the opposite direction and brought his medium pulse lasers online to the second and third target interlock circuits. The *Gallowglas* had gutted a *Hitman* from his command company, leaving it a smoldering heap tossed into the side of an apartment building. He'd been chasing it for ten minutes, and wasn't about to lose it now.

As the *Gallowglas* rounded the far side of the water tank, Archer locked on half of his pulse lasers—three of them—and fired. The shots were not aimed at the militiaman, but at the base of the water tank. It was a city reserve tank, probably for fire control. He didn't want to target it, but this was the final fight. Now was not the time to hold back. *Katya will castigate me for this afterward.*

The crimson bolts stabbed into the thin, metallic skin of the tank, and suddenly it collapsed. The rush of water was nearly 20 feet tall, and slapped into the side of the *Gallowglas.* The MechWarrior fought the sudden imbalance, but it hit their left leg with such force it was almost impossible. They fell

sideways into a ten-story office building, sending a shower of glass and metal raining down onto the street below.

General Christifori didn't hesitate. He unleashed the remaining pulse lasers at the suddenly stationary target. The scarlet bursts of light stitched the frontal glacial plate of the round cockpit. At first they seemed to do no damage at all, then the cockpit popped like a balloon. It imploded under the burst and instantly charred black inside. Smoke billowed from the holes made by the laser bursts, wisp-like, marking the end of the 'Mech. The heat in his cockpit had risen slightly, enough to make him start to sweat for the first time in a few minutes.

"Scratch that tally-ho I called," he said on the comm channel.

"Roger that," Katya replied. "We just managed to drive out that Demon tank that was pulling the hit-and-run. Chalk that up to the White Tigers. Fraser has the MA devices running. Anyone scanning this area of the city without our filters will think we have another twenty 'Mechs running around here."

"I wasn't planning on this militia," Archer said as he angled his *Penetrator* down a wide boulevard. Some small arms fire, mostly manpack PPCs, danced out ahead three blocks, signs of another firefight.

"Orders, sir?"

"Let's give them something to look at," he replied. "Katya, deploy into the city. Let them see you."

He first saw the Mech on his tactical display, then it appeared a few moments later. It was a massive *Daishi*. Lumbering down the street in its blue and white paint scheme complete with silver piping, he saw it approach and felt the streets rumble slightly under each thundering footstep. The plan had been to deploy the 'Mech and a few other decoys. This one was special, and Katya was piloting it.

The *Daishi* was painted to look exactly like the one piloted by Prince Victor.

"Got you on my scopes," he said.

"Roger that," she replied, firing a burst down the street in the direction where he saw fighting. Apparently from her angle she had a shot. "Looks hot down there."

"Yes, it does. You head down that street, I'll take your flank. Let that enemy infantry get a good look at you before you open fire. Then blast them."

"Why the pause?"

He juked his *Penetrator* out to the middle of the open street for a better angle as he watched an errant short-range missile snake into the air, run out of propellant, then drop into the side of a building, blasting a hole in the fifth floor. Flames lapped out from the hole.

"I want them to have time to signal their command that Prince Victor is on the field. Then they need to be put down. You have a war to win, Highness."

He heard her chuckle.

Jackson Davion stared at the image being relayed from the suburb of Portsmouth. That was the 'Mech—that damned *Daishi*. *Prometheus*. He had seen it before, studied the images from other battlefields. Too many other battlefields. It meant something. Victor. He was there, in Portsmouth. Reports from his sentries and infantry troops with scanning gear indicated there was at least three regiments operating there, possibly more.

Yes, it could be deception. That was why he had called in Simon Gallagher.

"So, is that him?" he asked, stabbing his finger at the freeze-frame image of the massive BattleMech.

"I have reports of a highly painted up and modified *Centurion* leading the strike on our satellite relay facility at Reamuth."

"*Yen-Lo-Wang*?" Kai Allard's deadly 'Mech.

"If the reports are accurate, and I have little reason to doubt them," Gallagher replied. "Taking out that facility is the kind of mission Victor would send his trusted friend to lead, don't you agree?"

Jackson said nothing for a moment. Instead, he stared at the image of *Prometheus* looming on the holographic display in front of him. He wanted to believe this was a diversion, a ploy. But it appeared to be a direct assault. Moving in the Fourth Avalon Militia had stalled the attack, bought him time to confirm who it was. Victor, Christifori, and the others had been in the city for an hour now. There was still time to drive them into the sea.

"Final recommendations, Simon?"

The older man flinched. "I believe this is the main assault."

"So do I," Jackson replied. *That is what makes me nervous.* "Very well."

"What are you going to do?"

"What I'm supposed to do: my duty. I'm sending our front-line units straight at Portsmouth. I will crush them because if I don't, Victor will do the same to me."

Archer pivoted his *Penetrator* at the waist. There was a slight metallic grind as the 'Mech turned, the result of a piece of armor that had been splayed back from a barrage of missile hits. Smoke rose from several places over Portsmouth, black, churning, rising high into the air. The streets had been chewed up from the feet of 'Mechs and the carnage of battle. Craters pockmarked the ferrocrete all around where he stood, some still spilling out grayish white smoke.

"Sitrep," he ordered.

Thomas Sherwood's voice came back in a crackle in his ear. "Forester's company reports Reamuth is green." Green, as in obliterated.

"Losses?"

"Too many. The Militia may be a hodgepodge unit, but they were tough. I'm down a full lance, sir. Falling back in good form to the city now."

"How's the new 'Mech?"

Sherwood chuckled, a rarity for him. "Let's just say I always wanted to try out the arenas of Solaris. This was the next best thing. I just wish my nephew had a holoimage of me in the cockpit of this beast."

Another voice cut in. "This is Ranger One," said the ragged voice of Captain Kraff. "Militia units have fled the city. I've lost half of my company, either down or dead. You'd think they were trying to tell us to leave or something."

Major Gett came on line. "Second Battalion losses are less, we're running at twenty percent down. I'm pleased to report our sectors are secure, sir."

Archer punched up the tactical monitors. "Okay then. If we've done our job, they're going to be coming for us any time now with everything. Get the sappers out. I want the main avenues of approach rigged with mines, traps, everything we brought with us. Clear out your fields of fire and establish fire zones. Get the artillery deployed at their assigned sectors and get your fire control teams in place."

"Do you think it worked sir?" Major Gett asked.

"I sure as hell hope so," he replied. "Otherwise this was the biggest waste of troops and material I've ever seen."

**PORTSMOUTH
AVALON ISLAND
NEW AVALON
CRUCIS MARCH
FEDERATED SUNS
24 MARCH 3067**

Artillery rounds ripped apart the street at the feet of Archer's *Penetrator*, spraying chunks of ferrocrete into the 'Mech's bird-like legs. Water surged up from one of the holes, an obvious hit on a water main. The cold water hissed into steam as it hit his legs—a warning as to how hot they were.

The artillery had been dropping all over Portsmouth. The spotters were either not in place or doing a bad job of directing fire. Many buildings had been hit, many streets had been so badly mauled they were impassable. It would be some time before life in Portsmouth returned to normal.

Archer turned slightly and brought his targeting reticle down on the advancing *Watchman*. It was already somewhat battered from fighting its way into the city, but was still a dangerous threat. A millisecond after he heard the tone in his ears from the target lock, he hit the primary target interlock circuit.

The heat in his cockpit soared as emerald green beams lashed out from the Clan ER lasers his *Penetrator* mounted. Both shots hit the *Watchman* in its left side. The beams cut like knives slicing through hot butter, searing through the advancing 'Mech's armor plating. The *Watchman* stopped for a moment mid-gait and seemed to quake where it stood. Archer knew that was an indication of ammunition cooking off deep inside its torso. It rocked in place for a moment, and a thick cloud of gray smoke churned out of the cuts from his lasers. The *Watchman*'s MechWarrior had managed to save their 'Mech, but apparently no longer had a taste for the fight. They limped off to the right, taking refuge behind a building.

Inside his neurohelmet, sweat stung the corners of his eyes as Archer walked through the rising column of water from the blasted water main in an effort to get a better angle. No joy. The *Watchman* had limped out of line of sight.

He stared at his tactical display and didn't like what he was seeing. Reinforcements from three different Davion regiments, all loyal to Katherine, had hit Portsmouth. The only saving grace was that they hadn't coordinated their attack as well as they could have, but had come in as they had arrived—albeit from different directions. Apparently Jackson Davion felt it was more important to hit them than to wait and coordinate. His third and second battalion had stubbornly been forced to give ground in their sectors, but they still held the waterfront port.

First battalion had suffered three waves of attack; the *Watchman* had been the last element of that third wave. Losses had been high, but they had only dropped back three blocks—three painful blocks. Most important to Archer was the time it was taking for the attackers. Just over three hours had elapsed from the time of the start of the battle for Portsmouth. In another hour, the *real* invasion would begin.

"Katya, how are you doing?" he asked.

A sigh came to his ears, a weary sigh. She wasn't normally a MechWarrior. Katya had been injured during her career, and had been relegated to commanding from a vehicle. Only recently had she been pressed once more into a cockpit, this time playing the role of Victor Steiner-Davion, piloting a duplicate of *Prometheus*. "I've got one leg that is just about gone, and have been hit just about everywhere else. I'm coming up on your flank right now."

He glanced over at the 'Mech and saw scars of black laser and pockmarks from missile hits. "You've looked better," he managed with a wry twist of humor.

"You'd almost get the idea these folks have something against the Prince." Her voice rang with sarcasm.

"Right," he said, his attention suddenly turned back to his tactical display. The approaching red dots on the monitor wasn't going to be good news. "I've got a lance of bandits closing down the street in front of us."

"I'm painting them too," she replied.

"Let them close in," he said. "The sappers will take care of at least the lead elements."

"Affirmative," she replied, sweeping her *Daishi* into line next to him. Together, they stared down the street.

The enemy 'Mechs came into view. Painted in urban camouflage, the lance of four 'Mechs were led by two medium *Nightskys*. Behind them, almost in formation, were a *Salamander* and a *Gunslinger*. None of this was good news. They were fresh, ready for a fight, and were rushing straight at them. The *Nightskys* were closing rapidly, moving with precision down the street between the 10-to-20 story buildings on either side.

A rumble came, and at first he thought it might be thunder, even though he knew differently. The street quaked, but it was the buildings on either side of the two lead *Nightskys*. The sappers had planted explosives in them, very carefully. He had reluctantly given the orders for them to lay waste to the city this way—it was necessary, bitterly so. The blasts had knocked out the structural supports on either side of the street. The buildings seemed to lurch toward each other and hit in the air above the charging BattleMechs.

For a moment, Archer wondered if the leaning buildings were going to hold each other up, each preventing the other from falling. They didn't. Gravity won. Thousands of tons of debris plowed straight down into the *Nightskys*. Both tried to outrun the trap, but there was no hope. The debris hit the 'Mechs hard, cutting off the two assault 'Mechs behind them. A rolling cloud of gray white dust churned up, blinding Archer's *Penetrator*.

The airborne dust seemed to linger forever, even though Archer was sure it was just a minute or two. He relied on his sensors to tell him what was out there, if anything. The collapsing of the buildings wasn't the only trick he had up his sleeve, it was just the most spectacular. He was also counting on the fact that the enemy would keep coming at him. *They want us out of here. In their minds, we are the only threat on this island.*

The *Nightskys* were history, but he picked up the faint magnetic reading of the assault-class 'Mechs on the far side of the debris-filled street. He tried to get a lock on them, but the intervening mountain of building rubble blocked a clear shot. Archer watched the tactical display and saw they were moving around, attempting to flank his position. Their move was obvious—if the direct path to him was blocked, they were angling to get down the street Katya faced.

"Specter One to Brain," he beamed over on the direct channel. "You're going to have company shortly."

"Tracking that already," she said. Archer moved his *Penetrator* off to her side.

"Let them come," he added. There was good reason. His street was not the only avenue that had been booby-trapped.

Archer didn't have a clear line of sight yet, but he knew they had come into range. Katya's *Daishi*, painted identically to that of the Prince, rocked under a wave of forty long-range missiles. The general reeled for a moment. Yes, the *Daishi* was a huge 'Mech, but for a moment he was unsure how anything could have survived such an attack. Smoke enveloped Katya, black, churning, sick smoke. Red and yellow flames lapped through the smoke. Archer waited. If she was out, he'd feel the thunder of her 'Mech falling onto the street.

The fall didn't come.

Instead, through the smoke, he watched her side-step towards him. She fired, her weapons pod fitted with a Gauss rifle. The slug was so fast it looked like a bolt of silver light streaking down the street where the missiles had come from. The arm recoiled slightly from the launch. Archer didn't see the results of the shot. He moved his *Penetrator* even closer to Katya's side.

The pair of assault 'Mechs were two blocks away, rushing forward like a tidal wave. Katya fired another nickel slug into the *Gunslinger*, hitting it in the right arm. The *Gunslinger*'s limb twisted backward under the impact, tossing armor plates. The Loyalist 'Mech didn't stop. In fact, its stride only slowed slightly, as if it was hesitating, but only for a second.

As they charged forward, they fired. The shots came down the corridor of buildings with full force and fury. One Gauss rifle slug burrowed deep into Archer's left side with such force that he rocked back in his seat and felt his ribs ache under the restraining straps. A burst of lasers slashed across Katya's chest, splattering globs of melted armor, like drops of mercury, into the air.

Archer dropped his sights on the *Gunslinger* and locked on. He fired, first the Clan-made lasers, then half of his pulse lasers. They hit the *Gunslinger* square on, mostly in the torso and legs. Armor popped off and danced down the street. The 'Mech came on.

The *Salamander* didn't wait. It launched another wave of missiles, a literal wall of warheads. Katya started to move the massive *Daishi* as if to dodge them, but to no avail. A few missed, racing past her 'Mech and further down the street. The vast majority hit her, blasting her cockpit, torso, and legs. The flames seemed to linger, hanging onto the 'Mech.

Archer sucked in a breath and hesitated like he had never done in combat before. *No...not her.*

The *Daishi* started to topple. She fired a Gauss slug down range into the *Salamander*, a snap-shot, one that seemed to be on target. It struck the *Salamander*'s right knee so hard the Loyalist 'Mech stumbled to the side and glanced off a building. Glass shattered and rained down onto the street from the running blow. The *Salamander* was still charging.

Right into the mines.

The mines had been hastily hidden, concealed in hovercars on the street, with trip lines carefully laid. Most were not even mines but ad hoc booby-traps, explosive-laden cars. They went off, first one, then another.

The *Salamander* was lifted by the concussion of the blast, tossed in the air slightly but appreciably. Its footing slipped mid-stride and the MechWarrior was obviously struggling to stay upright. It was a losing battle. Archer saw the armor on its left leg was all but gone. Myomer strands, severed in the blast, snapped and hung outside like torn muscle tissues. The *Salamander* hit the ground at almost the same time as Katya's 'Mech.

Her *Daishi* dropped face forward, grinding into the pavement with a sickening, metallic moan. Archer winced. Katya was down. Smoke billowed from half a dozen holes from the missile hits.

"Specter One to all commands, Brain is down. Send backup," he said as he locked onto the closing *Gunslinger*. Its six lasers lashed and pulsed out at him, a light show of green beams and brilliant red bursts of light seared his *Penetrator*. Several shots missed, but not nearly enough of them. His 'Mech seemed to scream from the impacts as armor melted and cut free from internal supports. A ripple of heat, suffocating, wrapped his body.

Damn you! Damn you all to hell! He fired. Not just one target interlock, but all of them. His ER lasers lanced out and caught the *Gunslinger* square on. The peppering crimson blasts from the medium pulse lasers seemed to hit everywhere. He knew at least one of the shots missed, but most found their mark.

The *Gunslinger*, its barrel chest puffing white smoke and a slick green streak from a severed coolant feed, still ran forward. The heat was searing in his cockpit as Archer sucked it in. It burned, it hurt, it reminded him he was still alive.

Archer glanced over at the *Daishi*. It wasn't moving. No. It had to move. She had to be okay. She had been with him from the start.

He was rocked suddenly from a hit to his leg, a Gauss slug. It hit with a *crack*, like a wet towel being snapped by his ear. The *Gunslinger* was sixty meters away and slowing, readying for the kill. He looked at his damage display and saw the red and yellow warning lights, indications of the damage he had taken. *Far too much in the red.*

Jabbing at the foot pedals, his *Penetrator* moved slowly, awkwardly. It was as if it was fighting him as much as the Loyalist 'Mech. The heat was playing havoc on it. He took a wobbly step forward and made sure he was still locked on target.

Archer waited what seemed like a lifetime for his ER lasers to recycle and recharge. Without even looking, he toggled one of them to the primary TIC and fired. The cockpit became an inferno. It didn't matter. If he cooked, he cooked. What was important was taking down this 'Mech.

The shot hit, barely, cutting from the right ankle of the *Gunslinger* upward to the thigh. It left a black steaming scar, sick, deep, hot. The *Gunslinger* was slowed as well. It aimed its Gauss rifles for another cycle.

They fired.

One shot passed his cockpit by less than two meters, the air-blast buffeting him hard as it whizzed past. A millisecond later the second one plowed into his left torso as if he had been punched in the stomach.

Archer lurched forward to meet the force of the shot, but he couldn't resist. The *Penetrator* that had carried him through so many battles was groaning under his efforts. A red warning light went off, flashing, a gyro hit. He contorted in his seat, as if shifting his own weight was somehow going to help. There was a popping sound somewhere down under him, deep in the bowels of the BattleMech. A moan filled the cockpit and his neurohelmet.

The ground seemed to rush up at him. There was a sickening *thud*, a metallic ripping sound. His head slammed into the cockpit seat as he felt himself being tossed around. A warning went off, but the sound seemed lost in the roar that filled his ears. Archer looked out his cockpit, ignoring the thin crack up the middle. The air was so hot it was almost impossible to breathe.

Across the way, only twenty meters distant, was the fallen form of the *Daishi*. He strained, stabbing at the foot controls. No response. Before the darkness overtook him, his last thoughts were not for his own safety, but that of Katya Chaffee.

Jackson walked into Katrina's office, the report in his hand. He had gotten the feed only a few minutes earlier. Perhaps it was the turn of luck they'd been waiting for. God knows they needed it.

"What is it?" Katrina demanded. "Word from Portsmouth?"

"Yes, Highness," he replied. "I just got confirmation from a unit in the city. The enemy still holds the city and the port facilities, but we are making headway. More importantly, your brother's 'Mech has been taken down."

"Victor, dead?" For the first time in a long time, Jackson Davion saw the look of pure joy, almost twisted, in the eyes of the Archon-Princess.

"We're not sure. I had assembled a special lance to take out the Prince and General Christifori, per your request. Headhunters. Both BattleMechs were taken down in battle, but we were not able to confirm the status of the MechWarriors. Victor's people overran the position a few moments after Christifori went down. Unfortunately, all four of our MechWarriors were apparently killed in the action."

"Acceptable losses if Victor is dead," she replied.

Jackson said nothing. *Not for the families of the men and women that had been sent to their deaths.*

"Can we send in other forces?" she asked, waving aside the deaths. "We need to make sure he is dead."

A knock came to the door followed by a military sentry. "Apologies for the intrusion, Highness."

"This had better be important," Katrina snapped.

"It is," the adjutant officer replied. "We just got reports of an invasion."

"We're aware of that," Katrina replied. "The situation in Portsmouth has been going on for hours."

"Highness," the officer said, obviously nervous. "These landings are on the north end of the island. Initial reports show multiple regiments dropping in. Prince Victor has been sighted on the field of battle. Kai Allard has been seen at the head of the Outland Legion, driving off to form flanking positions." The officer handed the report to Jackson Davion. His eyes raced through the materials.

"Impossible," Katrina said, rising to her feet. "Victor is dead. Christifori is dead. Allard is in Portsmouth."

Jackson threw the report onto her desk with what force he could. "It's not impossible, Princess. As was my initial fear, we have been duped. Portsmouth was a diversion. I'm going to pull the Seventeen Avalon and Twenty-Second Avalon Hussars out immediately to challenge these new landings. The Tenth Deneb will need to be extracted from Portsmouth immediately and rushed to the north, too."

"But Victor—"

"Victor has fooled us," Jackson said. "It may have cost him Christifori, but the cost was well worth it for him if he secures a beachhead."

"Damn him!" she spat.

Jackson said nothing. He simply saluted and turned. There was much to do. The war had taken a whole new twist.

REAR AREA FIELD HOSPITAL
BARRINGTON
NEW AVALON
CRUCIS MARCH
FEDERATED SUNS
25 MARCH 3067

His throat was so dry it hurt when he gulped. Archer knew the smell he was catching, the whiff of chemicals mixed with his own bad breath, meant one thing—he was in a hospital.

For a moment, he didn't want to open his eyes. He didn't want to know how bad it was.

The last memories he had were not good. Katya was down and not responsive. An almost fanatical pair of 'Mechs were rushing them. There was fire. His *Penetrator* had keeled over, baking him like an oven. It had been a long time since he had passed out due to heat build-up, but the memories of it were never fond.

There was no point stalling any longer. His eyes were caked at the edges, but eventually opened. Yes, a field hospital. The white curtain blocking his view was a clue. Shifting slightly in his bed, Archer's muscles ached, but he felt all of his limbs. That was a good sign. Turning, he saw an IV bottle hanging next to him. Yes, he was alive—battered, baked, but alive.

What about Katya?

He rose slightly in his bed, and was surprised he could. The privacy curtains on either side of him blocked his view, but a nurse emerged at the foot of the bed. Wearing green fatigues under a white smock, she moved in quickly to help him to a sitting position. "Take it easy, General."

"Situation?" he rasped, his voice barely audible.

"Relax, sir. Some of your personnel are here. They knew you'd want a full briefing. I'll get them." The fact that she wasn't hovering over him told him his own situation was not serious. He didn't matter anyway. Archer's real focus was his people, his command.

Lieutenant Thomas Sherwood entered first, followed by Captain Kraff. Both men looked all right, though Archer noted Sherwood had a bruise on his forehead that had to feel worse than it looked.

The nurse returned quickly with a glass of water and a bent straw. Archer took a long drag and the water stung his parched throat. He winced, and was almost embarrassed by the gesture.

His voice had returned. "What's the situation, gentlemen?"

Sherwood spoke first. "Major Gett assumed command and coordinated our extraction, sir. Our losses are significant, currently we show less than 32% operational effectiveness. We took one hell of a beating."

"The Loyalists took worse," Kraff added. "A *lot* worse."

Thirty-two percent effectiveness? The loss was staggering. Casualties and damaged equipment would account for a lot of that, but it still meant many good men and women dead. Killed under his command. *More blood on Katherine's hands...*

"What about the primary assault? Any word from the attacking force?"

"Reports in from General Sortek, Kai Allard, and General Sanchez all indicate they have secured a strong beachhead on Avalon Island with minimal losses. Fighting was rough, but a lot less than if we had not made our diversionary attack."

"What about Colonel Chaffee?" Archer asked.

There was a hesitation. The two officers looked at each other. He felt a knot in the pit of his stomach. "What is it?"

"The colonel was badly injured," Kraff said, minus his usual gruffness. "By the time we got to you, two 'Mechs were about to grind you both into greasy spots on the ferrocrete. It was some sort of headhunter lance; they fought right to the end. Damned fanatics."

"How is she?" he pressed.

Lieutenant Sherwood broke in. "She's going to pull through, but she's pretty busted up, sir. Her legs are broken—it looks like her cockpit got severely battered. She was lucky her fire suppression system kicked in, or she could have been facing severe burns." He paused for a moment. "She came around a few hours ago, and her first question was how you were."

Archer allowed himself a thin grin of satisfaction, if only for a few seconds. "I need to get back to duty. We have work to do. We've got to get the regiment back up to ready status in case the Prince needs us."

"General," a voice said from behind the white privacy curtain. A short, muscular man stepped around the corner. It was Prince Victor Steiner-Davion. "That won't be necessary. You and your personnel can stand down for now."

Christifori sat up a little more and gave him a salute, which he returned. "Sir, what are you saying?"

"General Christifori, the Avengers fulfilled their mission gloriously. I came here to tell you that, and to thank you. If it wasn't for your efforts, we would have lost many more people. Your people are tough as nails, tougher."

Victor nodded to the officers of the Avengers regiment. "You're going to be held in reserve, but I'm hoping we won't need your troops any more. God knows they've done their bit for king and country, as have you. But they've been rebuilt and refitted a lot in the last few years. The Avengers have helped win us a signal victory in the assault on Avalon Island. It's time for some of our other troops to finish this up."

"Sir, my men—"

Victor cut him off. "Archer, your troops are going to need you. You've suffered substantial losses. Trust me when I say this, if we need you, you and they will need to be ready. I'm just hoping it won't come to that."

"Sir." Archer stirred in his bed. "I was hoping to be there at the end."

"You are there, General," the Prince replied. "But I haven't forgotten my word to you months ago. You'll have to forgive my rush, but I'm needed elsewhere. When the time comes, you'll hear from me. Until then, your orders are to get your unit patched up." Victor glanced at his chronometer and nodded to Archer, who saluted him. He understood. It took a great deal for the Prince to come to the rear area when the fighting was still going on. It was a mark of respect. *I only hope I've earned it.*

"Simon," Katrina said, steepling her fingers in front of her. Her office fell eerily silent as she spoke. "You have let me down. You have let down the whole of the Federated Commonwealth. Because of you and your incompetence, my brother has been able to land his troops on Avalon Island."

Simon Gallagher did his best to restrain his nervousness, but Katherine could see it. A bead of sweat on the brow, a hand tapping on the arm of the chair. *Good, he understands his life is on the line, Champion or no.*

"Your Highness, I have already sacked the personnel responsible for this grievous error. From where I sat, with the intelligence at hand, the landings in Portsmouth looked to be the primary assault."

Katrina shot a glance at Jackson Davion, then back to her pet field marshal. "We are far too pressed right now for me to try and replace you, regardless of what I think of your competence," she fired back. "But know this—if Victor reaches this palace, you have plenty in your files he will find most amusing. You will, as will your family. I will see to that myself. Do I make myself clear?"

For a heartbeat, Simon Gallagher said nothing. Staring at her coldly, he understood the implications of what she was saying. For him, there would be no endgame. "I understand you completely, your Highness."

"Good," she replied. "Because this war is not mine alone. Everyone loyal to me stands to lose everything should we fail here.

"Everyone…"

General Christifori stood beside her bed. Two IV bottles fed Katya, keeping her alive and hydrated. The nurse had told him, advanced neurofeedback. The hits had set off an internal explosion that had sent a pulse of bio-electrical feedback into her neurohelmet and right into her brain. It was the bane of a MechWarrior. The condition was survivable, but painful.

Archer reached out and took her hand. It didn't move. She had been there with him from the beginning. In fact, it was her prodding that had convinced him to take a stand against Katherine. Now she was lying here, in a hospital bed, because he had ordered her into action.

Damn... Archer winced. If she were awake, he knew she would be pushing him, telling him not to waste time at her bedside. With Katya, the cause had been everything. Taking out Katherine had been the focus of her last few years. Injury would not stop that.

Christifori leaned over her. "I'm always counting on you to be my conscience, Katya. Now you can't. So what would you want me to do?" He spoke in a low tone, almost a whisper.

No response came. He didn't expect any. In his mind he heard her talking. Heard her words. He nodded. "All right then. Once more unto the breach, eh?"

He let go of her limp hand and turned away. Activating his comm unit, he signaled. "This is Specter One. What's the status of my 'Mech?"

"Sir," said a voice that could only be Major Gett. "Why do you want to know?"

"Major, I assure you I don't need or want a lecture. What is the status of my 'Mech?"

"Your *Penetrator* is little more than a shell, sir," she replied curtly. "It's going to take two days and two teams to get it operational. We don't have any reserve equipment not allocated."

"Then get those teams to work, priority one," he said. Turning, he gave Katya one last glance. "Yes, my friend, I'll end this thing once and for all."

APPROACHING THE DAVION PALACE
NEW AVALON
CRUCIS MARCH
FEDERATED SUNS
20 APRIL 3067

Sergeant Reed swung his battered *Lancelot* wide of the incoming missile salvo. The SRM carrier had unleashed a volley of death and destruction at his position from maximum range. The stubby missiles twisted and contorted, raining down all around him. His *Lancelot* quaked. Its right arm, already a mangled clump of metal, caught three warheads, twisting it even more. A puff of white smoke popped out from the elbow actuator, and he watched as the metal and myomer stump dropped to the ground. The 'Mech's weight shifted with the loss of the arm, but he easily compensated.

Suddenly, he saw something out of the right side of his cockpit. It was a BattleMech and, according to his tactical display, it was friendly. The massive, bird-like 'Mech was a dull, primer gray color, obviously repair armor plating. It stopped and leveled its giant arms out for a shot. He watched as glowing-jade beams stabbed at the SRM Carrier.

The boxy little tank was easily in range, and tried to make a break for better cover. The beams sliced into its flank armor, cutting long black slashes. Reed watched as oily, black smoke rose from the rear hit. The SRM carrier lurched to a sudden stop. Hatches opened and the crew began to crawl out. The smoke seemed to come from every seam, every crack, every hatch. Small wisps, then tendrils of twisted darkness.

Then it blew up, an orange ball of fire that engulfed everything around the SRM tank. The blast was massive and over in less than a second. The crew never stood a chance.

Sergeant Reed was stunned at what he had seen. If not for the 'Mech, a *Penetrator*, arriving, he might have been wiped out. He stabbed at his comm panel. "Whoever you are, thanks for the assist."

A very solemn, almost calming voice came back to him. "The Remagan boys are a tough unit. Watch yourself, trooper."

"Who are you?" Reed asked.

"Christifori," came back the voice. "General Christifori." Suddenly the *Penetrator* turned and ran off, obviously having detected another target.

Reed sat in his *Lancelot*'s command seat, his mouth hanging agape. He had heard stories from the other MechWarriors about Christifori. For the last few weeks, he and members of his unit had been operating as an independent command. Word was that Prince Victor had ignored the action. There had been rumors that Christifori and a lance or two of 'Mechs had showed up at several battles, the Avengers adding their fire in, almost always in the nick of time, then disappearing.

Some of the men said Christifori was sanctioned, that the Prince was using him to help troubleshoot battlefield areas...a firefighting unit. Word was his own regiment, Archer's Avengers, was being disbanded.

Reed had written it all off as rumors. Now, he saw differently. Christifori had appeared, saved his butt, then taken off.

Damn, I didn't even get a chance to thank him. He realized his peers were never going to believe what had happened.

FORWARD OBSERVATION POST
NEW AVALON
CRUCIS MARCH
FEDERATED SUNS
22 APRIL 3067

The hovercar was a staff vehicle, bearing two fender flags. The traditional flags of the defunct Federated Commonwealth had been replaced with handmade flags. One was a white flag of truce, the other was a single gold star above the symbol for the Federated Suns—the sign of the Marshal of the Armies.

Victor stood in his MechWarrior's shorts and t-shirt, hands resting on his hips as the car pulled up. The tiny flags stopped fluttering and the door opened. A regal man rose from the back seat. His uniform was pristine, his face was lean and tight. He was tall, and as he looked at Victor he had to look downward. There was a familiarity between the men, genetic. It was in the eyes and cheeks.

The drive had been short. Prince Victor's forces were just outside of the palace itself. The broadband carrier transmission had called for a cease-fire, which had surprised everyone on both sides of the conflict.

Jackson Davion stepped forward and saluted Victor Steiner-Davion. As he clicked his heels together, his spurs jingled. The gathering crowd of officers circling the staff car were surprised by the gesture. They were more surprised when Victor returned the salute.

"You called for a cease-fire, Jackson," Victor said coolly. "I assume your intentions are honorable, and this isn't some vain effort to buy you time."

Jackson's face betrayed no emotions. "No ploy, Victor. Katrina...Katherine sent me here to negotiate the surrender of the palace."

Victor paused, glancing at the man at his side, Kai Allard, then to the other officers gathered. As he returned his gaze to Jackson Davion, he crossed his arms defiantly. "Our terms are unaltered. Unconditional surrender. Your forces must stand down, surrender their armaments, vehicles, and BattleMechs. Prisoners not involved in war crimes will be paroled accordingly."

"I understand," he replied. "I know she will ask, so I must as well. What will become of her?"

Now Victor put on his poker face. "I will be honest, Jackson, our efforts have been concentrated on fighting the war. My plans for peacetime have been second-fiddle to our combat mission. I will say this, though. She needs to be surrendered to my forces immediately. Personally."

"I do not think that will be a problem," Jackson replied. "At this point, I think she expects that."

Victor nodded. "Her custody is important, Jackson. If you'd like, I can send an emissary with you to take her under arrest. That is the quickest way for us to ensure no one else dies in this conflict." His words were not hollow. While a cease-fire was in place, it was tenuous at best, and any small incident could cause it to erupt into full battle again. The war had been long, and the emotions tied to it ran very deep with the troops on both sides.

"I agree," Jackson replied.

Victor scanned the eyes of his officers gathered around the staff car. Each and every one of them had earned the right to go. A part of him wanted to be the one that went to Katherine himself. But this was a political opportunity, a chance to restore the lines of the Federated Commonwealth.

"General Christifori?" Victor called.

Archer stepped forward. Like Victor, he was in his MechWarrior gear. His t-shirt was soaked in sweat, having just been pulled from the lines.

"Highness?"

"I have one last assignment for you."

Katrina caressed the arms of the throne. Closing her eyes, she could feel them under her hands. This was the place her father had ruled from. It was a Davion throne, a throne of power. From this place, from this seat, the fate of the Inner Sphere had rested. It was hers, but in a few minutes, it would not be.

I'll be back...someday, somehow.

She heard footsteps in the room on the marble floor. Slowly, dangerously, she opened her eyes and saw the figures before the throne. An officer, a general, in a dress uniform. He had obviously been a last-minute addition; his face still showed some of the grime of battle. His face was familiar, but she did not focus on it. At least he was civilized enough to have dressed appropriately for court.

Next to him was Jackson Davion, her defrocked Marshal of the Armies.

"I have done as you asked," Jackson said formally. "Prince Victor has offered no terms other than your arrest and unconditional surrender. Given our current state, I felt compelled to accept."

She noticed he no longer addressed her as "Highness." It was already over—it had been so for some time.

"Very well," she said, waving her hand as if to dismiss him and his words. She rose slowly, almost wearily from the throne and took a step down to the marble floor.

"May I present the emissary of your brother. This is General Archer Christifori. General Christifori, this is Katherine Steiner-Davion." Jackson had not lost his formality or dignity given the circumstances. He waved his arm during the introduction as if court were in session.

Christifori stepped forward. There was no bowing, no averting of the eyes, no signs of respect for her authority. Yes, his face had appeared different in the holodisplay images. He was less imposing. Victor's public relations staff had done a good job.

Katrina stepped in front of him. "So you are Archer Christifori? Somehow I was led to believe you'd be much more."

His eyes met hers and for three seconds, said nothing. "Oddly enough, I was thinking the same thing."

"I suppose Victor sent you here to gloat?"

"No," Archer replied. "He chose me so the media could get a picture of me, a FedCom officer, leading you out of the palace. He felt the image would play well in the Lyran Alliance."

"According to my intelligence, you hate the media." Her words were coy, as if she were digging at his motivation.

He offered her nothing but a poker-faced stare. "I do. But this one time I'm willing to bend even my own rules. I owe that to my people."

"Your people? You mean my people."

"They ceased to be yours a long time ago," he replied.

She ignored the entire line of argument. "That's right," she said with a wry smile. *You petty little man.* "You lived on Thorin, if I remember correctly."

"Yes."

"And you blame me for your sister's death? How sad for you. I never even heard of you or your sister. Your entire involvement with this war was a mistake on your part. I didn't kill her; I didn't even order her death. You've been fighting for no reason at all."

Archer's face reddened slightly. *Good, I got to him.* "I'm not surprised you don't know her name. Petty tyrants often stomp on many people, and never know the names of their victims. Yes, Katherine, you didn't order her death, but you pardoned her killer. In many respects, that's worse."

"Watch your words, General," she said bitterly.

"I will not," he spat back. "You're not a princess anymore," he snapped back. "You're just a person. One that will be held accountable for her crimes."

"We shall see."

"Yes," Archer grinned. Reaching down to his belt, he held up a pair of restraints. "But that is the future. It is for people in pay grades above mine to ponder. This is the present. For now, Katherine, put these on, and I will take you to Victor. You can discuss your plans for the future with him. As of now, consider yourself under arrest and susceptible to the military code of justice."

She glared at the restraints. *Handcuffs? Who does he think he is?* "I will not put those on. I am royalty."

Archer said nothing. Stepping forward, he slapped them on her wrists. The metal was cold and hit her left wrist bone hard. It hurt—not much, but enough. "I assume you don't want me to carry you out of here for the media on my shoulder? Please—" he hesitated, "please say yes. Nothing would make me happier right now."

Katherine's jaw locked in anger. She stepped beside him, lowering her cuffed hands. He put his hand on the center of her back and led her out of the throne room. He would pay for what he'd done.

They all will pay...

THORIN MILITIA PARADE GROUNDS
ECOL CITY
THORIN
LYRAN ALLIANCE
15 SEPTEMBER 3067

Archer stood on the field inside the palace grounds, then headed to the podium. He'd been asked to take part in the ceremony inside, but had declined. His job was done. There was no need for the media to see his face. In fact, he was looking forward to obscurity. *I hope I can rebuild the family business...*

In front of him was what was left of Archer's Avengers. They stood at parade rest, perfect formation. Some were bandaged. Some, like Colonel Chaffee, had to have help to stand even after the months of recuperation during the trip home. She, like everyone else, had come to this place, for one last ceremony...one last gathering.

"My friends..." Archer began, his voice hesitating and almost cracking. "And you are my friends. We began this fight back on our homes. We fought in the Lyran Alliance, and even in the heart of the Jade Falcon *touman*. We went to Twycross and tangled with their best, plucking the wings right off the Falcon Guards.

"We all came for different reasons, but for one common goal—to end the reign of a tyrant. That has been done. There is no longer a need for the Avengers, not now. Prince Victor has sent formal congratulations to us as a unit. We have earned our pay and earned the respect of the people we left behind. Moreover, we've earned the respect of the men and women who are no longer in our ranks, those that died at our sides on the field of combat."

He paused, lowered his eyes for a moment. There were so many.

"I was going to do a long speech," he said, wadding up his notes and sliding them off the podium, "but that isn't necessary. What matters is this: the Avengers are family. If called upon again, we would serve. The time for service for most of us is now over. Some of you are being offered positions in the Thorin FTM. For those of you that take those commissions, I offer you the best of luck. I would say, 'make me proud,' but you all already have.

"But that is the future. This is now. Usually when a war is over, units like ours are disbanded. I have conferred with the Prince on this. We are not breaking up. You can't break up a family like us. On the books, we will still be listed as active duty. The reason is simple, there may yet be a time when the Avengers have to take up arms again.

My final command to you, all of you, for now, is go home. Put this damn war behind us. Be with your loved ones. If you make as good citizens as you did fighters, our people will always be proud of you, and so will I. Go to your families, return to your lives, but never forget our time together. Never forget when a handful of good men and women made a difference.

"Avengers, I salute you." Archer snapped into a pristine salute. The troopers went to attention and saluted back. There wasn't a dry eye staring back at him. The salt from his own tears stung the edges of his eyes. He didn't let his voice waver despite the desire to do so. Out of respect for those that faced him, he maintained his last bit of control and restraint. Not just for them, but for all of the troops he had commanded that were no longer alive, or were in a hospital somewhere. They deserved a moment of dignity.

"Regiment," he barked. "Dismissed!"

CENTURION
MEDIUM—50 TONS

DAISHI (DIRE WOLF)
ASSAULT—100 TONS

PLOG19

GALLOWGLAS
HEAVY—**70** TONS

GUNSLINGER
ASSAULT—**85** TONS

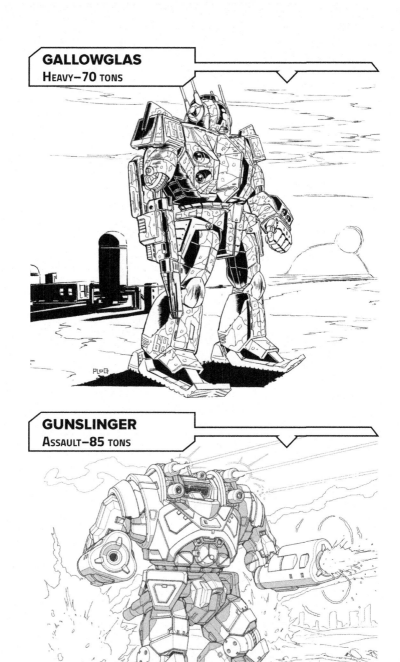

LANCELOT
HEAVY—60 TONS

NIGHTSKY
MEDIUM—50 TONS

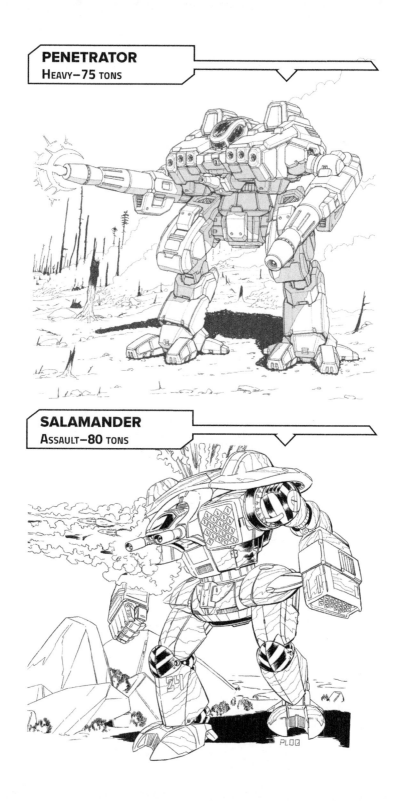

PENETRATOR
HEAVY—**75** TONS

SALAMANDER
ASSAULT—**80** TONS

WATCHMAN
MEDIUM—40 TONS

THE BACK ROAD

LOUISA M. SWANN

LUCAS FARM
OUTSIDE NAGOSHIMA
BUCKMINSTER
BENJAMIN MILITARY DISTRICT
DRACONIS COMBINE
17 AUGUST 3057

Sometimes you have to take the back road to get where you want to go. Not the most direct route, perhaps. But when you're running from the law, you learn to improvise or you end up dead. Somehow, those winding twists and turns led me to where I'm standing now—a field away from my old home, and twenty feet away from where I just buried my Special Forces uniform.

"Hey, mister. There's a dead guy in my daddy's field. You know anything about that?" The question comes from a pitchfork-wielding mini-person who somehow managed to get behind me.

Smart on his part, not smart on mine.

I study the youngster with interest. He looks to be about ten, yet I get the distinct impression he's much older. He's wearing a floppy-brimmed hat, so his eyes are in shadow. His work shirt and jeans are a bit on the big side, as if he's wearing an older brother's clothes.

The boy's accent is pure country, a breath of fresh air to my Dragon-stained lungs, and a reminder of just how provincial my childhood home has remained, in spite of being a prefecture capital. Buckminster always has been a place where people bow to the demands of life, not to the presumed authority of a conquering force, no matter how many years have passed.

"What's your name?" I ask, purposefully avoiding his question. I flex my calf, feel the knife sheath hard against my skin. Remember how effortlessly that knife slid into the cabby's gut. Instinct—born from years of special forces training—rears its long-toothed head, makes my hand itch to pull that same knife, to excise the threat now facing me.

No use wondering how killing got so easy. All it takes is time and experience.

"I said—you know anything about that dead man back there?" The boy shifts the pitchfork in his hand, angles the tines so they catch the sunlight oozing through overcast skies.

There are two reasons I came back to this farm on Buckminster: One—to find my roots. Two—to find my soul. I did not come back to kill boys who pretend to be men.

Sometimes the best way to bluff is to tell the honest truth. What makes the bluff work is the part you choose to tell. I jerk my chin in the general direction of the cab driver's body. "He tried to rob me. Brought me all the way out here and then came after me with a gun."

The boy licks his lower lip, turns the thought over in his mind. He keeps his eye on me, starts to lower the pitchfork—an opening I let pass—then stops, pitchfork still threatening.

"Why don't you tell that story to my pa?" He lifts his head and I get a good look at his eyes—dark brown, direct—Lucas eyes. Just like his daddy's.

The air smells of late summer—earth baked into laziness, like a mother about to give birth. I glance around, check the area for anyone else who might be hiding in the hip-high grasses. A wheat hybrid, from the looks of it. I pull a stalk between my fingers, stripping chaff and grain into my hand. Smell the rich, nutty scent. Harvest was the one time my daddy and I could work together without fighting.

"About time to get some AgroMechs working, isn't it?"

The question hangs in the air as I watch the boy's face charge with emotion—anger?—and go flat.

"Pa don't hold with 'Mechs of any kind," he says.

A breeze ripples across the field, takes me back down memory lane, and it's me standing in this harvest-ready field watching a MechWarrior stride down the road. Taller than the barn I'd grown up playing in. Aligned crystal steel armor on the outside, human heart and brain inside. Proud and ready to fight.

I'd known then I was gonna be a warrior. Not just any warrior. A warrior who could prove to my father just how wrong his simple beliefs were. I would become a member of the Draconis Elite Strike Teams—a dream I'd long ago realized.

A dream that would take away my ability to touch my emotions, that would tear my family apart.

"You're Phelan Lucas's boy, aren't you? I heard your daddy bought this place. This used to be my home. I grew up here." I hold my hands to the side, put on my best good-old-boy smile, but the boy's still suspicious. He isn't buying what I have to sell. "Come on now, put down the fork. Then we can have a nice, civilized conversation."

"How 'bout I keep my 'fork' and you start moving." The kid is young, but that pitchfork is full grown, with three nasty looking tines it would definitely hurt to run into.

I glance over my shoulder. Stare across the field on the other side of the road, where the boy's gaze keeps drifting.

Nagoshima is a distant smudge against the slate gray sky. It's not the city that draws the boy's attention, though. The sounds of mock battle drift toward us on a slight breeze that ruffles the grass and tugs the boy's hat brim. Familiar sounds. Even though they're too far away to see, I know what I'm hearing as well as I know the lines on my face.

BattleMechs. Engaged in a live-fire training exercise.

My own gaze follows the boy's and suddenly I'm back in the cockpit again, locking down my harness, stretching my chin to get comfortable as I slide the neurohelmet over my head, attach the biocables, and power up...

I cut the memories short, feel sweat slick beneath my arms. Piloting 'Mechs had been only one of my jobs, but the inside of a cockpit is not an easy place to forget.

The boy doesn't seem to have noticed my preoccupation. The 'Mechs are far enough away he can't possibly see much detail, yet a look of longing sits upon his face.

Would he still wear that same look if he knew how it feels to bake inside a machine, weapons firing salvo after salvo, the stench of sweat and fear oozing from your body like pus, while all around you people—real people inside their own machines—are dying?

I take a step forward and immediately stop as the pitchfork raises, its tines glistening with menace.

"Don't you come no further," the boy warns. His chin lifts, and I see the challenge in his eyes. I toy with the idea of meeting the challenge, but that was the old me. The new me has made a different choice: Stop killing and go home.

If only things were that easy.

"I like your caution, kid. Caution helps you live longer." I keep my hands spread and move toward the farm house at the far end of the field. Even though he can't possibly see the 'Mechs from where we stand, the boy can't resist one last glance toward the horizon as I pass by. His hunger matches the hunger I once felt.

"You know what it's like inside those machines?" I walk a little to the side so I can keep an eye on that pitchfork.

"You ain't no MechWarrior." In spite of his protest, the boy's eyes are wide. He lets the pitchfork drop a little lower.

"For a while, you feel like you're on top of the world, and nobody can knock you down." I remember well the feeling of accomplishment, of pride mixed with a bit of arrogance. "Then you start to get tired of the heat that bakes you like bread inside an oven every time you fire your weapons. Get tired of feeling scared. Get tired of the killing."

"I knew you weren't no Warrior. 'Mechs ain't scared a nothing." The boy's look turns to disdain. "One day I'm gonna be up there, riding one a them 'Mechs."

We walk a few steps in silence, me trying to figure out how to get out of this mess, the boy chewing on his lip as if trying to make up his mind about something.

"I thought your daddy didn't like 'Mechs?" I ask, more to keep the boy's mind occupied and his pitchfork in a less ominous position.

"Pa thinks they cause more trouble than they take care of."

"And you think he's wrong." Didn't surprise me to hear Lucas felt that way. He and my daddy went way back. I let my hands brush the heavily seeded grass as we walk, watch the breeze pick off the chaff and carry it away while the seeds fall to the ground.

"All's he cares about's planting and harvesting. 'Mechs take care of people." There's definitely a note of bitterness in my new friend's voice.

"Planting grain is an investment in the future," I say, ironically mimicking my own daddy's words. "Harvesting that grain is what keeps us alive, what keeps those warriors alive."

It had taken me years to see the truth in those words. Years filled with bloodshed and death. Deaths justified by the code of the Dragon, but not by my heart.

"They should be more careful when they come through, the 'Mechs, I mean. They're so big, they can't always see where they put their feet. I try to tell Pa that, but it don't matter to him. All's he sees are the crops they stomp into the ground."

Rebellion isn't new to Buckminster, a fact I can personally attest to. Rebellion had allowed me to leave home when I came of age; I plan on that same rebellion allowing me to return to that home.

"Your daddy's got a point."

The boy's point—a very sharp, metal point—presses through the back of my shirt. My cab driver's uniform shirt. Something I'm sure I'll have to explain when I meet up with Lucas.

The smell of roasting meat fills the air as we approach the farmhouse. My stomach responds to the tantalizing aroma in an almost violent fashion, reminding me I've missed several meals already today.

Telling me I'm home.

Funny how it doesn't feel like home. It doesn't feel anything except a little bit familiar.

I close my eyes and see chickens pecking in the yard, hear laundry flapping on the clothesline, taste the sweet tang of vine-ripe tomatoes. A small flock of Bucky browns, indigenous birds no larger than a ten-year old boy's hand, wanders among the chickens. My father always claimed the birds were nothing but a nuisance, but my mother loved the undersize bits of fluff. She refused to use anything but the iridescent brown feathers in pillows and quilts.

A cold, wet nose presses into my hand. I open my eyes, stare at the mangy creature sniffing my palm. A dune pup.

"You're quite a ways from home." I pat the pup's head, then rub my fingers hard against my pant leg. No one's quite sure where dune pups originated, but one touch of the wiry, sand-colored hair plastered against their skin like a thin sheet of armor is enough to set a body's skin crawling.

"*This* is his home," the boy says, and I nod. Home for boy and pup, yes. But not the same home I left behind.

We turn away from the white clapboard house with its sumptuous smells and lace curtains flapping in the windows and follow the mutt into the barn.

"Got my first whipping in this barn," I say, but the boy doesn't answer. I remember vividly the look on my daddy's face that day. I told him I wanted to be a MechWarrior. He said there were only farmers in our family. A lot of things changed that day.

My father.

Me.

I'd seen a lot of barns on a lot of different planets since then. One thing that's standard in any barn—round topped or pitched roof, old or new, red or gray—is the sweet scent of animal sweat mixed with fresh mown hay. A scent I've missed without even realizing it.

Funny how sharp memories can be when they're connected with smells, and how that same smell can bring fond memories forward to replace the bad. I can almost see my friends and I leaping from the loft into fresh-cut hay, challenging each other to see who can jump the highest, the furthest. Who can do double somersaults...

"Who you got there, Con?"

It takes a moment for my eyes to adjust to the darkness. At first, all I can make out is a shadow moving toward us. The shadow slowly resolves into a hulk of a man wearing the same type of clothes as the boy. Only the man's carrying a rifle in one hand, tipped behind him just enough I can't quite identify the make or model.

"I found this guy in the field, Pa. He killed a cabby."

Phelan Lucas pulls off his hat and wipes his forehead, looking at me all the while. He's older than I remember. What's left of his hair is steel gray. Wrinkles fill his leathery face. The wrinkles aren't laugh lines, though. They're the lines of a life hard-earned. The life of a man who doesn't fool around with games, who believes anyone or anything who threatens his family or his livelihood is better off six feet under.

Like a bug under a microscope, Lucas examines me from head to toe without moving. I could tell him my name, but I wait, wanting him to reach out to me, to somehow crack the shell of numbness that's grown so thick I can no longer feel the world.

His gaze meets mine, probing, assessing. All the years of training have built a self-assurance into my body that's almost impossible to hide. He sees this confidence. Knows I could kill him and the boy right now if I wanted.

And he's not intimidated. "You carrying any weapons?"

No partial truths here. The only way to deal with a man like Phelan Lucas is with total honesty. I move slow. Pull my right pant leg up high enough to show the edge of my ankle sheath. Let the pant leg slide back into place. The boy chokes back a startled yelp, but Lucas says nothing.

Sounds outside are muffled, like someone covered the barn with a heavy blanket. A large animal snorts somewhere deeper in the shadows. A hen cackles for a moment, then goes quiet. I can hear Con breathing—quick, fast little breaths that betray his anxiety. His father takes slow, deep breaths. Quiet breaths.

Breaths like mine.

I let a touch of a smile reach my eyes. Lucas's brow furrows in puzzlement.

"I know you," he says. Then his brow clears and he laughs. The end of the rifle dips down toward the floor. "You're Hendal's boy, aren't you?"

"Yes, sir." I should feel relief, but the shell hasn't cracked. Not yet.

"Didn't recognize you with that clown suit on and all." He pokes at the cabby's shirt.

"I borrowed this uniform from a man who doesn't need it anymore."

Lucas's gaze gets a bit more appraising. I begin to feel less like a bug and more like a mouse beneath a cat's paw. I lift my hands just slightly to ease his mind.

"I've had a bit of a run in with the authorities, Mr. Lucas. Seems they and I don't see eye to eye anymore." I visited my daddy's grave on the way out to this place. Tried to tell him he was right about the 'Mechs. Right about everything."

"Your pa always said you'd come back. Too bad he ain't here..." Phelan Lucas clears his throat. "So you're a deserter now, huh?"

Deserter.

The word rings in my ears. A man who should have killed himself rather than bring shame on House Kurita. Bad enough for a Combine MechWarrior to fail his duty—such a man would be dealt a swift death—but for DEST, death would take its sweet, torturous time.

I dip my chin in an almost nod, feel my face flush with heat.

"You weren't never in no 'Mech." Con's voice is filled with loathing.

"That's enough, boy." Lucas takes a deep breath and crams his hat back onto his head. He tucks the rifle into the crook of his arm and steps forward, right hand outstretched. "Good to see you."

I take his hand in a firm grip, matching his strength, but not offering more. "Likewise, Mr. Lucas."

Lucas chuckles, and I smile.

This almost seems too easy, but sometimes life's gifts are that way. You struggle along a rocky path, climbing mountain after mountain, and then suddenly the path opens up on a wide meadow and it's easy going—until you reach the next mountain.

"I need a place to stay for a while. Just until I get my feet back under me."

Con's scowl deepens. "We don't hold with deserters 'round here. 'Mech patrols shoot 'em deader than a squashed roach."

Lucas raises an eyebrow, puts a hand on Con's shoulder. "Go see if your Ma needs help with supper."

Con's face grows more sullen. He hangs the pitchfork on the wall and heads out the barn door without saying a word. Lucas turns back to me.

"Look, I got enough trouble with 'Mech patrols nosing around. If they find out I got a deserter hiding out here..."

"I watched a friend die, Mr. Lucas." How do you explain collapsing containment fields and 'Mech reactors self-destructing in a fiery inferno to a non-military man? "Her 'Mech burned itself up from the inside out with her trapped inside. Three of my lance went down with her."

Amazing how empty words can be when there's no feeling attached. I want to ache inside, to cry, but all I feel is nothingness, the cold void of space.

Lucas puts a hand on my shoulder, gives me a gentle shake. "Sometimes life ain't too kind. Your friend was doing what she had to do. We all do what we have to. It's how we survive."

Words. They fill the emptiness and then melt away as if they were never there. I shake my head, glance over at the pitchfork resting against the wall. "I should've died with them, but I'm still here. Why am I still here?"

Before Lucas can answer I hear rumbling outside. A distant sound like shuffling thunder. A familiar sound.

The sound of BattleMechs on the road.

"I think we have company," I say.

Lucas's expression doesn't change, but he steps forward and waves at me to follow.

We move deeper into the shadows. There's a storage locker at the back of the barn, with a heavy wooden door that swings open with a groan when Lucas tugs on the handle. He steps inside, switches on a light. "Plenty of fresh manure in the barn and a lot of hot air outside. Should mess up a 'Mech's monitors pretty good. Con wasn't fooling—these new guys can be pretty nasty if they get a bee in their helmets."

He smiles as if remembering I already know this.

The barn may have brought back some nostalgic memories, but closed-in spaces bring back memories of war. Of death. Of pain. I take a deep breath. Let it out slowly. Gather my energy like a coiled serpent ready to strike...

...and force my muscles to relax. I've already brought enough trouble to those I care about. I step inside. Look Lucas in the eye.

"How do you clean memories from your mind, Mr. Lucas? How do you let go?" I lean up against the wall, wrap my arms around my waist. "I can't get her picture out of my head. Every time I look at a 'Mech, I see her face, charred so badly I only know it's her because of the medallion she wore around her neck. For good luck, she said. But where was luck when her system malfunctioned? When she was trapped inside that burning hulk of metal?"

"If I had the answer to that question, son, I'd be doing more'n sitting here on this farm waiting for 'Mechs to tromp through my crops." Lucas starts to close the door, then stops. "I'll leave it cracked for you, but the light'll have to go."

I nod as he switches off the light and eases the door shut.

The room is pitch black until my eyes make the adjustment. Something rustles in the back. Habit forces my hand to the knife sheath, pulls the blade free before I make any conscious decision. A small slice of light sneaks through the cracked door and glows across my blade. I feel the edge, razor sharp and ready to kill. Listen for the rustle.

But whoever—whatever—is in the back of this room is quiet now. Listening for me.

Voices whisper in the corner of my mind. Living nightmares of the dead who can no longer speak. I press the knife against my palm to drive the voices away. Turn my thoughts to the barn and the last words I'd heard my father speak:

"Killing ain't the answer, boy. Never was. Never will be. You're nothing but two legs and a strong back far as the

military's concerned—a mountain mule willing to give his soul for a pat on the nose. Our place is here, working with the land. All killing ever got anybody like us is dead."

Sometime during the last few years my father's words, words spoken so long ago the memory was just a dusting upon my mind, began to make sense.

Doubt—in the system, in my superiors—crept through my being like an insidious disease, worming its way through my thoughts until every order was suspect, every action tinged with uncertainty. Yet I continued to follow orders until those same orders killed my comrades.

My friends.

The ground trembles—a vibration you can feel in your feet, but can't see with your eyes. I know from the feel the contingent approaching is small. Probably a single 'Mech on security patrol. From Lucas's reaction this isn't an uncommon occurrence, just an unwelcome one, though why 'Mechs are patrolling this area is something I can't quite figure.

Unless they're searching for deserters.

My heart skips a beat. My breath quickens. A small part of my mind notices the fear, the anticipation before the feeling slips away. My body is ready to react, like a well-oiled machine, a machine I no longer want any part of.

Another feeling slides through the crack that's starting to open in my shell. Shame. I came home looking for answers, not to hide in the dark.

I ease open the storage room door, look around before making my move. The barn appears empty. Hay muffles my footsteps as I steal across the open floor and take up position beside the huge doorway.

From my post I can make out the approaching 'Mech—a scarred BH-K305 *Battle Hawk*. Sunlight slants across the yard, bounces off the metal body in a flash of blinding light.

The machine stops, its huge legs casting shadows from the evening sun across the barn. Lucas stands calmly before the 'Mech, rifle resting in the crook of his arm.

Adrenaline stings my gut and pulses through my veins. Have I judged Lucas right? Is the man who now owns my daddy's house the man I think he is?

A gray-haired woman—sturdy as the land she helps tend—steps out on the porch. I can feel anxiety radiating from her straight mouth. She clenches a towel in her hands, wrings the cloth like a chicken being killed for dinner. Lucas waves her away. After a brief pause, she stomps inside and slams the porch door behind her.

I center myself, try to stem the flow of paranoia. My throat clogs as I watch the *Battle Hawk* shut down. The egress hatch opens and a chain link ladder clanks down the 'Mech's side. A pilot—dressed in legless suit and boots—steps from the hatch, his sweat-plastered hair glistening wetly in the sun. The man looks as out of place on this quiet farm as his 'Mech. He pauses at the top of the ladder, glances around, reaches back inside before descending to the ground, right hand hidden from view.

"Hello, Mr. Lucas. You planning on trouble?" The pilot wears a smile on his face, but his eyes are wary. He holds his right hand back by his side, gestures with his left at the rifle in Lucas' hand.

"Just scaring off critters," Lucas says. I start to relax. Things are going just fine—

Con runs out of the house, his face filled with defiance. "There's a deserter in the barn! He killed a cabby and threatened my pa!"

Lucas is startled. I can see the anger in his face from here. The confusion. I lean hard against the rough wood planks, feel a splinter slide deep in my palm.

The pilot's face isn't friendly anymore. "That's a serious accusation, son."

"There's no one in the barn but an old friend." Lucas lifts the rifle across his chest. He takes hold of Con's arm and pulls him tight to his side. "He's been helping us out, ain't that right, boy?"

The pilot stares into Con's eyes, but the boy doesn't answer. I can practically feel his hatred from here. His anger burns like mine used to burn, and I know it's only a matter of time. I tuck my blade up into my right sleeve, step out into the sunlight.

"Heard a commotion..." I fake surprise at the sight of the 'Mech. "Whoa. That's some machine."

The pilot glances up, surprise and suspicion written on his face. His right hand swings free and his eyes narrow as he studies the cabby's uniform. He glances at the barn. At Lucas. At Con. Back at me.

And I know he knows.

"This your deserter?" the pilot asks Con. He brings up his right hand, points the weapon he's been concealing in my direction.

"That's not necessary. Like I said, this here's an old friend." Lucas's big hand holds Con close.

The pilot scans the yard and his eyes come back to me. "You got some identification to go with that uniform?"

I nod. Reach in my pocket. Swallow and try to wet the dryness in my mouth. *I am more than what the military made me,* I remind myself. More than a killing machine.

That's why I came home. Not to kill, but to keep from killing. To find the truth behind my daddy's words. To find out why the man behind the machine died.

And maybe to bring him back to life.

But sometimes things don't always go the way we plan.

I pull out the cabby's ID and walk over to the 'Mech pilot.

"He's got a knife!" Con ducks out from beneath Lucas' arm and charges me from the side.

The pilot spins, weapon flashing in his hand. Lucas raises his rifle as the pilot fires a shot that creases my leg. The leg stings with pain, but I block it so swiftly it might not have happened. I dodge behind the laundry, feel the years of training, the years of battle struggle to take over.

Death is what identifies me. Killing's all I know. All I have known since I was little more than Con's age.

"No!" Con's voice slices through the air just as the rifle cracks. The boy crumples to the ground, Lucas reaching for him like a drowning man grabs for rope.

I dive into a forward roll, come up beside the pilot. He stares at the boy on the ground, at Lucas kneeling by Con's side. Red coats my vision, painting pictures of MechWarriors falling, burning...

The instant kill zone between the fourth and fifth intercostal spaces is where I've been trained to strike, but that would be too merciful.

I shove my knife deep into the man's gut. "You didn't have to hurt them," I hiss as warm blood spills out over my hand, a dark flow that matches the darkness inside me.

His eyes turn to mine, his glare filled with disdain, and he spits in my face.

I push the blade deeper, give it a twist, watch the light fade from his eyes before pulling my knife free.

"Lucas?" The woman's panic-tinged voice shrills across the yard as the porch door slams. I whip around, ready once again to defend myself. It takes a moment for reality to sink in. For the battle haze to clear from my mind.

Lucas sits crumpled on the ground beside Con. His eyes are red, tears streak his cheeks.

"I was trying to distract him," Lucas whispers. "But Con got in the way."

Red seeps from Con's side. I kneel down, pull aside his shirt. Glance at the wound.

"It's a clean shot," I tell Lucas. "Through and through. He'll be okay as long as you get him to a doctor."

Con's mother shoves me aside and pulls her son to her breast. I give the woman room. Breathe deep the dust-laden air.

MechWarrior blood sticks the cabby's shirt to my ribs. I clean my blade on the shirttails—the blade I should have used to end my own life rather than bring the shame of a deserter upon the House of Kurita—and slip it back into its sheath.

"You're nothing but a yellow-bellied coward," Con says. He pushes his mother away, but his gaze—filled with hatred and pain—stays fixed on me.

Lucas stands. Grabs my arm.

"You can't stay now." His voice is raspy, his eyes filled with an apology I know he'll never make.

"I know." I try to keep the desperation from my face, but I know he's seen it. "It's just that..."

"Coming home's not always the answer," Lucas says.

Con's face grows hard as a 'Mech's armor. He struggles to his feet, leans briefly on his mother, then straightens. "He's a damn deserter. He don't have no home."

The bitter statement slices at my heart in a way I'd thought I'd never feel again. I draw a deep breath, let the feeling run through me. Someday the boy will understand.

I look deep in Con's eyes, at the determination, the desire.

Then again, maybe he won't.

I pause a moment to let the pain in my knee subside. The wound will take a long time to heal, I know that from experience. My soul will take longer, but the shell's been broken now. I glance back into the barn, let my gaze linger on the loft, draw the sweet hay scent deep into my lungs, feel the pain stab my heart once more.

And turn to leave.

"I'll hunt you down, you know." Con's voice is flat and low, the way it was when he first confronted me. Lethal—like a poisonous snake. "When I get my 'Mech..."

"Con!" Lucas's hand is raised as if to strike his son. He lowers it slowly. Lines drawn heavy by life's hand deepen on his face, revealing the battle within.

A battle my own father lost.

'Mech against 'Mech. Machine against human. Father against son.

There's a chance my soul will heal.

But another soul will slowly leach away, minute by inexorable minute, until boy becomes man.

And man becomes machine.

BATTLE HAWK
Light—**30** tons

COMMERCE IS ALL

STEVEN MOHAN, JR.

CANOPIAN PLEASURE CIRCUS *BACCHANAL*
HIGH ORBIT OVER TRONDHEIMAL
ILLYRIAN PALATINATE
5 JANUARY 3033

Captain Douglas Berg stepped into the Hook-Up, the first outer-ring bar on the Canopian Pleasure Circus *Bacchanal,* and felt his jaw tighten.

The bar's cheap sound system transformed the pounding music into one long screech punctuated by a back beat so deep he felt its throb in his teeth. The bar was dimly lit except for occasional flashes of blue-white light that left him blinking away bright afterimages. The air was filled with a foul, blue haze and the mingled smells of tobacco and marijuana.

Sweat and desire.

He'd been on less chaotic battlefields.

How'd he let Sully talk him into this?

Thank god the Hook-Up was located in the outer ring, where the DropShip's spin was maximum. After seeing how weird this place was, he had no desire to visit one of the zero-G places.

He turned to go and felt a strong hand clamp down on his arm. "Not trying to get away, are you?"

Berg turned to see his good friend, Lieutenant Jason Sullivan, staring at him, a broad grin stretched across his ugly face.

"Who, me?" Berg asked innocently.

"C'mon," said Sully in a slurred voice that told Berg the infantry officer was already well into his cups, "Might as well 'ave a good time." He sobered for a moment. "If Little Bob has his way, it'll be your last."

H. R. "Little Bob" McIntyre was the ruthless dictator of the Circinus Federation, a gang of thieves, cutthroats, and rapists dressed up to look like a real government. The latest intel indicated the Circinians were mobilizing troops and assembling DropShips. All signs pointed to a Federation invasion of the tiny Illyrian Palatinate.

And if that happened, Berg, Sully, and the rest of the mercenaries in Thor's Army would be in the middle of the fighting.

But that didn't mean that everyone in the Periphery had to know about it.

"This is not the place," Berg hissed.

"You think they don' know?" said Sully, waving at the crowd with his glass. "Th' whole *sector* knows."

"All right, stop it," said Berg sharply, grabbing the other man by the tunic.

"Why do ya' think the circus's in town," asked Sully fiercely, "if not to collect our last few coins before the invasion comes?"

Berg slowly let go of his friend. He didn't have an answer for that. It was rare for the Canopian pleasure ships to range through the Periphery as far coreward of the Magistracy as the Palatinate, and here was the *Bacchanal* hanging in orbit about Trondheimal.

Sully grabbed him around the back of the neck and pulled Berg's face close to his. "So 'ave a good time, Dougie." Then he let go of his friend and stumbled off into the semi-darkness.

Berg glanced around the room and sighed. Little chance of that. He waved for a drink without bothering to tell the 'tender what he wanted and a glass of something appeared before him. He took a sip. Bad vodka. Good enough.

There was plenty of skin on display at the Hook-Up, a good time for the asking. Long, platinum hair. Or white-blond. Or red. Blue eyes, violet eyes, emerald eyes. Heavy breasts barely bound by shimmering silver tops that accented rather than covered.

It was crass. It was obvious.

It was boring.

Berg had promised Sully he would come to the bar, and he'd come. He downed his vodka in one quick toss, turned to go.

And saw her.

She was nothing like the other women in the bar. She wore a dress the color of midnight that somehow managed to be sexy and classy at the same time. It hugged the curves of her slim body, which were nice without being overdone. Her skin was the color of rich mocha, and set off nicely by gray-green eyes.

Berg tried to swallow and found he couldn't.

She reached the bar and summoned the 'tender with a look. He set a drink in front of her Berg bet wasn't bad vodka.

He stepped forward and slapped a C-bill down on the bar. "For the lady."

She frowned. "That's really not necessary," she said coolly.

The 'tender sat down a second drink to match the first.

"But it would be my great pleasure," Berg said. "Perhaps there's someplace we could go. And, uh, talk," he said quickly.

Her gaze flickered to the MechWarrior insignia on his collar and then back to his face. "I don't think you and I have anything to *talk* about."

Berg blinked. He had to be the only man who could strike out in a pleasure circus. "Well, please take the drink anyway," he said. "I insist."

She opened her mouth to protest, but a deep voice behind Berg said, "Thank you. I will."

Berg turned to see a Circinus officer reaching for *his* drink. The man's head was shaved except for a brown topknot that hung halfway down his back. The golden skull insignia on his black leather uniform made him a captain, though the indigo battle tattoos covering his face and neck suggested he was an extremely well-traveled captain.

"What are *you* doing here?" Berg snapped.

The Circinian officer smiled, a gleaming shark's smile. "Canopus is not party to the dispute between Illyria and the Federation. And my money is as good as anyone's, Captain…"

"Berg. Douglas Berg."

The Circinian smiled. And I am Car Negdren." He drained the shot glass and set it down on the bar with a sharp *clack*. "Thank you, Captain. Perhaps you'll let me return the favor some time."

"Sure," said Berg tightly. "*If* we run into each other again."

"Oh, I'm sure we will," said Negdren. The beast slipped his arm around the woman's waist like he owned her. "Ready to go, Arissa?"

"Quite ready." The pair turned to leave, but not before the beautiful woman named Arissa offered Berg a dismissive smile that cut deeper than any wound he'd ever received in battle.

After the incident in the bar, Berg would've left the *Bacchanal* on the next Trondheimal-bound shuttle if not for his buddies. It was a warrior's duty to watch his comrades' backs, even on leave. Especially if there were Circs about. So Berg drifted moodily through the mutant freak-shows and skin palaces and gaming emporiums, partaking of nothing but the occasional drink and keeping his eyes open.

Unable to think of anything save the woman, and how she'd gone off with that pig, Negdren.

Sometime during his wandering he found himself at a small hatch labeled The Chapel of Stars. Berg wasn't a religious man, but he had a sudden longing to find a quiet corner in which to be alone. So he slipped a token into the lock slot and waited for the hatch to cycle.

He stepped into a dark space lit only by starlight. The chapel was a ferroglass bubble cast into the shape of a church's nave and thrust out from the ship's hull, so worshippers would feel like they knelt in the very palm of God. Berg shut the hatch softly behind him and took a careful step forward. Here, noise felt like heresy.

Slowly his eyes adjusted to the darkness and after a time, Berg realized he was not alone. A woman knelt close by in the thin light of the stars, head down, hands pressed palm to palm.

"Great Father," she whispered and her soft, clear voice startled Berg. *It was Arissa.* "Please look after little Katrina, who fate long ago placed in your care. And give me the strength to do what must be done."

She's praying, Berg realized, mortified. "Arissa," he said softly.

She jumped to her feet and turned on him. "Are you following me? How dare you!" He could see the fury written on her face even in the darkness.

Berg held his hands up. "I'm sorry. I didn't mean to—"

She reached out to slap him, and he caught her wrist in his hand.

She jerked away from him. "Let go of me."

Berg instantly let go.

She rubbed her wrist, and Berg saw a sneer twist her pretty lips. "The brave warrior," she said derisively.

"I'm sorry," he said again. "Did I hurt you? I didn't mean to."

"No," she said bitterly. "You never *mean* to."

"Hey," said Berg. "You don't know me."

"I know you better than you know yourself."

"Why do you hate me so much?" asked Berg.

"You're a mercenary," she said. "Men pay you to fight."

"What do men pay you to do?" he shot back.

This time she did slap him, hard enough to sting. Hard enough he tasted blood. She stood with her legs apart, hands clenched into fists, breathing hard.

She was standing very close to him, close enough that he could hear the angry rasp of her breath, almost feel the rapid rise and fall of her chest, smell the scent of her: soap and sweat and rose petals.

"Look," he said as calmly as he could, "As long as there are men like your precious Negdren in the universe, there needs to be men like me, too."

She fixed him with a hard stare, then stepped past him and stalked out of the space.

Berg was at a bar, quietly nursing the pain with a low-rent bourbon, when she found him again. He knew it was her even before she spoke, because she put her hand on his shoulder and leaned up against him so her mouth was right next to his ear. He felt the softness of her breasts pressing against his back.

"Hades Black Label?" she said lightly. "I would've thought a MechWarrior could afford better."

Berg didn't turn around to look at her. "My father always said, 'If you're gonna get drunk, no sense doing it on the good stuff.'"

"Sounds like a wise man," she said.

Berg didn't say anything. He just sipped his bourbon and stared straight ahead.

"I've acted badly," she said after a moment. "Let me make it up to you."

"Are you offering me a date or a business proposition?" he said bitterly.

"I'm offering you an apology," she said firmly.

Berg considered not answering, just sitting there until she went away, but her smell was on his uniform now, on his uniform and in his head. He thought about it for a minute, but there was never any doubt about what he was going to do.

He turned around to face her.

She stared down at him, those gray-green eyes locked on his, searching for something.

"Dinner?" he said gently.

She broke into a wide smile. "That would be nice."

Arissa picked a Polynesian restaurant whose bulkheads were wrapped in a hologram that showed silver moonlight tracing a path across a tranquil black sea. If Berg had been sitting on sand rather than a fine leather chair, he would've believed he was actually on the beach.

Torches set at each table provided flickering, yellow illumination, lending the illusion that they were the only diners in the restaurant. Arissa ordered for them: white wine, braised sea bass on a bed of island vegetables, and for dessert fresh pineapple cut by the waiter right at the table.

For most of the meal they ate in silence, but afterward, Berg looked at her and said, "I kept wondering why you didn't like me. But that was really the wrong question, wasn't it?"

Arissa moistened her lips.

"The real question is, why don't you like soldiers?"

She looked down and took a deep breath. "I'm from Niue."

He looked at her blankly.

"It's a small world, barely bigger than a large moon," she said softly. "It's not even on most star charts."

And then something clicked into place in Berg's head. Some scrap of dusty intel about a little world chewed from top to bottom by two pirate factions each looking for a place to call their own and the innocent population caught in the middle.

Berg opened his mouth. "I'm—"

"What?" she snapped. "Sorry?" She shook her head and drew a deep shuddery breath. "No, strike that. *I'm* sorry. This isn't about you. It's just hard for me to remember that sometimes."

"Is that—I mean, when you mentioned Katrina—"

She looked up sharply and those gray-green eyes told him there were still some questions she would not answer.

That's okay, he thought. *No more questions.* He wasn't going to be just one more soldier that hurt her.

Gently, he reached out and took her hand in his.

Sometime in the middle of the night his watch buzzed insistently, tickling the inside of his wrist. He swam slowly

back to consciousness. Arissa was a lump of soft warmth pressed against his back. He took a moment to answer the summons, allowing himself the indulgence of remembering the brush of her lips against his, the feel of her body under his hands, the smell of her filling him up.

It was all he could do to make himself get out of bed.

He found his comm and flicked it open, read the message. One of his troopers, Corporal Toggleson, had been detained by Ship Security on a D-and-D.

Then he glanced down and saw something by the dim blue light of the comm's screen, something not right. The corner of a currency note stuck out from one of Arissa's dresser drawers. Curious, Berg slowly pulled the drawer open and picked up the note.

Five hundred bones.

Circinian currency.

A currency that was useless anywhere but the Federation.

He glanced down into the drawer. It was hard to tell in the dark, but there was maybe twenty, thirty thousand bones in all. Far too much money for the pleasure of a woman's body. He glanced over at Arissa sleeping in the bed.

No matter how beautiful the woman.

What had Negdren said? *My money is as good as anyone's.* Berg remembered the man's combat tattoos. Tattoos that suggested Negdren should be a major, or more likely, a colonel. Now why would a Circinian colonel pretend to be a captain? Maybe because he didn't want to draw attention to himself while he was running an operative.

"What is it, Douglas?" Arissa asked in a slurred voice that told him she was still half-asleep.

He dropped the note back in the drawer and quietly slid it shut. "The ship picked up one of my men on a drunk and disorderly. Gotta get him out of the dock."

She sighed in her sleep. "Hurry back," she whispered.

Yes, thought Berg bitterly, *hurry back, said the whore to the mercenary.* If love and duty could be sold like commodities, why not trust as well?

As soon as he had dressed and left Arissa's quarters, Berg pulled out his comm and punched in Sully's access code. It took eight rings before a groggy voice said, "Ye—"

"Sully, this is Berg. Toggleson's gotten himself in some trouble. I need you to go get him out of the dock."

"Look, Dougie, I don't think I can—"

"This is a red tactical tasking, Lieutenant Sullivan. Noted and logged. Berg out."

Red tactical tasking. That meant an automatic court martial if Sully failed to come through. Berg hated to pull rank on his friend, but he couldn't afford to have someone from Ship Security call Arissa's quarters looking for him.

He headed quickly to a staircase that led to a mezzanine that looked down on the row of rooms where Arissa's was located. When he reached the top, he ducked down behind the railing.

He didn't have long to wait.

Ten minutes after making the call to Sully, Captain—or rather, *Colonel* Negdren—appeared at Arissa's quarters and rapped on the door. Berg's stomach clenched and his mouth tasted dry. So much for Arissa being half-asleep.

So much for a lot of things.

He slipped back down the stairs and hid behind the bend in the wall.

Negdren was only inside for five minutes. Not enough time for anything fun.

Only enough time for a pick-up.

The door clicked open, and Berg stepped out from his hiding place. "Hey, you son of a bitch. What do you think you're doing?"

Negdren looked up sharply, and then a smirk stole across his face. "Well, what do you think I'm doing, Captain?"

Berg pointed a finger at Negdren. "She's mine. You stay away from her."

Negdren held his hands out in an expansive gesture. "She belongs to anyone who has the asking price." If possible, his smile grew even bigger.

Berg smiled back and then he kicked up and in, the toe of his boot contacting solidly with Negdren's groin.

The air went out of the Circinian, but the colonel was a tough old bird. He didn't go down as Berg had expected. Instead, he came out swinging.

Berg blocked the first punch and the second, and then he staggered back, his ear ringing and one whole side of his face numb. Third time's a charm.

Berg delivered a long, sweeping kick, hoping to knock Negdren's feet out from under him, but the colonel nimbly danced away from Berg's boot and then hammered home with one of those roundhouse punches.

The world went black for a moment and when Berg managed to get his eyes open, Negdren knelt over him, his topknot draped over his near shoulder, an insufferable smile warping his tattooed face. "You shouldn't fight dirty with a pirate, Captain. We invented it."

Berg tasted the salty tang of blood. He groaned and half-closed his eyes.

Negdren leaned forward and whispered, "You know, Captain, she was beautiful. The best I've ever—"

Berg's hand snapped up like a striking snake, closing around Negdren's topknot and jerking down. The move caught the colonel off balance and unawares. He tumbled over, and his head slammed to the deck.

Berg scrambled to his feet. Negdren managed to get to his hands and knees, his shoulders sagging and his head hanging down.

Berg hesitated. He wouldn't hit a man once he was down. Then he thought of Arissa, and his steel-tipped boot lashed out and caught Negdren squarely in the face.

The colonel fell and moved no more. The stain of crimson against the white deck told Berg he had at least broken Negdren's nose.

Berg glanced down the hall to make sure no one was coming, then he bent down and began searching the colonel's person, stopping only when he found the data crystal he knew had to be there.

In the end, there was no reason for Berg to go back. He had quickly copied the crystal and returned the original to Negdren's prone form. Negdren would wake to find his crystal still there, and so would conclude the fight had truly been about a woman.

On the eve of battle, Illyria would know the Federation's mind.

And there was no reason to go back for Arissa, now that he knew *exactly* what he was to her.

Then he saw those gray-green eyes, remembered the smell of her, and none of the logical reasons mattered...

An hour after the fight, he found himself back at her quarters.

Arissa opened the door before he could knock. She wore a shimmering silk robe the cool color of dark grass. Berg couldn't help noticing it barely reached her knees, and she obviously wasn't wearing anything else underneath.

She stepped aside to allow him in.

"Who is Katrina?" Berg asked, his voice hard.

"That is none of your—"

"*Who is Katrina?*" he roared.

Arissa's jaw set, but after a moment she said, "My sister. She was my sister. She was five." She swallowed. "When the pirates killed her."

"You were praying for strength," Berg said angrily. "Praying in her name. Strength for what, Arissa?" He held up the copy of Negdren's crystal. "Strength enough to betray Thor's Army and Illyria?"

"No," she whispered. "Strength enough to pretend I didn't want you. You know how long it's been since a man wanted to *talk* to me?"

Berg's heart melted.

And then he remembered her sleeping innocently in the bed. And Negdren arriving at her room not ten minutes later. "You tell a pretty story," he said coldly.

She tilted her head, an expression of hurt sketched across her face. "Please, Douglas—"

Berg's hand slashed through the air, cutting her off. "No. You came to me because Negdren sent you to me."

"It's true that Negdren wanted me to come to you. It's not true that's why I came."

"I have the crystal, Arissa."

"Have you read it yet?" she asked sharply.

Berg opened his mouth, but before he could say anything she bent down and retrieved a reader from the table. She thrust the device at him.

Berg slowly took it from her, attached the crystal, and began to scroll down the small screen. "I never told you any of this," he said slowly. "And...this is wrong. There aren't three lances of 'Mechs on Reykavis, only one. And there isn't a reinforced battalion on Trasjkis. That force is no more than company strength. And..."

He looked up. "These are all lies."

She nodded. "Lies Negdren will believe. Because he thinks I got them from you."

"They make us look much stronger than we really are."

"Yes, they do," said Arissa tightly. "And so there will be no war. Little Bob will look at this intel, and he'll think twice about attacking Illyria."

Berg swallowed. "I—"

"Don't bother to thank me," she snapped. "I did it for Katrina. Not for you."

He reached for her, gathered her into his arms. She pulled back for a second, then collapsed against his chest, her body shaking with silent sobs.

"It's okay," Berg whispered. "You sell your body, and I sell my life. But there is a part of us—"

"Yes," she whispered back. "A part of us that cannot be sold."

EN PASSANT

PHAEDRA M. WELDON

**SANDOVAL CASTLE
ROBINSON
DRACONIS MARCH
FEDERATED SUNS
7 OCTOBER 3065**

The *click* of Päl Wyndham-Sandoval's polished boots echoed off the corridor walls leading from Duke Sandoval's library and study. The braid of his topknot swung around to brush his cheek. He swept it away with an impatient hand. The sword, which went with his dress uniform, bumped against his left thigh, and with every determined step he ground another piece of his own frustrations beneath a heel. Within an hour of his arrival on Robinson, the world had turned one-hundred and eighty degrees.

Servants stood aside in the wide hall to let him pass. He acknowledged them with barely a nod. Broad events preoccupied his thoughts: James Sandoval no longer directed the course of the family dynasty. Mai Fortuna no longer led the Robinson Rangers. Tancred Sandoval now bore the ducal title, and he had shifted Robinson's support in the ongoing civil war away from Katrina Steiner-Davion to her brother, Victor.

Päl's life had been altered by events beyond his control. Just as it had when Arthur Steiner-Davion was assassinated. He had been in that stadium, seated with other Battle

Academy cadets, listening to Arthur's address when explosions rocked the proceedings.

Events born of that calamity had played out at an alarming speed, enveloping him each time he caught his breath. Then-Duke James Sandoval, blaming the attack on the Draconis Combine. Tancred, choosing not to rejoin the Rangers. Päl had been tapped to take his place, promoted to leftenant. The young scion feeling like a chess piece being shifted about a board.

Returning to his family's estates on Exeter, saying goodbye to his wife and newborn son, and leaving to join the First Rangers for their ill-fated assault on House Kurita.

However, no matter the whys or the what-happeneds since his last visit to Robinson; Päl was excited to see his parents. They had been in the room earlier, when Tancred arrived to accept the mantle of dynasty leadership, but not for the military planning session that followed. Päl had so far managed only a handful of words with them.

Turning a corner in the spacious Sandoval Castle, he found them waiting just inside the foyer doors. His father, a roundish man of medium height and receding hairline, had once served with the Rangers. Päl had grown up on his father's stories of 'Mech battles, and considered it destiny that had stepped in to make the baron's son a MechWarrior and an officer.

The Baron Exeter took a few steps toward Päl, his expression dark and his mouth open to speak, but the baroness stayed him with a hand on his left arm and a calm smile to her son.

Baroness Margarette Wyndham-Sandoval was a proud woman, rich in the heritage of the Sandoval family. Päl had always seen his mother as one of the pillars of the family, the one whom others looked to for guidance. As her son, he had always done as she wished, and she had never guided him wrong. The Baroness was a strong and silent partner beside his father, and he loved them both. He only wished, at times, his mother's stolid and stoic appearance in court had not carried over into her duties as mother.

Päl pulled the dress-white gloves from his hands as his mother directed them with a nod to the doors, and beyond to the waiting Avanti stretch hover sedan. He opened the car's door for his mother and gave her his hand as she gracefully stepped in. His father gave him a tight smile, placed a hand on his son's arm, then bent down to enter as well.

After the doors were closed and the car was underway, the baron could contain his curiosity no longer. "Well?" He raised a graying eyebrow at his son.

Päl shrugged. Tancred's loyalties were no secret, although the particulars discussed behind closed doors might be. But he had never kept information from his father. In only a few sentences, he relayed the meeting's proceedings—including Tancred's plan to ease relations with Theodore Kurita.

His words garnered exactly the reaction he'd expected from his father.

"*What?*" the baron's voice boomed inside the sedan. "Is the man mad? How can he give up those worlds to the Dragon? This is outrageous!" He traded a glance with his wife, who nodded. "Unacceptable!"

Päl was no longer so certain. He turned his attention to the passing scenery, considering.

It was early autumn on Robinson, and the display of browns, oranges, yellows, and reds reminded him of fall evenings at home, spent with Khim. He missed her terribly after almost three years apart, and felt guilty for abandoning his son at such an early age. After the unit's disastrous retreat from Ashio, Päl had remained on Mallory's World with the rest of the regiment. He'd sent word to his mother, asking if he should request leave to return home until the First received new orders.

His mother had advised him to remain on Mallory's World. She had taken a lead in his son's education, and Päl shouldn't worry himself with such details. According to the baroness, Päl was where he needed to be, in support of the duke's orders. And so he'd remained with his regiment, wrote letters to his wife Khim every day, and practiced with his knives.

Until Mai had tapped him to accompany her here to Robinson for a meeting with the new duke.

He sighed as he finally looked back at his father. "That's the way it is, Father. And truthfully, I see no flaw in what he proposes."

The baron's eyes widened. "You *support* Tancred in this nonsense? Turning the loyalties of Robinson toward Victor."

"I support the decisions of my commander and duke, sir, as any good soldier would. You taught me that." Päl clasped his hands in his lap. The filtered sun glinted off the gold of his Battle Academy ring. "Tancred feels our attentions are wasted attacking the Combine." He paused for a beat. "I agree."

"You can't be serious..." the baron began. "James would never have allowed such a thing."

Päl kept silent. The young Wyndham-Sandoval knew not all decisions were the right decisions—and sometimes one had to make a choice on his own. That much he'd learned during the battle on Ashio, when choices in battle saved or destroyed lives. Where officers played their soldiers and their regiments like pieces on a chess board. After the retreat, he had begun to see himself and his fellow soldiers as the pawns—those pushed out in front—expendable, to protect those with the power.

And there might come a time when Päl would need to make a choice with his loyalties, but now wasn't it.

"Päl, answer me. Are you serious?"

Päl leaned forward. "Yes. I am. Father, I'm a MechWarrior, and a son of the Sandoval dynasty. I supported the former duke in his decisions, and I will support Tancred's orders as well." He wanted to add how he knew his cousin had warned Mai not to lead the Rangers into Combine territory. Tancred's reasons had been sound, and proven right in the end.

"In support of Victor? Päl, have you not been paying attention? He's in league with the Draconis Combine. Everyone knows he's sleeping with a snake. How can you trust a man who's in bed with the enemy? How can Tancred know Kurita will accept concessions and not wait until our forces are drawn elsewhere on foolish attacks against our own people then attack our worlds, murder our children, and rape our worlds for their own—"

The baroness calmly reached out and put a firm hand on her husband's knee. She gave no other sign, her gaze drawn out at the passing scenery as the Avanti stretch-sedan began its crawl along the drive to the Wyndham-Sandoval estates.

The baron fell silent.

Chill wind caressed the beaded sweat on Päl's forehead as he closed his eyes and opened his other senses. He smelled the crisp decay of autumn leaves, heard the soft, whispering shuffle as the wind tossed them about on the grounds of the gardens. He cocked his head to his right shoulder, felt the bite of steel between the index finger and thumb of both hands.

With a spin, he directed and controlled the blade from his right hand to the top of the target, then followed the release of his left blade to the bottom, forming a double-strike he'd perfected years ago. He saw in his mind's eye where the blades would strike the target. That was the key—to know the direction and visualize it.

The spin completed, Päl came to land in a crouch, the thrown blades now replaced by new ones pulled from hidden sheaths beneath his clothing. The simultaneous *thwack* as the blades hit the tree twenty meters away brought a smile to his face. The first of the afternoon.

My son doesn't know me.

Again, the realization yanked away his momentary glee, and he lowered his arms and straightened. He recalled the young boy's formal bow—his son's dark, even gaze that measured and sized up the room, analyzed things in an almost combative style. Much as his mother did at times when she entered a room.

I don't know my son.

"Päl?"

The familiar voice of his wife brought his thoughts into a happier place as he turned to see Khim and Chauncy approaching. Khim held a large ceramic mug with the Wyndham-Sandoval crest painted on the side. She was just as beautiful now as the day he'd met her. Her dark, raven hair contrasted with his own blond tresses, now held back in a single ponytail at the base of his topknot. She was the night to his morning. She was his place to run to when the world turned chaotic and cruel.

And he loved her unconditionally.

Chauncy's stately form was the opposite of Khim's. She was a short, elderly woman, rising to Päl's shoulders, with wiry, gray hair and a cherub face. His former nanny and foster-mother had lost weight since he'd seen her, and her skin, though usually pale, seemed much more so in Robinson's evening light.

He retrieved and resheathed his knives and stepped toward them.

Other than Khim, Chauncy had been the only member of the house to greet him with a smile and a warm embrace. Just as she did now. "What are you two doing out here?" he took the offered mug from Khim and kissed her cheek. The cup warmed his fingers as he inhaled the aroma of spiced wine.

"Com'n to fetch you in to get ready. Guests are already arriving." Chauncy clasped her thick hands in front of her green skirts.

Päl had completely forgotten about his parent's social event to supposedly welcome their son home from the war. He groaned.

"Forgot, didn't you?" Khim's voice wasn't as light as it had been earlier when he'd arrived home. They'd spent most of the first hours of his homecoming in private, rediscovering each other again.

Päl nodded. "This party is little more than an excuse for my mother and father to renew their presence within the family. It's all politics—which I will never participate in."

Chauncy gave him a light laugh. "You're a Sandoval, Päl. It will pull you in anyway."

"Not if I stay with the Rangers." He sipped the wine and felt its warmth spread through his extremities. It was indeed becoming colder in the advancing evening. "I've no time to worry about the larger picture there." He flashed back to the last battle on Ashio, and then quickly tucked it away. *I can't think of fallen friends now.*

"And why the long face?"

He shrugged.

Chauncy put a hand on his shoulder. It felt warm and comforting. There was so little contact outside of private rooms in this house, or on his family's estates on Exeter.

Päl handed the mug to Chauncy. He absently pulled his knives from their sheaths and in unison began weaving their blades between his fingers. He looked at his wife, whose own gaze was locked on his hands and their movements. She looked extraordinarily pale in the waning light and her eyes were wide holes filled with shadows.

"Khim?"

She looked up into his eyes.

It was the knives. Khim had always hated his knives.

"I'm going in, Päl." She turned, and then paused. "You need to get changed."

He watched her walk away as he continued moving the blades between his fingers.

"She's not much into your choice of weapon, is she?" Chauncy shifted her position and set the mug on a nearby garden bench.

He shook his head. "No. And with our earlier discussion of our son's education..." He let the sentence trail off as he turned and abruptly threw the knives into the dark. He spun, retrieved his second set in a fluid movement born of practice and control, and threw again.

Chauncy followed him to the tree and stood beside him as he judged their placement.

Four blades in a cross pattern. Shoulders, neck and lower abdomen. He pulled them from the tree and resheathed them before reaching deep into his trouser pocket to retrieve his Battle Academy ring.

"You still have that thing?"

Päl nodded. It had been a gift from his father. Päl's abrupt promotion and draft into service had precluded his official graduation, so Marquin believed it was right he have one. "Yeah, but I learned knives from Master DeGigli before I had the ring. I can't wear it and throw. Disrupts my aim."

He gestured for her to step toward the house and he followed. "I'm sorry I've been away so long, Chauncy."

"If you're thinking of me in that, and hurting my feelings—please don't. You're my life's work, child. And even if I didn't give you life's first breath, I was there when you learned your greatest lessons."

She gave him a sideways look. "But if you're fretting about your son, he's a Wyndham-Sandoval, Pål. Keep that knowledge close. He's the baroness' pet project." Chauncy pursed her lips. "I think at times she sees him as her own."

Pål nodded as the two trudged up the hill and through the gardens to the estate. *Another pawn for the board.* And yet, as they walked, he didn't know where that thought had come from.

Khim's ire eased as she helped him get dressed. Layering on bit after bit of his dress uniform became almost a game between them, and Pål believed they might not make it to the party.

She left first, answering a summons from the baroness. Pål finished the final touches and checked himself in the mirror. He looked presentable enough, an officer of House Davion.

He moved to the bed where his knives and their sheaths lay. He yearned to put them on, but didn't want to anger Khim. If she saw them or suspected he wore them at a social event, his nights afterward could be...uncomfortable.

With a sigh, he wrapped them in their case of black velvet and placed them in the drawer of his nightstand.

The murmur of voices and laughter filtered up from the downstairs to the family's apartments. Pål left the suite and walked to the stairs.

A movement to his right stopped him at the first step. A figure in dark clothing stood near the door to his father's private study. The figure turned and froze when he saw Pål, then turned away from him and headed down the opposing hall.

Päl chased after the man. He didn't know if the dark-clad figure belonged in the estates or if he was an intruder. Although, guests usually didn't run away.

He rounded the corner of his father's study to face an empty corridor. The intruder had vanished.

Päl concentrated on the hallway, and pushed aside the ambient noise from the party below. He calmed his breathing and sought out each nearby sound.

A door opened behind him. Päl dodged back behind the bend in the hallway. He peered around the corner to see several courtly dignitaries, family and close friends, file into his father's study. Curious, the baron's son tiptoed back down the hall to the side door he'd discovered as a child. It was hidden deep within the ornate decoration of the wall. He had found it once while following the baroness about the halls. His mother had used the small door several times—yet its existence had never made him wonder why.

Until now.

Dust tickled his nose as he eased in, careful not to allow his sword to clang against the floor or walls. Gray smudged his white dress-gloves and he brushed them on his pants. There was only a bench and when he sat, the walls pressed in on his knees and back. His dress sword made stealth difficult, but he managed to sit and look out through the room's peephole.

The study was filled with more than ten stately dressed men. Several women stood to the side, among them his mother, the baroness.

The baron stood at his desk and raised a hand. Quiet descended.

"I'm sure you've all heard of the new Duke's plan to pull troops from Combine space and move against Katrina in support of Victor."

Some of those in the audience nodded, others looked about with shocked faces.

The baron nodded. "You that are gathered here are the few remaining that still support Duke James Sandoval's belief that the Draconis Combine is the enemy, not our ally. Word was given to me this morning by a reliable source that House Kurita will move against the Federated Suns. They will not accept the new duke's offer of an accord, but will be swift in their revenge of our attacks on their worlds."

Päl frowned. What was his father talking about? That wasn't what was discussed in the meeting he'd attended that morning. Tancred had seemed confident that Theodore Kurita would agree to the terms set for a cease-fire. Päl had always believed the duke's son a viable leader, not easily taken by rumor and innuendo.

Where had his father gleaned this information?

"Marquin," a man in a blue brocade coat raised his hand. "Are you saying we're all in danger?"

"I'm saying the new Duke is making us vulnerable by pulling our troops away from the border." He shook his head. "I stand here before you to give warning. I myself fear for my family's safety. My own son participated in those attacks on House Kurita. My own family is at risk."

"They wouldn't dare!"

Päl didn't see who had spoken. His own thoughts wrapped around what his father said. *This is ridiculous—there had been no mention of any possible attacks of retribution.*

"I'm afraid they might, Peter." The baron put his hands on his desk, palms down, and leaned toward his audience for emphasis. "Tancred isn't thinking—he's too caught up in his friendship with Victor to see the truth. The Combine *cannot* be trusted. It will take a new assault by them on a Davion world to prove we are right. I pray it doesn't come to that..."

The baroness moved then, her eyes narrowed in his direction. Had he made a noise?

Once outside the hidden room, Päl straightened his uniform's vest and adjusted his sword as he turned back down the hall toward the grand staircase.

The Baroness Magarette Wyndham-Sandoval stood at the hall's end, her hands clasped together before her. Her face was composed, and belied only a small amount of surprise. "Päl?"

"Mother." He increased his step, heels clicking on the tiled floor.

"What were you doing back there?"

He furrowed his brow. "I thought I saw an intruder earlier. I had been on my way downstairs to join Khim when I saw him." He shrugged. "I'm afraid he got away."

"An intruder?" Her expression changed little, but he did see her gaze flick downward, to his sword.

Päl glanced down at the dust-smudged glove he rested on his sword hilt.

He looked up at his mother. Her smile at him did not touch her eyes.

A chill traveled down his spine.

Päl and Khim stood in the dinner reception line for nearly half an hour, greeting guest upon guest. Faces blurred with names, and he felt a dull pain creep along the base of his skull. The muscles around his mouth ached, and he worked his jaw back and forth as he preceded his parents into the dining room.

Most of the conversation centered around the transfer of power to Tancred Sandoval, who had declined tonight's invitation, begging pardon and needing to attend to his own family.

Several guests asked Päl on occasion to retell the battle of Ashio—some wanting the bloody details of the Rangers' retreat while they ate. But the young MechWarrior wasn't ready to recount to strangers some of the more painful events of his life, and bowed out with grace and politeness most becoming a baron's son.

As the meal ended he excused himself, pleading a headache, which was the truth. The baron escorted Khim toward the veranda, where he and the baroness had planned an extravaganza of fireworks.

Päl went down into the kitchens in search of Chauncy. The house mistress claimed no knowledge of where his nanny had gone. Remembering aspirin in the medicine cabinet of his and Khim's apartments, the Baron's son took the steps two at time, pausing only briefly at the top to cast a glance at the door of his father's study.

So much of what he'd heard earlier jumbled about in his head. He suspected his father had lied to those family members—for he doubted Tancred would have agreed to work with Theodore Kurita if he suspected sabotage. And Päl believed the lie was meant to turn their family's support away from Victor.

Political intrigue and posturing was what had killed Arthur. Päl wanted no part of it. In the field there was no place for such games, but here within the walls of the Sandoval family, that was all that seemed to exist.

Once inside his darkened bedroom, Päl pulled his sword from its sheath and set it on his bed. With a sigh, he tucked his gloves into his belt and strode into the bathroom where he turned on a single light. Ignoring his tired reflection in the mirror, he found the aspirin and swallowed several without water.

An old, familiar noise, one he'd not heard since childhood, came from the bedroom. It was the sound of the old service door beside his and Khim's bed. As a small boy Päl had often hidden inside that door, and sometimes traveled the tunnels behind it for adventure. But he'd sealed it years ago.

He looked from the bathroom to his bedroom. He saw nothing at first, and feared the events of the day—especially spying the intruder earlier—had him jumping at shadows. But since caution had often saved him in battle, he turned the bathroom light off to shroud himself in darkness, then crouched behind the door's frame to peer out at the bedroom.

Light from the hall gave subtle illumination to a movement in the wall to the right of their bed. As he suspected, someone was opening the hidden door. From the secret entrance came a dark-clad figure that crouched once they gained admittance. The door closed behind them with a *click*.

Päl couldn't be sure if this was the intruder from before. He couldn't see the figure's detail in the shadowy light. The figure stood and pulled something from within the folds of their garment.

Light glinted off metal. Recognition gave him pause. They had a Nakjima pistol.

An assassin.

Päl's sword lay on the bed, between himself and the intruder. His knives lay nestled within the drawer of his nightstand. He had no readily available weapon.

From the assassin's movements, he read that his presence was still unknown. It was best to remain hidden, and to watch. The dark-clad figure crept to the bedroom door. With their free hand on the frame, they looked from the left to the right, as if checking for someone, then left, closing the door behind them.

Once he was gone, Päl ran to the bed, grabbed his sword. He then pulled his knives from the drawer and tucked them, unsheathed, into the belt of his dress uniform. He then moved to the door and peered cautiously around. There was no sign of the assassin.

With his sword ready, Päl moved to the stairs and caught the fleeting glimpse of dark robes at the foot of the stairs as the figure turned to the right in the direction of the ballroom.

Once at the foot of the stairs, Päl told a guard of the intruder. "Gather the others and find him."

The guard nodded to the baron's son, then turned just as Päl's father and mother approached from the other direction.

"Päl, where have you—"

He put up a hand to silence Marquin. "I believe an assassin has entered the estate from the old door of my bedroom. I've alerted the guards."

"An assassin?" Marquin Wyndham-Sandoval's usually ruddy expression had gone quite pale. "In my home?"

"Where is Khim? I need you to take her out of here, but don't panic the guests. I'll find him." He turned to go.

The Baroness pulled on Päl's arm as her son turned away. "Päl—Khim went to look in on your son. She's gone to the open nursery." The open nursery was on this floor—opposite the ballroom.

My son.

Päl ran as fast as he could toward the nursery wing. His feet pounded against the tiled floor as guests yelled after him, curious as to his alarm. He hoped none would follow.

When he entered, the room was dark. Autumn moonlight filtered in through the open windows, casting shadows over the bed and crib. Päl held his sword ready. The light flashed off his blade as he crouched low and looked into the bed where his son should be sleeping.

It was empty.

In the dark, he heard the familiar sound of a weapon powering up. He moved out of the way as a blast lit up the room, the weapon's energy discharge narrowly missing his head to splash off the far wall.

The assassin stood just inside the door. He held Khim in his arms, her windpipe cut off by his left hand. He held the pistol aimed at her temple.

Päl's heart froze.

"Drop your sword." The assassin's voice was deep, unassuming. The baron's son found no accent, no place to claim the man's heritage. "Drop it."

"Where is my son?" Päl dropped the sword to the ground with a loud *clank*.

"I don't know where your son is—he's not why I'm here."

"Then who is? My wife?"

The man's head moved back and forth slowly. Päl couldn't make out his features in the subdued light. The assassin turned the pistol on Päl and fired again.

A bright flash illuminated the room. Päl had anticipated such a move, though, and lunged for the safety of a nearby toy-chest. But this time he hadn't moved fast enough, and as he landed, he realized the intruder's Nakjima had struck its target. His left shoulder burned, as if someone was holding a hot branding iron to his muscle and bone. He stifled a cry as he landed on the burned flesh and was able to right himself into a crouch.

Khim called out to him, but her voice was abruptly silenced. The assassin had closed his grip on her throat.

"Who sent you?" Päl reached down to his belt and pulled out a set of knives. Their cold, steel blades felt good in his hands. He peered around the box. The assassin had pulled Khim back several meters, into the shadows.

The lack of light did nothing to sway Päl's confidence, but the injury to his arm did. The pain when he rotated it experimentally was solid, and it would grow more intense until it was treated. He felt the warm trickle of blood down his chest as he sized up the distance and speed he would need.

To compensate for his handicap, he needed an opportunity—a second when the assassin wouldn't be expecting an attack from the dark.

The assassin shifted.

That was the opportunity Päl needed.

Too late, he realized he still wore his Battle Academy ring. He aimed, allowing his knowledge of position and skill to determine the best placement of his weapons. He might have made better aim if only his left shoulder hadn't protested with sharp fire, or his ring had not caught the knife's edge.

But fate was on his side and the right knife found purchase in the assassin's weapon hand, the blade piercing the palm. The assassin yelled and dropped the weapon.

His second knife shot wide to Päl's right, and embedded itself in his wife's side beneath her breast. Blood streamed down her milk-white dress.

"No!" Päl dove forward to catch his falling wife as the intruder released her and fell back into the corner's shadow. She clung to him, her eyes wide.

He lowered her to the floor as he realized the assassin was moving toward the door.

Vengeance drove him as he pulled the second set of knives from his belt. He narrowed his eyes as he studied the shadows, turned a practiced ear to the sounds of footsteps and gauged their distance. Päl pulled his ring from his finger and set it on the floor. The assassin stumbled near the nursery's entrance and Päl let fly his weapons, shutting out the fire that burned through his shoulder with the movement.

A cry of pain answered the baron's son as he struck his target. The man collapsed in an untidy pile.

Khim was hurt badly, bleeding to death. Päl had to take care of his wife, but there were things he had to know. Duty pulled him in two directions, and he was too-recently a soldier.

With a glance at Khim, he moved across the floor to the felled enemy. The assassin lay on his side and Päl pulled him onto his back. Both knives had found a home in the man's neck, one on either side. Blood fountained over Päl's hands as he grabbed the man's collar and pulled him close.

"Who sent you?"

The assassin shook his head.

He pulled the attacker closer. The coppery smell of blood was everywhere. *No time!* Päl had to attack quickly and with ruthless strength. How his mother would handle it.

"I will know your name. Give over your employer, or I will see your family held accountable for your treachery this night."

The man shuddered in Päl's hands, and he feared the assassin would expire before speaking. When the attacker opened his mouth, blood pooled over the sides as he whispered in a gurgled voice, "The Baroness Wyndham-Sandoval."

Päl released the man, and the assassin's head smacked against the floor. He was dead, his last breath uttering the one name Päl had never thought to hear. He stood on shaky legs and moved away as if afraid the man's body would ignite in flame. He stared at the dead man, his mind a jangle of unfocused thoughts.

He lied...it had to be a lie.

Chauncy came to the door at that moment, her arms filled with stacked blankets. She yelled and dropped the blankets when she saw Päl standing over the dark-clad corpse. Her gaze traveled back to her charge and her hands flew to her mouth as she went to him, staring at his bloodied uniform. "Päl, you're..."

He put up a hand. "I'm fine." Though the pain from the assassin's weapon was now a debilitating vice around his shoulder. He turned and headed to his wife, so still on the floor. He knelt beside her as Chauncy joined them, the house-mistress' hands gentle as she touched Khim's neck to find a pulse.

"She's alive," Chauncy said, then looked into the gaze of her grown charge. "What happened?"

"He came in through our rooms—the old door," Päl reached up and rubbed at his temple, unaware of the blood he smeared across his brow. "Mother said Khim had come here to check on our son."

The house-mistress' eyes narrowed in confusion. "Päl, your mother had me bring him into my apartments before the party started. Away from the noise…"

His gaze fixed on Chauncy's wizened face. Päl swallowed back the nausea that threatened to overwhelm him, though he was uncertain at that moment if it were a reaction to his injury, or the realization his mother had just attempted to have him assassinated.

"Päl?"

He blinked at the pommel of the knife protruding from his wife's chest. He knew better than to remove it. It would only hasten her bleeding. He saw the glint of his ring beside her and with a burst of anger he grabbed it and tossed it across the room. He hissed at the pain in his shoulder that threatened to pitch him into unconsciousness.

He bent and kissed his wife tenderly on her cold cheek, then stood on uncertain legs. "Watch her, Chauncy. I'll send for a doctor."

Päl knelt beside the assassin and retrieved the Nakjima, then moved slowly out of the nursery toward the elevated voices below.

Guests had spilled out of the ballroom and were now creating a ring of enclosure about the baron. Many had been muttering and whispering among themselves. As news spread, the crowd grew louder.

"It was as the Baron warned, the Dragon has come."

"The snakes have tried to kill the Baron's son!"

Someone else was more certain. "Dead. He must be dead!"

Päl stood in the shadows beneath the stairs, away from the guests. His shoulder burned and again he felt himself grow light-headed. He watched with distant fascination as the panic spread. Simple words, spoken with just the proper emotion—and all of them would turn on Tancred. Realization of what his true standing was within the family did not come as a surprise, but more as a sad revelation. *I am a pawn. Nothing more. Nothing less.*

Carrying the Nakjima, Päl Wyndham-Sandoval stepped forward. Sharp intakes of breath greeted him as the crowd parted to allow him through. Many, seeing his bloodied uniform, gasped. His father leaped forward, braced him with a hand on either shoulder, and then grabbed the weapon from his son.

"Nakjima." He nearly spat out the name. "Combine manufacture."

Neither the baron nor baroness appeared overly worried about Päl's condition. But then, his father was lost to his hatred for House Kurita.

His mother, though, was calm. Far too calm. He found her eyes, and just below the surface of her calm, proud mask, he saw the truth of what the assassin said.

She wanted the family's loyalties turned, as did his father. As did most of those here in this room. But she had been the one willing to sacrifice her only son to achieve it. And why not? She had a new grandson to raise.

The truth was there and gone in an instant. As Margarette Wyndham-Sandoval stepped from behind her guests, a grand show of concern washed over her face toward her son. "Päl, was it the Dracs?"

He matched her gaze with his own and said, simply and quietly. "No." He turned to the nearest guard. "Please, could you summon a doctor? My wife..."

But the baroness wasn't going to be ignored. She moved even closer to Päl, the flash of her eyes toward the crowd of guests making it obvious to her son that she knew she was on stage. It was time to call the play together. "But it has to be." Her eyes narrowed. "How do you know it is not?"

Päl kept his voice even, though the fatigue he heard in his words was genuine. The pain in his shoulder was like a smoldering fire, constant and fierce. The loss of blood was making it difficult to stand. The guard hurried off to summon help for Khim, so Päl allowed himself a moment. "Because he told me."

"He told you?" The baron stepped forward. "Tell us, Päl. I demand to know!" A murmur of assent swept the assembled nobles. When the baron looked to his wife for support in his demand, however, he found only stony silence. Frowning, glancing between his wife and son, the baron fell back on the will of the crowd. "Who did this?"

A hush settled as all eyes turned to Päl. His own vision wavered, though nothing could erase the still image of his mother, standing close enough for assumed concern, yet far enough away should her son betray her to the assembly. He blinked several times, willing himself to stay conscious. Focused.

He narrowed his eyes at her. Their very way of life depended on his answer, and he knew the use of ruthlessness at that moment. Understood it, for like his mother, who had wagered the life of her son on the turn of history, Päl too had put the assassin's family on the table to force the confession that now would change his life forever.

He swallowed, blinking with sluggish control as the world seemed to spin slower around him, and looked to his father, who stood within the nexus of this moment.

Päl saw the board clearly now—saw the position of the pieces. The game had just started. The baroness held the kingdom in white—but it was Päl who now controlled the black. He saw the carefully placed moves that might have sent him and Khim to their deaths.

Two moves of a pawn across the board.

In truth, he knew she hadn't expected him to live.

But there was a little-known move in chess called the *en passant*, where the first move of a pawn with two squares can be met and defeated by one move of the enemy's opposing pawn.

"Päl! Who has done this?"

With a sigh, the baron's son moved his gaze from his father's red, flushed face to rest it calmly upon the serene visage of his mother's composure.

"Katherine Steiner-Davion."

DESTINY'S CHALLENGE

LOREN L. COLEMAN

THE NAGELRING
THARKAD
LYRAN COMMONWEALTH
2 SEPTEMBER 2721

Coming down off Wolstenholme Plateau, one of the Nagelring's primary live-fire and piloting ranges, Alek Kerensky heard the order passed for line abreast formation. He scratched at the scale of dried sweat crusting inside his elbow. Swallowed hard against a metallic aftertaste. Throttled forward his 80-ton *Striker*.

Two months out of summer-long OCS training, starting his first full year as a Star League cadet, the controls were fast becoming familiar in his sweaty hands. But he still overcompensated for the increased speed by swinging the BattleMech's massive arms too quickly, and his cockpit dipped side to side, side to side.

Alek knew his 'Mech appeared to stagger forward with a drunken swagger. Like a space-naval crewman on his first shore leave. A popular underground video, posted on the Nagelring's *OurSpace* network, ran thirty seconds of footage of Alek's lurching *Striker* set to hornpipe music. The aspiring (and anonymous) director had even dug up some ancient cartoon footage of an animated sailor with bulging arms and a corncob pipe, ending the homemade vid with a bray of corny laughter. No doubt, an "A" for creativity.

At least this brand of hazing came with fewer bruises. And no trips—yet—to the hospital.

"Waiting on you, Cadet Kerensky."

As usual.

Cruising forward at forty-three kilometers per hour, Alek's BattleMech finally joined the three other *Striker*s being paced by Colonel Baumgarten's *Pillager*. The *Striker*s were massive, hulking brutes. Blocky. Bow-legged. But in great demand among Nagelring cadets because of their assault-class weight and heavy weaponry.

By comparison, the *Pillager* was a much more refined design. Linebacker shoulders and a tapered waist. With maneuvers behind them, Colonel Baumgarten had deactivated

his BattleMech's Light Polarization Shield. The Nagelring's CO walked with a graceful stride not many could command from a 100-ton machine. Proud. Stately, even.

It wasn't unknown for Baumgarten to lead training exercises, but never before on such a small scale. A short romp out with only four cadets, two of them on remedial training programs and Alek a "green" trainee running two years behind the usual curriculum?

Something was in the wind.

Whatever it was, it would have to keep. The cadets all knew what came next. Remedial training or not, C.O. or not, it was tradition, and tradition carried a great deal of weight in the Lyran Commonwealth.

Possibly even more in the Star League.

The five assault-class BattleMechs paraded forward beneath a powder-blue sky and Tharkad's retreating autumn sun. Music suddenly blasted in over Alek's comms system, piped onto an auxiliary channel reserved for parade functions and other non-essential military maneuvers. The brassy shout of trumpet and saxophone caught him off guard, especially when it was joined on the next beat by a distorted guitar. He had been expecting some kind of speed-music tune from Ceramic Monkey or Nolo Contendre, groups battling it out for the top two worship spots among the younger generations on Tharkad.

Grunge-jazz was *not* the norm. Certainly it wasn't tradition.

Then again, who was going to argue that with the academy's commanding officer? His school, his rule.

The unusual, the out of place, held a special fascination for Alek. So Baumgarten's choice of music distracted him for an extra heartbeat. The other three *Strikers* pushed forward, getting the jump on him as all would-be MechWarriors raced the last five kilometers back to one of the Nagelring's 'Mech hangars. A "friendly competition," supposedly. Outside of academia—even within it—Alek had rarely known those two words to go together.

Still: "'The illusion which exalts us is dearer to us than ten thousand truths,'" he whispered.

As usual, words from the immortal Russian poet stood him in good stead. Being able to recognize the race for what it was—an illusion to foster some sense of worth through harmless competition—helped Alek attack the challenge in a methodical manner.

Throttling forward, pushing his *Striker* to its maximum speed of sixty-five kilometers per hour, Alek worked his controls and pivoted hard for a small rise to the east. Slogging uphill would seem to make little sense to his fellow cadets, who raced each other forward onto open ground. Though if they had reviewed the topographical data on this area, they would have seen that the open range ahead—three kilometers up, and after a sharp dogleg— would force them onto a harder slope before the final downhill run to the 'Mech hangar.

Alek planned to run what looked like an easier, parallel course today. Taking advantage of the terrain, as his new courses in Strategic & Tactics always recommended.

"All things being equal," Major Kiault had lectured, "the commander who takes advantage of the battlefield's underlying terrain will have a distinct tactical advantage."

A passable paraphrasing from Sun-Tzu's *The Art of War*. A theory Alek would attempt to put into practice today.

Over the rise and down a shallow slope on the far side, Alek twisted and turned along a path through slash-cut timber. It cost him valuable time, he knew, avoiding piles made from shattered trees and uprooted stumps. Not so much, though, as the "usual" route would take. Should take.

In long, four-meter strides, he ate up the ground in his *Striker*. Burning up one kilometer. Then two. Working his controls exactly as he'd been taught to build muscle memory which might—they threatened—save his life one day.

But the 80-ton BattleMech seemed to have a will of its own. It fought back with each swing of the arms, which rotated out a little too far. As each step fell a bit short of a running BattleMech's optimum stride. He felt it. That awkwardness. The neurofeedback circuitry, so finely attuned to his nervous system, impressed on him a sensation of sluggishness. As if he himself was attempting to run with a length of rope tied between his ankles, just shy of his best stride.

"Come on," he cajoled the 'Mech. "Move!"

According to his heads-up display, he had pulled even with the other cadets, though just barely. They were coming around the dogleg, starting to fight the uphill slope he had avoided. But they were still in open territory, and he had a tall stand of poplar and ash cutting him off from the final leg of the race.

At a full run, he splashed through a small stream, leaving a half-meter deep footprint in the boggy ground, then plunged into the wood. His *Striker*'s swinging arms tore branches away with little complaint. Where trees leaned in too close, he shouldered them aside or trod over them. The thin poplar boles snapped like twigs beneath the BattleMech's metal-shod feet.

Insulated in his cockpit, Alek heard barely more than a distant *crunch* and bark of shattered wood. His rearview monitor, however, showed the swatch of destruction he left behind. A new path, several meters wide, of tortured branches, uprooted trees, and earth churned over by wide, blade-like feet.

Powerful.

And unnecessary.

Breaking free of the wood, Alek saw he had already lost the race. Two *Strikers* pushed by him on a dead run, storming forward as only 80 tons of assault machine could do. The second one cut in close, nearly bumping shoulders with him. Alek wrenched furiously against his controls, avoiding the collision by scant meters. Swinging wide as the third and final *Striker* gained ground, pulling up even with him.

Less than two kilometers out, now running parallel to a paved access road, Alek saw the 'Mech hangars squatting up ahead like oversized Quonsets. A tall fence tipped with razorwire guarded this end of the sprawling Nagelring complex, though a full thirty meters had been pulled back in anticipation of the arriving BattleMech patrol. It was any cadet's race still.

Any cadet but Alek.

Slow but certain, he lost ground to the other cadets. According to his instruments, he had his throttles pegged high at the *Striker's* maximum speed of sixty-five kilometers per hour. Somehow, though, the others coaxed just a little bit more out of their machines. Striding out just a bit longer. Turning slightly sharper.

Alek fell fifty meters back. Then a hundred.

Still a kilometer out, trailing by two hundred meters, Alek finally slacked off on his throttles. He passed through the barrier fence at a controlled fifty kph, resigned to his last place finish.

He knew what awaited him at the hangar. Helping the technicians check all systems shut down on every 'Mech. Picking up after the other cadets who would all grab a shower and a fresh uniform before the post-training review with Colonel Baumgarten, leaving their sweat-soaked cooling vests draped carelessly over the back of their command chairs or—in the case of any high spirits—hidden somewhere within the hangar for him to find, clean, and turn in for a maintenance check.

Friendly competition. And tradition.

"Dearer to us," he whispered, throttling back into a walk, "than ten thousand truths."

Every school, course, and instructor had their system. Routines a student could adopt, flowing along the path of least resistance, learning, excelling, with a minimum of difficulty. Or, in standing out, making waves and drawing attention.

Leon Trotsky had said ideas that enter the mind under fire remain there securely and forever. But with his own experience at Tharkad University still fresh in his mind, Alek had no immediate desire to stand out from the crowd. Difficult enough that everyone knew how he had entered the Nagelring, and what those trials had cost four senior cadets: Three expulsions; one on probation and lucky, in the minds of most instructors, to still be enrolled in this prestigious academy.

No one harried Alek anymore—there were no more suspicious visits to the infirmary for him to explain—but neither did they go out of their way to include him. To most of the other cadets he was still an unknown, a social burden to be accommodated while awaiting some kind of final group consensus.

Accommodation was all right with Alek. Accommodation left fewer marks.

So while everyone around him nervously held their breath, Alek bent his efforts toward this new training. Taking on nearly double the workload of an average cadet in an effort to make up for his two-year late start. Keeping quiet. Adopting the local routines.

Surviving a post-training debrief with the Nagelring's *Kommandant,* Alek merely had to sit up tall in his seat, take copious notes in his log book, and say "Yes, sir!" with sufficient confidence whenever asked a question.

Usually the question being: did he understand?

In academics, when Alek had been a full-time student of Tharkad University, instructors had often pushed him to form his own opinions. To challenge any "accepted wisdom," and seek the higher truths.

Here, they seemed more interested in knowing that he understood exactly what they wanted him to know.

"Dismissed," Colonel Baumgarten finally said, though he stayed after for a few moments to help the two remedial cadets with some finer points from the day's exercise.

Alek slipped away quietly, returning to the 'Mech hangar on his way to the cadet lockers. Still dressed in combat togs and lacking the shower the others had been able to grab, his cooling vest was damp and beginning to smell like stale body odor, and his bare skin itched under a layer of dried sweat

What MechWarrior trainees laughingly called a uniform wasn't much more than combat boots, shorts, and a thin tank top worn beneath their cooling vest. Welcome in the sauna-like heat that often flooded a BattleMech's cockpit. Not so much after. Especially with Tharkad's sun in full retreat and the taste of an early winter in the air. The afternoon chill rose gooseflesh on his arms, his legs.

Or maybe it was something else entirely.

The truth was, Alek often took a chill entering the 'Mech hangar. Like entering the underworld cavern of some mythological beast. And inside, four massive titans of war. The now-deserted hangar tasted of damp ferrocrete, coolant, and old welding. Gloomy, with the large hangar doors rolled shut, overhead lighting barely held back the shadows. He padded by softly, quietly, as if worried to wake the slumbering giants.

"Afraid of the dark?"

The voice shattered the stillness, startling Alek. He tensed. It was a voice he'd come to recognize. The fourth member of his new training lance.

"A pleasure, as always, Cadet Ward."

"Stuff the formalities, *Alek*. Just what are you doing here?"

Resigned, Alek turned to face his fellow cadet. Patrick Ward stood just inside the side door, dressed in a tailored cadet's uniform, arms crossed over his chest. Raven-black hair and green eyes the color of malachite, ramrod straight posture, strong jaw—he had the look of young nobility, even though Alek knew he hadn't much of a pedigree.

Patrick still wore a red "warrior's badge" on his tunic's right breast, which he'd earned in his second year at the Nagelring. Quite obviously missing, however, was his gold Honor Squad braid. That, along with all academic credit for his third year, had been stripped from him by the Nagelring's cadet review board due to his participation in events surrounding the Spring Reception, the harassment of Alek, and the injury to Elias Luvon.

Some cadets felt expelling him would have been kinder.

"I'm training to be a MechWarrior," Alek said.

The other cadet shook his head. "You're up to something, but I don't believe that's it."

Alek knew himself well enough to accept that Patrick was not so wrong. Elias Luvon had been hurt, and hurt badly, when Alek had struck out in fear and anger. Joining the military, Alek had assured himself, then, that he would simply be retaking control of himself. But did anyone ever have that kind of control, even over their own lives?

The illusion which exalts us...

He shrugged. "I'm not doing this out of guilt over Elias, if that is what you are thinking. Though, yes, I believe I have something to prove here."

"To whom?" Patrick pressed. He had an intense manner, as if he could focus his entire being on one specific problem, and thereby defeat it.

"To the only person it makes sense to prove anything to," Alek said with a slight touch of exasperation. "To myself."

Patrick considered that for a moment. "Fair enough," he finally said, though he didn't sound persuaded. "I think that's an honest answer. Though I'm still not convinced it's the truth."

Neither was Alek, and that bothered him more than he was likely to admit.

"'Deep in my song, safe from the worm, my spirit will survive,'" he recited from Pushkin's works.

Patrick frowned. "He said you had a thing for dead Russians. That one of them?"

"Who said?"

Another frown. "Doesn't matter."

Which meant Elias, most likely. The specter hanging over both of them from the Archon's Spring Reception bound the two together. It also created a wall that would not be easily breached. Certainly Alek had no desire to delve into the morass with Patrick Ward, one of his former tormentors, but he also sensed an opportunity. One he could not back away from easily.

"It is one of my so-called 'dead Russians,' yes," he admitted. "Now let me ask you. What are you doing here?" He stepped forward. "What are you *really* doing here?"

Patrick didn't answer for a long moment. He stood there, staring down Alek. Possibly he was crafting some kind of careful answer. Possibly he'd just walk away.

Then he glanced off to one side, at the nearest of the 80-ton *Strikers* racked back into its bay.

"Growing up," he said softly, slowly, "I could not imagine anything more magnificent than piloting a BattleMech."

"And that brought you to the Nagelring?" Alek suddenly wanted to know. *Needed* to know.

The other cadet shook his head. "Can you think of one childhood fascination that ever measured up to its expectations?"

Without thinking, Alek stepped over to join him, looking up at the titanic machine that dominated all around it.

The tick of cooling metal could still be heard. Shovel-blade feet. Bulging midsection. Hatchet-edged cockpit. Massive arms swinging down almost to the knees. Settled into their bow-legged stance, partially cloaked by the shadows, the 'Mechs looked like childhood monsters biding time inside massive closets.

"No," he offered. Shivered. "But maybe these could come close."

Patrick grunted a noncommittal response, and an awkward silence descended between the two cadets. The kind, Alek knew, that often stretched out into refreshed hostility. He wasn't certain he wanted to let this bridge into the enemy camp fall so easily, though.

"You said earlier you were not convinced I was telling the truth." Alek swallowed hard, his throat tight. "What made you say that?"

Patrick paused, as if considering his words, then, "If you are really trying to prove something to yourself, why are you holding back?"

"Who says I am?"

"I do. As could anyone who's seen you pilot a 'Mech or work the simulators. Or seen your neurological response curve—that test they ran on you back when you were in the hospital? You're green, but you should still be better than you're showing. You're either coasting, or you just don't care. Either one could get somebody killed someday."

"And you followed me here just to tell me *that*?" Alek bit off the question with something close to anger. Anger at himself for kicking open this door. Inviting the rebuke, which had more teeth to it than he would have thought.

"I followed you here," Patrick said, "for the same reason I cut you off on the training run today. I wanted to learn something about you."

Alek remembered that. Breaking through the trees to have one of the other *Striker*s cut him off. Having to veer out wider than he'd planned.

"So what did you learn?" he asked.

Patrick clasped his hands behind his back. For a moment, Alek thought the other cadet would simply turn and leave without answering. Then he shrugged. "You're not stupid, Kerensky. I'll give you that. And you aren't weak, either. Maybe you'll even make a decent MechWarrior. Someday."

"And?"

"And maybe you aren't a complete waste of my time. As it has been pointed out to me, my options at the Nagelring this year have been slightly curtailed. It's been suggested that I get to know you. I'm considering it."

"So what's stopping you?"

"The truth?" Patrick looked from the nearby 'Mech to Alek. Then back again. "I'm not sure yet if I want to be your friend."

And with that, he did turn away. Toward the side entrance leading back to the briefing room. Leaving Alek behind, still staring up at the *Striker*.

Then, pausing at the door, Patrick asked suddenly, "So what's stopping *you*?"

The question caught Alek off-guard. He felt something rise to the top of his mind, shoving aside all the rationales and all the other excuses he might have mustered. He knew it immediately for what it was.

The truth? It seemed to be the day for it.

Alek stared up at the *Striker*, not knowing—no longer caring—if he were alone or if Patrick still stood at the doorway. "This whole thing." He looked around the empty 'Mech bay. "All of it."

Then his voice dropped to a simple whisper. The way in which most basic truths were spoken.

"It scares the hell out of me."

PILLAGER
Assault–**100** tons

STRIKER
Assault–**80** tons

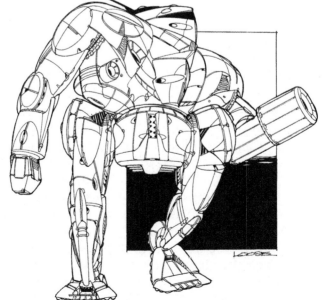

ABOUT THE AUTHORS

Ilsa J. Bick is a writer as well as a recovering psychiatrist. She is the author of prize-winning stories and novellas, and has written such *Classic BattleTech* tales as *Break-Away* and *The Gauntlet, Books I* and *II*, as well as the MWDA novels *Daughter of the Dragon, Dragon Rising*, and *Blood Avatar*. Other work has appeared in *SCIFICTION, Talebones, Beyond the Last Star, Star Trek: New Frontier: No Limits*, and *Star Trek: Voyager: Distant Shores*, among many others. She has several *Star Trek: Starfleet Corps of Engineers* e-books to her credit, and her next *SCE* e-book, *Ghost*, is forthcoming. Her first published novel, *Star Trek: The Lost Era: Well of Souls*, cracked the 2003 Barnes and Noble Bestseller List. She lives in Wisconsin with her husband, two children, and other assorted vermin.

Randall N. Bills has served as the *Classic BattleTech* line developer, continuity editor, art director, and a primary author/ novelist for almost a decade, where he's led the publication of over fifty products for that universe. He also served as the *MechWarrior: Dark Age* continuity editor, working for WizKids to help in the creation of that original universe—including its thirty full-length novels—and was the driving force behind the coffee-table art/universe book *MechWarrior: Technology of Destruction*. In addition he's published fiction and game design in the *Shadowrun, Earthdawn, Crimson Skies,* and *Vor: The Maelstrom* universes. As well as publishing eight novels set in the *Classic BattleTech/ MechWarrior* universe, he's one of the lead writers kicking off the *Adventure Boys* series of Young Adult fiction as published by the Adventure Boys Company. He lives in the Pacific Northwest with his beautiful wife Tara, and three busy children: Bryn Kevin, Ryana Nikol and Kenyon Aleksandr...oh, and Jak O' the Shadows, a red-tailed boa.

Loren L. Coleman has been a novelist, game designer, and all-around literary hatchet man for over fourteen years. Regularly published since 1995, his first *BattleTech* novel, *Double-Blind*, hit bookstores in 1997. In the last ten years he's published over twenty novels, including nine for *BattleTech* and a trilogy to help re-launch the world of *Conan the Barbarian*. Counting up all short stories and game-related sourcebooks, he has well over two million words in print—most of them involving a media tie-in project of one type or another. Most recently Loren has edited two DAW anthologies as well as a six-series set of Young Adult works for Adventure Boys, Inc. When he isn't writing or launching new ventures, Loren plays Xbox games, collects far too many DVDs, and holds a black belt in traditional Tae Kwon Do. Currently he resides in Washington State with his wife Heather Joy, two sons Talon LaRon and Conner Rhys Monroe, and daughter Alexia Joy.

Jason M. Hardy is a beloved storyteller, international peacemaker, and revered philosopher who always enjoys the opportunity to write his own bio. He is the author of the *MechWarrior: Dark Age* novels *The Scorpion Jar, Principles of Desolation* (with Randall N. Bills) and the forthcoming *The Last Charge*, along with the *Shadowrun* novel *Drops of Corruption*. He's contributed a number of stories to the BattleCorps website and, with the editor's indulgence, will continue to do so. He lives in Chicago with his wife and son.

Kevin Killiany has been the husband of Valerie for over a quarter of a century and for various shorter periods of time the father of Alethea, Anson, and Daya. Since the late nineteen-sixties, Kevin has been an actor, a drill rig operator, a photographer, a warehouse grunt, a community college instructor, a drywall hanger, a teacher of exceptional children, a community services case manager, a high-risk intervention counselor, and a paper boy. He is currently a writer, with stories published in a variety of universes—including

Star Trek, *Doctor Who*, *MechWarrior*, and of course *Classic BattleTech*. He is also an associate pastor of the Soul Saving Station in Wilmington, NC.

After experimenting with numerous occupations, **Louisa Swann**, a native Californian (ack! She admits it!) settled on writing as her long-term mental aberration. During her excessively loud oral dissertations (proven integral to her writing process as evidenced by numerous short story sales to DAW, Pocketbook, and BattleCorps), husband and son shake their heads and mutter something about "the muse." In the interests of survival, husband Jim acquired an 80-acre compound complete with coyotes, frogs, and screech owls to serve as nightly backup band for a raving writer's rants. Interdimensional traveling provides fodder for the muse, allowing Louisa to discover wonderful new places like the *Classic BattleTech* world and put them on her list of favorite places.

Steven Mohan, Jr. lives in Pueblo, Colorado with his wife and three children and—shockingly—no cats. When he is not writing he works as a manufacturing engineer. He has sold more than twenty stories to BattleCorps, including the Jihad serial *Isle of the Blessed*. He appeared twice in *Total Warfare*, and has done work for several upcoming *Classic BattleTech* sourcebooks. His original fiction has appeared in *Interzone*, *On Spec*, *Polyphony*, *Paradox*, and several DAW original anthologies, among other places. His stories have won honorable mention in *The Year's Best Science Fiction* and *The Year's Best Fantasy and Horror* and he was nominated for the Pushcart Prize for his alternate history tale, *A Monument More Lasting Than Brass.*

Blaine Pardoe is an author of science fiction and military history books. He has written numerous BattleTech/MechWarrior books and books on Count Felix von Luckner (*The Cruise of the Sea Eagle*) and an upcoming book on Frank Luke, Jr.

Michael A. Stackpole is an award-winning author, game designer, computer game designer and podcaster. In 2006 he and Brian Pulido won the Fade-In magazine scriptwriting contest grand prize for the script *Gone*. At DragonCon, Mike's writing podcast, "The Secrets", took the first-ever Parsec award for writing-related podcasts. When not writing or podcasting, Mike enjoys indoor soccer and salsa dancing. Both are similar—it's all in the footwork—but for one you get to dress up nicely. His web site is www.stormwolf.com.

Robert Thurston has been writing science fiction and fantasy since the early 1970s, after attending the second and third Clarion SF Writing Workshops. When the first collection of stories from Clarion was published, his story "Wheels" was awarded first prize; the story later became the basis for his novel *A Set of Wheels*. He has written over a dozen novelizations and original novels, including *Alicia II, Q Colony, BattleTech, Robot Jox,* and nine *Battlestar Galactica* books. He lives in New Jersey with his wife, Rosemary.

Phaedra Weldon is the author of several *Classic BattleTech* stories/novellas, including the continuing Sandoval Saga, *En Passant* and *Epaulet Mate*. She has also authored the Isis Marik series, *The Art of War*, and is currently working on the multi-layered Jihad series/novella, *A Distant Thunder*. Her other publications can be found in various DAW anthologies, as well as works in the Star Trek universe for *Starfleet Corps of Engineers*, and *The Next Generation* series, *Slings and Arrows*. She is also the author of the ACE Fantasy series *WRAITH*, released June 5, 2007, and is currently working on book II, scheduled to be released in 2008.

BATTLETECH GLOSSARY

AUTOCANNON

A rapid-fire, auto-loading weapon. Light autocannons range from 30 to 90 millimeter (mm), and heavy autocannons may be from 80 to 120mm or more. They fire high-speed streams of high-explosive, armor-piercing shells.

BATTLEMECH

The most powerful war machine ever built. First developed by Terran scientists and engineers, these huge vehicles are faster, more mobile, better-armored and more heavily armed than any twentieth-century tank. Ten to twelve meters tall and equipped with particle projection cannons, lasers, rapid-fire autocannons and missiles, they pack enough firepower to flatten anything but another BattleMech. A small fusion reactor provides virtually unlimited power, and BattleMechs can be adapted to fight in environments ranging from sun-baked deserts to subzero arctic ice fields.

DROPSHIP

Because interstellar JumpShips must avoid entering the heart of a solar system, they must "dock" in space at a considerable distance from a system's inhabited worlds. DropShips were developed for interplanetary travel. As the name implies, a DropShip is attached to hardpoints on the JumpShip's drive core, later to be dropped from the parent vessel after in-system entry. Though incapable of FTL travel, DropShips are highly maneuverable, well-armed and sufficiently aerodynamic to take off from and land on a planetary surface. The journey from the jump point to the inhabited worlds of a system usually requires a normal-space journey of several days or weeks, depending on the type of star.

FLAMER

A small but time-honored anti-infantry weapon. Whether fusion-based or fuel-based, flamers spew fire in a tight beam that "splashes" against a target, igniting almost anything it touches.

GAUSS RIFLE

This weapon uses magnetic coils to accelerate a solid nickel-ferrous slug about the size of a football at an enemy target, inflicting massive damage through sheer kinetic impact at long range and with little heat. However, the accelerator coils and the slug's supersonic speed mean that while the Gauss rifle is smokeless and lacks the flash of an autocannon, it has a much more potent report that can shatter glass.

IFF

Short for "Identification Friend or Foe," this is a system of signals from an onboard transponder that can be detected and used to identify the vehicle, especially in combat.

INFERNO

A special, shoulder-launched missile designed as an anti-'Mech weapon. It explodes several meters from the launch tube, spraying the target with white phosphorus or a similar flammable compound in a jelly base. Infernos are not carried aboard 'Mechs because of their flammability.

IR

Infrared is light at wavelengths too long to be seen by the human eye. Infrared radiation is emitted by heat sources such as running engines or living bodies, and can be detected by equipment designed for use in the dark.

JUMPSHIP

Interstellar travel is accomplished via JumpShips, first developed in the twenty-second century. These somewhat ungainly vessels consist of a long, thin drive core and a sail resembling an enormous parasol, which can extend up to a kilometer in width. The ship is named for its ability to "jump" instantaneously across vast distances of space. After making its jump, the ship cannot travel until it has recharged by gathering up more solar energy.

The JumpShip's enormous sail is constructed from a special metal that absorbs vast quantities of electromagnetic energy from the nearest star. When it has soaked up enough energy, the sail transfers it to the drive core, which converts it into a space-twisting field. An instant later, the ship arrives at the next jump point, a distance of up to thirty light-years. This field is known as hyperspace, and its discovery opened to mankind the gateway to the stars.

JumpShips never land on planets. Interplanetary travel is carried out by DropShips, vessels that are attached to the JumpShip until arrival at the jump point.

LANCE

A BattleMech tactical combat group, usually consisting of four 'Mechs.

LASER

An acronym for "Light Amplification through Stimulated Emission of Radiation." When used as a weapon, the laser damages the target by concentrating extreme heat onto a small area. BattleMech lasers are designated as small, medium or large. Lasers are also available as shoulder-fired weapons operating from a portable backpack power unit. Certain range-finders and targeting equipment also employ low-level lasers.

LONG-RANGE MISSILE (LRM)

An indirect-fire missile with a high-explosive warhead.

MACHINE GUN

A small autocannon intended for anti-personnel assaults. Typically non-armor-penetrating, machine guns are often best used against infantry, as they can spray a large area with relatively inexpensive fire.

PARTICLE PROJECTION CANNON (PPC)

One of the most powerful and long-range energy weapons on the battlefield, a PPC fires a stream of charged particles that outwardly functions as a bright blue laser, but also throws off enough static discharge to resemble a bolt of manmade lightning. The kinetic and heat impact of a PPC is enough to cause the vaporization of armor and structure alike, and most PPCs have the power to kill a pilot in his machine through an armor-penetrating headshot.

SHORT-RANGE MISSILE (SRM)

A direct-trajectory missile with high-explosive or armor-piercing explosive warheads. They have a range of less than one kilometer and are only reliably accurate at ranges of less than 300 meters. They are more powerful, however, than LRMs.

SUCCESSOR LORDS

After the fall of the first Star League, the remaining members of the High Council each asserted his or her right to become First Lord. Their star empires became known as the Successor States and the rulers as Successor Lords. The Clan Invasion temporarily interrupted centuries of warfare known as the Succession Wars, which first began in 2786.

BATTLETECH ERAS

The *BattleTech* universe is a living, vibrant entity that grows each year as more sourcebooks and fiction are published. A dynamic universe, its setting and characters evolve over time within a highly detailed continuity framework, bringing everything to life in a way a static game universe cannot match.

To help quickly and easily convey the timeline of the universe—and to allow a player to easily "plug in" a given novel or sourcebook—we've divided *BattleTech* into eight major eras.

STAR LEAGUE
(Present–2780)
Ian Cameron, ruler of the Terran Hegemony, concludes decades of tireless effort with the creation of the Star League, a political and military alliance between all Great Houses and the Hegemony. Star League armed forces immediately launch the Reunification War, forcing the Periphery realms to join. For the next two centuries, humanity experiences a golden age across the thousand light-years of human-occupied space known as the Inner Sphere. It also sees the creation of the most powerful military in human history.

(This era also covers the centuries before the founding of the Star League in 2571, most notably the Age of War.)

SUCCESSION WARS
(2781–3049)
Every last member of First Lord Richard Cameron's family is killed during a coup launched by Stefan Amaris. Following the thirteen-year war to unseat him, the rulers of each of the five Great Houses disband the Star League. General Aleksandr Kerensky departs with eighty percent of the Star League Defense Force beyond known space and the Inner Sphere collapses into centuries of warfare known as the Succession Wars that will eventually result in a massive loss of technology across most worlds.

CLAN INVASION
(3050–3061)
A mysterious invading force strikes the coreward region of the Inner Sphere. The invaders, called the Clans, are descendants of Kerensky's SLDF troops, forged into a society dedicated to becoming the greatest fighting force in history. With vastly superior technology and warriors, the Clans conquer world after world. Eventually this outside threat will forge a new Star League, something hundreds of years of warfare failed to accomplish. In addition, the Clans will act as a catalyst for a technological renaissance.

CIVIL WAR
(3062–3067)

The Clan threat is eventually lessened with the complete destruction of a Clan. With that massive external threat apparently neutralized, internal conflicts explode around the Inner Sphere.

House Liao conquers its former Commonality, the St. Ives Compact; a rebellion of military units belonging to House Kurita sparks a war with their powerful border enemy, Clan Ghost Bear; the fabulously powerful Federated Commonwealth of House Steiner and House Davion collapses into five long years of bitter civil war.

JIHAD
(3067–3080)

Following the Federated Commonwealth Civil War, the leaders of the Great Houses meet and disband the new Star League, declaring it a sham. The pseudo-religious Word of Blake—a splinter group of ComStar, the protectors and controllers of interstellar communication—launch the Jihad: an interstellar war that pits every faction against each other and even against themselves, as weapons of mass destruction are used for the first time in centuries while new and frightening technologies are also unleashed.

DARK AGE
(3081–3150)

Under the guidance of Devlin Stone, the Republic of the Sphere is born at the heart of the Inner Sphere following the Jihad. One of the more extensive periods of peace begins to break out as the 32nd century dawns. The factions, to one degree or another, embrace disarmament, and the massive armies of the Succession Wars begin to fade. However, in 3132 eighty percent of interstellar communications collapses, throwing the universe into chaos. Wars erupt almost immediately, and the factions begin rebuilding their armies.

ILCLAN
(3151–present)

The once-invulnerable Republic of the Sphere lies in ruins, torn apart by the Great Houses and the Clans as they wage war against each other on a scale not seen in nearly a century. Mercenaries flourish once more, selling their might to the highest bidder. As Fortress Republic collapses, the Clans race toward Terra to claim their long-denied birthright and create a supreme authority that will fulfill the dream of Aleksandr Kerensky and rule the Inner Sphere by any means necessary: The ilClan.

CLAN HOMEWORLDS
(2786–present)

In 2784, General Aleksandr Kerensky launched Operation Exodus, and led most of the Star League Defense Force out of the Inner Sphere in a search for a new world, far away from the strife of the Great Houses. After more than two years and thousands of light years, they arrived at the Pentagon Worlds. Over the next two-and-a-half centuries, internal dissent and civil war led to the creation of a brutal new society—the Clans. And in 3049, they returned to the Inner Sphere with one goal—the complete conquest of the Great Houses.

Printed in Great Britain
by Amazon

46049360R00198